Love Pour Over Me

By
Denise Turney

Love Pour Over Me

Copyright 2012 Denise Turney,
All rights reserved.

Copyright 2012
Chistell Publishing

Published by eBookIt.com

Scriptures are taken from the
New International Version of the Bible.
Copyright 1985, Zondervan Corporation

All rights reserved. No part of this book may be reproduced in any form, except for the inclusion of brief quotations in a review or article, without written
permission from the author or publisher.

Chistell Publishing
3300 Neshaminy Blvd. Suite 589
Bensalem, PA 19020

Cover: Tywebbin Creations

ISBN-13: 9798812872953

Love Pour Over Me
People say that love is enough, but is it <u>really</u>? Is some heartache too painful to recover from?

******

<u>What early readers are saying about **Love Pour Over Me**:</u>
"**Love Pour Over Me** *is a book that readers can relate to. It examines the human condition and splendidly shows how one can triumph over adversity."*

Adrianne Daniels
Ohio School Teacher
******

"With **Love Pour Over Me**, *Denise Turney has done it again! Turney is a very talented writer who knows how to bring a story to life."*

Caroline Rogers
Co-Founder, C&B Books
******

<u>About the Author of **Love Pour Over Me**</u>:
Works by **Denise Turney**, international radio host and author of **Love Pour Over Me** have appeared in periodicals such as *Parade, Essence, Sisters In Style, Madame Noire, Obsidian II, The Bucks County Courier Times, Halogen TV, The College of New Jersey Literary Review, Trenton Times* and the *Pittsburgh Quarterly*

"And now these three remain: faith, hope and love. But the greatest of these is love."
I Corinthians 13:13

Dedication
For Gregory

Table of Contents

SECTION I..................................1..

Chapter One 1

Chapter Two 14

Chapter Three........................27

Chapter Four..........................36

Chapter Five...........................44

Chapter Six 61

Chapter Seven.......................84

Chapter Eight.........................96

Chapter Nine........................110

Chapter Ten..........................118

Chapter Eleven.....................123

Chapter Twelve 136

Chapter Thirteen..................153

Chapter Fourteen 167

Chapter Fifteen 175

Chapter Sixteen 183

Chapter Seventeen 189

Chapter Eighteen 194

Chapter Nineteen 209

Chapter Twenty 223

Chapter Twenty-One 239

Chapter Twenty-Two 251

Chapter Twenty-Three 266

Chapter Twenty-Four 285

SECTION II (12 years later) 301

Chapter Twenty-Five 301

Chapter Twenty-Six 314

Chapter Twenty-Seven 328

Chapter Twenty-Eight 336

Chapter Twenty-Nine 342

Chapter Thirty 359

Chapter Thirty-One 364

SECTION III 366

Chapter Thirty-Two 366

SECTION I

Chapter One

It was Friday afternoon, June 15, 1984. Raymond Clarke lay across his bed. An empty bowl of popcorn was on the floor. Snacking did little to ease his excitement. In less than three hours his year round efforts to prove himself deserving of unwavering acclaim would be validated in front of hundreds of his classmates. Tonight was his high school graduation, the day he had dreamed about for weeks. He knew his grades were high enough to earn him academic honors. Even more than his grades were his athletic achievements. He hadn't been beaten in a track race in three years; he won the state half mile and mile runs for the last six years, since he was in middle school. People would cheer wildly for him tonight.

The television was turned up loud. "Carl Lewis threatens to break Bob Beamon's historic long jump record at the Olympic Trials in Los Angeles this weekend," an ESPN sportscaster announced. "Beamon's record has stood for sixteen years. Lewis . . . "

Raymond got so caught up in the mention of the upcoming Olympic Games that he didn't hear the front door open.

"Ray," his father Malcolm shouted as soon as he entered the house.

"What?" Raymond leaped off his bed and hurried into the living room. "Dad?"

"What? Boy, if you don't get your junk--"

Raymond watched his father wave his hand over the sofa, the place where he'd thrown his sports bag as soon as he got home from graduation practice at school.

"Get this sports crap up," Malcolm growled.

Silence filled the house.

Raymond grabbed his sports bag, carried it into his bedroom and tossed it across his bed.

His father exited the living room and entered the kitchen. Like a dark shadow, frustrations from spending ten hours working at a drab automobile plant where he drilled leather seats into one Ford Mustang after another while his line supervisor stood at his shoulder and barked, "Focus, Malcolm. Get your production up," followed him there. It was in the furrow of his brow and in the pinch of his lip. "Ray."

Raymond cursed beneath his breath before he left his bedroom and hurried into the living room. Seconds later he stood in the kitchen's open doorway.

He watched his father toss an envelope on the table. "Letter from Baker came in the mail. Something about you getting some awards when—" He reached to the center of the kitchen table for a bottle of Steel Fervor. He'd stopped hiding the alcohol when Raymond turned five. The alcohol looked like liquid gold. Felt that way to Malcolm too. "you graduate tonight."

Malcolm took a long swig of the whiskey and squinted against the burn. He tried to laugh but only coughed up spleen. "You're probably the only kid in the whole school who got a letter like this. Everybody up at Baker knows nobody cares about you. Letter said they thought I'd want to let all your relatives know you're getting some awards so they'd come out and support you."

Again Malcolm worked at laughter, but instead coughed a dry, scratchy cough that went long and raw through his throat. "We both know ain't nobody going to be there but me and your sorry ass. Don't mean nothing anyhow. They're just giving these diplomas and awards away now days." On his way out of the kitchen, bottle in hand, he shoved the letter against Raymond's chest.

Raymond listened to his father's footsteps go heavy up the back stairs while he stood alone in the kitchen. When the footsteps became a whisper, he looked down at the letter. It was printed on good stationery, the kind Baker High School only used for special occasions. Didn't matter though. Raymond took the letter and ripped it once, twice, three times --- over and over again --- until it was only shreds of paper, then he walked to the tall kitchen wastebasket next to the gas stove and dropped the bits inside.

"Ray."

He froze. From the sound of his father's voice, he knew he was at the top of the stairs.

"Give me that letter, so I'll remember to go to your graduation tonight."

Raymond twisted his mouth at the foulness of the request, the absolute absurdity of it. He didn't answer. Instead he turned and walked back inside his bedroom. He grabbed his house keys and headed outside. At the edge of the walkway, he heard his father shout, "Ray."

Raymond didn't turn around. He walked down the tree lined sidewalk the way he'd learned to walk since Kindergarten – with his head down. He stepped over raised cracks in the worn sidewalk, turned away from boarded windows of two empty dilapidated buildings and told himself the neighborhood was just like his father – old, useless, unforgiving and hard.

A second floor window back at the house went up. Malcolm stuck his head all the way out the window. "Get your ass back here," he hollered down the street.

Raymond sprang to his toes and started to run. His muscular arms and legs went back and forth through the cooling air like propellers, like they were devices he used to try to take off, leave the places in his life he wished had never been. It was what he was good at. All his running had earned him high honors in track and field. He was Ohio's top miler. He'd made *Sports Illustrated* four times since middle school.

"Ray."

"Yo, man, you better go back," Joey chuckled as Raymond slowed to a stop. Joey, a troubled eighteen-year-old neighbor who dropped out of school in the tenth grade, leaned across a Pontiac Sunbird waxing its hood. "If you don't, your old man's gonna beat your ass good."

"Aw, Ray's cool," Stanley, an equally troubled twenty-one-year-old who pissed on school and failed to get a diploma, a man who couldn't read beyond the third grade level, said. He stood next to Joey. His hands were shoved to the bottoms of his pants pockets. "And we know the Brother can run. Damn. We all can run," Stanley laughed.

"Ray, remember the night we ran away from that Texaco station, our wallets all fat?" Joey laughed. He talked so loudly, Raymond worried he'd be overheard.

"Thought we agreed to let that go," Raymond said. He looked hard at Joey then he looked hard at Stanley and the nine-month old deal was resealed, another secret for Raymond to keep.

One glance back at his father's house and Raymond started running again. He ran passed Gruder's an old upholstery company and Truder Albright, a small, worn convenience store, all the way to the Trotwood Recreation Center six miles farther into the city.

Houses were larger in Trotwood than they were in Dayton, lawns filled with flowers that swayed in the wind; neighborhoods were quieter too. As a boy when his father drove him through Trotwood on the way to the Salem Mall, Raymond told himself that this is where his parents and he would have moved to and lived, had his mother not fallen in love with another man, had she stayed.

Raymond sat in the bleachers at the recreation center watching an intramural basketball game for well over half an hour, until he felt certain Malcolm had, in a rare respite, drunk himself into a modicum of civility. When he turned over his wrist and saw that it was after five o'clock, he ran every step of the six miles back home.

The living room was empty. Raymond heard a noise akin to the rise and fall of a buzz saw. He frowned toward the stairs and mumbled, "He's asleep," while he exited the living room and entered his bedroom.

ESPN was still on. He went straight to his closet and pulled out his favorite pair of black nylon dress pants, a crisp white button down shirt and a tie. Fifteen minutes later he was showered, dressed and standing in front of his bedroom mirror.

His father was drunk. That he knew. It always went this way, every night. Like a religious habit, he'd spent his childhood watching his father drink half a bottle of whiskey every evening after he arrived home from work. When he was a little boy, he'd sit across from Malcolm at the kitchen table swinging his legs back and forth like a pendulum clock watching Malcolm turn a new shiny glass bottle up until it reached empty. He always brought a toy into the kitchen with him then, a race car or a plastic airplane. He'd push the toy back and forth across the table and sing out, "Voom. Voom," but he never took his eyes off his father. It was a time gone, like cement, down into Raymond's psyche.

But that was years ago. Since then Raymond had gotten into a few fist fights and had gone on more than one stolen car joy ride with neighborhood boys he hoped would take him in as a good friend, but who never did.

He dodged cops when they knocked on the door last spring. He'd just returned home from school; mercy abounding, Malcolm was still at work.

With their stiff blue caps squarely atop their heads, the cops questioned Raymond about the robbery at a nearby Texaco station, a wrong - for Raymond - birthed out of a last ditch effort to gain a neighborhood friend but now a source of pain and regret.

Raymond's academic and athletic reputations convinced the cops that he was innocent. His refusal to rat out Joey and Stanley kept them from going to prison for the third time in less than two years.

Never mind that Joey and Stanley kicked his butt when he was a kid until he bore new bruises, ones not put there by Malcolm. Never mind that cops badgered him, pounding Malcolm's living room table and promising, "Ray, if you tell us what part Joey and Stanley played in the heist, we'll make sure nothing happens to you and we'll go light on them." Raymond didn't tell. If not for him, Joey wouldn't be waxing his car right now and Stanley wouldn't be standing around trying to find something interesting to do.

Despite the run-in with the law and Malcolm's drunken rages, verbal assaults that burst forth into outright physical beatings when Raymond reached puberty, Raymond had found a way to stay alive. He had made it to seventeen.

He was running a brush across the top of his hair when the phone rang.

"Hello?"

"Ray. Raymond Clarke?"

"Speaking."

The man laughed. "Big night for you."

Raymond placed the brush atop his dresser. "Who is this?"

"You'll come to recognize my voice soon enough," the man joked.

"Coach Carter? Coach Reginald Carter?"

"Yes. Wanted to call and congratulate you on graduation tonight. Have a good time, Son. Look forward to seeing you on campus in what, one, two weeks?"

"Yea," Raymond nodded. "Soon."

"Congratulations again, Ray. You deserve it. Heard you did better than good this year. Heard you did great."

"Thanks."

Raymond opened his hand and watched the receiver fall gently against its cradle. A bird squawked outside his window and he stared across his room at nothing in particular. He couldn't count the number of calls he'd received from college track and field scouts over the last two years. He told his father about none of the calls. When Malcolm pushed and demanded, "Where you going to school next year, boy," Raymond always told him what he knew he wanted to hear. He always looked right at his father and told him, "Ohio State."

With the phone dead and Coach Carter's voice gone, Raymond returned to the living room and sat on the sofa in silence. The front door was open. Through the screen door, warm summer air carried the scent of fried pork chops, chicken and hamburger from neighboring houses into the living room.

Because Malcolm's kitchen table was bare and the refrigerator held only beer, wine coolers, a bowl of two week old broccoli, a pint of cottage cheese and a celery stalk, Raymond served himself an evening meal through his nose. As if he could get full on the smell of food, he tilted his head back and inhaled in long, slow breaths.

In the living room, the second hand on the battery operated Ingraham wall clock ticked and slid forward, ticked and slid forward. Soon Raymond had the phone in his hand again. "Yo, Paul," he said to his high school track teammate, the one guy who gave him good athletic competition, someone he considered a real good friend. "When are you leaving for the convention center?"

"Five minutes. Man, you know we have to be there an hour before the ceremony starts. I'm running late as it is—" He paused. "You need a ride?"

"Can you swing by and get me on your way?"

"My mom and dad are driving."

"I mean, Man, please. Help me out." He sighed. "Even though I got my license a year ago, you know my dad's not gonna let me drive his Camaro."

"Your pops ain't coming?"

"Yo, Paul, Homey," Raymond begged.

"A'right. A'right."

The Dayton Convention Center was packed. Four hundred students – their purple and white caps and gowns making them the focal point of attention -- filled the front of the main auditorium. A mass of parents, grandparents, aunts, uncles and cousins sat in the raised seats at the back of the room.

The program started with a slew of speeches, enough to make the students wriggle in their seats. Over time, the evening began to take on an unwanted hue. A stale fatigue came into the air, started to make the graduation ceremony feel boring.

Then a good thing happened. Principal Bernard Jones approached the microphone and everyone in the auditorium sat up.

"And now," Principal Jones said, "it's time to hand out the diplomas."

Cheers went up and drowned Principal Jones' voice. Like confetti that had been tossed toward the ceiling, it was a long time before the cheers came down.

It was eight o'clock. Raymond told himself not to but he turned partway and glanced over his shoulder. It was as if he'd suddenly been plagued with dementia, because he forgot the years of abuse heaped upon him with Malcolm's calloused hands. He wanted Malcolm to walk through the convention center doors sober and real proud like. He wanted Malcolm to be glad to call him his son.

"To the students, as I call out your name, please stand and make your way onto the stage." Principal Jones flipped through a stack of stapled papers then he pushed his mouth close to the microphone and said slowly, "Sharon Appleseed."

A loud round of applause, whistling and "way to gos" pierced the air. It went on like that for more than an hour, until all but two students had received a diploma – Raymond and Janice Thompson, a bright sixteen year old who sat in a wheelchair due to spina bifida.

Principal Jones sang Janice's praises. Hers had been a stellar academic career right from the start. "She's earned her way onto the Honor Roll every year since the Seventh Grade. She was voted to Girls State by our finest instructors. She has won three presidential academic citations. And," Principal Jones laughed, "I'm sure her parents appreciate this most. She has earned a full scholarship to Spelman College in Atlanta, Georgia." Principal Jones' hand went out. "Ladies and gentlemen," he beamed, "Please stand and congratulate the Class of 1984's Salutatorian, Janice Thompson."

Janice pushed the wheelchair toward the stage and everyone stood and applauded wildly. Amid the swell of noise and the sea of people, Raymond looked over his shoulder and searched every face for Malcolm. His gaze darted in a crazed fashion.

Then he felt a tap on his shoulder. It was his friend, Paul. They sat next to each other. "Yo, Man, is your pops coming?"

Raymond turned away from Paul, faced the stage and stood tall, head up, shoulders back.

When Paul tapped him again, he jerked his shoulders hard and shrugged him off.

The auditorium grew quiet.

"And now, it's time for us to bestow the top honor." Principal Jones smiled before he said, "This young man has earned high commendations academically and athletically."

In short intervals, Paul, several members of the track team and Raymond's high school track coach turned and looked to the back of the auditorium toward the entrance doors. They prayed for Malcolm to show.

"Damn," Paul muttered when he turned around and faced the stage for the eighth time. He bumped shoulders with the guy who stood next to him. "That asshole ain't coming." He lowered his head and his voice. "Ray's pops ain't coming."

"This young man has earned All-City, All-County, All-State and top national honors in cross-country and track and field. In fact, twice he's been listed as the top high school miler in the country by *Sports Illustrated* and *Track and Field News*. He has earned four Presidential academic citations. He's been on the Honor Roll since the Seventh Grade." Principal Jones scanned the auditorium for Malcolm. When he didn't see him, he spoke slower and started to make things up in the hopes that time would become Raymond's friend.

"I remember when he first came to Baker. He was a scared young man, but not anymore." He pursed his lips and gave Raymond a nod. "He's ready to take advantage of the full scholarship his achievements have gained him." Principal Jones glanced at the doors.

A few students and several parents squirmed in their seats. Some people glanced at their watches as if to say "Come on".

"He has maintained a 4.0 grade point average since the ninth grade. He hasn't missed a day of school since the third grade." The doors demanded his attention again, but no one came through them.

"Ladies and Gentlemen, please congratulate Baker High School's Class of 1984 Valedictorian, Raymond Clarke."

Paul clapped until his hands stung. A few students stood in their seats and hollered out, "Go, Ray!" Before long a chant went up. All the students pumped their fists in the air and shouted, "Ray-mond! Ray-mond!"

Raymond's heart beat wildly in his chest. He clamped his teeth down against his bottom lip and jailed the rising emotion. He extended his hand when he neared Principal Jones' side.

"Well done," Principal Jones told him as he handed him his diploma. He patted Raymond's back. "You did a fine job, Son." He shook his head, "A fine job."

The chain lock was on the front door when Raymond got home that night. He jiggled the chain and tried to get it to slide open. When that didn't work he walked to the back of the house and tried to open the rear door, the one leading to the backyard. He cursed as he realized a chain lock was on the back door as well. Then he looked for an opening. He was in luck. The kitchen window was ajar just enough to allow him entry. He grunted and pushed up. The screen didn't even bang when it landed in the sink. He crawled through the window like a thief.

When he reached the stairs, he saw a flicker of light coming from the second floor. "Dad," he called out softly, then louder as he made his way up the stairs. "Dad."

A newly pressed blue striped suit coat hung across the chair in the corner of his father's bedroom. The television was turned down so low it sounded like it was humming.

"Dad?"

The bed was empty, covers bunched together near the foot. The shade to the room's one lamp was tilted as if someone had punched it.

"Dad?"

Raymond walked across the hall. He started to scream. "Dad?" He ran back down the stairs. "Dad?" he screamed as he made his way through the house.

He saw the shadow, curled and bent like an old man, at his bed's edge. Silence was his escort into his own room.

Malcolm stood slowly. His body leaned right, from his shoulders to his ankles. His hands were clenched. His eyes were slits. "Why didn't you tell me?" he demanded. His hands, then his arms and legs quaked. He took heavy Frankenstein-like steps toward Raymond. "Why didn't you tell me? Why didn't you tell me?"

When no more than a few inches separated them, Raymond saw the red in his father's eyes.

Malcolm stepped forward again, and this time, Raymond stepped back. He prepared to duck. "Tell you what?" he stammered. Fear had gone into his body. He felt like, instead of blood, electricity was coursing through his veins.

"Why didn't you tell me?"

"What? What, Dad?" Raymond screamed. "Tell you what?"

Malcolm took one last step forward then he thrust his hands open and threw bits of paper in Raymond's face. The paper fell against Raymond's nose, his mouth.

"Why didn't you tell me you were graduating today?" Malcolm's body shook. He turned and looked for a chair, the bed, someplace to sit down. "After all I've done for you," he cried. "You tore up the letter. You-you-you just walked off and left me upstairs a-sleep," he shouted and slurred.

"You knew," Raymond said. "I thought you'd just come. I couldn't be late. I had to go, and we both know how mean you can be when I wake you up."

"Augh," Malcolm grunted. He took a swipe at Raymond's face, but lost his balance and only grazed his nose.

"I wanted you there," Raymond tried. "I looked for you."

Malcolm balled his hand and raised it. This time his hand landed in the center of Raymond's forehead. Just now Raymond hated his father enough not to be afraid of him, one hard emotion swapped out for another.

Again and again Malcolm's fists landed across Raymond's nose, his shoulders, his chest. Malcolm was so inebriated his fists fell away almost as soon as they found their spot. "Who did it, Ray?" he openly wept. "Who fed you? Hunh? Who clothed you? Hunh? Who made sure you got to that damned school? Hunh?" He went to point at his chest, but ended up leaning back so far, he fell across the bed. "Hunh?" he asked again when he sat partly up. "Not your mother. She left when you were just a kid. Who?" he demanded. "Who?" he stood and shrieked. "Who took care of you?"

"You-did," Raymond said. His teeth were clenched so tight his jaws ached.

"You better believe it was me—" Malcolm began. He didn't finish. The bed caught him seconds before vomit spewed out of his mouth.

Raymond stood by the door with his white button down shirt and tie still on. Then he came back into the room, used the hem of his shirt to wipe vomit off his father's mouth and tucked his father into his bed.

He spent the night on the living room sofa. ESPN hummed in the background. He looked up at the ceiling and wondered if he should call Coach Carter first thing in the morning and tell him that he wasn't going to come to university after all, because he had to stay home and take care of his sick father, a middle-aged man who had not started to drink until after his wife left him for a has-been professional football player when Raymond was only two years old. "Or," he wondered while he stared up at the ceiling, "Should I just go hundreds of miles away from here?"

Chapter Two

At nine o'clock the following morning, Malcolm woke with a numbing hangover, the remains of last night's potent whiskey. His face was washed yet unshaven. Stubble circled his chin. "Ray, where's your help?" he growled as he steadied his way down the stairs.

Raymond leaned forward on the living room sofa. "I put—"

Malcolm waved him off. He leaned across the kitchen table and unscrewed the top off a bottle of Steel Fervor and gulped the liquor until it burned in his throat.

Seconds later he entered the living room and flung his hand out at Raymond. "Said where's your help? You eat like a damn animal. I'm not gonna pay to feed you."

Raymond shoved his hand to the bottom of his pants pocket. When he pulled it out again he pushed two crisp twenty dollar bills at Malcolm, money he'd earned from a weekend job at the Salem Mall.

"Be here when I get back," Malcolm demanded. He snatched the bills out of Raymond's hand. Money, as it often did, worked like magic on him and he softened. "Want something?"

"Nah."

Seconds later, he was out the front door. "Don't go nowhere," he called back. "Be here to help carry the groceries in." When Raymond didn't respond, he stopped. "Ray?"

"Yea. I'll be here."

Raymond listened to the red and black Chevy Camaro, the car he'd spent a failed year begging Malcolm to let him drive just once, back out of the side drive then he jogged into his bedroom and pulled his sports bag from beneath the bed.

His hands were shaking. It all seemed so easy last night while he lay across the living room sofa, convincing himself to make his exit while Malcolm, as usual, shopped for scant groceries on a Saturday morning. He hadn't planned on being emotional; he was just going to grab his stuff and go. After years of abuse he should be able to just leave, but his body was starting to feel tight, like thick rope knots were in his shoulders, his back and in his throat. He'd felt this way too many times before when he was a boy hiding behind the furnace. "Damn it," he cursed while he ran his hand beneath the mattress then over the closet shelves.

"I didn't leave a trace, no letters from Coach Carter, no school admissions forms," he finally pronounced. "Malcolm will never know where I am."

He went into the living room and called a cab. "Shit," he cursed when he looked up at the clock and saw it was nine-twenty. Malcolm bought so few groceries, even though the grocery store was more than fifteen minutes from their house, he knew he'd be home before ten-thirty. "I should have called for a cab sooner." He spent the next twenty minutes pacing the living room floor.

When the driver pulled along the curb and honked the horn Raymond ran toward the door. Then he turned back. He went into his bedroom and looked at the Honor Roll certificates nailed to the walls; some of them were ten years old. His gaze swept across track trophies placed atop his bedroom dresser. An envelope lay beneath one of the trophies.

Inside the envelope was a black and white photo of his mother. Raymond found the picture when he was in Kindergarten. He'd been rummaging through boxes in the basement when he discovered the photo. It was shoved to the bottom of a cardboard box that was so old it smelled of mildew. *"Love Jennifer,"* was all that was scribed in the picture's bottom right corner.

This time when Raymond looked at the picture he saw it. His mother had the same wide nose and full lips he had. Her eyes were wide and dark brown like his too. *"She's why he hates me,"* he told himself. *"I remind him of her."*

Raymond heard the cab driver honk the horn again. He thought about grabbing the envelope but he left it beneath the trophy. Over the years he'd pulled it out at least three to four times a month and looked at it. He imagined his mother as a warm, loving woman when he was a boy. Now all he felt was abandonment when he thought of her.

Posters of Carl Lewis and Edwin Moses hung at the sides of the window. The television was off, but turned to ESPN. His blue terry cloth bath robe hung over the closet door knob. His two pairs of dress pants, several pairs of socks, three sweaters, one dress shirt, underwear, track shoes and two pairs of sweat pants were shoved inside the sports bag he carried over his shoulder. He wore the only other clothes he owned.

When Raymond heard the cab driver lay on the horn, he hurried out of the house. For seventeen years this had been home. Despite the abuse he'd suffered at his father's hands, the house's familiarity made him feel safe, but not safe enough to stay. He imagined that Malcolm was at Kroger arguing with a produce clerk about the color of the lettuce, one of the few food items he ever came home from the store with.

Raymond figured Malcolm thought a head of lettuce was all the produce a growing young man needed. He knew that, if not for the many times he ate at Paul's house, he'd probably be malnourished. Except for Thanksgiving, Malcolm never brought home more than two bags of groceries a week. The bulk of his money went toward liquor.

Raymond closed and locked the front door then he dropped his key inside the mail box. A ghost haunted him; it pulled at him with so much force it felt stronger than he was. It was the shadow of a boy who didn't want to leave, who wanted to stay and beg for his father to love him.

On the sidewalk and as if remains of decency in Malcolm and his relationship had called to him, Raymond turned and looked back.

The cab driver honked the horn and leaned towards the passenger window. "Yo?" In seven minutes it would be ten o'clock.

Turning away from the house, Raymond stepped toward the cab.

"Where to?" the driver asked as Raymond scooted across the back seat.

"The Fifth Avenue Greyhound bus station."

"You got it," the driver said as he pulled away from the curb.

The cab bumped its way down the street. Despite his vow not to, Raymond kept glancing out the window.

He saw Ms. Nipson, a nosy neighbor who lived two houses down and across the street, part her living room drapes and glance out onto the street. She stared at the cab while it went by. "Damn," he cursed.

"Hey," the cab driver said peering into the rearview mirror and smiling at the red and white Ohio State t-shirt Raymond wore.

Raymond glanced at the driver. "Yea?"

"Aren't you that track star from Baker?"

Raymond chuckled. "Yea." Seconds later, he frowned out onto the street as they passed Gruder's, a place so forsaken Raymond marveled that it was still open.

The cab driver peered into the rearview mirror again. "So, you graduated yesterday?"

Raymond gave a nod. "Yea."

The volume in the cab driver's voice went up. "Saw the write up on your graduation in the paper."

"Yea."

"You did good, Man."

"Thanks."

"Makes the city proud."

Raymond responded, "Thanks." He nodded once. "I appreciate that."

"Saw all those awards you won. You're the man around here, on a national level too. Unbeatable. That's what I say . . ."

While the driver droned on, Raymond stared out the window at Joey and Stanley. Their hands were jammed to the bottoms of their pants pockets. Their heads were back. They leaned against the outside of Truder Albright. The store's marred screen door slammed to a close when a customer entered it.

Raymond laughed, and for a scant second, the driver stopped his incessant chatter. He leaned into a sharp right turn, steering the cab farther away from Green Street. "What's that?" he asked Raymond.

"Nothing. I was just thinking about two dudes I used to get into it with when we were younger, two dudes I'm glad to be saying good-bye to." He laughed. "They were back there standing outside an old building looking like they had nothing better to do. Hard to believe they used to be the coolest cats in town."

"Goes that way sometimes."

The driver and Raymond didn't speak another word the remainder of the trip. Every now and then they did glance at each other. They were strangers and for the rest of the trip while they absorbed themselves inside their separate thoughts they stayed that way.

Close to the center of town, the cab inched alongside the curb outside the Greyhound bus station. Raymond handed the driver twenty dollars, grabbed his sports bag and climbed out. He moved fast enough to keep from turning around. He didn't have practice leaving. He wasn't good at it. He'd never done it before.

As soon as he exited the cab, a gust of wind brushed down across his face. He almost stepped into the path of two adolescent boys popping wheelies on their five-speed bikes and yelping the lyrics to *New Edition's* hit song "Candy Girl" while they sped down the sidewalk.

Years before Joey, Stanley and he held up the Texaco gas station the three of them used to ride their yard sale bikes down Green Street popping wheelies, their near flat tires catching at cracks in the sidewalk.

Raymond tugged on the bus station door and went inside. The lobby was more empty than full. A few older women, their weight having ballooned as they aged, sat in the waiting area. Large shopping bags and suitcases were pushed close to their legs. Some children played hand games near the exit doors while their parents stood in one of the ticket lines. Several out-of-state university students milled about looking for something to do while they waited for their busses to pull up for loading.

Raymond leaned across the long service counter. "Philadelphia," he said as soon as the clerk looked up from her copy of the *Dayton Daily News*. "*Cincinnati Reds Hammer the Atlanta Braves*" was splashed across the top of the sports page.

"Round trip?" the clerk asked with a courteous smile.

Raymond shook his head decidedly. "No," he said. "One way. I'm not coming back. Ever."

Forty-five minutes later, he sat on a crowded Greyhound bus pondering his future. He turned away from the other riders and gazed out the dirty bus window most of the bumpy ride. Each mile the bus covered made his hometown of Dayton, the gas station hold-up and especially Malcolm, a permanent piece of history, forever behind him.

Fourteen hours into the trip, an army of insects were splattered against the large bus window making it hard to see. Night had come across the sky. Hardly anyone talked now.

"Philadelphia," the driver announced. She jarred Raymond away from sleep. "Philadelphia," she said again.

As the bus inched inside the terminal, Raymond stretched his tired, stiff limbs and stood. He peered out the bus window and admired Philadelphia's rising skyline. Images of Malcolm combing the neighborhood screaming out his name, his thoughts racing, his heart pounding, rose in his mind, but he shook his head and pushed the images aside. He was in a new place now; he had a new home -- a clean slate.

He grabbed his sports bag and got in line behind other riders. Single file they inched, one slow step after another, off the bus.

Tops of lofty buildings saluted the stars in a way they didn't in the daytime when government employees and business workers rushed back and forth across the noisy streets.

Philadelphia's sticky night air combed Raymond's skin and whisked up his nose. He frowned. The odor near the bus terminal was funky, stale and sweaty. Candy wrappers, dirty napkins, empty soda cans and shreds of paper littered the ground.

Raymond turned in a circle, not sure which way to go. Cars sped down Filbert Street heading deeper into town. Prostitutes coursed the night in high, narrow heels and pants so tight anyone walking behind them could tell they didn't have on panties. Music blared on battery-operated radios. A dog barked in the distance.

"Need a ride?" a thin, ebony skinned cab driver called out to Raymond.

"Sure do," Raymond answered. "325A Walnut Street," he told the driver as he slid across the cab's back seat.

Fifteen minutes later, the cab pulled in front of an open field behind which were several brick apartment buildings, their roofs tall and wide.

The cab driver glanced at the lights coming away from the apartments. "325A Walnut Street."

With a single wave, Raymond stepped away from the cab and moved across the expansive campus. He squinted through the night and asked a couple snuggling on a bench at the center of the lawn how to reach Roddin College House.

"Keep walking," the blond haired guy wearing a t-shirt with 'Ride it out' printed on the front said. His girlfriend kept her head buried against his chest. "When you reach the end of the lawn, take a left." The guy's pointing finger rose. "See that tall building over there?"

Raymond followed the guy's finger. He nodded. "Yea."

"That's Roddin."

"Thanks, Man," Raymond said. He slapped palms with the guy, pulled up on the strap of his sports bag and resumed his walk across the lawn.

A short muscular dude looked up from behind a long desk with a plate nailed to it that read *Roddin House Resident Director*. "Name?" the guy asked, his mouth twisted in irritation.

"Raymond Clarke."

"Room 712," the guy said, holding out a key. He looked like he hadn't missed a day of lifting weights in a decade. "You have the apartment to yourself until we find you a roommate." He glanced at the registry. "Coach Carter's sponsoring you." He looked up with a crooked grin, one not bearing compliments. "Track star, hunh?"

Raymond laughed. "Something like that."

"Yeah," the guy growled.

"Is there a problem?" Raymond asked, stepping back.

"Nah," the guy mumbled. "You're the last check in I was waiting on before I go home." He cut his eyes at Raymond. "I got parties to get to."

Raymond took the key. "Didn't mean to hold you up."

"Don't worry about it," the guy responded dryly. He stood. "Name's Walter."

"Cool," Raymond said, trying to clear the air. "Good to meet you, Man."

Walter unclenched his jaw and pointed over his shoulder. "You can take the elevator behind us, and trust me, Man, I would." He worked at a chuckle. "Those stairs are a bitch." As Raymond hoisted his sports bag onto his shoulder and walked to the elevators, Walter turned and peered at him out of the corners of his eyes.

The elevator went up like a slow yawn. After Raymond got off on the seventh floor, he went two doors to the left and there he was, at his new home, apartment 712. He unlocked the door, went straight to his bedroom and fell across the bed. His bones ached with the heaviness of fatigue. The fourteen hour bus ride had exhausted him.

Soon he was on his feet again checking out his new home. The first room he went into was a small kitchen. Inside was a stove, a sink, a half-sized refrigerator and a short counter – no table. There wasn't room for one. He smiled as he exited the kitchen and walked down the hall. Although he was tired, he was pleased. He'd never had his own place before. In his overview, he saw two bedrooms, his and one for his roommate . . . whoever that turned out to be. Each bedroom was equipped with a twin bed, a desk, a chair, a dresser, a closet and a working table. At the apartment's hub was a spacious living room with a large window hung with light blue drapes covering much of the right side. Raymond parted the drapes, unlocked the window, pushed it ajar and peered out.

The next half hour passed with haste, like the early morning was begging for trouble to happen.

Raymond looked up at the radio/alarm clock on a corner of his bedroom work table; it was two-thirty. In seventeen hours no one had shouted at or cursed him. He felt odd, naked. Beneath the surface, far below his conscious mind, he longed for conflict. He wanted the thing he hated but had grown so used to he missed it.

He dumped the contents of his sports bag onto his bed, grabbed a pair of shorts and a towel and headed for the bathroom.

The cool shower water tingled as it splashed his skin. When he stepped out of the shower, the fresh scent of lavender soap trailing him, he had on what he always wore to bed, a long loose pair of shorts, no underwear.

He flipped the channels on the color television at the edge of his bedroom dresser. PBS,

Love Pour Over Me

Nickelodeon, BET, MTV and Lifetime shows whizzed by as he clicked the remote control. "Is this it?" he asked while he looked at the television. "This is all there is to do in this city?"

He gawke d at sce ne s of downtown Philadelphia, Broad Street with its shops and businesses, and Race Street with its nearby canals and historic sites. Next neighboring eateries and a new science exhibit at The Franklin Institute flashed across the screen. He stopped clicking channels and dropped the remote onto the bed when he heard Harry Kalas shout, "Mike Schmidt went for two homeruns in tonight's game against the New York Mets." A rerun of the night's game where the Phillies played and defeated the New York Mets aired next.

That was it. Raymond lay back on the bed. He gazed up at the ceiling. Mention of Mike Schmidt, the Phillies all-star third baseman, brought back memories of happy times he'd spent with Malcolm. They never missed a baseball game when Raymond was a kid. They either tuned in to the game on television or took the Camaro to Cincinnati and watched the Reds play at Great American Ball Park.

The TV droned in the distance. Harry Kalas' exuberance rose, "Mike Schmidt catches a fly ball to third base and . . ."

Outside the resident hall, in the top limbs of nearby sycamore trees, blue jays rested on twig piles until rain started to fall. A single bat flapped its way across the sky, staying away from lamp poles and building corners. And one mile from campus locals blasted bullets at a man who'd been bent on making it rich in the drug trade, his fate sure to make its way into the early morning newspaper.

Oblivious to the ensuing murder, Raymond turned on his side in bed, breathed deeper and went gently into sleep's embrace. He was free of the bullets that tore at then ripped through the man's skin, his organs for now.

As the guy's blood stretched out across the street in downtown Philly, rain poured out of the sky and pounded the city of Dayton. Rivers rose and puddles found their way over curbs and against the edges of houses as Malcolm, with way too much liquor on his breath, shouted at the police in the Third Street station to help him find his son.

****

It was Sunday and twelve o'clock in the afternoon. Roddin House was quiet; most of the guys were sleeping in after a hard night of partying.

"Morning," Raymond called out to Walter after he climbed down the seven flights of stairs and neared the exit doors.

"What's happening?" Walter shouted from his place behind the main desk, careful to be warmer toward Raymond than he had been when they first met, not wanting to draw attention to himself.

"Nothing much, Man," Raymond said. He didn't miss a step. "Have a good one."

Walter looked up from a recent issue of *Ebony* magazine. "You too, Ray. Take it easy." A second later he raced outside after Raymond.

"What is it?" Raymond asked after Walter grabbed him by the shoulder and turned him around.

"I almost forgot. I thought I saw something about you on the news this morning." He searched Raymond's face. "Were you supposed to go to Ohio State?"

"Nah," Raymond shrugged. "Where'd you hear that?" His gaze shifted down. While Walter watched him so hard the side of his face started to feel hot, he mentally retraced his steps. Finally he nodded and told himself, *"Everything's cool. I cleaned my room back home like a Navy recruit. Dad doesn't know I'm here."*

Walter's chatter broke up his concentration. "Thought I heard you were missing, but," he tapped Raymond's shoulder and laughed. "I'm so tore up from partying earlier this morning, I don't really know what I heard."

"Whatever, Man," Raymond chuckled nervously. "All I know is the story wasn't about me. I'm good. I'm right where I'm supposed to be." He nodded. "Be cool."

As soon as Raymond turned around, hot glare from the sun blinded him. He raised his hand and used it as a makeshift visor to ward off the sun's rays.

Walter watched Raymond, with his newly trimmed fade, walk away from him. Walter didn't trust anyone. He wasn't a fool. He figured, at some point, everyone would turn out to be just like him, sneaky and slick like dirty oil.

Oblivious to Walter's growing curiosity, for the next several hours, Raymond walked in and out of libraries, lecture halls, arts buildings and athletic centers to become familiar with the campus. He also wondered if Walter really got information that he was supposed to be at Ohio State from the television.

"Ah, forget it," he finally said after he tired of trying to figure out what Walter knew. He didn't want to pry further. He was new around here and he didn't want to draw any undue attention to himself.

He ventured into the surrounding neighborhood in search of record shops, particularly those with hard-to-find old-school jazz cuts, songs by Duke Ellington, Charlie Parker, Norris Turney, Theo Monk and Miles Davis. His search didn't lead him to good music. Instead it led him to good food and drink, specifically a string of quaint coffee and pastry shops on University Avenue.

A door away from one of the coffee shops, a trio of police cruisers sped down the street, their sirens blaring. Raymond didn't turn; thanks to the rising violence in West Dayton, he'd seen his share of police cars. Mixed in with the noise from the police cruisers were vanilla, chocolate mint, hazelnut, cinnamon and raspberry coffee scents. The scents hung heavy in the air. Aroma from the coffee blended and thickened and weakened the lingering scent of blood from last night's shooting until hardly a memory of the killing remained in the area. The early morning rain had even washed away much of the chalk that had outlined the dead man's body, but the rain could not rid of the desire to get even for a crime that connected rage, dirty money, a dangerous appetite for snooping and celebrity.

Chapter Three

Raymond entered each coffee shop just so he could drink in the rich, sweet aroma. Coffee. It was the one thing Malcolm made for him. Thanks to Malcolm, Raymond had been drinking coffee since he was three years old.

That first day in Philadelphia, Raymond ordered four cups of coffee. He drank the coffee as if, with each swallow, he would gain the strength to navigate a new life on his own.

The last cup of coffee was a mild hazelnut from Corner Flavor, a café a mile away from campus. He paid for the drink, grabbed his receipt and hurried outside into a mass of human traffic.

Just as he did, a tall, muscular man with shoulder-length dreadlocks, pedaled down the sidewalk in front of him. The man's elbow - poked out to provide balance while the man sat on the small bike seat - bumped Raymond's forearm, and, before Raymond could steady the cup in his hand, the hot coffee splattered the man's sleeveless knit shirt.

The man stopped.

Raymond's face was drawn down, evidence of an apology.

The hint of a smile adorned the man's face. He brushed coffee drops off his shirt then he extended a hand toward Raymond. "Don't worry about it, Dude. It wasn't a big deal. I'm cool."

The man pedaled away from the café. The ten-speed bicycle he rode ambled slowly down the avenue, popping up ever so slightly each time the bike's wheels rode over an elevated crack in the sidewalk. The bike almost stopped when the man reached the spot where the murder took place.

Raymond stood on the sidewalk outside of Corner Flavor. Wind brushed through his hair while he stared at the University of Pemberton football logo on the back of the man's shirt. He watched the guy turn his head from side to side, as if he was a detective inspecting the area, checking it for bullet shells, hair fibers, anything that could betray the story he told cops.

Two hours later at the University of Pemberton's main bookstore, at the time of day when the sun is gentle and its heat soothes rather than burns the skin, Raymond stared into the chiseled face of the guy he ran into outside Corner Flavor.

The guy looked at him, but didn't speak.

As a perfunctory greeting, Raymond tilted his head skywards and said, "What's happening?" He extended his hand. "My name's Raymond."

The guy returned his nod. "We meet again," he laughed. "Name's Anthony. Anthony Thompson. Straight out of Knoxville, Tennessee," he bellowed, like Knoxville was home only to kings. A second later, he added, "Welcome to UPemb."

"Thanks." Raymond said. He felt like he was standing in front of Paul, one of the few good friends he had back home. "I see you put your bike away. And," he added, "You play football, right?" He chuckled at the question. Anthony's broad shoulders, his large choppy hands, wide rubbery neck and thick skull gave the answer.

"I've been play—" he stopped talking and followed Raymond's gaze.

Four women, their chests jutting out beneath cotton blouses, stood on the top steps of Hotel Pemb. Raymond couldn't stop looking at a short, mocha colored woman who wore large loop earrings, a pair of tattered jeans and a rust-orange sleeveless blouse.

"She ain't for you," Anthony laughed.

"There are four women over there," Raymond said. "How do you know which one I'm looking at?"

"Yea, right. We both know who you're looking at."

Raymond eyeballed him with a tight brow, like he wasn't going to accept anything short of an outright apology. "Why wouldn't she be for me?"

"Look how she's dressed. Look at her sun scorched jeans." He chuckled. "She's more my boy

Doug's type than she is yours. She's a free-spirit." With a shake of his head, he added, "Never know what you're going to get with a woman like that."

"So, I'm uptight and predictable? You don't even know me. Damn. We just met."

"Naw, man. I was just saying."

Silence passed between them.

"She's not your type. That's all I'm saying. It's nothing against you. Oh," he added in an attempt to shift the conversation, "You're right. I play ball. This is my second year. I'm a running back." He grinned unashamedly. The fact that he was as handsome as Denzel Washington took his stud status way up.

A crowd of sports enthusiasts hurried across the street. They ignored Raymond, didn't even give him the respect a child gave a ghost. They approached and circled Anthony like he was the only man in the area. They peppered him with, "You're gonna kick butt this year." "You're gonna break the NCAA rushing record." "Nobody can stop you." "You're gonna land the cover of *Sports Illustrated*."

Anthony soaked up the attention, let it fall down on him like summer rain. "Word," and "Damn straight," he shouted back to the fans. At the same time he continued his conversation with Raymond.

"Gotta get some place soon?" Anthony asked.

"No. I'm cool," Raymond answered.

"Good. We can hang out." Anthony pushed his dreads behind his ears and waved at another fan who called out, "Pemb can't be stopped," as she passed him on her way out of the bookstore.

A guy wearing a cut off UPemb t-shirt, up high enough to show off his beer gut, bumped Anthony's shoulder. "Gonna take the team undefeated this year, Man?"

Anthony tilted his head up. "You know it. Gonna pound the sense out of those other teams. I'm a beast. I'm unstoppable."

The guy gave Anthony a thumbs-up then he walked to the other side of the street.

"What?" Raymond asked with raised brows while he looked at the backs of the fans. "You a celebrity?"

"I'm the man around here, Dude. I play ball. You're gonna see soon enough." He smiled like a fox. "I score a few touchdowns every now and then."

Raymond noticed another a group of students whose eyes widened upon sight of Anthony. Without thinking, he stepped back out of the way. "Looks like you score more than a few touchdowns," he mumbled. "My gut tells me that you'd cost the entire team a game if you walked off the field."

Anthony stared across campus at nothing in particular. In the distance a trio of blue jays flew away from a building roof. A cloud of steam blew up out of the roof vent behind the birds. With a vacant expression in his eyes, Anthony said, "Comes with a price." He paused. "A high price."

"You don't seem to mind it."

Anthony shrugged.

"Ant-ne. Ant-ne," a baritone voice called. The voice came from a tall lanky man sporting long, brunette dreads.

"Doug," Anthony turned and hollered. His smile widened. "Over here," he swung his arm. "Come meet Ray."

"What are you guys over here talking about?" Doug asked, his hands waving. "Not going to dismiss a brother, are you? And," he wanted to know, "Where were you last night? I called your dorm I don't know how many—"

Anthony squinted. "Don't worry about that now."

Doug didn't give up. "Hope you didn't go to that club over on University Avenue."

The frown on Anthony's face said it all. He turned sharply, looked down the bridge of his nose at Doug and just-like-that, the subject changed.

"Ray," Anthony said. "This dude is Doug, my dear brother straight out of Sicily." He swung his arm around Doug's shoulder and tightened the grip. "Can you believe this brother came all the way over here from Italy just to attend the University of Pemberton? Wasn't running from the law, had no epiphany or anything, just wanted to come to the City of Brotherly Love to go to school." He laughed. "Dude loves home designing." He squeezed Doug's shoulder so tightly, Doug's right foot lifted off the ground. "He's majoring in design."

Raymond gave a slow nod.

Without wondering about the deeper identities of the men facing him, he took Doug's hand inside his own and shook it.

"Where did you two meet?" Doug asked Raymond while he glanced at Anthony.

"I was coming out of Flavor Corner," Raymond told him.

"The café on University Avenue?" Doug asked. "Isn't that the spot where—" One glance at Anthony and he bit down on the question he longed to ask.

"I was walking around trying to become familiar with the area," Raymond said. "There are a lot of nice little shops and places to hang out around here."

"This your first time in Philadelphia?" Doug asked. He opened his arms.

Raymond admired the green and silver eagle on the front of Doug's jersey, emblem of the local professional football team.

"Yes. And from the looks of it I'm going to like this city. Heard New York's not too far up the road. Just take the turnpike and you're in Manhattan in no time, something like two hours."

"Absolutely," Doug said, nodding energetically. "New York's not too far up the road." He stepped back and smiled. "Glad to meet you, man. Hang out with us and we'll get you settled in quicker than you'd ever do on your own. We know this town, and this campus. Nobody except the guys who built the place knows Pemb like Ant-ne and me. Stick with us. We know where to go and," he shot Anthony a telling glance. "We know where not to go."

The men talked for a few more minutes. As they stepped away from each other, Doug laughed, and, looked directly at Raymond. Doug cupped his hands together as if he was praying, then he pushed his hands toward Raymond and asked, "Did Anthony almost knock you over with that bike of his when you were coming out of Flavor Corner? He hardly pays attention when he's riding that thing." He walked backwards, away from Anthony and Raymond.

Anthony waved and blurted, "No, I didn't almost run him over. I'd only do that if you were coming out of the café."

Mirth hung between them like a thread. It bonded them closer one to the other -- the good, the bad -- the dark secrets.

With one last joke, they turned away from each other and headed in separate directions.

That night, Raymond lay on his back in bed and contemplated recent changes in his life. As if she was tied to a string in his mind, the woman he saw outside the Inn lodged herself in his thoughts. Only once did he think about Malcolm and wonder if he was okay or if he was drowning in loneliness now that he had what he'd spent years shouting he yearned for – to be in the house alone.

While the air conditioner blew, he thought about climbing beneath the bed covers, but he crossed his legs and decided against it. When he arrived at the campus early Sunday morning, Walter told him that he had no roommate. Initially, he felt slighted as he watched other students who lived in the resident hall laugh and joke their way back to their apartments in pairs. But after meeting Anthony and Doug and reading a Walter Mosley novel when he got back to his apartment, he hoped UPemb never landed him a roommate. He liked solitude. It was a familiar feeling that had grown warm and quaint over the years, like a heavy winter coat.

Outside his room fireflies flickered across the sky like bursts of light. Crickets chirped a chorus that grew louder as the night thickened. Student athletes laughed and chatted beneath the flood lights outside Roddin. Their voices rose and fell with collective excitement and reached all the way inside the resident hall.

The late June temperatures had dropped twenty degrees since noonday. Stray cats milled the streets. Car horns blared in the distance.

Inside the resident hall, a myriad of male voices could be heard. Doors opened and closed with regularity to allow men on the floor to shout jokes and empty threats packaged in laughter back and forth to each other.

Raymond took it all in with quiet reserve. That is, until a knock at his apartment door demanded his attention. He turned away from his bedroom ceiling, a place he had fixed his gaze while he thought about the woman he'd seen earlier in the day.

"Ray," a voice called with force from the hallway.

Raymond pursed his lips and pushed off his bed. He knew it was Walter. "Damn," he moaned while he walked into the living room. "Coming," he hollered when Walter started to pound the door.

Raymond cracked the door open. "What?" he asked.

A slither of light came inside the apartment from the hallway. "We found you a roommate," Walter said. He stepped to the side and a tall thin, Mexican, much of his face covered with a bushy beard, appeared.

"Hi," the man said, his hand was extended and his beard curled at its ends. He carried a heavy duffel bag across his shoulder. His voice boomed, "My name's Patrick."

Raymond eyeballed Walter then Patrick. He didn't speak nor did he shake Patrick's hand.

In a second attempt at friendship, Patrick extended his hand closer to Raymond. "Said name's Patrick." His voice was colder, tight, unlike it had been when he first introduced himself.

As Patrick entered the apartment, slowly so as not to bump Raymond, out in the hallway Walter stifled laughter. He smiled while he watched Raymond tighten his brow and fix his gaze on Patrick's face.

Raymond turned with a scowl and walked across the living room floor; his feet landed hard enough to create an echo. Just as he was about to walk out of the living room into the hallway he stopped. Turning and glancing at the door, he snarled, "Aren't you gonna shut the door?" at Patrick.

Patrick shoved his hand against the door. It closed so hard it shook on its hinges. He followed Raymond into the hallway then stepped beyond him to the left, passed the bathroom. His green duffel bag lay on the floor next to the front door.

Raymond stood outside his own bedroom door watching Patrick check out the apartment, but not for long. Soon he was in the living room again, hunting for something to harangue Patrick about. "Yo, Man!" he shouted from the living room.

Turning away from the entrance to his new bedroom, Patrick asked, "What?"

After Raymond rolled his eyes toward the ceiling he asked, "Are you just gonna leave this big, ugly ass bag sitting in front of the door?"

Patrick cursed beneath his breath then he stomped inside the living room. He grabbed his bag with one hand, pulled up on the handle and carried the bag into his bedroom. This time before he entered the bedroom, he gritted his teeth and asked, "Is this my room?" Before Raymond answered, he added, "The one with the desk, dresser, bed and nothing else?"

Raymond didn't respond. Instead, he walked into the hallway, turned right, entered his bedroom and closed the door.

Patrick saluted the closed door with his middle finger.

Chapter Four

A note was pushed beneath the door of Apartment 712; its side was neatly folded and kept in place with a single staple. After he unlocked the door and tossed his chemistry and American literature books across his bed, Raymond opened the note. It was dated September 7, 1984. Raymond had been at UPemb for nearly three months. For him, life over the past few months had been mostly good, untarnished by hidden rage and anger, since Patrick and he had started to work at a friendship, and now this.

His gaze raced back and forth across the paper. A frown tore at his face, tightened it and made him look ugly.

"Ray, stop by my office tomorrow. Your father called. I want to see how I can help." The note was signed Dr. Eric Davis, President of Student Affairs.

Hurt and ire built up from the abuse he'd suffered at his father's hand poked at Raymond. He balled the note up. Before he knew it he was clenching his fist.

"Must have left a letter from UPemb somewhere back home in my bedroom," he complained. *"But I checked,"* he consoled himself. He clenched his fist again. *"He probably saw the picture of Mom under the trophy, and that set him off."*

His box springs shook and squeaked when he fell down across the bed. "Damn," he muttered. He turned onto his stomach and opened his chemistry book.

Chemistry was his first required course to earn an engineering degree, and in just one month, he had scored a D on his first two tests. He tried to read but his thoughts kept going back to Ohio.

"Why?" he asked with disdain, *"Didn't you check your room better?"* He bit down on his bottom lip until it hurt.

He flipped the chemistry book's pages until they blew up cool air. He told himself to study, but he couldn't forget the note.

He'd always suffered at his father's hand. He couldn't count the times Malcolm picked him up from kindergarten drunk. Teachers and parents would stare at Malcolm then they'd invariably turn and stare, sadness filling their eyes, at him, the little boy standing in the corner with a shrunken look on his face.

"Come on, boy," Malcolm would call with a fling of his wrist just before he reached out for him. Years of drinking tamed his tongue; he scarcely slurred but every teacher at Kindergarten knew he was drunk.

It took Raymond several weeks to figure out that the quicker he responded to his father's requests -- the faster he ran behind him -- the better it went. But this incident on the second day at Kindergarten was five-year old Raymond's first lesson in public embarrassment, and he still had a lot to learn.

"Bye, Ray," a pudgy boy had giggled and waved. He'd befriended Raymond at once, since the first day Malcolm brought Raymond to the school. Raymond and the pudgy boy played together during recess. They took up for one another when other kids picked fights with them.

Raymond picked up his book bag, the one with Batman sketched across its back. He reached out to hug the boy, but Malcolm clamped down on his arm then yanked it.

"Da-de," Raymond cried. He wiggled and tried to free himself from Malcolm's grasp.

"Shut your punk ass mouth," Malcolm growled into Raymond's ear. He tightened his grip until the flow of blood in Raymond's arm pinched and slowed.

Then Malcolm stood, raised his voice above its former whisper, smiled and nodded at the teachers. "Have a good evening," he told them. "Thanks for taking care of my boy."

Raymond cried all the way to the car. Teachers and other parents looked on in horror but no one did anything.

Years and miles removed from the Kindergarten incident, yet filled with the bitterness of its ache, fury boiled beneath Raymond's skin while he lay on his bed in his college apartment. The old bitterness threatened to grind its way into tears. He searched for a place to dump the emotion.

The blare of loud, banging Salsa music came at him like a gift. He stood, threw the note into the garbage, scowled and stomped across the hall to Patrick's room.

He hammered Patrick's door with his fists. He jerked the knob and tried to shove the door open but it was locked.

"Turn your music down," he shouted.

"Yo, homeboy," Patrick hollered from his study desk. Words sounded like they curled before they rolled off his tongue. His grandmother's thick Mazatlan accent rested on every word he spoke. It was as much a part of him as was his grandfather's love for deep water fishing. "I'm just playing my music." He smiled. "I like it loud."

"I don't care if you do like your music loud. Turn it down," Raymond hollered at Patrick's closed bedroom door. "I was in my room trying to study."

"Here," Patrick said after he jerked his door open. "Here's a pair of headphones. Put 'em on."

"Like hell," Raymond snarled. "Turn that garbage down. I don't want to listen to that Mexican cha-cha crap banging in my ears." He let the headphones slip through his hands. They landed on the floor between them. "I'm trying to study."

It was without conscious intent, without a conscious knowing, but Raymond did it anyway. He kept talking to Patrick, a man he had started to believe could become a friend.

"Have a big test coming up," he continued. He looked to the right, in the direction where Patrick stood outside his bedroom door. When Raymond glanced inside the bedroom, he saw that Patrick's blanket was pulled tightly over the top of his bed then folded beneath the bottom of the pillow nearer the bed's crest, evidence of tidiness.

Patrick turned and walked farther inside his room and sat on the edge of the bed. He listened while Raymond rattled on.

"I bombed the first test the professor gave." Raymond shook his head. "If you take Chemistry this year, don't take Professor Whitler. He's boring. He talks in these long monologues. He never asks a question unless he's sure nobody knows the answer and he never has time to meet with students after class. Yet," he chuckled, "right after a test he always stands in front of the class and tells us how he's available for consultation." He laughed. "But he never makes the time to meet with anyone."

His gaze rose and landed against Patrick's bedroom mirror. Through the mirror, he noticed the Mexican flag nailed to the back wall. It seemed to explode with bright red, white and green colors evenly dyed onto a thick cloth, and looked smaller than it actually was. Everything in the room, including the waist high, forest green duffel bag that leaned against the side of Patrick's bed and the towering speakers out of which the Salsa music blared, looked smaller through the mirror.

"I don't know one student Professor Whitler's met with and I asked everybody in class." He swallowed hard. "They all said no. Everyone in class is struggling." He shook his head. "Professor Whitler's only there to embarrass us. He doesn't care how hard we work. He wants to take his insecurity out on us. I mean, this dude never ask a question unless he's certain no one knows the answer."

He bent and picked the headphones off the floor, walked inside Patrick's bedroom and placed the headphones on the dresser. "Sorry about earlier, Man."

"It's all right," Patrick grinned. "I'm having a bit of trouble in my political science class, so I understand. Plus, you're busy with cross-country. You've got a full plate."

"Cross-country's the easy part," Raymond shrugged. "Coach Carter and the guys on UPemb's cross-country team are cool." He smiled. "They remind me of a few guys on my high school track team back home."

"Where's UPemb ranked so far this year?"

"First in the Northeast, third nationally. We race Princeton next weekend."

"Is the meet here?" Patrick asked.

"No," Raymond told him. "It's in Jersey."

"I might come," Patrick said.

"If you do, you can ride up with me. We usually drive our own cars to meets unless they're more than 50 miles from campus. And," Raymond added, "Not a lot of people come out to our cross-country races." A smile broke out across his face. "Now, track." His smile widened. "People pack the stands to watch UPemb's track meets, at least that's what Coach Carter and the more senior athletes on the team tell me."

"How long have you known Coach Carter? Sounds like you like him."

"I talked with him a few times on the phone when he was recruiting me, but I've only known him in person about as long as I've known you."

"He's got sandy blond hair?" Patrick asked. "He's usually at the student center early in morning sipping a cup of coffee and carrying a clipboard in his arm?"

"That's him," Raymond smiled.

"He's always talking with somebody when I see him."

"People like him," Raymond said. "Coach Carter never puts a person down. I don't care how much they're struggling. He always finds a way to make things work out without cursing, pointing fingers and making people feel badly."

"Homey's always laughing when I see him," Patrick added. "My kinda guy." He gazed across the room. "Not like my old man," he said, the volume in his voice lowering.

Raymond turned away from Patrick and looked into the hallway.

"My old man drank," he said, looking up at Raymond. When Raymond met his glance, he added, "Way too much."

"Ho-how's yo-your mom deal with it?"

Patrick's brow rose. "Never heard you stutter before."

"Nah," Raymond said, waving his hand. "I can only imagine what it must have been like for you growing up like that."

"Like what?" Patrick asked.

"With your dad drinking."

"It was hard," Patrick responded somberly. "But my mom took most of the blows." He squinted. "He was real mean to her. I think about her all the time."

"Are they still together?"

As if he hadn't heard Raymond's question, Patrick continued, "My old man hasn't drunk anything except water or milk in five years. Doctor told him if he did he'd be digging his own grave." He chuckled dryly. "That sobered him up real quick. And, yes," he added, "my folks are still together." He shook his head. "My mom ain't never leaving. She's one of those old timey wives. She's in it for the long haul. But," he sighed with relief. "My old man doesn't beat on her no more. He stopped doing that five years ago too. Still," he said, gazing across the room again. "I worry about my mom. There were a lot of mean years."

"It's good your dad stopped drinking," Raymond said.

"What about you?" Patrick asked. "Are your folks still together?"

"Nah. Nah," Raymond quickly answered. "But they're cool," he nodded.

Silence filled the room for a few awkward seconds. Then the guys returned to a safer topic, sports. "Yeah, Homey, I see Coach Carter almost every morning when I'm heading to my political science class."

"Coach Carter's cool, but his work outs are tough," Raymond said, shaking his head. "Ran fifteen quarter mile runs before I came home today. Only had a minute break between them. Coach said it'll get our speed up. Quarter mile intervals do work. I ran eight of those when I was in high school, but," Raymond moaned, "this is the first time I've run fifteen sets." He shook his head again. "Quarter miles are butt kickers."

Patrick leaned forward on his bed. "I say if you do the hard stuff, you'll reap the hard to reach rewards."

Raymond nodded approvingly. When he looked up, his and Patrick's gazes met.

"Remember when I first got here?" Patrick laughed.

"I hadn't been here long, but I enjoyed having the place to myself," Raymond admitted.

"I could tell."

"Sorry about that, Man."

"Nah," Patrick waved. "It took a week, but we've been cool ever since. Although you do stay holed up in your room studying a lot, and more so over the last two weeks."

"That chemistry course is kicking my butt."

"Let me know if you want me study with you," Patrick offered. "I'm pretty good at chemistry."

Raymond walked toward the door. "Thanks, Man." He forgot about Malcolm and the letter from Student Affairs as he entered his own bedroom. He opened his chemistry book and stretched out across his bed. Then, and without meaning to, he turned and looked at the wastebasket, and the memories of Malcolm started to surface, haunt him all over again, make him afraid that Malcolm would come after him, create loud, ugly scenes that would leave him with but one unfortunate choice, that would force him back home.

Chapter Five

Patrick was right. For Raymond, the hard work did pay off. Two weeks ago, he won the men's NCAA five mile cross-country championship in a record setting twenty-two minutes and forty-four seconds, and now he had his sights set on winning the national indoor half mile and mile championships.

Upcoming competitions helped to keep his mind off Malcolm. They made time pass quickly, weeks feeling as short as days and months as short as weeks. It was late November. Raymond had settled into a comfortable groove.

The respite was a reward in itself. Yet, Raymond knew that if he continued to compete in cross-country, indoor and outdoor competitions, his mind and body keying up for the next big race, he'd soon wear down. He'd lose a step, and start to become an easy prey for the other runners who always trailed him, close on his heels, anxious to lean ahead of him across the finish line, breaking the tape before he did.

Yet, despite what he knew and felt, Raymond kept pushing himself. He lengthened his stride as he walked to his apartment. He shoved his hands in his pockets and thought about the last thing Coach Carter said to him less than ten minutes ago when they bumped into each other in the Student Center. Coach Carter had been sipping a cup of almond coffee. He held a brown briefcase, the one he kept track workouts in.

"You know I'm not a morning person," Raymond laughed as soon as he saw Coach Carter, the mid-evening sky starting to darken. He met Coach Carter's gaze. "But, believe it or not, to get an edge on the indoor competition, I've been getting up at six a.m. every day this week and putting in an eight mile run. Today's the only day I didn't get up early," he told his coach. "Plan to log a brisk run tonight though."

Coach Carter shook his head. "We're both doing our homework." He tapped the briefcase. "I just spent the last hour working on practices." He placed his hand on Raymond's shoulder and smiled approvingly. "You know, Ray," he said, "I knew you had a champion's mentality the first time I saw you run. I keep telling you what a rare talent you are, but you're always so modest." His smile widened. "You're gonna go far in track and," he paused, "in life."

Raymond glanced at the floor. He felt hot, symptom of his growing embarrassment. Compliments made him nervous, as desperate as he was to receive them. "I appreciate that, Coach," he finally looked up and responded. "Heading home for the day?" he stepped forward and asked.

"Yeah, and I better get there soon," Coach Carter answered as he turned over his watch. "Or my wife's gonna cook my grits."

"Better get out of here then," Raymond chuckled.

Coach Carter tightened his grip on the briefcase's handle. "If I ran as fast as you do, I'd be there," he snapped his fingers, "just like that."

"You've got a beautiful family, Coach. Running fast is no match for that."

"Thanks," Coach Carter said. "Other than the quick run, what else is on your schedule for the evening?"

"Think I'm gonna go to the weight room and lift."

Coach Carter smiled, nodded his approval and said, "I love your drive, the way you go after what you want. We just might win it all this year." He paused. "In both indoor and outdoor track and field." He looked at Raymond, his star athlete, intently. "You're a big part of that, Ray." He paused and wagged his finger. "But remember that in between working out you should take time to rest and have fun. Life's for living. Enjoying yourself is a big part of that."

"Will do," Raymond said as he slapped palms with Coach Carter. They waved good-night to each other, turned and headed toward the Student Center's opposite exit doors, Coach Carter toward the parking lot and Raymond toward Roddin House.

The wind picked up and Raymond quickened his pace. As he neared Roddin House, he continued to think about what Coach Carter told him until he started to hear music.

Through an open Roddin House window, a Miles Davis cut spilled outside, filling the area with music. Wind shook trees and tossed leaves across the ground. Chill filled the air.

Patrick looked up from where he sat on the living room sofa. Colored pencils, drafting rulers, a slide calculator and electrical wires were spread out across the coffee table.

"Finally got Professor Whitler to see the light," Raymond said as he closed the apartment door. He threw his keys onto the living room end table and walked toward the sofa. "What are you making now?"

"Not sure yet," Patrick answered. "It's for this weekend's science fair. I'm going connect it my criminal justice class. You know. Do something different."

Raymond had grown accustomed to Patrick occasionally leaving simple words like 'to' out of sentences when he spoke English. The only times he heard Patrick speak Spanish were the few times he overheard him talking on the telephone with his mother, a loving and gentle woman who enjoyed visiting local Mexican markets just so she could meet and talk with friends, or with his father, a man Patrick described as coarse, a man who loved the water, foamy waves lapping up off the ocean at the edges of the Mazatlan shore. Patrick talked fast then, like a typewriter clanging along at over two hundred words a minute.

"Create a new way to pick up fingerprints to help catch dudes that shoot a man for nothing in this city," Raymond said.

"It takes more than fingerprints catch an offender, Homey. You have to get to know a person to know what they're capable of doing."

"So every cop knows every murderer?"

"No, Amigo. That's not what I mean. You have get inside the head of an offender to know what drives and motivates him. A lot of that has to do with what hurt the offender when he was young."

When Patrick peered up, Raymond looked away from him. "I almost forgot about the fair." He snapped his fingers. "Even with all the electrical stuff you keep around here it almost slipped my mind. Remind me come Saturday. I'll be there."

"Esta chido. What's this about Professor Whitler?"

"He's going to let me take the last test over so I can get my G.P.A. up. He knows I'm busy with track. And what's *esta chido* mean?"

Patrick released a hearty laugh. "It means 'cool.'"

A smile hid in Raymond's voice. More Spanish. It came like a gift to Raymond. It made him think that he had Patrick's complete trust.

He said, "Coach Carter didn't even have to call Professor Whitler. I got through to Whitler myself."

He exited the living room and walked into his bedroom. His rustic, hooded jacket dropped onto his bed when he lowered his arms and shook his shoulders.

"Going to see writer, August Wilson's, play *Fences* tonight?"

"No. I'm going out for a run." He reached inside his closet and pulled out a black and white sports bag. "Despite what they tell you, practice is never over."

"Oh," Patrick said, "Can't believe I almost forgot tell you. Student Affairs called hour ago. Homey," he laughed. "You better get down there and talk to Dr. Davis. He's not someone you want to ignore." He turned away from Raymond and glanced at his science project. "Must be important."

"I met with him when I first got here. No need for me to go back down there."

"Okay, Amigo," Patrick shrugged. "But if it was me, I'd at least call Dr. Davis."

"Besides," Raymond moaned. "I know what it's about."

"What if it's your parents? I only hear you talk about them once since we--"

"I told you my mom's been out of the picture since I was a kid," Raymond snapped. A second later, shame nipped at his conscience. "Nah," he said, his voice absent its previous edge. "It's not them."

Yet, he knew the call from Student Affairs was about Malcolm. The second letter he got today from the office made that clear. He and Malcolm hadn't spoken since he left home over five months ago. Malcolm was trying to reach him, but he had other pressing matters to tend to.

"And," he told Patrick, "I don't want to get into this right now." He clutched the sports bag, grabbed his keys off the end table and headed for the front door. "I'm going for a run."

Just as he touched the knob, he returned his attention to the living room. Guilt nagged him. Whenever Patrick was without his girlfriend, Sandra, he invited him along.

"Want to come?" The question was a means to assuage his guilt. He almost prayed that Patrick would stay at the apartment.

Patrick stood. His back was to the bay window and the outside dark that enveloped the campus. The soulful rhythm of Miles Davis' "Nerfertiti" found its way inside the apartment. It came in like a whisper, real low and funky, as if the trumpet was creeping its way around the residence hall.

"You going to lift first?" Patrick asked.

"Nah. First I'm gonna run. I can meet you at the gym and we can lift together if you want."

Patrick nodded. "I got you." He walked down the hall and entered his bedroom. He pulled a pair of sweats out of the closet. He already had on his red and white high-top Converse sneakers.

"You know what?" he said in a change of mind. "If you don't run too fast, I'll run with you."

Raymond chewed his lip and shifted his attention to the floor. He almost lost the conference cross-country championship race to Dwight Gooding, a junior at Indiana University, a month ago. Through the grapevine he'd heard that Dwight was twice as hard to beat in the outdoor mile than he'd been in the men's five mile cross-country run. After the winter holidays, the outdoor track season would begin. Raymond had no intention of feeling the threat of a loss in an event he'd won since he was in the ninth grade. "Damn," he moaned to himself. He knew Patrick would slow him down.

Patrick watched Raymond's shoulders slump. "That's all right," he said with a wave of his hand. "Go ahead and run. I know how much it means to you. I know Coach Carter's counting on you to help take the team over the top at the nationals this summer." Turning back toward the living room, he added, "I didn't really want lift weights tonight anyway."

Raymond took in a deep breath and straightened his spine. "Nah, Man. Let's go. Coach and I talked a few minutes ago. This is gonna be a good year for the track team." He nodded. "I'm gonna work hard to help the team win the national indoor and outdoor championships. Ohio State beat UPemb for the indoor title last year. UCLA took the outdoor national title." He shook his head. "I'm not going to let that happen again. Plus," he paused. "Next week we have our first indoor competition against Cornell." He looked at Patrick. "I'm not gonna lose." He shook his head again. "UPemb's not gonna lose." After he nodded, he said, "You want to run. Come on." He tilted his head towards the door. "Let's go."

With his familiar boisterous laugh, a sound that boomed with annoying loudness, Patrick bounded to Raymond's side. "Let's go, Brotha," he shouted."

"I'll match your pace," Raymond said. "I was going to go all out, but if you want to come, I'll slow down." He raised a finger. "But just this once."

On Roddin's main floor, they bounded outside into the cool autumn air. Raymond led the way.

"Hard to believe eye-spy Walter's not on duty tonight," he remarked flippantly. "That dude's always minding somebody else's business like he doesn't have business of his own. Can't trust that--"

Patrick glanced at him out of the corners of his eyes. "Ain't nothing wrong with Walter. Walter's cool. He's funny. We always enjoy a good talk whenever I see him while he's on duty." His next words came out slow, with great care. "He's in the know."

After he pursed his lips, Raymond said, "Whatever." He changed the subject. "The gym's only a few blocks away. I say we run a few miles, go to the gym, lift then run back."

Ten minutes later they were a mile into campus. Night thinned the longer they ran allowing them to see several feet ahead with ease. Their white hooded sweat jackets alerted drivers to their whereabouts. Raymond breathed easier the longer they ran. He tried not to, but his stride opened. A few seconds later when he heard Patrick sucking on air, he shortened his step and slowed down, like a horse pulling up in a race.

"Thanks, Brotha."

"How far do you think you can go?"

"Another mile and then we head to the gym."

Raymond rolled his eyes. Since noon he promised himself a brisk run. It was his way to unleash his disappointment, one pounding quick step after another, disappointment come upon him after the woman he had the hard crush on cut her eyes at him when he saw her outside the Student Center. "I-I don't mean any harm," Raymond stammered after the woman glared at him, wounding him deeply with her hard, cold stare. As he prepared to enter the Student Center and she to walk away from it, she bumped his shoulder, nearly knocking his African history book out of his hand. Then raising her head and moving her shoulders back, she walked passed Raymond like he hadn't been standing next to her. He watched her cross the lawn. He didn't stop watching her until he saw a guy jog across the grass, and, joining her side, take hold of her hand.

"*I should have known she wasn't single,*" he told himself while he walked inside the Student Center earlier in the day, scent of the woman's Charlie cologne at his back. He'd been watching her for months, since he saw her outside the Inn at Pemb. He'd spent weeks getting up the nerve to talk to her.

Patrick and he ran up Locust Walk, over to University Avenue, then jogged back to Walnut Street. Several blocks later, they stopped so Patrick could catch his breath before they turned and jogged to the gym.

At the entrance to the gym, Patrick bent over. His hands braced the tops of his knees. He took in and released deep breaths. "That was a good run. And, why'd you damn near stop when we got to University Avenue?"

"I was thinking about something I heard when I first got here," Raymond answered. He glanced at the gym. "*Only the fittest survive*" was printed across the glass door.

"Which was?" Before Raymond answered, Patrick laughed and said, "Seems like a lot happened when you first got here. Student Affairs called you. You met Anthony and the crew--"

"Believe it or not," Raymond interrupted. He looked over his shoulders. Patrick and he were outside alone but still, he lowered his voice. "First night I got here there was a shoot out. Some dude got killed."

Patrick searched Raymond's face. "You didn't know the cat, did you?"

"Nah," Raymond frowned. "I had just got here. I didn't know anybody. Next day Doug kept trying to say something about a club on University Ave--"

"What?"

"Noth-Nothing." He met Patrick's glance. "Honestly."

"*Pues si*," Patrick laughed. "If you say so."

Raymond opened the gym door. "It's not about what I say." He pursed his lips and shrugged. "It's a fact. I'm giving you straight talk."

"All right, Homes."

"Gotta watch you criminal justice types. You're always out looking for a clue."

Upon entrance to the gym they were met by an array of dumb bells, nautilus machines, weight benches and dead weights spread across the cement floor. Many of the students occupying the gym were football players or body builders.

As Raymond neared the middle of the weight room and a free nautilus machine, a loud voice rang out. It seemed almost to call to him. He looked up and searched for the voice's owner. He didn't know the short, stubby man with one long narrow scar running down the side of his face that looked like it was placed there by an angry woman's sharp fingernail. But what the guy said arrested his attention.

"I was born and raised in the streets. Can't nobody tell me nothing. I know more than all of these rich, comfortable punks who call themselves professors."

The guy's hard words met a chorus of laughter.

Raymond listened to the laughter until he heard its tightness. The brashness with which the guy spoke made it clear that the guy felt he was the gym leader.

"I run this campus. If somebody steps to me wrong, all I have to do is nod." The guy raised a finger to his head and pulled it back like a shooter pulling the trigger on a gun. "And that's that."

Raymond turned away, rolling his eyes and twisting his mouth. He'd heard his share of bullies tossing out threats. He knew a coward when he saw one.

"Who are you rolling your eyes at?" the guy's voice bellowed at Raymond's back.

Raymond didn't turn. He continued to face the nautilus machine. He felt Patrick's gaze hot against the side of his face, measuring the breadth of his courage. All eyes were fastened upon him, waiting to see what his next move would be.

He hoisted a leg over the nautilus machine's bench, pulled off his sweat top, grabbed the bars at the sides of the machine and, with a deep breath, began to push out a set of two hundred pound reps.

"You didn't hear me?" The voice was closer, right at Raymond's back.

Raymond grunted and pushed out another rep.

"Soft jock. You ain't nothing."

After he inhaled, Raymond grunted out another rep.

"Punk ass track runner. And," the guy scowled so hard he looked like a snarling dog, "just because you hang out with a slick football player, don't mean nothing." He gritted his teeth, "That motherfucker's gonna get his too. Payback's a bitch," he added, his tall fade poorly trimmed and the tattoo of a cross on his right shoulder, while he turned and walked away from Raymond. Not another word passed between them.

Forty minutes later Patrick and Raymond finished their work out and left the weight room. Cool, brisk air dried their sweat, creating white patches on their skin. Most of the run back to Roddin, neither mentioned the insults that the guy had barked at the gym. Raymond busied himself by swatting moth flies. "These bugs are biting me like I'm a pork chop." He said, slowing his jog to a crawl. "Who do you think's gonna win Saturday's basketball game, us or St. Joe's?"

"You joking? St. Joe's. They're good," Patrick said. "The Hawks' point guard boss. Homeboy's got smooth jumper."

Raymond agreed. "Villanova, St. Joe's and Temple are the teams around here when it comes to basketball."

"You gonna check the game out?"

"I don't know," Raymond answered. "I was thinking about going to Zanzabar Gold and catching some live jazz." He snapped his fingers. "Hey, talking about music, have you heard Grover Washington Jr.'s latest cut?"

"Inside Moves?"

"Right," Raymond said.

"I heard *Watching You, Watching Me* on WJJZ the other day. It's tight." He glanced at the side of Raymond's head. "You thinking about copping it?"

"For sure," Raymond answered. "Grover Washington Jr.'s old school. He knows jazz from the root up."

"Yea, but he plays mostly smooth jazz now."

Raymond shrugged. "Man's gotta earn a living, and that's what's hot these days."

"*Si.*"

"Besides I don't think he'd go too far away from old school. That root's in his soul," Raymond laughed. "It's what he came up on."

They talked in pop-pop-pop rhythm, like they were singing. Reminiscent of a man leading a band, Patrick's hands swung in the air while he talked. His voice rose as loudly as he kept his music.

On this night while they jogged from the weight room back to Roddin, Malcolm's recent letter to Student Affairs weighed heavily on Raymond's mind. It pinched at his thoughts akin to how the moth flies wouldn't let up on his skin. The letter arrived at UPemb this morning. One of the Student Affairs secretaries put the note inside an envelope, sealed it with tape and stuck it under Raymond and Patrick's apartment door. Even with the letter, Raymond knew Malcolm didn't know where he was.

He imagined that Malcolm had sent a letter to every school in the country that had a decent track program. It was a crap shoot, darts being thrown in the dark. He knew Malcolm wouldn't know where he was for sure until he called or wrote him back. National sports television and radio shows didn't cover college track and cross-country like they did basketball and football.

But the letter brought echoes of the familiar pain from home. Its rocky, jagged mood stuck to Raymond like ice picks. "You owe me, boy," Malcolm, his handwriting scribbled and hard to read, began. "I'm the only one who took care of you after your mom walked off with her new lover. You'd of been dead. You were just a baby. That's right," he wrote, the ink smearing across the ruled paper. Even without the smell of hard liquor, Raymond knew his father was drunk when he penned the letter. "Your dear precious mama who you insist on loving so much walked off and left you when you were just a baby so she could cuddle up with a has been football player. How's that for a trade off?" Again the ink was smeared. If Raymond hadn't known better, he would have sworn that his father had been crying.

"I was only twenty-eight years old. Left me to figure out how to raise a kid all by myself. I'd been through enough." The writing grew choppy, as if Malcolm was jabbing at the paper. "My dad beat the life out of me when I was a kid. You think I'm hard on you? I ain't been half as hard on you as my old man was on me. You had it easy. Married your mom and thought I'd finally get to rest and enjoy life. But no. Bitch walked off and left me to raise a kid all on my own. Trifling whore."

At this point in the letter, Raymond wanted to snatch the receiver out of its cradle, bang out 555-2323 on the dial and shout to Malcolm that it wasn't his fault that his mother left. Seconds later, he wondered if he'd cried too much as a child. He wondered if he'd become a burden at just two years old.

One more paragraph, and to his own surprise, he did snatch the receiver out of the cradle but he never dialed the number. He knew Malcolm would laugh at him. He knew the loud taunt would rip across the wire and echo throughout his bedroom. He knew its loud, reverberating noise would push tears into his eyes.

He wanted to tell Malcolm about the woman he met on campus. He wanted to tell him about the passing grade he was earning in Chemistry, a course he'd long struggled with. He wanted to tell Malcolm how well he was doing in track, but he didn't. He hung the phone up and kept Malcolm and his relationship the way it was – cold and distant.

As if to shift Raymond's thoughts, Patrick lengthened his stride. As they neared Roddin he began to enjoy the feel of air moving in and out of his lungs. The wind no longer felt like an enemy, as if it was punching him in the chest. He started to enjoy the run. He talked without struggle. "Lionel Hampton is another homey who's versatile with his craft. My mother took me to see Hampton perform live in Mexico City one time. I was just a little boy." He smiled as if images and sounds from the long ago experience were seeping through the memory so strongly that he looked like he'd just walked away from the concert, Lionel Hampton's white dress shirt wet with sweat much like his t-shirt now was, his fingers entwined with his mother's, his small head turned, looking back at the maestro as if he was more magic than man.

"I fell in love with jazz the day I heard Lionel Hampton play." Patrick's smile widened. "Hamp put it down."

He leaned into the turn. "Miles Davis is another dude who has a new album out . . ."

While Patrick talked, Raymond's thoughts volleyed back to Malcolm. Had he called Malcolm, he was going to tell him that he set the national cross-country record a few weeks ago. That would have made Malcolm proud.

In fact while he ran around the final turn of that cross-country race, and his muscles tightened with lactic acid, he thought of Malcolm. The larger Malcolm's image grew in his mind's eye, the harder he pumped his arms, and the faster his legs turned. Wind knifed his lungs but he only raced faster. He sprinted through the finish line like he was halfway through an eight hundred meter race.

He would have told Malcolm about the 'A' he earned in Social Science. He would have told his father a lot of things, each of them able to make Malcolm proud, to bring him what he drank hard liquor in search of. Although it had never done so before, Raymond told himself again that his achievements would have made Malcolm feel big, feel like he belonged.

"It's good to see Miles back in the saddle," Patrick continued. "It's good see another maestro strong again."

"Yea," Raymond mumbled.

"Low talking dude, that Miles," Patrick chuckled.

Raymond nodded.

"Not like that loud mouth braggart at the gym."

Raymond bit down on anger. He used the emotion like a shield. He promised himself that if he saw the guy from the gym again he'd pound blood out of his face. He'd make him feel sorry for bringing him pain, for making him feel small.

"Hey," Patrick said. "We're back."

Roddin was a few yards ahead of them. Light came away from the resident house windows and landed on the sidewalk.

"We had good run," Patrick said. He peered at the sky. "We finished in time. Feels like it's starting to rain. And," he added while he squinted through the night. "Looks like Anthony and Doug are coming this way."

"Anthony, then Doug leaned forward and slapped Patrick across the back.

"Haven't seen you homeboys in awhile," Patrick said. His voice was loud, like he was shouting. "Good to see you."

"Shut up," Doug waved, turning his torso partly away from Patrick. "We keep telling you to come to some games with us, but you always back out," he added, glancing at Anthony as if seeking his approval. "You're such a girl, Patrick."

"I'm not big sports fan. I'm into science. Ray can tell you." He nudged Raymond's shoulder. "There's a science fair at Robert J. Amerie Hall Saturday. If you want go to that, I'll go with you. I have an exhibit at the fair."

Anthony's eyes widened. "Really? What's your exhibit?"

Patrick laughed. "Nah," he said. "I'm not gonna tell you. Plus I'm not sure yet myself. I'm still working on it. Come to the fair and you'll find out what my exhibit's about."

"How long have you been into science?" Anthony wanted to know. "I think that's cool, man. Science always kicked my butt. If I passed science it was a miracle."

"I liked science since I was four. Guess how I knew I wanted to be scientist?"

"How?" the men asked as a group.

They talked their way back to Apartment 712. They stayed long enough for Patrick and Raymond to shower and change into jeans. Raymond topped his jeans off with a soft black and yellow sweater while Patrick wore a clean UPemb sweat top. All four men wore a hooded jacket.

They went back into the night amid light rain. They walked to a local diner. Grilled cheese sandwiches, hot soup, and buttered vegetables seasoned their conversation which swung from science to soccer to track and field to whether or not UPemb's football team would make it to the BCS Bowl next month to Doug's other great love -- theatre. Raymond even thought about pulling

Anthony to the side and asking him if he knew the loud mouth guy from the gym, but he decided to let it go.

They stayed at the diner for two hours. It was ten o'clock when they stood to leave. Raymond walking with his head down, suddenly looked up.

She came through the door with her shoulders raised. Long, loose curls bounced against her back. A pair of low-cut jeans showed off her curvy, petite frame. Dark mahogany lipstick made her mouth look like luscious fruit. An umbrella was in her hand.

Raymond's breath caught in his throat.

He watched her head swing from side to side. Water sprinkled her shoulders. When she stood still her big brown eyes focused right on him and his opened mouth. He wondered if she remembered him from the Student Center and the Inn at Pemb.

She tried to hurry beyond him, but the doorway was clogged with people slowly making their way in and out of the diner. If she took two more steps forward, her body would collide with Raymond's.

"Can we talk?" Raymond wanted to ask. Yet, all he did was stare at her.

Patrick cupped his hand around Raymond's elbow then pulled.

Raymond didn't move. His gaze remained fastened on the woman's face. Her cheeks were rosy as she had just come indoors out of the brisk temperature and the falling rain.

"Brenda," a rich alto voice, belonging to a tall, mocha skinned woman, called from inside the diner. "Over here."

"Excuse me," Brenda said while she moved her umbrella to the side, pulled in her stomach and inched beyond Raymond.

"So, your name's Brenda," Raymond said.

Anthony went to his toes. The rain was coming down hard and he didn't have an umbrella. "Ray. Come on, Man."

Brenda blushed but she didn't turn. Too many people in the diner knew her boyfriend, a man who didn't tolerate a woman he was seeing showing interest in another guy.

Raymond didn't move. It was as if he was frozen, all of his attention fixed on Brenda.

After a few seconds, the sensation of Raymond watching her intently caused Brenda to do more than blush. Glancing ever so slightly over her shoulder at him, she said, "And your name is Ray."

He grinned. Just as he reached out for her, the woman who had called to Brenda earlier waved. "Come on, B," she hollered.

"Coming, Cynthia," Brenda shouted back.

Raymond stepped in front of Brenda, preventing her from moving through the crowd. Smiling, he told her, "My name's Ray-mond Clarke." With that he exited the diner and walked into the falling rain, remembrance of Brenda filling his thoughts with promise and his body with pleasure.

Chapter Six

It was December 14, 1984. Raymond hadn't seen Brenda in two weeks, since the night they bumped into each other at the diner. He thought about her every day. Her soft smile and the scent of the Charlie cologne she wore lingered in his memory.

UPemb's first major national indoor track and field meet being a month away, he also hadn't jogged with Patrick again. He told himself that he couldn't afford to. Coach Carter signed him up to run the eight hundred and fifteen hundred meter runs at the indoor competition, New York City's Albright Invitational. The fastest time Raymond had run in practice in the eight hundred meters was one minute and fifty-eight seconds. His fastest fifteen hundred meter run clocked in at three minutes and fifty-six seconds. Both runs were clocked outdoors. Raymond knew to give himself a chance to win the Albright Invitation on January 12 he had to shave several seconds off both distances.

"Eat three to four eggs and a little cheese in the morning," Coach Carter told him at the end of yesterday's practice. "For lunch and dinner, load up on protein and carbohydrates. Trim back on sugar. Do that for a week and we'll measure the results. You're ready mentally," he told Raymond. "We just gotta get your times down a little before we head to New York."

Raymond nodded obediently. "Sure thing, Coach." His voice came out loud and strong, but that's not how he felt. In fact, he stayed at the track after the end of practice so he could time himself at both distances again, his teammates gone home and Coach Carter busying himself in his office next to the men's locker room.

Half an hour after practice ended, Coach Carter walked out of his office. When he reached the entrance gate to the track, he turned and looked over his shoulder. "Ray, why are you still here?" he asked. He held the familiar briefcase.

"Thought I might get in another run," Raymond shrugged and answered.

Coach Carter laughed. "Come on," he said as he swung his arm over his shoulder. "Let's go. No need in you wearing your legs down. That won't help us," he chuckled. "And besides tomorrow's the big football game. I'm sure you and your friends will be tailgating and rooting Anthony and the rest of the UPemb football team on." After Raymond caught up to him, Coach Carter shook his head and stretched his free arm across Raymond's shoulders. "We gotta win tomorrow and make it to the BSC Bowl, Ray. "If we win tomorrow, it'll be the first time in the school's history that the football team made it to the BSC Bowl."

They reached the parking lot and Coach Carter removed his arm from Raymond's shoulders. "Big game tomorrow, Ray. I'm not an avid football fan, but even I'm going to tomorrow's game." He chuckled. "My whole family's going to be there." He patted Raymond on the back. "Go home and help pump Anthony up for the game. We'll focus on track and get ready for January's competition on Monday. And come on," he added. "I'll give you a ride to Roddin."

The following morning Roddin House was abuzz with the prospects of UPemb winning a historic spot at the BSC Bowl. The biggest football game of the year had arrived, the final game of the regular season that would determine whether UPemb made it to the BCS Bowl. As odds would have it, their opponent was long time rival, Norte Dame. Game tickets sold out a week ago. On and off campus and bar after game party RSVP lists were so long, students had begun to organize smaller private parties in their dorm rooms. Out-of-town pro football scouts had booked their plush Philadelphia hotel rooms days ago. NBC-10, KYW, ESPN, Action News and local Trenton and Delaware television sports crews were on campus in their station vans.

Outside Roddin, as frost clung to lawns and students donned gloves, tailgate parties -- the sweet aroma of smoked barbecue wafting through the air -- lined up one behind the other north of UPemb's football stadium. All around campus beer flowed like water, especially at main hubs like the Student Center and Elixir, a popular on-campus eatery. Cheerleaders, budding models and other curvy women with gorgeous faces strutted toward the game in tight jeans and low-cut blouses. One guy filled their thoughts – Anthony Thompson.

"Homeboys," Patrick called out in his booming voice. Its sound went through the opened apartment door and echoed down the hallway.

Heads turned. Right away everyone looked at Patrick's beard, the reddish brown hair having grown nearly twice as thick since Patrick moved in with Raymond. The beard, it was Patrick's trademark. So too was his voice that was usually so loud people on the floor rolled their eyes and cursed beneath their breath when Patrick got to talking real good.

Snack crumbs and meat scraps littered the apartment. Except for a few chips, pretzels and Doritos no other pre-game food Raymond and Patrick bought yesterday remained.

"Damn," Joe Joe, a guy who lived across the hall, moaned. He looked through his own opened apartment door into apartment 712. "Pat's always talking so damned loud." He swung his foot at his door and slammed it closed.

"Pat! *Amico!*" Doug said. He took a swig of his ginger ale. "What do you want?"

"Ready head to game?"

"Let's do this," Anthony said. He leaped off the sofa. For the last week he'd answered countless game questions put to him by eager reporters. He was ready to get on with it. "Everybody's coming out to watch me beat down on Notra Dome," he exclaimed. "By the end of the third quarter, those greasy cats are gonna be sorry they stepped on the field."

"See you at the stadium," dudes from upstairs told Anthony. They took turns giving him one-arm hugs.

Across the hall, guys grabbed their UPemb jerseys and car keys. "Go hard on those wannabes," they shouted. Raymond stood and rounded the corner and went into his bedroom. "Where's the rest of your crew, Ant-ne?" he asked while he reached to his closet's top shelf.

Anthony looked from Patrick to Doug. "You all are my crew," he answered. "And," he wanted to know, "What are you looking for?" He almost walked around the corner, but he stopped himself. He knew now wasn't the time to hammer Raymond with questions.

"Time to head to the big game," Raymond answered. "I gotta go correct." He pushed aside a stylish fedora hat and a pile of button down shirts until he saw the yellow and black Timberland boot box at which instant he smiled. "Last weekend I bought a pair of mean Timb's. It was that or get the new Adidas."

"Speaking of looking for something," Anthony teased in effort to clear his mind. The biggest game of his life was less than two hours away. He couldn't waste another second trying to figure out why rumors around the club shooting had resurfaced. "How are things going with you and that woman Brenda?"

"None of your business." Raymond chuckled. "That's how things are going. Things are going none of your business."

Laughter came back to Raymond from the living room. "Homeboy's in love," Patrick teased. "That woman's your wife, Ray." Patrick's smile faded. In its place were a straight brow and a square jaw. "You're gonna marry her."

Doug grabbed a handful of chips and pretzels, sipped his ginger ale and sat forward on the sofa. "That woman doesn't love or *amore* you, Ray." He munched the chips. "Sure. She's nice." He shrugged. "But she's not into you. You want a woman who's head over heels in love with you, a woman who doesn't want to go one single day without you. You want to marry a woman who's going to adore and obey you. You don't want to marry a woman who's just being *amichevole* or nice."

Raymond snatched his hand away from the closet shelf; a pair of blue and white Adidas that he only wore twice fell to the floor when he did. Several long, pounding strides and he was back inside the living room. At the sofa's edge he glared at Doug. "You ever love a woman? Ever have a woman love you?"

He was met with silence.

"Don't tell me whether a woman loves me or not," he continued, "Because you don't know what you're talking about."

"Hey, pal, I was just playing," Doug offered, looking from Anthony to Raymond. "Don't go nuts."

"Yea, Ray. Calm down." Patrick raised and waved his hands through the air like he was directing a frenzied orchestra song. "If you love this woman, you love her. I can look at you and tell you have feelings for her. Despite how many times you say there's nothing going on between you two, I know there is. You go quiet when she comes around."

Raymond's attention swung from Doug to Patrick. The glare in his eyes remained. He read his friends' thoughts, and quickly said, "I'm not scared of her."

As if he hadn't heard the bark in Raymond's voice, Anthony buckled his knees and fell across the empty space at the end of the sofa. He burst out laughing. Seconds later when he stood, he was still laughing. He reached across the living room chair for his team jacket. "Let's get to the game," he demanded. "I gotta play ball."

After he pulled on the new Timberland boots, Raymond looked over his shoulder at Doug and Patrick. His brief row with them was forgotten, pushed back into time as if it never occurred. "Ready?"

Patrick stood. "Let's go. Anthony?"

"What?" Anthony asked from the hall. He didn't turn. He knew his friends were behind him.

"You riding with us?" Patrick asked.

"I'm gonna ride with, Ray," he said. A second later, he glanced across his shoulder at Raymond. "Mind giving me a ride back to my place so I can pick up my jersey? Would call my mom and dad but they already left for the game." He chuckled. "They're acting like kids. My whole family is pumped up. They got in two days ago."

Despite his public bravado, Raymond found Anthony to be one of the coolest, most humble dudes he'd met. "It's cool your family is excited about the game," he said. "And yes. I'll drive you by your place." Zipping his jacket, he added, "We can all cram inside my car, but Patrick, if you drove, Doug and you can go on over to the stadium and hold me a seat."

Patrick tossed his car keys into the air then Doug and he headed for the elevator a few steps ahead of Anthony and Raymond. On Roddin's main floor, all four men raced outside to their cars.

Walter stood in the hallway between the elevators and the men's room, the place where he'd run as soon as he heard Anthony's and Raymond's voices. His back was pressed against the hard cement wall. Slow tight breaths went in and out of his nose, picking up the faint odor of dried piss that lingered around the men's bathroom door. His gaze darted and roved, struggled to pick up the slightest shadow, the hint of someone approaching.

Patrick turned on the sidewalk and looked back at the empty main desk for Walter, a guy he'd shared more than a few good laughs with since he'd arrived on campus.

Sun rays hit Raymond's sparkling clean black and silver Hyundai Excel. A new cherry air freshener strip swung from the mirror. The smell of Armor All covered the car's vinyl seats.

"When did you get your ride?" Anthony asked.

"A few days ago." Raymond said turning the key in the ignition.

After he tapped the horn at fellow athletes living in Roddin, Raymond pulled away from the curb. "I heard you moved into the apartments over on Chestnut."

"Man, where have you been?" Anthony said. "I moved in there a week ago." He laughed. "Can't get laid like a grown man living in those crammed dorms. In fact," he added while he pointed. "Turn down this street."

The Excel cruised down 34th Street. UPemb football banners hung out of dorm and apartment windows. The backs of trucks and RVs were scribed with game slogans like *"Go Pemb!" "Beat Notra Dome!"* and *"Mighty Bears 12-0!"* Already street vendors were out selling their wares: UPemb t-shirts, hooded sweat jackets, skull caps and team action posters, most of Anthony high stepping across the end zone.

As if he had nothing to do with the festivities, Anthony raised a brow and leaned toward Raymond. "You haven't been to the apartment? I thought I invited all of you over. Man, visit. You know you're my homeboy." He shook his head. "Now, mind you, it's not the Hilton."

"As long as you like it."

"I do. Life's good. Everything's cool. Just feeling pressure. That's all." He folded one leg across the other. "Know what I mean?"

The Excel pulled up to a traffic light and stopped. Several dudes wearing UPemb jackets and carrying a large white cooler walked across the street in front of the car.

"Nobody's said a word to me about the shooting," Raymond blurted. Anthony had asked him about the shooting outside Club Zone, a club less than a mile off campus, several times since the night they walked from the diner through the falling rain back to Patrick and his apartment. It was the same night Raymond bumped into Brenda. "Is somebody after you?" Raymond had pulled Anthony aside and asked that night a week ago. Raymond didn't tell Anthony about the braggart at the gym, his words still jagged, sharp and disrespectful when Raymond thought about them. But it was the guy's threats that caused Raymond to worry about Anthony.

Since he posed the question a week ago, to Raymond it seemed like Anthony was digging for information, trying to figure out what he'd heard since he'd come to campus. "I only know what you told me last week. I mean, what can I say?" He shrugged. "I had just arrived to Philly the night the shooting happened."

Anthony searched Raymond's face. "Sorry to dump that on you, Man, but I had to tell somebody, especially with talk about the shooting coming up again." He shrugged. "And after I started talking, you asked me what I knew too."

Raymond's hands tightened around the steering wheel. He continued to look directly ahead while he gazed through the front windshield.

"I just—I just had to tell somebody. And like I said, I was just at the club. I didn't know those dudes that got to scuffling." He gazed out of the window. All week he told himself to focus. Even after hours of studying Notra Dome on film, particularly their bulky, defensive lineman Philip Walters – this year alone Philip had 15 sacks and more than 58 tackles -- Anthony wondered if he was ready for kickoff.

"It's not illegal to go to a club," he said. "I was having a good time like everybody else. Next thing I know I'm sitting in the club and I hear guys shouting then there's shoving then running. Then I heard pop-pop-pop out in the street." He shook his head. "That's the end of my involvement with the shooting."

Raymond stared at him. They'd gone over this so many times, and yet, he heard himself ask a familiar question. "So you were still in the club when the shooting took place?"

Anthony's eyes roved back and forth. He was silent. It was as if, although he had been at the club, he was waiting for the right answer to come to him. "Like I keep telling you," he said, "I was coming out of Club Zone when these dudes ran out of the club behind me. They drew their guns, chased this other cat down the street and shots rang out. That's all I know."

"First you said the guys ran out before you did."

"Aw, Man," he whined with a wave of his hand. "I don't remember the exact details."

"Whatever."

A second later Raymond heard himself talking again. "Okay, so you didn't do anything. That being the case, why do you keep sweating what happened that night?"

Anthony tossed his head back and let loose a rip roaring laugh. "Man, you don't know anything about the press and being famous. The two go together. They create intrigue. The combination sells papers, makes money."

A quartet of women, their hair blowing in the wind, darted across the street in front of the Excel.

Raymond slammed on the brakes, sending Anthony lunging forward then quickly back against the headrest again. "Watch where you're going," he shouted after he rolled the window down.

The women kept running. They were headed toward the football stadium. Unaware that Anthony was in the car they didn't even turn and look over their shoulders at Raymond.

"Yea, but if you didn't have anything to do with what happened that night," Raymond said after he rolled the window up and turned the heater down, "Then there's nothing to report."

Anthony rolled his eyes. "Dawg, Ray, Man, are you slow? There doesn't have to be anything to report," he barked. "All there has to be is someone famous placed at the scene." He spread then shook his hands. "That's all it takes."

Raymond shrugged. "Whatever. That's all over with."

Anthony grew quiet.

They went down another block and stopped at a red light. Raymond turned and eyeballed Anthony. "What's going on?" Before Anthony answered, he assured him that, "I haven't said a word about this to anybody, not even to Doug or Patrick. Not a word. Patrick doesn't know you were at the club on the night of the shooting. Doug has his suspicions for whatever reasons." He shrugged. "Doug's from the Old Country. He's no stranger to murder and mayhem." He shot Anthony a telling glance. "But he doesn't know anything for certain as best as I can tell."

"Good," Anthony sighed. "I don't need this getting all mixed up."

Raymond looked at him. "You told me that case was closed." He paused. "What's the deal?"

"Heard a few dudes talking—"

"Screw that, man," Raymond said with his face turned up and tight. "People talk. That doesn't mean anything."

"Naw. This is different. This time this little sawed off shotgun of a dude--" He stared out the car window. If he could disappear right now, he would. But he was the campus star, the biggest man at school. Even if he did run away, wherever he went someone would notice him. "--Dude's always popping off at the mouth. He hangs out around the gym. Thinks he's tough."

While Anthony described the guy, Raymond's mind traveled back to the night Patrick and he went running then stopped at the gym and pushed out several reps. Even now he could hear the stubby guy barking out threats.

The light turned green. Raymond pressed the accelerator and they turned onto Chestnut Street. They pulled in front of a row of gray cement apartments. As soon as Raymond opened his car door and looked up at the apartments, he turned up his nose. "Ugly," he moaned.

Once inside the apartment and while he waited for Anthony to grab his gear, Raymond surveyed the living room and the kitchen. Empty water bottles and energy drinks were spread across the sofa. Several pairs of dirty jeans were tossed across the room's single chair. There was so much dust on the television, with the power turned off the screen looked gray.

Books were stacked on the floor next to the television. Sports posters, mostly of Walter Payton, Barry Sanders, Bernard King and Earl Campbell, were tacked to the kitchen walls. A framed picture of Anthony's girlfriend, Aretha, a tall, voluptuous woman with a bright smile and a pretty face, was on a corner of the coffee table. Raymond looked at the picture and wondered if Aretha knew she was one of many women in Anthony's life. Recently washed dishes filled the plastic drainer; but it was obvious that the dishes had been dropped and shoved rather than placed inside the drainer, a clear sign that Anthony hated to wash tableware. In the center of the kitchen table, like a beacon of hope, was an assortment of brightly colored silk flowers.

"So what's this dude going around saying?" Raymond shouted from the living room.

While Raymond studied the apartment, Anthony rushed through his bedroom. He snatched his cleats, jersey, helmet, socks, jock strap, skull cap, jeans and a sweatshirt. "That I started the beef between the guys at the club. That if it hadn't been for me, the fight wouldn't have happened." He paused. His shoulders dropped, lending him the appearance of a defeated man, not a champion. "That because of me a guy's dead."

"And it's—"

"A lie," Anthony shouted, his shoulders rising and fight again in his spirit. "It's a straight up lie. But I hear this dude knows people, and I don't need trouble." He was shaking his head when he walked out of his bedroom carrying his gear. "I don't need trouble," he repeated. He grabbed his door keys off the top of the television. "Let's roll."

"Do you need to call your coach before we leave? It's going to take us, what, fifteen minutes to get to the stadium?"

"Nah. Ten minutes tops." He rushed back into his bedroom and grabbed his cordless phone off his nightstand. Seconds later he raced back inside the living room. "Just called coach. He knows I'm on my way."

They ran out of the apartment.

"So go on about this dude with the loud mouth," Raymond said when they reached his car. He wanted to know more. He had to know more. He had to know if this guy was the same person who accosted him at the gym.

"From what I hear, he hangs out with a bad crowd. I don't know how much he's been talking, but if he doesn't stop, something's going to happen. Philly is not the city for this kinda trash talk."

"What's he look like?"

"Aww, Ray," Anthony waved in a sudden change of mood. "I don't want to talk about this right now."

"Yea," Raymond nodded. Even though Anthony let go of the subject, Raymond continued to relive the night at the gym. He also thought about the first night he arrived in Philadelphia.

They sped down the street, made several quick turns then raced toward Bruce Jordash Stadium. The closer they got to the football stadium, the more congested traffic became. In some spots, they literally stopped.

Horns honked. Ticket scalpers worked their magic and souvenir vendors walked between cars shouting, "Get your game program for only five dollars! Get your game program for only five dollars!"

It took tight maneuvering but Raymond made his way in and out of different lanes until he reached the back of the stadium, the area where only coaches, football players and their closest relatives were allowed to park.

Anthony leaped out of the car. "Thanks," he bellowed over his shoulder at Raymond while he raced down a long tunnel that led to the coaches' offices and the locker room.

Feeling much too alone, especially with the memory of a faceless stranger who was shot the night he arrived in the city, Raymond stepped outside the Excel, locked the door and headed toward the stadium. He wasn't halfway across the parking lot when voices, thick with labored breath, called out, "Ray."

Raymond turned. Running from the far end of the parking lot were Patrick and Doug.

Patrick reached him first. "Anthony already went inside?"

"Yea. We just got here. You know Anthony. He's always pushing the button when it comes to keeping a schedule. Tell him to be somewhere, I don't care what time it is, and he finds a way to be ten minutes late."

"Homeboy," Patrick said with a raised brow and a lopsided grin. "You sure that's all it was?"

Raymond gave him a hard probing look and he silenced.

After Doug caught up to them, they walked shoulder to shoulder from the parking lot to the stadium. Students flirting, jostling for seats, laughter and endless conversation greeted them. It was an hour before kickoff, but the stadium was already half full.

In the lull of conversation that had meandered between him and his friends, Patrick turned his back to Doug. He leaned against Raymond's shoulder and whispered, "So, what took Anthony and you so long get here?"

Raymond's face was so tight when he faced Patrick he looked like he was squinting. "What? We all practically left at the same time. It didn't take us long to get here." He shrugged. Patrick's tone concerned him. He wondered if Patrick was starting to put pieces together, overhearing rumors about the club shooting.

"With the traffic, I'm surprised we got here when we did," Raymond quickly added. "And why are you worried about when we got here? What counts is that we're here." A second later, he chuckled. "Look, Man. I came here to watch the game."

"Aw, homeboy," Patrick jostled. "You're my *amigo*. I'm just telling you be mindful of who you're real homeboys are."

Raymond fed him silence. He was tired of being at the center of confusion.

"You and me. We're cool," Patrick said. "Just make sure you know details on people you consider a friend."

"Have you been talking to that nosy Walter?" Raymond blurted. "I see you chatting him up. If anybody needs to watch who they hang out with, it's you. And," he added, hoping to deflect the conversation, "I don't have any friends that you don't."

"Humph."

"What does that mean?" He pushed Patrick so hard he fell against Doug and nearly knocked him over. The woman sitting next to Doug spilled half her cup of water across her lap.

"Sorry," Doug told the woman while he moved off of her. "What's wrong with you?" he turned and asked Patrick with a tight brow, his hands bursting away from his chest toward Patrick.

Patrick laughed. "Ray's just mad that someone's onto his boyfriend Anthony."

"Shut up, Patrick," Raymond barked. "I don't want any part of your Inspector Gadget bullshit. You want to be a private investigator so bad, you're about to piss your pants. But you're just a freshman like the rest of us, so you have to wait your time."

"Absolutely," Doug chimed. "Pat, you better cease talking to Walter so damned much. That nosey dude will get your ass killed."

Over ninety minutes later they sat amid eighty thousand screaming fans. University of Pemberton banners soared across the sky. A loud buzzer signaled the start of halftime. UPemb was ahead of Notra Dome by two touchdowns, both scored on ten yard runs by Anthony.

The UPemb band, their blue and red uniforms brightening the area like a painted backdrop, marched across the grassy field. Horns blared and drums thumped. Over head a blimp with the words "Go Bears" floated across the sky.

"Wanna get a hot dog and a soda?" Doug leaned forward and asked.

"Sounds good," Raymond said. Initially it was with reluctance then a growing acceptance that he said, "Patrick, come with Doug and me to the concession stand." He told himself to treat Patrick the same as he always had although he was starting not to trust him. On top of that they were roommates and he didn't need anymore hard relationships in his life.

The guys talked and laughed so much while they made their way down the steps, they didn't see the mass of students moving in the same direction. And Raymond didn't see the long facial scar on the guy standing four people over from him.

The guy watched Raymond out of the corners of his eyes. He'd seen Raymond in the Excel with Anthony earlier in the day. He'd been parked on the corner behind the cover of a large Elm tree when the Excel crossed over Chestnut Street.

"Look at line," Patrick moaned as soon as he reached the bottom of the bleachers.

When Raymond and Doug stopped joking around and looked up they gasped.

"*Mannaggia*," Doug cursed. Despite the growling in his stomach, he thought about turning back.

Raymond searched the area for a let-up in the concession stand lines. His gaze scanned over the top of the scarred guy's head. When he turned and looked to his side, in the spot where the guy once stood, the guy was gone.

"Patrick," Raymond said while he glanced to his side again. "Did you see—" He stopped. It was true that he wanted confirmation that the guy he'd seen was the guy from the gym, but they weren't here to hunt for a trouble maker, and he wasn't certain that Patrick was the person to seek answers from anymore.

The line to the concession stand wrapped around the corner toward the bleachers. Students inched forward, heel-toe, heel-toe. A myriad of conversations mixed in the air.

Doug moaned, "We've been standing in this line for I don't know how long. Does everybody in this city want a stadium hog dog right now?"

"Homeboy, stop complaining," Patrick advised. "We've been waiting too long back out now." He shoved his hands inside his coat pockets and told a joke, its punch line sounding too much like an old Richard Pryor "Mudbone" tale.

Raymond reached the concession stand counter first. The cashier's long brunette hair was pulled into a bun and covered with a white knit mesh. The woman twisted her mouth when, after two seconds, Raymond didn't rattle off his order.

"I'll take a hot do—" Glancing to his right, Raymond stopped talking. His tongue caught in his mouth. In the line next to him was Brenda. She was standing so close to him, the strawberry scent of the shampoo she washed her hair with last night whisked up his nose. The longer they stood beside one another, the more the mild, fresh scent worked its way toward becoming Raymond's favorite.

"Hey," the cashier called out to Raymond.

Brenda looked at him and their eyes locked.

As if she'd done something worth repentance, Brenda quickly turned away and pulled down on her jacket hem.

The cashier rolled her eyes. "Sir?"

Brenda peered at Raymond.

Raymond stifled the grin that threatened to widen his face. "One hot dog, a pretzel with mustard and an ice water, please," he said while he looked at Brenda.

"Mustard's over there," the cashier said. She pointed to a row of tables lined with napkins, plastic silverware and condiments.

So she wouldn't appear to be staring at Raymond, Brenda turned and followed the cashier's finger. Raymond didn't take his eyes off of Brenda.

"Come on, Ray. Hurry! Hurry!" Doug begged. "Give the lady your order and come on. Customers like you are probably the reason this line's so long to start with."

"He actually was one of the quicker ones," the cashier said while she placed the hot dog, pretzel and ice water in Raymond's opened hands. "You wouldn't believe how long some people take to ask for a burger or a hot dog."

Raymond stepped out of line and waited for Brenda to be served. He swallowed hard when she turned away from the concession stand, pretzel in hand. "Cashier said condiments are on these tables," he noted in a broken, uneasy way, while he walked alongside Brenda.

She didn't respond. She also didn't intend to put mustard on her pretzel, but she found herself standing at the table next to Raymond.

"Don't you run track?" she finally asked.

"Ye-Yes," Raymond stuttered. "Surprised you would know that." His mouth felt dry. He sipped his water. His palms felt sweaty. He tightened his grip on the cup, hot dog and pretzel. "Never seen you at one of our track meets."

He squeezed mustard atop the curves of his pretzel then he held the bottle out toward Brenda's pretzel. "You want some?"

After Brenda ran her hand over the top of her hair, she said, "Yes. I-I'd like some. But not a lot," she quickly added. "And," she said after Raymond topped her pretzel with dark yellow mustard and they stepped away from the table, "I don't have to go to the school track and field meets to know who you are. Everybody knows you're one of the top middle distance runners in the country, definitely the best on campus."

While Raymond bit into his hot dog, Doug and Patrick, sodas and hot dogs in their hands, nudged his back with the points of their elbows. "Come on," Doug said. "We should get back to our seats. You know how people steal seats when you go missing for too long."

"I'm talking," Raymond turned and told them. His jaw was plump with bits of chewed hot dog. His brows were creased. "I'll catch up to you. My butt ain't that big. I'll squeeze back in next to you two."

"*Idiota*," Patrick mumbled. "Fool around end up having to stand." He cut his eyes at Brenda. This was a football game, an event for males to bond, not a place to strengthen a relationship with a woman. They all could have brought their girlfriends. This wasn't supposed to be a honeymoon; it was a football game. And although Doug nor Patrick mentioned it, it was as if Raymond had broken a code when he stayed behind with Brenda.

"Damn," Patrick whispered while Doug and he walked past Raymond and Brenda toward the bleachers and the subdued noise of a crowd awaiting the start of the second half of what was turning out to be a promising football game.

Raymond's choice to talk with her rather than to hang with his friends didn't escape Brenda. She smiled unashamedly when she looked up at him. "You can go back with your friends if you want," she said, but she hoped that he would stay with her.

He swallowed the bite of hot dog. "And wait to see you whenever we just happen to bump into each other on campus?" He shook his head. "No way. I'm not letting that happen." His shoulders rose. "Who knows when that could be, and besides," he added, "This is the first time I've seen you that you talked to me." He shook his head again. "I was starting to think you didn't want to extend a simple hello in my direction."

"I'm not stuck up if that's what you're implying."

"Did I strike a sensitive nerve?" He raised the hot dog sandwich to his mouth then he lowered it. "People going around saying you're stuck up?" Before she could respond, he added, "Certainly wasn't me. I don't think you're stuck up. Scared. Now that did cross my mind." He bit into his sandwich. He smiled while he looked up at her and chewed the hot dog and bun.

She grinned. "You think you're wise."

"You didn't answer my question."

"I've heard people say I can be stuck up." She shrugged. "But who can't be? I'm quiet. I keep to myself. I find that often gets misinterpreted as being stuck up."

"I tried to get you to say 'hi' a few times. I wasn't trying to get your phone number or address. I just wanted a 'hello', and you turned away from me. Although," he chuckled, "you did say about four words to me when we ran into each other at the diner." While he watched her gaze at the ground, he wanted to apologize for discomfort she felt, but he didn't. Her previous efforts to dismiss him created a wound that had deepened over time.

"I'm sorry." She scarcely spoke above a whisper. "I'm sorry," she repeated. "I didn't mean to hurt your feelings."

"No. No," he responded. "I bounce back quickly." While he talked he asked himself why he didn't simply accept her apology. It angered him that he felt he had to act as if she hadn't injured his feelings. It was like he was standing in front of Malcolm choking back emotion, forcing himself to behave as if nothing Malcolm said pierced his psyche.

She looked at him and his steeliness melted.

"Well, really," he said while they walked toward the bleachers, "It did hurt when you didn't acknowledge me and I do accept your apology. Thanks for offering it." He paused. "Say. What section are you sitting in? I think everybody at school is at this football game," he chuckled. "Maybe we're not sitting that far apart."

"Section D. And," she added with a downward gaze. "I'm not alone."

"I didn't think you would—"

"I came with another guy," she told him bluntly.

"Oh."

"It's not going to work."

He turned to walk away. "Well, it was nice talking—"

She pulled on the back of his jacket. "I'm not talking about you and me." She almost grinned. "I don't know if we'd work or not. I was talking about the guy I came to the game with. We're not going to work. I know that for sure."

"And you came to the game with him?"

"I have a hard time doing things I feel might hurt another person's feelings."

He laughed. "You didn't have a problem hurting my feelings."

She pursed her lips. "And to think you weren't even going to admit you were hurt."

"Okay," he conceded. "Who is this guy?"

"It means nothing to you. I'm trying to find a way to let him go gently."

"I was going to ask if you'd sit with me for the rest of the game. Section D is above where my friends and I are sitting. In time this guy would have gone hunting for you and saw us sitting together. He would have gotten the message then."

She chuckled.

"Why didn't he go get your food and drink for you?"

"He didn't want anything and I get what I want all by myself."

Raymond laughed. "You're super independent?"

"Absolutely," she answered without batting an eyelash. "But not because I went and got my own pretzel."

"It's good that you're independent." He moved his water and pretzel into the same hand. With his free hand, he brushed her forearm. "The only thing about trying to be too independent is that it gets you out of balance. And no," he added with a shake of his head. "It's not a woman thing. It happens to men way more than it happens to women. At least I think it does. When we try to be too independent, we shut ourselves off from love." After a brief pause, he added, "I ought to know. I've fallen into that trap enough times myself." He stuck his chest out and teased. "But I felt like a big strong man then."

In the quiet space that danced between them, he heard what he'd just said. The revelation surprised him. It was as if he was listening to a stranger who looked just like him. Never before had he been this forthcoming, not even with himself. For a brief instant he forgot what it felt like to be afraid that he could be hurt.

Brenda laughed unashamedly.
"I like that," Raymond said.
"What?" she asked.
"Your confidence."
"Well—"
"Brenda," a male voice from further up in the stadium called out sharply. "What's taking you so long?"

Raymond looked into the bleachers. He stared into the face of a tall, lean man. A tweed Trilby hat covered his head. Tan leather gloves, with a stripe of red across their front, warmed his hands. His nose was short and narrow. His eyes were small, almost beady; they were so dark they looked black. His face was long like his body. His features were sharp, distinct. He wasn't the type of man passersby could miss even if they passed him on a crowded street.

Raymond looked back at Brenda. Not until he saw the shrunken look on her face, even her shoulders had lowered and seemed to cave in, did it occur to him that he'd faced her in order to measure her reaction to this new man's presence. What he saw sent a chill up his spine. Soon his hands were balling into fists. Silently, as if he were merely a spectator at a more harrowing competition than the rousing football game, he watched the exchange between Brenda and the man unfold.

"Brenda?" the man tried again. He walked to the bottom of the bleachers and leaned around the edge.

Out of the corners of his eyes Raymond saw Doug and Patrick glance at him.

"Brenda?" the man said for the third time.

She almost shouted. "Give me a chance to answer."

The man's eyes swelled. "Well," he said. "I'm waiting."

"The line at the concession stand was long," she told him. "I'm just getting back." Her patience expired and she added, "If you had gone with me, you wouldn't be standing there with that dumb look on your face wondering where I was." A second later and as if she read Raymond's mind, she added, "Byron."

Raymond's brows shot up. He looked away from Brenda. Now he had a name to connect to the man. He wanted to thank her. "I gotta go," he finally said. "My friends are waiting on me. I want to finish watching the game."

"Say?" Byron called out when Raymond moved beyond him.

Raymond turned.

"Aren't you friends with Anthony Thompson, the baller?"

Raymond met Byron's stare. "Yes," he answered. "I am. And you?"

Bryon chuckled dryly. "I was just asking because I thought I saw you hanging with Anthony at the Student Center a few times. I thought you might know each other."

"Yea, I know Anthony. He's one of my best friends."

"That's good," Byron responded with a slow nod. "I'm sure Anthony would tell you how un-cool it is to hang around another guy's lady. Know what I mean?"

Raymond's brows creased. "Hanging? I was just making conversation."

"As long as that's what it was," Byron said. He turned his back to Raymond and reached for Brenda.

"Look man," Raymond growled while he turned and walked up the steps toward Byron who struggled to grab Brenda's hand, "I just met you."

"Ray," Patrick stood and screamed. He curled his hand toward his chest. "Come on. The game's starting."

"Take that nonsense someplace else," one of the students who sat close to where Raymond, Byron and Brenda were congregated growled.

After he met Brenda's glance, Raymond gave her a nod to tell her that he'd be in touch.

Chapter Seven

The score was 28-23; Notra Dome was winning. Only thirteen seconds remained in the game. UPemb had the ball. It was first and eighteen on Notra Dome's forty-two yard line, a long shot.

Jim Towsley, UPemb's sophomore quarterback, stepped behind the line of scrimmage. He scanned the field; he was determined to get someone on UPemb into the end zone. He looked to his right and stepped back again. Tim Jones and Mark Patterson, UPemb's wide receivers were covered.

Notra Dome's defensive lineman, Philip Walters, glared as he pushed and shoved UPemb's offensive line out of the way player by player and made his way across the field toward Jim. "You're going down," he growled at Jim as he charged so hard across the field his cleats churned up mud.

Closer to the goal posts, Anthony forearmed a Notra Dome tackler and sprinted down field. Two Notra Dome players, a safety and a defensive back, sprinted after him. They ran so hard Anthony heard their feet land against the muddy turf.

This was it. There wouldn't be a second chance. If Anthony didn't find a way to score now nothing else he'd done in his football career would matter.

With a final grunt, Anthony stretched his arm and waved his hand. The Notra Dome safety leaped into the air seconds after he did.

Jim took one last step back then he hurled the football into Anthony's hands, just before Philip Walters soared across the field and landed on top of Jim.

While Jim lay on the ground gasping for air, Anthony turned sharply and sprinted toward the end zone.

Philip pushed to his feet and shouted a string of obscenities. He raced alongside the rest of Notra Dome's defensive line toward Anthony.

A Notra Dome defensive back grabbed the back of Anthony's muddy jersey and brought him toward the ground. Clumps of mud splattered into Anthony's eyes, blinding him. Despite how hard he pulled up with his forearms, he felt himself slipping, moving closer to the earth.

Philip ran at Anthony diagonally across the field, his eyes yellow with anger, his heart pounding with determination.

Anthony shook the mud away from his eyes, stretched out his forearm and threw the defensive back off his shoulder. Racing toward the end zone, he didn't notice Philip's foot slide beneath the heel of his right cleat.

Anthony stumbled forward. The football popped out of his grasp and sprang into the air. Philip lunged against his right shoulder then reached for the football.

The crowd was on its feet, cheering wildly.

The ball spun in the air. Then Anthony fell hard on the ground. The ball was snug in his hands.

Philip fell on Anthony and tried to snatch the football out of his hands, but two referees blew long on their whistles, sending a piercing noise through the air.

For a second, everything stopped. Then the two head football coaches ran down the sidelines and started screaming obscenities. "It's our ball," Notra Dome's head coach Johnny Woodson screamed until the veins at the sides of his forehead fattened and pulsed.

"No. Bless it all," UPemb's head coach Mark Flint hollered. "We scored." He pointed at Anthony who lay gasping for breath on the ground. "He's in," he claimed as he shook his pointing finger. "He's in."

Calls up to the booth followed by two huddled on-field referee conferences preceded the field judge's walk to the edge of the end zone.

A hush reined over the crowd.

The field judge raised both of his hands, signaling the touchdown, and the UPemb football players, coaches and fans erupted into loud celebration. Raymond, Patrick, Doug and the entire

UPemb stadium waved its hands wildly through the air. Students pulled their hats and caps off and tossed them up like champagne corks aiming for the sky. Confetti sprinkled down out of the top of the stadium like colored rain. Firecrackers zoomed and banged. Cheerleaders and diehard fans raced to the center of the field. Anthony's parents and extended family cheered and shouted from the sky box. UPemb players hoisted Anthony atop their shoulders and carried him, their fists pumping and saluting the sky with victory.

Around them, like weary battlers gone too long into the heart of a winless clash, Philip Walters and the other Notra Dome football players ambled about the field with their heads down. They shook a few UPemb players' hands with the limpness of a hard defeat, then slowly resigned themselves to the long walk back to their locker room and the air conditioned bus that awaited their arrival at the edge of Frankfort Field.

Less than two hours later after they showered, celebrated the historic win with family and gave round after round of television and newspaper interviews, every UPemb football player headed to Club Zone. Their girlfriends--women so beautiful their faces looked more the work of Michelangelo than that of Maybelline--hung on their bulky arms.

"I'm gonna spend more time with my family," Anthony told his teammates as they left the stadium.

"What?" Jim asked. He shook his head defiantly. "Nah," he said. "You're coming with us." He pulled on Anthony's arm.

"Plus," another UPemb player said, "Your folks left for home in Tennessee a few minutes ago." The guy laughed. "I saw you telling them bye."

"Aw, damn," Anthony whispered low enough so as not to be overheard. A second later he raised his voice. "Can't we hang out somewhere else just once?"

His plea fell on deaf ears.

The spirit of celebration was thick in the air and as if he had no choice, Anthony followed his teammates to Club Zone.

"Man, do you think we ought to do this?" Raymond asked when he caught up to Anthony outside the club. Before Anthony answered, Raymond turned and looked out at the street. He didn't see the color red, but he knew a man's blood had spilled into the street on the night he arrived to Philadelphia.

"Nah," Anthony told him. "I don't think we should go in. But," he shrugged, "What can I do?"

A second later Raymond wavered. "Ah," he sighed. He'd been *odd man out* his entire youth back home in Dayton. He wasn't up for filling that role tonight. "If you don't go in. You know," he said, "Show your face, then whoever's spreading the rumors could take it that you're hiding."

"Exactly," Anthony nodded. And one thing was certain; Anthony Thompson was nobody's coward.

"Just one thing," Raymond added, his voice lowering to a whisper as he leaned toward Anthony's ear. He glanced over his shoulder at Patrick and Doug. "If any trouble gets started in here, give me your word that we're all leaving – you, me, Patrick and Doug. There are gonna be a lot of people drinking tonight. I wouldn't be surprised if somebody didn't start a problem, but if they do. And," he added. "I mean, at the first sign of trouble, give me your word that we're all going to leave."

Anthony looked him squarely in the eyes. "You have my word."

For hours Club Zone was paradise to men with raging hormones. When the DJ, a bald headed white dude with a goatee who knew a smooth R&B cut when he heard one, played slow songs, the guys stroked their dance partners' narrow spines and, the songs needling on, they slid their hands over and gripped the willing women's thick backsides. Concern that word of their flirting and sensual hip stroking would get back to their girlfriends didn't cross their minds once.

After all, Sandra hated football so she wouldn't have come to the game if Patrick had paid her to. Doug's girlfriend, Maria, was in Tuscany, Italy attending her younger brother's wedding and Anthony's girlfriend, Aretha, had caught a red eye out of Philadelphia International to Birmingham, Alabama to be with her grandmother, a woman whose health was failing so badly Hospice had come in. The woman Raymond loved – Brenda -- hadn't become even a mere friend of his yet.

When the guys weren't on the crowded floor dancing they were talking loudly at their table. While they talked they sipped ice water, gin or wine and told jokes, some of them funny. Raymond didn't touch a drop of alcohol. He did rip off a string of satirical jokes based on life in the 1970s, reminiscent of the comedic giant, Sinbad.

"This place is banging," Anthony shouted across the table to his friends. He raised his recently refreshed glass of wine and clinked glasses with them. "Nobody throws a party like Club Zone."

Larry Graham and *Grand Central Station's* "The Jam" blasted across the club's gigantic speakers. Before the band got halfway through the funky R&B cut, Doug, plenty of wine and gin in his system, hurried away from the table. He cupped his stomach with his hands and prayed that he'd make it to the toilet in time. At the bathroom's doorway he hollered "Pardon me!" to a guy wearing a pin-stripped suit. The guy took one look at Doug's contorted face, stepped to the side and provided a clear path to the bathroom.

Doug shoved his hands against the bathroom door, pushing it open. He emptied his stomach at once, bits of the liquor and hot wings he'd consumed at the club spilling out onto the floor. He spent the next several minutes on his knees hurling stank vomit into the public commode.

Back at the table Patrick tapped Raymond's forearm. "Think Doug's all right?" he asked.

Raymond stood. He ran his hands down his pants then grunted. He didn't want to care for a man who drank too much. Yet, he felt obligated to look out for Doug. "Let me go check on him," he said before he walked away from the table.

Moments later he came out of the bathroom with one of his arms wrapped around Doug's waist. Doug leaned so much of his weight into Raymond's side, they both were unsteady as they walked, one slow step in front of the other, back to the table.

"Let's roll," Anthony said in a tone that didn't leave room for discussion.

"How're we gonna get Doug home?" Raymond wanted to know.

"I'll drive him back to his dorm," Patrick said.

After he grabbed his own car keys, Raymond tightened his grip around Doug's waist and walked his friend back to Patrick's car. "Me and Anthony'll follow you," Raymond told Patrick.

"That's all right, *Amigo*," Patrick said. "I got experience at this." He looked somberly at Raymond then slowly, he smiled, the bond of shared experience born in heartache, moving between them. "Remember?"

Raymond gave Patrick a tight-lipped grin. As the guys made their way into the night they could still hear the club music banging. They knew there'd be parties going all night. After they got Doug into bed, they knew they could go back out and hang at another club.

At the top of University Avenue, Patrick flipped on his blinkers and honked his horn.

"Catch you later," Raymond hollered out his window. He and Anthony continued their drive up the avenue, the road and sidewalks quiet as most of the people who attended the football game where at parties or back at their dorms.

The Excel ambled down the avenue at a comfortable pace, until Anthony looked into his side view mirror. "Yo. Is that dude following us?"

"Who?" Raymond asked.

Anthony squinted into the side view mirror. "The dude behind us in that Mustang."

"Nah, Man," Raymond laughed. "Why would some dude in a Mustang be following us? I don't know anybody who drives a Mustang." He turned and looked slowly at Anthony. "Do you?"

A piercing noise snatched away all remaining time Anthony had to answer. Mixed in with the night's music two shots, released from the clip of a 45 magnum, rang out. One of the bullets busted Raymond's right tail light. The other bullet scraped the side of the passenger door, inches away from where Anthony sat.

Everything sped up. Being shot at had a way of pushing the clock forward. Raymond slammed the accelerator to the floor, leaned and turned the Excel sharply to the right. He didn't bother with blinkers. He just drove like his life depended on it.

"Take the next left," Anthony ordered. His pulse rose and, due to the wine he'd drunk at the club, his head started to pound.

Raymond sped down the street; his eyes opened so wide they felt stretched. He kept glancing into the rear view mirror. His hands started to sweat; they almost slipped off the steering wheel. The Mustang was only several yards behind them.

The Excel's tires squealed into the left turn. "Where to now?" Raymond asked.

Anthony opened his mouth so he could breath. He was too scared to think. "Haul ass," he shouted. "Just haul ass until we lose this dude."

Lakeside's "Fantastic Voyage" played on the radio, but neither Raymond nor Anthony paid attention to the hit song as they sped further away from campus into less familiar parts of town.

Fear clutched Raymond's heart, everything was happening too fast. The longer Raymond drove, the sweatier his hands became and the thicker night grew. Soon he was squinting, struggling to see several feet down the road. The further they sped away from campus, the more Raymond hoped the Mustang's driver had an ounce of sanity, enough to want to avoid a shoot-out in the middle of the city.

Anthony pointed and screamed, "It's a dead end!" He raised his hands to shield his face against the blow.

A cement wall blocked their path. The Mustang's headlights blared through the Excel's rear window as it picked up speed and rammed the back of the Excel.

Raymond turned the steering wheel sharply to the right to avoid the wall and found the entrance to an alley. When the Excel emerged onto the street, he followed up with a sharp left and two more sharp rights.

At the end of the next block, Anthony hollered, "Take this right!"

The Excel's tires spun, digging black burn marks into the street as it rounded the corner. At the corner's edge, the right front tire caught on a large rock. Force from the break in the car's speed sent the Excel careening to its side and bumping its way over the curb.

Raymond clutched the steering wheel as the car scraped a row of residential mailboxes and dug up grass and dirt as it continued to barrel down the sidewalk. At the end of the street he lost control and the car rolled hard into a ditch.

Anthony cursed while he kicked at the passenger door. Raymond used his shoulders then his legs and feet to push the driver's side door open. He crawled onto the ground on his hands and knees. Then he ran around to the Excel's passenger side and got Anthony out.

House porch lights came on. Curtains parted and home owners peered onto the street.

Moving in low strides Raymond and Anthony made their way out of the ditch, across the top of the street then down a narrow alley. Every few seconds they glanced over their shoulders for the Mustang. The alley was too narrow for a car to fit in, and they knew that they could out run any man in the city. They ran, stride for stride, gifted middle distance runner and football star, all the way back to campus.

It was 3:30 in the morning when Raymond and Anthony reached University Avenue, their appreciation for life way up. Their fear of death was as fresh as the wounds that covered their bodies. The top of the street was quiet.

Raymond stooped over to catch his breath then found himself staring at the lighted sign above Coffee Flavor, the spot where his path first crossed Anthony's. The word 'coffee' dredged up a powerful association in Raymond. He thought about Malcolm, but the reflection didn't have long to stay.

"I told you I was gonna get you, motherf—"

The voice was familiar. Raymond turned in time to stare down the dark barrel of a 45 magnum.

The Mustang, its over worked engine pushing steam through the hood, was parked on the other side of the street. Raymond's gaze roved back and forth between Anthony and the guy holding the gun. He stood between two men who, at this point in the chase, appeared equally foreign to him.

"Why are you doing this—" Raymond tried to ask.

"Shut up," the guy holding the gun ordered, his voice full of bite.

That's when Raymond saw it. Even in the thick darkness he made out the large tattooed cross on the guys right shoulder. Quickly he searched the side of the guy's face for the scar, and there it was like a mark on a road map, a sign of sorts. The guy from the gym. Before Raymond knew it, he lunged at the guy.

The gun flew into the air. It landed on the ground with a thud. When Anthony looked down at the weapon, it looked to be no more than a heavy toy, certainly not strong enough to tear a man's head clean off his shoulders.

He stared at the gun in frozen curiosity. The longer he looked at the weapon the more fascination with its power crept into Anthony. He smiled before he snatched the gun off the sidewalk, then he grabbed the back of Raymond's shirt. "Come on," he demanded while he pushed Raymond's arms down, away from the guy's chest. He didn't need anybody to see him, not now. He needed to escape.

Raymond stood over the guy from the gym. His fists were clenched. "If I ever see you again—"

Anthony pulled on Raymond's shirt. "Come on," he shrieked. He scanned the street for cops, someone out for a bite to eat, anyone who could finger him. "We have to get out of here."

En route to Roddin, Anthony wiped his fingerprints off the gun with the hem of his shirt then, and with a great amount of reluctance, he dropped the weapon inside a tall wastebasket. Its weight pushed through balled paper towels, napkins, Styrofoam cups and shreds of paper until finally the gun landed at the bottom of the wastebasket, several feet beneath the garbage it had fallen through.

Walter was sitting at the main desk when Raymond and Anthony stumbled, out of breath, inside the resident hall.

"Y'all look tore up," Walter stood and said, his mouth twisted into a lopsided grin, while Raymond and Anthony made their way to the elevators.

"It was a tough—"

"Partying," Anthony interjected before Raymond could finish his statement.

Walter hurried behind Anthony and slapped his back. His hand landed between Anthony's shoulder blades, the place where the impact from the Excel's roll into the ditch hurt most. "You did your thing," Walter said while he patted Anthony's back. "UPemb's going to the big dance."

"Straight up," Anthony nodded. He urged Raymond toward the elevators. He didn't want to have to start making small talk; he knew how chatty Walter could be. If they didn't get to apartment 712 now, he knew Walter would start drilling them with questions.

Anthony hurried inside the elevator and jammed his finger on Floor Seven. But he wasn't quick enough.

Walter turned and, in a shout, asked, "Did y'all hear about that shooting tonight?"

The elevator doors closed slowly, without a word from Anthony or Raymond. Patches of mud clung to their clothes, making it obvious that they hadn't just been out partying.

"Think he knows anything?" Raymond asked Anthony when they stepped onto the seventh floor.

"Who?" Anthony inquired.

"Walter," Raymond said. He looked at Anthony with disbelief. "You know I'm talking about Walter. Who else would I be talking about? The dude in the Mustang?" Irritation crept into his voice. He stomped away from the elevator, creating distance between Anthony and him. Memory of the gunshots followed him down the hall. After he turned his key in the apartment lock, he pushed the door open.

The living room was dark. Aware that he had another event in his life to hide Raymond rounded the corner and peered inside Patrick's room. He breathed a sigh of relief when he saw Patrick sleeping with one arm wrapped around his girlfriend Sandra's stocky frame.

Raymond pulled Patrick's bedroom door closed, toning down the couple's choppy breathing that threatened to turn into full blown snores, then he made his way back inside the living room. Anthony was sitting on the sofa. The apartment was quiet.

Raymond did what he always did when it was dark and quiet in the apartment and he felt alone. He walked to the living room window and looked across the city. Philadelphia's skyline, its buildings saluting the heavens and office and housing lights sparkling into the night, never ceased to amaze him.

He didn't know why but he wondered what Malcolm was doing. He wondered who Anthony really was. He wondered what Walter really knew.

He wondered who he could call to help pull his car out of the ditch.

He shifted his weight from foot to foot and peered down onto the street. His mind froze, stilled like the night. Beneath the glow reflecting off the corner street lamp he saw Walter. He was talking with a guy Raymond couldn't place.

Exhausted with the night's events, Raymond turned away from the window. A second later, he spun around and looked out onto the street again. Something about the guy Walter talked to demanded his attention, wouldn't let him go.

Chapter Eight

It was January 7, 1985, the Monday after the end of UPemb's two week winter break. Snow covered lawns and sprinkled sidewalks separating campus buildings. Christmas wreaths decorated a few residence hall windows. Raymond lowered his head against the cold wind and walked to Student Affairs. The few times he raised his head, even though he figured seeing her was a long shot, he looked across the area for Brenda.

He'd spent the two week winter break alone in Apartment 712, Patrick, Doug and Anthony having gone home to visit with their families out of town. Raymond had gone back to University Avenue twice, and his cupped hands working like small shovels, dug through the garbage can Anthony tossed the gun inside, but he never found the gun. The morning after the car chase, before the sun rose all the way in the sky, he called a tow truck to pull his Excel out of the ditch. It took less than three days to get dents knocked out of the Excel and his taillight replaced. Except for a brief thirty second television report the day after the shootout that announced, "Gun shots rang out near University Avenue late last night. Cops are checking to see if the incident is gang related," Raymond hadn't heard anything about the confrontation; still he prayed that details of the harrowing escape would remain hidden, undetected.

TV sitcoms airing holiday specials and local radio stations playing classic Christmas songs of joy and love, he also picked up the receiver and dialed Malcolm's telephone number every weekday during the break. He always called when he knew Malcolm was at work. He just wanted to hear his father's voice on the answering machine, have something to remind himself that, like his friends, he had a family back home too. He only left a message once.

The sky having darkened and the apartment starting to feel too quiet, Raymond pulled on a hooded sweat jacket and walked outside to a pay telephone just off campus, closer to Center City. Malcolm's telephone rang eight times before the answering machine turned on. It was two days before Christmas. Raymond shifted his weight from foot to foot, then casually and as if he was merely ordering a pizza, he pulled the receiver close to his mouth and said, "Merry Christmas."

He slammed the receiver in the cradle when emotion caught in his throat, moistened his eyes. His father had wounded him deeply over the years, berating him in front of neighbors, punching him in the face and breaking his nose several times and coming home so intoxicated once he knocked Raymond on the floor as soon as he discovered Raymond had left a quart of milk on the kitchen table until the milk had started to sour, had started to smell. Malcolm leaped upon the then ten-year-old Raymond that evening and wrapped his thick, oil stained hands around his throat. Raymond kicked, shoved his hands against Malcolm's forearms and thrashed his head from side to side trying to free himself, but he was the smaller of the two, and Malcolm was more than drunk, he was in a rage. Despite the fact that Malcolm hadn't missed a day of work in ten years, his supervisor wrote him up earlier that day, told Malcolm that he had placed the wrong parts in more than a dozen cars during the month. "I apologize, Sir," Malcolm responded to his supervisor. "I'll do better."

Hours after the meeting with his supervisor, alcohol mixed with rage in Malcolm, turned his eyes red. His fingers clamped onto Raymond's throat, leaving marks. His own neck started to ache from strain, he leaned over Raymond and choked his throat so wildly. After awhile Raymond's body stilled against the kitchen floor. His head no longer thrashed. Malcolm leaned back, his heart racing. He grabbed Raymond's wrist and placed two fingers against his veins. When he didn't feel a pulse, he shook Raymond then he started to weep and curse into the room. He pressed his hands, one atop the other, against Raymond's chest, the way he'd been taught in a CPR course he took at work when he first got hired. He leaned over and blew into Raymond's mouth. It took several seconds, but soon Raymond coughed and opened his eyes.

It took Raymond less than ten minutes to jog back to Roddin from the pay phone. He was glad that he'd left his father a message, relieved that he'd dialed him from a telephone number that wouldn't reveal his whereabouts. He loved Malcolm in a way that meanness and abuse had not been able to dissolve, but he never wanted to see him again.

A group of women leaned against a wall talking when Raymond opened the door to Student Affairs. He tilted his head upwards toward the women, a signal of "hello" then he walked toward Dr. Davis' office. He wasn't in the office long when Dr. Davis started asking him questions; he prayed none of the questions would lead to the shootout.

He looked away from Dr. Davis and scanned the large plush office for the fifth time. "I talk to my dad two, three times a week," he stammered. He'd only been in the office a few minutes, if that, and already he knew which of the plants were real and which were artificial. He even picked up the scent of the Pine Sol the cleaning man scrubbed the floorboards with late last night.

Dr. Davis clasped his long, narrow fingers together, joining them at their round ends. He leaned back in his high back leather chair and searched Raymond's face. He'd had his share of probing conversations with troubled students. Despite what Raymond thought or tried to conceal, Dr. Davis knew a problem when he saw one.

"Are you sure?" Dr. Davis asked while he, the mature, experienced educator, gazed at Raymond, the young trying-to-find-his-way kid, over his horn rimmed glasses.

Raymond stared at the titles to the books neatly placed inside the bookcase at the back of the office. Literature, chemistry, advanced psychology and team building texts sprinkled with a few Langston Hughes and Paul Laurence Dunbar poetry volumes filled the cherry wood case. He turned away from the books and worked up an answer before Dr. Davis had the chance to pry further.

"I'm sure." His face was set. He looked certain of himself.

"Then I don't understand," Dr. Davis said.

Raymond turned away from examining a Jacob Lawrence painting nailed to the office's back wall. He peered at Dr. Davis. Soon he was glancing at the painting again, anything to calm his fears.

"Raymond."

"I'm going to respond to you," Raymond told him. He looked right at Dr. Davis. "This whole thing is odd." Even while he talked, he appreciated that Dr. Davis not once asked him about the campus shooting. He was glad that the school, the police, no one who could afford to talk had discovered that Anthony and he were involved in the crime. He didn't need to answer more questions. As it was, he had so few answers. Plus the Albright Invitational indoor track and field meet was on Saturday. He knew he had to stay focused on the meet if he planned to defeat Indiana University's star middle distance runner, Dwight Gooding, in the eight hundred and fifteen hundred meter runs.

"What whole thing is odd?" Dr. Davis asked.

"Me sitting here in your office," Raymond told him. His shoulders rose. "The calls and the letters your office keeps sending me."

Dr. Davis leaned forward in his chair. "Your father has called this school several times since you enrolled."

"I talk to my father," Raymond shouted, jumping to his feet.

"Sit down, Son," he said. "Let's talk about this," he nodded. "Let's get to the bottom of this. Today."

"I don't know why he keeps calling here," Raymond said. His chest felt tight. "And I certainly don't know why he writes the school."

"Your father's trying to reach you, Raymond."

Raymond turned his palms up. "I talk to my father. I call him every week. He's the first person I called when I got here."

Dr. Davis pushed his glasses down onto the bridge of his nose. Then, peering up over the glasses' top edge, he looked at Raymond.

"I mean, I know it's odd," Raymond stammered. "But that's just the way my father is."

"Is he experiencing a form of dementia?"

Raymond paused then he lied. "He doesn't like to talk about it, but he does forget things sometimes." He nibbled his lip and scanned the office. Nothing had changed about the Lawrence Jacob painting since he last examined it, but he looked at it again anyway. "I hope he's all right." He met Dr. Davis' glance. "I'll go home in the next few weeks and check up on him."

"I think that's a good idea," Dr. Davis said. "But I still want to talk with you."

"About what?" Raymond asked, his voice growing edgy.

"About your father and the content of his phone calls."

"So he asks for you every time he calls the school?"

"No," Dr. Davis said. He leaned back in the chair. "He always asks for you when he calls. Every time your father calls here he asks this office to get in touch with you and have you call him. He says he doesn't know where you are, but he thinks you're here. He said he's called more than a few colleges looking for you. Several times he's mentioned that you were supposed to be at Ohio State. He said you got a scholarship from Ohio State." Dr. Davis spread his hands. "He said he would drive up here and check on you but that his car is old and wouldn't make it and that his mind won't hold up under a long bus ride. Your father said he's scared to catch a plane."

Raymond's face expanded into outright incredibility. He gasped and clutched the sides of the chair he sat in. "My father told you he was scared?"

To Raymond it was inconceivable . . . Malcolm being scared. After all, the one nurturing constant about Malcolm was his ability to never be afraid. It was one of the reasons Malcolm wanted to be home in case Dayton's corruptly skilled burglars targeted their house. More than to avoid having to go out and buy a new television or VCR to replace stolen ones, Malcolm wanted to be home so he could give the thieves a serious beat down.

Nobody was going to take advantage of Malcolm Clarke, not anymore. He'd spent enough years suffering beneath the hand of his own father. Now it was his turn to administer the hard blows.

Raymond sat across from Dr. Davis and told himself that if Malcolm had been in the Excel when the driver of the Mustang fired shots, Malcolm would have slammed on the brakes and sent the Mustang crashing into the Excel's bumper. Then Malcolm would have kicked the Excel's door open and sprinted back to the Mustang. Even now he saw Malcolm snatching the driver out of the Mustang, tossing him to the ground and stomping him with his steel work boots.

The Excel wouldn't have rolled into a ditch if Malcolm had been there. The Mustang's driver wouldn't have walked away either; he would have been rolled off University Avenue in an ambulance stretcher.

"Raymond," Dr. Davis repeated in a raised voice, trying to interrupt Raymond's thoughts.

"Raymond," Dr. Davis tried again.

With a quick jerk of his head, Raymond looked up. "Hunh?"

"We were talking about your father."

"Oh, yes. Yea. Like I said I'll go see him in a few weeks." He squirmed in the chair then he sat erect. He nodded, hoping that was all that needed to be said.

Dr. Davis smiled, the kind of smile that didn't send his lips curling up at the ends. "We were talking about how often your father contacts the school and tries to reach you." He studied Raymond, his smooth forehead, his eyes opened like half moons, his pursed lips and his fingers that wouldn't stop fidgeting with the chair's arm rest.

"Your father said he only thinks you're here because of a letter he came across in your bedroom. He said you just up and left home." He tilted his head and peered inside Raymond's eyes. "Is any of this ringing a bell?"

"No," Raymond responded flatly. "I don't know what my dad's talking about. I told you I'll go home and check on him. He might need to adjust his medication."

"Okay. All right," Dr. Davis said. "But the next time your father calls here, I'm going to ask him to hold while we locate you." He looked hard at Raymond. "Understand?"

Reluctantly Raymond nodded, then stood and excused himself from Dr. Davis' office. He kept loosening and clenching his hands while he walked out of the building that housed Student Affairs. Malcolm's blood shot eyes, his bitter face and his hard, mean voice nipped at him, haunted him.

As he walked across campus, making his way between lecture halls and administrative buildings to Roddin House, he thought about Malcolm. Soon he was reminiscing and back in the third grade. Because it was the day before winter break, elementary school had let out early. The school bell was still ringing like a siren when eight-year-old Raymond grabbed four books out of his locker and raced alongside his classmates toward the school's exit doors. Cold wind blew through the doors into the school when the first group of kids pushed them ajar and ran outside.

Kids pulled on their coats, drew hats down over their heads and pushed their hands inside gloves. They talked and laughed while they stood with their friends or siblings at the front of the school. Raymond talked briefly to a few kids, but mostly he stayed by himself. Every now and then he looked onto the street to see if Malcolm's car was approaching.

Half an hour passed. Only a handful of students were still standing at the front of the school, Raymond being one of them. The cold air thickened, started to feel like blades pricking Raymond's skin.

Moments later, Raymond watched the last two students climb inside the back seat of a station wagon. "Is someone coming to get you?" the woman driving the station wagon leaned across the front seat and asked, glancing up at Raymond.

"Ye-ye-yes," Raymond nodded. When the woman didn't turn away from looking at him after several seconds, he smiled until his teeth showed. "My father's coming," he told her in a raised voice.

The woman sat erect, waved at Raymond and pulled away from the sidewalk.

An hour went by. Raymond had started to shiver. He'd placed his books on the ground and buried his hands at the bottoms of his coat pockets. He turned and looked at the school doors, thinking about re-entering the building. A second later, he hurried around the side of the building. The parking lot, the place where teachers parked their cars and trucks, was empty except for a Volkswagen that was parked behind a shed, but Raymond didn't see the car. Tears pooled in his eyes until he heard a car's engine nearing the front of the school. He wiped his eyes, sniffed hard, keeping mucus from rolling out of his nose, and ran to the front of the school. He lowered his arms to his sides while he watched a red and silver Pontiac Sunbird drive to the end of the block. Five minutes and three cars later, he started to cry. *"Stop being a baby,"* he scolded himself inwardly. *"Stop crying like a punk."* He continued to berate himself, but the tears did not stop falling down his face.

He looked back at the school. The main hallway was empty, like kids had not filled it less than two hours ago. When he turned back around, he bit down on his bottom lip until he pricked it and it started to bleed.

"Be at the front of the school as soon as I pull up," Malcolm told him in the morning. "I'm not waiting on you, so you better be there."

"School's letting out an hour early today," Raymond said as he closed the top on the cereal box. Then he sat at the kitchen table and ate a bowl of cereal.

Malcolm rolled his eyes. "I'll take off from work early. It's gonna cost me money," he mumbled, "but I'll be by the school on time. But," he wagged his finger and added, "I'm not waiting on you. If you're not out there when I pull up, I'm driving off." He poured himself a bowl of cereal and sat down next to Raymond. "Hear me?"

"Yes," Raymond answered.

"Yes, what?"

"Yes, Sir."

"So, what 'chu learning in school?" Malcolm asked, making small talk with his son as they both ate a bowl of Shredded Wheat.

"We're doing multiplication and division in math," Raymond answered, a smile nipping at the corners of his mouth. He liked sitting next to his father eating breakfast. Once or twice a week his father scrambled eggs or made a pot of Cream of Wheat or oatmeal and fixed him toasts before he drove him to school. Many of the breakfasts were silent, neither of them talking. Occasionally they discussed sports competitions they watched on television the previous evening. Sometimes Malcolm asked Raymond how he was doing in school while they ate.

The morning before winter break twelve years ago had been one of those mornings when Malcolm seemed happy to have Raymond as his son, a morning that caused Raymond to lower his guard, to stop trying to protect himself from his father's meanness.

He kicked at the school grounds for several more moments. Despite how hard he sniffed, snot dripped down his nose and across the top of his mouth. He wiped it away with the back of his hand, spreading snot across his gloves.

The sky began to darken. "Ray, do you have a ride home?" a familiar voice asked from inside the school.

Raymond turned and looked up at Ms. Fletcher, the school principal.

"I'm getting ready to leave for the day. Before I leave I always check the grounds to make sure all the kids are safe. I thought surely all the kids would have been picked up by their parents by now." She smiled faintly. "Do you want to come inside and call your father?"

The idea seemed like a charm to Raymond. He walked back inside the school and, as Ms. Fletcher turned away from him, he blew a kiss up to the ceiling, thanking God that he hadn't been alone the way he'd thought. He hurried ahead of Ms. Fletcher into her office. As soon as he reached the secretary's desk, he stepped up on his toes and grabbed the telephone. His fingers hurried across the dial. He waited while the line rang at Malcolm and his house. He let the line ring fifteen times then he glanced over his shoulder at Ms. Fletcher. She sat patiently in a chair across the room.

Raymond turned his back to her, pressed his finger against the receiver and redialed home. Again the line rang fifteen times.

"Come on, Sweetheart," Ms. Fletcher finally stood and said. "I'll drive you home. Your father must have gotten busy at work."

Even as he watched Ms. Fletcher grab her coat and pocket book, Raymond figured that was a lie. Malcolm hardly ever worked overtime, and when he did, it was only during the summer. Malcolm told Raymond he only worked overtime during the summer so he'd be sure neighbors would be outside washing their cars, watering their lawns or sitting on their front porches, fulfilling the role of makeshift babysitters for Raymond until he got home.

Raymond walked timidly, stiffly to Ms. Fletcher's Volkswagen at the back of the school. He glanced at the shed before he slid across the passenger seat, marveling at how the shed had concealed the car from his view earlier. He didn't say much the ride from the school to Malcolm and his house, and even then, he only spoke to answer questions Ms. Fletcher asked him. He knew she only asked him questions about school and how he was doing in his classes to keep the car from being too quiet. He figured he was the only kid from school she'd driven home, everybody else's parents making sure to pick them up soon after the final dismissal bell rang.

He'd walked home from school twice, but after he got chased for two blocks by a Rottweiler he never attempted the four mile trek again.

"Thank you, Ms. Fletcher," he said as he scooted off her car's front seat and grabbed his four books. "Thank you very much," he looked up and nodded.

"You're welcome, Sweetie," Ms. Fletcher said before she put her car in reverse and backed out the side driveway.

Raymond hurried onto the front porch. He pulled his key out of his coat pocket and unlocked the front door. When he turned, he was surprised, howbeit relieved, to discover Ms. Fletcher sitting in her car at the edge of the sidewalk.

He entered the house, waved back at her and she pulled away from the curb and drove down the street.

The first place Raymond went after he peed in the toilet was the kitchen. As he'd done that morning, he poured himself a bowl of cereal, sat at the kitchen table and ate dinner.

Half an hour later he washed the dirty bowl in the sink, placed it in the drainer and walked back inside the living room. He turned on the television and stretched out across the sofa, glad that school was out for the next two weeks. He laughed while he watched an episode of *My Three Sons*. Before the show ended, he drifted into sleep.

It was dark outside by the time Malcolm arrived home. "Get up, boy!" Malcolm kicked at the sofa and ordered.

Raymond's torso shook against the sofa, but he didn't sit up.

"I said, get up." Malcolm screamed, kicking the sofa harder.

Raymond blinked several times then opened his eyes. "Dad," he tried as he sat up.

Malcolm leaned over him, the smell of hard liquor heavy on his breath. "How did you get home?"

Raymond shook his head, as if doing so would help him to fully awaken. "Ms. Fletcher gave me a ride."

"Didn't I tell you about riding with strangers?"

"She's my school principal—"

"Shut up," Malcolm snapped. He pointed his finger and shook it in Raymond's face. "I told you not to ride with strangers. Just because that woman's your principal doesn't mean you know her, does it?"

Raymond sat silently.

Malcolm leaned close to him, nearly falling over onto the sofa. "Does it?"

"No," Raymond said, shaking his head slowly from side to side. "But she seems nice—"

"I said shut up." He stood and started pacing the floor in front of Raymond. "I went up to that damn school and sat outside in my car in that damned cold waiting for you, looking for your ass."

Raymond spread his hands and raised his shoulders. "I stayed for about two hours. I even called here—"

"Are you accusing me of lying, boy?"

Raymond leaned back on the sofa. "No, Sir."

"I'm tired of fooling with you." His eyes narrowed. "Sick of this shit. I'm so tired of being weighed down by you, looking after you, taking care of you."

"Was I suppose to just stay at school all night—"

"I drove up to that school looking for you, and you weren't there. Got me burning up my damn gas for nothing."

"I waited—"

"Almost lost my damn job trying to get out of that hard assed plant. Boss wouldn't let me leave right away. Those bastards actually asked me to pull a double. I walked out two hours into my second shift so I could pick you up from school." He gritted his teeth. "I bet I waited outside that damn school for nearly five minutes on you, and here you are," he added, tossing his hand up, "sitting on your ass at home. And yeah, I went by the bar," he admitted after he entered the kitchen. "You don't know what kinda day I had."

Raymond sat on the sofa and listened to his father curse for ten minutes, much of his rage and profanity aimed at him. Then he stood, walked to the kitchen doorway and asked, "May I go into my room, please?"

"Sure," Malcolm growled.

Halfway to his bedroom, eight-year-old Raymond stopped and turned back. He stood in the kitchen doorway like a ghost, like somebody only partially there. "Sorry for making you waste your time coming to get me," he said then he turned, walked into his bedroom and shut the door.

****

Ten years having passed since the start of winter break in the third grade and exiting Dr. Davis' office moments ago, Raymond hurried across campus. Worried that Malcolm would contact Dr. Davis again, making a mockery of his attempts to reconstruct his life by adding stretches of contentment, joy and triumph to it, Raymond didn't lower his head against the cold wind. His thoughts filled with memories of Malcolm, a man Raymond was desperate to escape, rid himself of like dirt gone down a drain after a hard shower. Over the coming days, the only things that broke up haunting memories from Raymond's childhood was his focus on Saturday's Albright Invitational and musings about when he and Brenda would see each other again.

Chapter Nine

The day Raymond had pushed his body to points of excruciating pain for, Saturday, January 12, 1985, had finally arrived. Runners, long jumpers and discus and javelin throwers, their family members and track and field fans filled New York City's John Albright Center. Anthony, Aretha, Patrick, Sandra and Doug drove up in Doug's Pontiac Sunbird early that morning, Aretha and Sandra swapping stories about recent *Young and the Restless* episodes, the guys talking about new videos airing on BET. Raymond and the rest of the UPemb track team rode up from Philadelphia Friday night on the team bus. Most of the two and a half hour bus ride, Raymond thought about Brenda. Because he didn't have her telephone number nor knew what dorm she lived in, he could only hope that she saw the flyers posted around campus advertising the indoor invitational. Silently, he prayed that she'd see the flyers and drive up to watch him race.

Despite his longings to relax, Raymond not only daydreamed about Brenda, imagining himself holding her, their faces gently pressed together while they sat on the Jersey shore watching seagulls soar and squawk across the sky above them, he also worried that he might lose today's races. He only slept two hours last night and he and his team mates checked into their hotel rooms at ten o'clock. For breakfast instead of loading up on carbohydrates like Coach Carter instructed, Raymond only ate two pieces of unbuttered wheat toasts.

"Ray," Coach Carter said as Raymond headed toward the starting area. He grabbed Raymond's arm and pulled him close as the announcer gave the call for the eight hundred meter run. "Get on the inside and let Dwight be the front runner for the first three laps. Stay on his heels, no more than three to four steps behind him." He looked Raymond in the eyes. "Take him at the start of the fourth lap and don't let up." He released Raymond's arm and tapped him on the back. "He can't catch you. Nobody out here can catch you if you do what I just told you."

Seconds later, a race official stood in front of the runners. "Men, I'll give you a two count start then I'll sound the starter's pistol," he began instructing the field of twelve runners.

The official finished repeating the race instructions that Raymond had heard dozens of times over his track and field career, then stepped back and said, "Runners take your marks."

Raymond stepped behind the starting line then pulled off his red and blue sweats. He almost glanced into the stands, searching for Brenda. He dared not glance to his right at Dwight Gooding for fear that it would jinx his performance.

The twelve runners standing still behind the starting line, the official raised the starter's pistol and pulled the trigger. Sound of the gun's blast sent the runners sprinting across the line. As newspaper sports writers in New York City predicted and wrote in their columns, Dwight led the pack. His tall, thin frame ran down the straightaway then leaned into the first turn smoothly. Raymond ran three men behind Dwight.

At the start of the second lap, Coach Carter glanced at his stop watch and yelled at Raymond to, "Move up!"

Raymond opened his stride. His muscular arms pumped through the air, pulling him closer to Dwight.

"Come on, Ray," his teammates cheered.

Anthony, Doug and Patrick stood in the bleachers. "Take that dude, Ray!" they shouted as they pumped their fists in the air.

Aretha, her fingernails recently polished and her hair styled in loose curls, stood next to Anthony clapping and cheering Raymond on.

Sandra wrapped her arms around Patrick's waist and exclaimed, "Ray's gonna win."

Two laps later, Dwight was still out front.

"Now, Ray!" Coach Carter jogged to the edge of the indoor track and screamed.

Raymond inhaled deeply, increased his pace and ran on Dwight's heels. Midway around the turn he started to run alongside Dwight. Soon Dwight and he were running stride for stride. As they came out of the turn, Raymond pulled out front. He raced down the backstretch like a gazelle. When he felt his thighs tighten he ran faster.

"He's on you, Ray!" Patrick screamed.

"Run faster!" Anthony hollered.

"Beat this guy, Ray!" Doug begged, his fists pumping the air.

Dwight sprinted next to Raymond.

Coach Carter grimaced when he saw Raymond leaning back. He knew his star athlete was fatigued. The finish line was twenty yards away. "Ray!" he yelled, "Go all out! Give it all you've got!"

Raymond gritted his teeth and tried to lengthen his stride, but his tight muscles would not extend, allowing Dwight to move ahead of him. Raymond glanced out of the corners of his eyes and saw Coach Carter hang his head. He spent the next ten seconds racing to catch Dwight. They were less than two yards from the end of the race when Raymond sprinted as hard as he could, pulling alongside Dwight.

At the finish line Raymond leaned forward, causing his chest to break the tape ahead of Dwight. Boos sounded in the stands, Dwight's many fans openly displaying their disapproval of Raymond's win. As the fans booed, Raymond walked to the side of the track and interviewed with three television reporters.

Doug, Patrick, Sandra, Aretha and Anthony cheered and clapped in the stands. As Raymond stepped away from the reporters, Coach Carter hugged him, patted his back and exclaimed, "Way to go, Ray. You just gave us a big win." Then he stepped back, shook his finger and advised, "Before you run the fifteen hundred make sure you stretch and warm up real good. You got tight out there in that eight hundred meter run."

Raymond spent the time between his next race jogging, stretching and doing deep breathing exercises. Less than two hours after the eight hundred meter race, he won the fifteen hundred meter run in three minutes and forty-eight seconds, setting an Albright Invitational record. Through Anthony, Doug and Patrick he found out that Brenda wasn't at the track meet. Even though he didn't expect her to be there, hope that she would created a bitter sting in his heart, but he didn't let it show.

After the team returned to UPemb that night with their first place trophy, Raymond and Coach Carter stood outside the school bus discussing the prospects of the team winning its second competition, the Martin Field Invitational in Baltimore, Maryland.

"Reginald Barnes, Yale's premiere middle distance runner, won't give you nearly the trouble Dwight did," Coach Carter told Raymond.

Raymond chuckled. "I ran against him in high school at an AAU meet. I beat him then. I know how to run against Reggie. If UPemb wins the sprints, we should get our second team win of the season."

They always talked like this, coach and gifted athlete. Their conversations stayed light, that is unless the team was close to losing a meet which only happened once since Raymond's arrival and that loss came during the cross-country season.

After coaching track for sixteen years, Coach Reginald Carter knew how to relax his way into a national title. It was his forte. He also had a knack for connecting with athletes. He genuinely cared about them and it came across.

He hadn't been this relaxed when he was Raymond's age. For him, grace had come over time, one hard experience after another. He'd also been blessed to enjoy twenty-two years of marital intimacy to a licensed psychotherapist. He watched his wife, learned from her. Her inner light and clarity helped to strengthen his communication skills, brought him an added tranquility.

Throughout his career, he'd never seen a middle distance runner as talented or as committed as Raymond. He'd also never seen an athlete as complex. Raymond always seemed to be pushing for something.

"You want me to give you a ride back to Roddin?" Coach Carter asked after they finished discussing their next track meet. He started walking toward his truck.

Raymond followed him. "Nah. Think I'm gonna go for a walk and clear my head."

Coach Carter nodded once, mainly out of habit. "What's on your mind?"

Raymond back pedaled. "I was just--" He shrugged. "Ah," he scowled. "My dad's been checking up on me." He grinned then he laughed.

"Things are good with your pops and you?" Coach Carter examined Raymond's face, his eyes and his brow, closely. He was a man himself. He knew how men hid emotions behind a shroud of bravado and unreal strength.

"Yea. He just wanted to talk." Raymond shrugged and lied. "You know."

Coach Carter pulled off his baseball cap and ran his hands over his short, red curly hair. "Okay," he said. "But it sure is cold out. I wouldn't stay out here long."

"I'm not," Raymond said, walking across the parking lot alongside Coach Carter. "Just gonna do a little thinking, then I'm heading back to my apartment."

Coach Carter tapped his shoulder. "Have you told your pops how well you're doing in track?" He paused. "And in school, for that matter?" The smile on his face was a welcome sight for Raymond. He never could seem to get enough praise despite his efforts to keep people from heaping it upon him.

"He knows."

Coach Carter turned and eyeballed Raymond curiously.

"I talk to him," Raymond nodded. "I tell him."

"Man, if you were one of my boys, I'd be up here several times a month just so I could check out your races." He chewed a stick of gum robustly. "You got the goods, Ray. You got the goods."

They reached Coach Carter's truck and Raymond looked across the mostly empty lot, before he said, "Have a good night, Coach. It was a good meet today."

"Hey, Ray," Coach Carter tried again, looking at the back of Raymond's hooded sweat jacket. "It's really cold out. Take that walk some other time. Hop in my pick-up. I'll give you a lift."

The ten year old Ford bumped its way to Roddin. During the ride, the two men talked about Coach Carter's three sons, a Richard Pryor standup television special and baseball. Country music played on the radio. Fishing gear and an old rusty tent clanged against the sides of the truck bed while the vehicle made its way down the street.

"These apartments are a lot nicer than the ones I stayed in when I was going to college," Coach Carter said as they pulled in front of Roddin.

"They're cool," Raymond responded. He opened the passenger door, grabbed his sports bag and stepped out. "Hey, Coach. Thanks for the ride."

"Yea," Coach Carter said, sticking his head out the driver's side window. "And hey, Ray," he called out.

Raymond neared the driver's side door.

"If you ever need to talk about anything, your father, family back home or anything, just give me a holler."

"Thanks."

They slapped palms and headed in separate directions.

As Coach Carter headed down the street, Raymond hurried up the steps to Roddin.

The main floor was quiet when Raymond entered the residence hall, sign that most of the guys were either in their apartments or outside hanging with friends.

Walter pulled the January 1985 issue of *Ebony* above his brows, concealing his face, when he looked up and saw Raymond entering.

On his way to the elevators, Raymond glared over his shoulder at Walter, telling himself Walter's nosiness bore a sinister essence. He tightened his jaws and wished Walter and his paths had never crossed. Yet, now that they had he approached Walter wearily, as if one wrong move, one ill timed comment or question would set off a chain of events that would find him making an early morning paper, details surrounding the last moments of his life, sounding too much like the guy who'd gotten gunned down the first night he arrived to Philadelphia.

Several steps beyond the main desk, he turned. "What's happening, Walter?" he asked between pursed lips.

Walter shrugged. "Nothing."

Raymond chuckled as he peered at Walter's back, then he walked to Walter's side. "You ain't lost for words and you know it. Everybody on campus knows that. And--" he began, walking close enough to Walter to make out the words in the article.

As Walter peered over his shoulder at him, Raymond squeezed his lips together, keeping himself from asking Walter who the guy was he saw him talking with the night of the shootout. Ever since that night three weeks ago, he'd wanted to ask Walter about the guy, but he kept stopping himself.

Walter scowled. "You're sizing me up?"

"Nah," Raymond shrugged. "You just seem different, not like your normal talkative self."

Walter placed the magazine on the desk and raised his voice. "I ain't gotta talk to you or nobody else. Don't go worrying about whether I talk or not." He stood and walked within inches of Raymond's nose. "If anybody's got to watch what they say and who they say it to, it's you and your boy, Anthony."

"Yo, Man, what are you talking about—" A second later, Raymond rolled his eyes, and released a thick breath. "You've been all up in my business since I got here last summer."

"Last summer?" Walter asked with arched eyebrows. "Are you talking about that time I told you I heard you were supposed to be at Ohio State?" He shrugged. "So what?"

"Tell you what, Walter," Raymond advised, "You mind your business." Walter met his glare and he added, "Stay out of mine."

"Hey, Man," Walter chuckled, suddenly changing his attitude. He extended a hand toward Raymond. "Ain't no beef between you and me." He nodded. "What do you say we keep it that way?"

After he pulled his sports bag over his shoulder, Raymond shook Walter's hand. "Cool," he said. Then he walked heel-to-toe back to the elevators. As the elevator doors closed in front of him, he made a note to talk with Anthony. The look in Walter's eyes when he mentioned how he needed to watch who he talked to made him feel uneasy, sent a chill up his spine.

Chapter Ten

Raymond's heels hit the Student Center linoleum floor in loud clunks. He shoved the game room door open. "Yo, Anthony. Where have you been?" His voice was tight. "Haven't seen you in what? A week?"

Anthony shrugged.

Raymond stormed over to his friend. He stared at the video game screen, then turned and stared at Anthony. "I can't believe you're in here playing a video game. With everything that's going on, you're playing a video game."

"Aw, man," Anthony waved off, "I already got grilled about the gun."

Raymond's brows rose. "What?"

"Dude who was driving the Mustang," Anthony began, "His name's Michael." He didn't look up to measure how Raymond was taking the information. "He said the gun's mine." He laughed.

"Michael," Raymond said dryly. "So his name's Michael." A second later he pursed his lips so sharply they looked twisted. "He's the same dude who gave me a hard time at the gym the night Patrick and I went lifting."

Anthony's gaze strayed momentarily from the game monitor. "Oh, yea?"

"Yea," Raymond frowned. "That was months ago."

"So, what did he say?"

"He said he runs this campus and can have a man exterminated with just a word."

Anthony punched the game controls. His fingers and thumbs popped up and down in rapid succession while he watched Pac Man speed down an open lane.

Bewildered at Anthony's reaction all Raymond could think to say was, "This is what happens when you grow up around crime. It stops seeming like a big deal after awhile." He thought about Stanley and Joey back home. He could almost hear sirens screaming their way down Green Street and Gettysburg Avenue.

"Yes and no," Anthony said. "Since last year's shooting whenever I hear police cruisers screaming down city streets, I can hardly sleep."

He swerved the game controls; Pac Man rounded corners, avoiding Shadow and Bashful only to run into Pokey and Speedy. "Ray, you don't have to worry about that loud mouth anymore."

Raymond looked at Anthony. "What do you mean?"

Anthony's fingers moved fast as he maneuvered Pac Man out of another tight spot. He almost laughed while the diminutive character spun his way down a clear path. "I got called down to Dr. Davis' office."

"That makes two of us," Raymond said.

Anthony chuckled. "Cops met me there thanks to Michael." He frowned. "Dude nearly cost us our lives and he rats to the cops." He murmured an expletive and punched the controls hard. "That punk said the gun he shot at us with was mine."

For the first time since Raymond entered the center, Anthony acted as if he was worried that he was talking too loudly. He turned and searched the room visibly relieved to discover that except for a handful of guys huddled in a corner at the other end of the room, Raymond and he were alone.

"Good thing I wiped that gun clean," he said. "If I hadn't, no telling where I'd be right now. And," he added, "Before you ask, nothing's changed. I've always told you the truth." His hands slid off the game controls. He stopped playing Pac Man long enough to look Raymond in the eyes. "I had absolutely nothing to do with the first shooting or this one."

It came to Raymond -- the never ending string of madness, the way a choice once made and acted upon continued to unravel long after it started. He'd experienced it at home with Malcolm. He'd grown up around it. Yet, he also knew how he walked away clean as a whistle after Stanley, Joey and he robbed the Texaco station two summers ago.

While he watched Anthony play Pac Man, he realized that Anthony wasn't going to tell him what role he played in the first shooting. He hoped Anthony told him the truth when he declared his innocence, but his own marred history wouldn't allow him to believe that.

"Where'd they find the gun?"

"Aw, man," Anthony frowned, "you know that dude went back and got the gun as soon as we ran off. Cops told me his fingerprints were all over that thing."

"So, dude fingers you. Cops come by the school, but they don't want you to know they're on to you."

Anthony stared at the game screen. He looked frozen, still as a mannequin. "What do you mean, on to me?"

"It was just a figure of speech," Raymond said. "So you're called to Dr. Davis' office where you're met by the police and then you're grilled for what, one, two hours?"

Anthony's fingers and thumbs popped up and down again on the controls. Pac Man gobbled up a string of pac-dots.

"At least an hour. I told them the same thing I told you because that's all there is." He paused. "The truth never changes."

"Can't argue with that." Raymond looked around the room. When he returned his attention to Anthony, he asked, "Did you tell them about the chase?"

"I didn't mention you once."

"That's not why I asked," Raymond said.

To which Anthony laughed.

"These last few weeks have been crazy," Raymond said. "UPemb won the BSC Bowl and classmates treated me like a celebrity, simply because I knew you. Glad that's over with," he sighed. "We have enough to think about with school alone."

Anthony fidgeted with the game controls. His mind was miles away.

Memories of gunshots rang in Anthony's ears. The anxiety-laden noise accompanied scenes pushed up from his subconscious, haunting memories of the car chase. He started to breathe longer, slower – one strained breath after another. For a brief moment, sadness crept over him. He felt remorseful for having pulled Raymond into his problems but he didn't apologize.

Next to him, Raymond turned his feet on their sides. For him, days spent training and studying, nights spent at jazz clubs, the Jersey shore, and sporting events with his friends over shadowed the car chase. He didn't believe Anthony when he told him that his hands were clean, that he was completely innocent of last year's club shooting, but he'd forgiven Anthony.

Like buoys trying to stay afloat in deep sea water, the men stood shoulder to shoulder in silence. Their own private thoughts were all that came to them until Anthony turned away from the game and said, "It's time for change, man." Returning his hands to the controls, he mulled recent transformations in his life. "That's why Aretha and I have been going to this church over on Arch Street. When I went home my mom told me she heard the pastor, a guy named Bishop Moore, preach at a large conference in Tennessee a few months ago. She said Bishop Moore is a big dude who preaches straight from the bible. She said Bishop Moore's real involved in the community, giving back to the poor and hurting." He tapped Raymond's shoulder. "My mom said every year the church serves more than 32,000 people free meals. It owns ten apartment units in Philly and uses the apartments to provide housing to folks who lose their homes in fires or other natural disasters."

Raymond looked at Anthony with growing curiosity. Although he thought Anthony was polite, considerate of other people's opinions and outgoing, making it easy for people to feel comfortable in his presence, he never guessed Anthony had religious inclinations. He'd rarely heard Anthony talk about church, and the few times he did, Anthony had always been talking about an experience his mother had in church.

"The church on Arch Street works with local and regional organizations to empower the community," Anthony continued, no longer playing the video game. "It holds literacy and computer training programs and stress and financial management workshops and clinics."

Raymond nodded.

"My mom said Bishop Moore's in touch with the community, not walking around with his head in the clouds." He chuckled. "She should know. My mom knows a good preacher when she sees one. My brothers, sisters, dad and I went to church on Sunday mornings when we were kids, but that was about it. We didn't go to church three to five days a week like some families do. After we grew up and moved out my mom got more involved in church. My dad still mainly goes only on Sunday morning, but my mom," he smiled, "she's a hard core Christian, always in church, dancing and shouting." He gazed across the room. "Even when I try to hide it, my mom can tell when something's bothering me." He returned his attention to Raymond. "She said going to church would help, would make it right."

Chapter Eleven

It was March 17, 1985. Athletes and spectators started making their way out of Baltimore, Maryland's Smith Field. UPemb had just won the national indoor track and field title, thanks to Raymond outperforming the competition in the eight hundred, fifteen hundred and four hundred meter runs.

Raymond had only had three short weeks to train for the four hundred meter run, a race he hadn't competed in since the tenth grade in high school. Coach Carter had pulled him aside after practice nearly a month ago and asked him to compete in the race. "It's the only way the team's gonna beat Michigan," he told him.

"All right, Coach," Raymond nodded.

Even Raymond was surprised when he was clocked at forty-eight and twelve seconds in the race, setting a meet record. His aim had only been to win, giving UPemb valuable points.

Teammates padding him with compliments, Raymond was halfway beneath the overhead at Smith Field, on his way to the team bus when he looked up and saw Brenda sitting with her roommate in the stands. Raymond's heart raced so fast he feared his hands would start shaking. His body stilled, but his thoughts filled with fantasy.

Brenda wore a pair of faded jeans and a white blouse with ruffles. Her face grew flush when Raymond met her glance. She turned away from him briefly, but emotion wouldn't stop tugging at her mouth. Seconds later, she grinned bashfully and looked directly at him.

"Tell Coach I'll be at the bus in a few minutes," Raymond tapped a teammate and said. Then he ran into the stands, taking the steps three at a time. "You came all the way to Baltimore," he teased as he ran a hand across Brenda's forearm, enjoying the touch of her soft skin. Seconds later, he extended a hand toward Cynthia, Brenda's roommate. "Hi, my name's Raymond's," he smiled and told her.

"Nice to meet you. I'm Cynthia," she grinned, "And I know who you are," Cynthia told him. "You hang out with Anthony Thompson," she said with arched brows, "And now I see," she added glancing at the track, "you're a champion in your own way."

"Thank you," Raymond chuckled. He returned his attention to Brenda. "So, when did you get in?"

Cynthia grabbed her purse and stood. "B, I'm gonna go to the bathroom."

"I'll be here when you get back," Brenda told her.

"So," Raymond said, filling the seat Cynthia previously occupied. "Talk about a surprise."

"I was going to come to some of your other races, but I couldn't get away," Brenda said, nervously pulling a strand of hair behind her ear.

He leaned forward, so he could get a better view of her. "You still seeing that guy?"

She was slow to answer.

Raymond sat back. "I understand," he told her. Then he added, "I think."

"I just have a hard time breaking—"

"Ray!" a UPemb long jumper shouted up into the stands.

"I'm coming," Raymond stood and told his teammate.

"Coach said come on! Bus is getting ready to pull out."

"We never seem to have enough time, do we?" Raymond asked Brenda.

She looked up into his eyes then feeling emotion prick her skin, causing the hair on her arms to rise, she turned away from him and looked across the track.

"I gotta go," Raymond told her reluctantly. He waited for her to meet his gaze. "Say?"

"What?" she uncrossed her legs and asked.

He smiled softly at her. "Can I have your phone number?"

"Ray!" his teammate leaned closer to the stairs and shouted.

"I'm coming," Raymond turned and assured him.

"I-I-I," Brenda stammered.

"I don't bite," Raymond teased her.

"I can tell," she assured him. Her face grew flush again. She reached inside her purse and pulled out a pen and a note pad. She wrote fast. When she finished, she folded the paper and handed it to Raymond.

"Thanks for coming to watch me race," he told her. "I appreciate it." He nodded. "It means a lot to me." He gently stroked the top of her hand as he grasped the paper her telephone number was written on. Then slowly, as if he didn't want to let the moment go, he leaned forward and kissed the side of her face.

"Ray!" his teammate screamed from the bottom of the stands. "Come on!"

Raymond walked slowly backwards down the steps. Nearer to the bottom of the steps, he smiled and told Brenda, "I'm gonna call you tonight." Her gaze met his and heat coursed through his body; begging him to hold on to this moment.

He scarcely boarded the team bus before Coach Carter came looking for him. Later that night, he telephoned Brenda; they talked for more than three hours. That Sunday, she borrowed Cynthia's car and followed him to Arch Street African Methodist Episcopal (AME) Church, a place Raymond had been worshipping at for several weeks, since he ran into Anthony playing video games in the Student Center. Brenda had thought about riding to church with Raymond, but she feared someone who knew Byron might see them in the same car together.

Raymond had been eager to introduce Brenda to Bishop Moore, a powerfully influential man. "She's nice, insightful and intelligent, a wonderful woman," Bishop Moore said, turning from Brenda to Raymond the Sunday morning Raymond introduced Brenda to him. Turning back to Brenda,

Bishop Moore said, "Hope to see you next Sunday and at Wednesday's bible study and prayer meetings." He smiled at Raymond again. "Raymond regularly comes to both. He's even led some of our prayer meetings."

Raymond hadn't expected it, but going to church brought him a sense of grounding, a foundation that made him feel whole, like nothing was missing from his life. He read four to five chapters of the scriptures a day, no less than two chapters in the morning and two chapters at night before retiring to bed. He had even started thinking about ways he could align his life with biblical precepts, letting go of the unwillingness to completely forgive Malcolm and adding more spiritual focus to his daily routine. The church's parishioners took him in like a family member, hugged him, shook his hands and kissed the sides of his face when they saw him. They filled up gaps in his life, drew him into their religious practices and beliefs, heaping their approval upon him as he started volunteering to lead prayers and read scripture. Although gone unspoken, more than to learn about religious precepts, stacking them one upon the other like bricks with which to erect the remainder of his life, Raymond attended Arch Street AME three to four times a week because he craved for the parishioners, people he deemed morally upright, fair and longsuffering, to accept him.

****

Sakura cherry trees, their blossoms exploding into white clusters, stood in the narrow gap of land that separated two aging row houses. A grandmother, her knee high stockings rolled down to her ankles, sat on the front stoop of one of the row houses. Three toddlers, plaits and ribbons in their hair, ran back and forth on the sidewalk below the stoop.

Anthony sat across the street from the houses in the used yellow and black Nissan 300ZX he bought a month ago.

"What a friend we have in Jesus" played softly on the Nissan's radio. Song . . . it was the only inspiration Anthony wanted anymore. He'd started going to church to feel peaceful amid talk about the shooting. It worked for awhile then a new trouble, a shift Anthony didn't see coming, took place.

Opposite Anthony's sports car, a little boy popped a wheelie on his five-speed bicycle then pedaled down the sidewalk. A loaf of buttermilk Wonder bread, something the boy's mother had sent him to the store for, hung from a bag off the bicycle's handlebars.

"The inner city," Anthony mused. *"It never has what you expect."* He peered across the street at the cherry trees then he laughed. *"It always has more than you think you'll find."*

On the other side of the street, parishioners exited the church's wide double doors, the day's sermon recently ended. They chatted, hugged and waved to one another as they made their way to their automobiles, most parked in the massive lot at the rear of the church, a few, like Anthony's 300ZX, parked on the sides of the street.

Bishop Moore stepped onto the church's front porch, the front zipper to his long burgundy and white pastor's robe open, exposing his sweat drenched white dress shirt. Adults surrounded him, patting his back and smiling up into his face, thanking him for delivering another emotionally rousing sermon. Children waved pictures of Christ before him, their personal impressions of the messiah, that they'd drawn earlier in the morning during Sunday School.

Turning his head and looking out over the street, Bishop Moore spotted Raymond, one of the newer members of Arch Street, someone Bishop Moore saw promise in. He'd already started thinking about asking Raymond to head up the church's young men's group. "Thanks for coming again, Ray," he waved, his voice booming. "Stay the course."

"Have a good one, Bishop," Raymond waved back from halfway across the street as he headed toward Anthony's car. "Loved this morning's sermon on Pharaoh and reaping what we sow."

"Glad to hear it," Bishop Moore said, just before he turned away from Raymond and entered into a conversation with the chairman of the deacon board.

Raymond opened the passenger door, and Anthony looked away from the cherry trees.

"Why'd you leave early?" Raymond asked as soon as he scooted across the passenger seat. He didn't give Anthony time to answer. "You just got up and walked out of church before Bishop Moore finished his sermon—"

"Did you hear how many times that man said hell? Ain't hard to tell what he's thinking about. He actually grinned when he preached about Pharaoh drowning," Anthony chortled.

After he turned the key in the ignition and pulled away from the curb, he continued with, "All that man does is tell people God's gonna punish them. He says it in an ain't no skin off his back, matter-of-fact kinda way. He doesn't want forgiveness." He felt Raymond's gaze burning against the side of his head, but he didn't look away from the street. "Oh. Bishop Moore'd never come right out and say it," he added after he turned the radio up. "He might not even know it, but he wants folks to be punished. He doesn't love people. He wants to see people get theirs."

With a flip to the right blinker, he rounded the corner. "Maybe there's somebody he wants to get back at." He shrugged. "His mother." He shrugged again. "His father. Maybe there's somebody he'd like to see God punish." He glanced at Raymond. "Know what I'm saying?"

"He's a pastor."

"You're going to defend him? Forget the preaching part. You can't see there's no forgiveness in that man? You can't see the anger chewing away at him?"

"Your mother's the one who recommended the church. What are you talking about? You're the one who brought me here? You were gung-ho on Bishop Moore a month ago."

Anthony chuckled. "My mom wants me to walk the straight and narrow. Now I see why she led me here."

Tramaine Hawkins' rich voice filled the airways. She sang the hit gospel song, "Changed."

While the song played on the radio, Anthony sighed. "My mom was wrong about this church." Seconds later, he looked at Raymond with disbelief. "You can't see it?"

Raymond shook his head decidedly. "You can't attack a man of God."

"And what are we?" Anthony asked as he pulled up to a stop sign and peered down the street. A brown and white station wagon drove across the lane in front of them.

"If God created us, then aren't we God's men too?"

"Well—"

"Come on, Ray. Who are these special people God talks to while God goes mute on everyone else?"

Raymond shrugged.

"I get you wanting to be close to God." He tossed his hand out. "A few weeks ago we were running for our lives. We got shot at. I see where you're coming from," he nodded. "We need someplace where we can feel safe." He laughed. "It's the reason I came to church. We need to chill. I get that."

"But," Anthony continued. "Now I know I don't need to be in a building to be close to God." He laughed. "If that was the case God wouldn't have started talking to people until men stacked bricks on top of each other and some dude stepped back and called it a church."

"I get you, Man."

"If that was the case, God never spoke to Adam--."

"I get it, Anthony."

"All I'm saying is don't go blind trying to be what someone tells you to be."

"Strange coming from you," Raymond said, his voice taking on an edge Anthony hadn't heard since the night of the shooting. "The guy who's been taking orders from one football coach after another since he was in grade school." This time when he laughed his voice went out like a cockatoo; it screeched and rocked.

Anthony pounded the good reverend's persona that much harder. "Bishop Moore's the reason Patrick and Doug stopped going to church."

"Aw, come on. And," he chuckled, "Only reason Doug stopped going was because you did." Raymond shook his head. "Doug'll do anything you say. He just wants to gain your approval."

"No," Anthony disagreed, shaking his head vigorously. "They got tired of those screaming, hell, shame and guilt sermons. Where's the freedom in that? I thought Christ came to set us free, not make us feel guilt and shame. We can get plenty of that outside church. There are enough folks to crack on us for days right out in the street."

"He doesn't preach that way all the time."

Anthony laughed. "We haven't been going to the same church these last four weeks then."

"Maybe Bishop Moore does preach hard, but he's a good man."

"I'm not saying he's not. But you don't know him to defend him."

"I know he's a preacher."

"Okay, Ray," Anthony nodded patronizingly. "Whatever you say." He drove down Girard Street with Shirley Caesar's "No Charge" playing on the radio.

"Like I told you before, my parents took me and my brothers and sister to church when we were coming up. I know what it feels like to be around a preacher who cares about folks." He shook his head and tossed his hand over his shoulder in the direction of Arch Street. "And that ain't it."

"Shoot," Anthony smiled. "Every Sunday morning my mom would get up and cook a slamming breakfast." His smile widened. "Eggs, grits, bacon and homemade buttermilk biscuits." After he ran his tongue around his mouth, he said, "Gospel music would be playing on the radio." He looked across the street at a stretch of row houses and said, "Loved those Sunday mornings." He savored the memory. "Loved them."

"I hear you," Raymond said. He looked out the front windshield at nothing in particular. His voice sounded distant, like he was deep in thought. "You see how kids run up to Bishop Moore at church?"

"You see how he seldom drives to church with his wife?"

"She gets there after he does."

"Yo, Man, he never talks about himself, but he's always talking about somebody else. Talks about big time preachers who make a mistake, like it's something he could never do. And, yo," Anthony continued, "Notice how he calls out people in church who've been sleeping around or drinking without giving their name?"

Raymond shot Anthony a quick glance.

"People walk out of church whispering." Speaking in mock soprano, he mimicked the congregants. *"Child, who do you think pastor was talking about this morning?"*

Raymond leaned toward the passenger door.

"All right. I'll stop," Anthony said. "You have a right to respect the man."

The 300ZX pulled up to a red light. A woman dressed in a wide hemmed skirt and knee length black boots crossed the street in front of the 300ZX. "Nice," Anthony purred while he watched the woman's hips sway.

"And," Anthony added when the light turned green and he pressed the accelerator, "What did you forget? You said you went back in church because you forgot something."

"I got everything." Raymond folded his arms then clasped them against his chest.

"Yo, Man. What's wrong with you?"

"Nothing," Raymond answered with a quick shake of his head. "I'm straight."

"A'right," Anthony said. "If you say so." He wasn't up for a fight.

They rode the rest of the way in silence. Ten minutes later they pulled in front of Roddin.

"Ain't that the dude who lives across the hall from you and Pat?" Anthony asked. To get a better view of the guy, he leaned across the seat in front of Raymond, causing Raymond to lean all the way back so he wouldn't bump him. "His name's Joe Joe, ain't it?"

Raymond looked out the window at the guy. "Yea."

"He's tight with Walter, ain't he?"

Raymond looked out the window at the guy again. He knew better than to trust Walter, but the guy -- other than a lot of boasting about affairs he'd had with women, he hadn't heard so much as a peep out of him. "I've seen him and Walter talking. He started to tell Anthony about seeing Walter talking with a guy he was certain was Michael the night of the car chase but he stopped himself.

Anthony squinted. "I've seen that dude somewhere else before." This time he leaned so far across the seat, Raymond had to lean back until his spine hurt to get out of his way. "Damn, that dude looks familiar," Anthony said.

"Yea," Raymond shrugged.

"You're not listening," Anthony snapped. He sat erect. "You've been in your own world since we left church. I still don't know what you ran back inside to get."

"I signed up for a newsletter, okay?"

He stared at Raymond's down turned mouth. "Cool."

They sat in the car and talked for several minutes. Every now and then they chuckled dryly, the kind of laugh that took work. When their

Love Pour Over Me

conversation started to wind down, Anthony said, "I'm not going back to church."

"I don't know," Raymond murmured.

"You don't know what?"

Raymond reached for the door handle. "I feel at home there, and," he added when Anthony shifted the car from 'park' to 'drive', "You think one minute you need church and the next minute you don't?"

"You're not my father, Dude."

With one kick of Raymond's leg, the car door opened. "Have a good day," he told Anthony, his mouth as straight as a pencil drawn line. "You go hang out with your sports friends."

"What the hell does that mean?"

Raymond turned sharply. "Do you have to curse?"

"It never bothered you before. Damn, Man," Anthony moaned, "You act like you just spent ten years in a church. From what you told me about your childhood, nobody took you to church when you were a kid. So why are you acting like this? You think it's your job to judge me?"

"I'm not judging you. I just don't know why you want to stop going—"

"You made a comment about me hanging out with my sports friends. You were being crash, and you know it."

"Okay. So I apologize."

"All right," Anthony said. His face was tight.

It stayed that way until Raymond stuck his head inside the car and they slapped hands.

"You want to hang out?" Anthony asked when he sat up.

"Nah. I'm going up to my room. I think I'll watch some TV."

"You all right, Man?" Anthony asked.

"I'm cool."

"All right."

"Be cool." Raymond closed the passenger door and walked toward the resident house.

"You too," Anthony called out as he pulled away from the curb. Seconds later he was gone down the street.

As Raymond approached Roddin House he heard Joe Joe tell his huddle of yes-men, "Woman was so sprung, I had to shut off my phone to keep her from calling me."

Raymond threw his hand up to the guys and nodded. "Joe Joe's always lying," he chuckled while he walked through the doors. "He didn't shut his phone off because of a woman. AT&T cut his phone off because he didn't pay his bill."

"What's up, Ray?" Walter asked from his station inside the main corridor.

"Hey, Walter," Raymond answered back. He kept his distance. As far as he was concerned, being friends with Michael, Walter was someone he had to watch closely. Yet, he also knew that he had too much dirt in his own past to press the issue.

Walter flipped the pages of a *Black Enterprise* magazine. "What's happening?" he asked slyly.

"Everything's cool," Raymond said heading toward the elevator. As soon as he stepped aboard, he closed his eyes. When he opened them again, Walter was staring at him coldly.

The elevator doors shut and Raymond went up.

"Yo, Patrick," Raymond called out when he unlocked the apartment door. He walked through the living room then he turned and went down the hallway that separated Patrick and his bedrooms.

"That's right," he said with a snap of his fingers. "Patrick went bowling with Sandra."

Four hours later, Raymond sat alone in the apartment, reading the Psalms, trying to figure out why Walter kept eyeballing him. Conversations seeped into the living room. Students recently returned from barbecues, bike rides or the movies opened their apartment doors and spilled into the hall.

As he turned another page in the bible, Raymond thought about joining the other students in the hall then he dismissed the notion. With each passing minute he told himself that Bishop Moore was right. People didn't take life seriously enough.

Like film beginning to coat the eye, change came upon Raymond. It made him reticent. It set him on a path that would gain strength with each advancing day, with each repeated thought – as if a long string of dominoes, stacked one against the other, had been hit – had gone off, sailing across a floor, predicting the outcome of the end of his life.

Chapter Twelve

It was a balmy Saturday, May 11, 1985. Brenda caught a plane to Tennessee earlier in the day. She and Raymond had been seeing each other sporadically for nearly two months, usually at church or by the lake at Fairmont Park, a place where Brenda didn't expect to run into Byron.

Her sister, Virginia, picked her up from McGhee Tyson International Airport on Alcoa Highway in Knoxville as soon as her plane landed. They headed straight to Asheville, North Carolina.

"These tulips are gorgeous," Brenda told Virginia as she knelt in the flower bed. She breathed in the tulips' fruity scent and looked across the field at her sister. "I'm so glad we came to Biltmore House and Gardens. I always wanted to visit this place."

Purple azaleas, white carnations, yellow tulips and black roses sprouted on rolling hills like classy ladies in exquisite wide-brimmed hats. Opposite the flowers, and as if they were planted to balance the earth with edible color, rows of turnip greens, lettuce, tomatoes, blueberries and strawberries went on for acres. Above them stood oak and willow trees, their tops pushing up toward the heavens, their limbs stretching out large and stately while they swayed beneath the sky's gentle breeze.

Virginia rubbed her thumb and forefinger delicately across the petals of an opened rose. "I am so glad that you came home for a visit," she told Brenda. "Coming here straight from the airport was a good idea. I thought you'd enjoy visiting Biltmore." A gust of wind blew a rose petal against her chin.

When she stood her gold and diamond Swarovski bracelets and matching earrings clinked. The sensuous Estee Lauder perfume she wore with a touch of honey scent filled the air with a light sweetness. "My place is about an hour from here." She ran her hands across her Stephen Burrows' jeans and brushed dirt away from her slender hips. "Ready to go?"

"Sure." Brenda's gaze swept up and across Virginia's *perfect* figure. Since they were teenagers, Brenda wished she looked and dressed more like her older sister.

They talked their way back to Virginia's silver BMW.

"Girl," Virginia said with a swing of her polished fingernails, "Did I tell you? I met this handsome man at Strut's a few weeks ago."

"Struts?"

"It's a jazz club in East Knoxville," Virginia announced gaily while she combed her hand over her recently permed hair. "I forget that it has been awhile since you went out on the town with me now that you're at school in Pennsylvania."

She tapped Brenda's forearm. "Struts is like that club Zanzabar Gold you tell me about."

"So what's this guy's name and how's he treating you?" Brenda wanted to know.

Virginia smiled until her teeth showed. "The gentleman's name is Scott. Scott Lawry," she added. "He owns and manages real estate. He was already in the club when I came in. I'm not sure if he caught my eye because I was sitting by myself while my girls were on the floor dancing their butts off or if he caught my eye because I felt him staring at me from across the room." She didn't hide her blush.

"Go on," Brenda said as she pulled down on her t-shirt she noticed that her fingernails were slightly chipped and an old greasy stain spread across the shirt's bottom front. "Tell me about this guy and the night you two met."

"As soon as I looked at Scott," Virginia said after she stuck the key in the ignition and brought the engine to a purr. "He got up and crossed the floor." She tapped Brenda's shoulder. "Let me tell you, he didn't waste any time. He came right to me." She backed her BMW out of the parking lot and made her way onto the highway. "He told me he saw me the second I walked into the club."

"Yea?"

"I had the time of my life that night. Scott and I talked for hours." She smiled. "B, that man is so handsome I had to keep reminding myself that he was real."

"Scott is naturally attentive," she continued. "From the first time we met, he has always listened, completely listened, to me." She glanced into the rearview mirror, pulled into the fast lane and zipped past a Honda Accord. "Scott knows how to love a woman. You ought to see how he shares himself with me." She giggled. "He said he was drawn to my energy. Oh, and," she added, "He has a younger brother named Michael who lives in Philadelphia." She grinned. "Can you believe that?"

The BMW ate up miles of road. They sped by businesses, restaurants and gas stations. Virginia talked about Scott for more than half an hour, until they neared Knoxville, at which time Brenda flashed a toothy grin.

"I met this guy named Raymond," she blurted as if she had no concern for the statement's impact.

"Raymond?" Virginia asked. "Raymond?" she asked again as if she needed to be sure that she'd heard her younger sister reveal that the glow on her face was due to a man. "What happened to you and Byron?"

Brenda went on as if she hadn't heard Virginia. "You know how men are fun loving but they want you to think they're serious when you first meet them?"

"No. I do not know," Virginia responded curtly. "If a man is into you, he is into you. People who seem serious are just that," she added coldly. "They are plain serious." She paused. "Maybe he's hiding something."

"No," Brenda said flatly. "He just doesn't let go as much as his friends do. That's all." She gazed out the window. "Raymond's right like rain."

Virginia shot her a chilly glance.

"Raymond listens to me the way Scott listens to you. He doesn't interrupt me. He doesn't laugh at me. He's not mean." Her bottom lip quivered, as if some painful time shared with Byron had taken hold of it. "He doesn't make me feel small."

"And Byron is—"

Brenda answered slowly, reluctantly. "We're still together." She almost laughed. "Byron probably wouldn't break up with me unless he was furious." She looked across the road. "He has a nasty temper. Let him get good and mad and he might call it quits. Then again," she added, "He might not end our relationship even then. I'm like a centerpiece in his life, someone who's always there." Her voice lowered. "I stay with him even while he runs around with other women—"

"Byron's not the type of guy who cheats—"

"Oh, Byron cheats," Brenda said through clenched teeth. 'I'm just dumb enough to stay," she added somberly. She quickly added, "Can you believe he told me that I'm a good business investment, because I make him look by being smart and pretty?" She turned away from Virginia and looked out the passenger window. "I know you might find this hard to believe, but Byron's calculating. When he gets mad, he treats me like he's playing a game of chess that would cost him too much to lose. He can be really mean. And," she added in a lowered voice, "he doesn't love me."

"Damn it," Virginia cursed. She'd spent years imagining herself spoiling Byron's and Brenda's beautiful children, her nieces and nephews. This was too much. Brenda hadn't bothered to ease her into this shocking news. She'd just come right out and said it, and Virginia wasn't going to digest it whole, as if it didn't mean anything. "Stop lying," she demanded.

"You don't know Byron like you think you do—"

Virginia rolled her eyes. "This is the guy you fell in love with in your senior year of high school. Byron was everything to you, Brenda!" she shouted. "He's one of the nicest guys I've ever met."

Brenda was silent. She watched a McDonald's truck go by on the opposite side of the highway.

"B?"

"I wanted to spend the rest of my life with Byron," Brenda answered when she turned and faced her sister. Her voice was strong, not rocky with tears the way it had been months ago as she watched Byron and her relationship fall apart. "I wanted us to be happy together. I spent hours dreaming about the love we would share. I saw us growing old together." She almost smiled. "Then Byron started shutting me out, ignoring me."

"B."

"No. For real. There were times when I was so upset after a fight we had, I walked around campus in a stupor. There were times when I felt numb with pain.

"All relationships come with—"

Brenda raised her voice. "I felt caged, Virginia, and there were times Byron didn't call or visit all evening. I'd later hear from my roommate Cynthia or someone else that he'd had been out having a high time with other women."

"Those are rumors," Virginia insisted. "If you think it's tough living with a man," Virginia admonished in her proper Southern accent – not the lazy, slow vernacular so many folks around her used – "wait until you have to live without one." Her tone hurt. It brought no comfort to Brenda, once the little girl who looked up to her in search of protection.

Brenda leaned into the passenger seat. When she glanced out the window she saw a Shoney's Big Boy. She pointed. "Remember when Mom and Dad would take us to Shoney's and we'd get those huge strawberry pies they serve?"

"You have not changed," Virginia laughed. "You are switching the subject."

"It's not like you want to hear what I have to say."

"B, since we were in high school you dreamed of being with a man who would make you feel at home inside his love. You said that yourself." She flipped on her blinkers and turned off the highway onto a side street. "I cannot count how many times you said that when we were in high school."

"That was before I started dating. I was still living in a fantasy world when I walked around saying that. After a few years of dating, I became disenchanted with the soul mate search. Dating is a waste of time. 'Go out with another cute boy,' Mama would tell me. I can hear her now. 'You're too pretty to spend a Friday night at home,' she would say. After awhile Dad started saying it too." She sighed. "Mama always pulled Dad into it. And so I'd keep dating. I knew what Mama was trying to do. She wanted to make sure I was taken care of after I left home. Both she and Dad wanted to see us married to successful businessmen."

"That's a good thing to wish for a woman."

Brenda shrugged.

"How do you think Mama is able to enjoy that beachfront house Dad and she have in sunny Miami, Florida?" She didn't wait for Brenda to respond. "That gorgeous four bedroom house they have on six acres of land. Dad is the reason Mama can enjoy that. Mama has not worked since we were born, if she worked a day in her life at all."

"Times have changed."

"I know but a good man makes a woman's life easy. Byron can give you that," she was quick to add. "But you insist on jacking that up."

Brenda shrugged. Part of her wanted to laugh at the way Virginia laid down her proper, genteel mannerisms and picked up street talk just-like-that. A larger part of her wanted Virginia to stop being mad about Raymond and simply be her friend.

"Life is all about relationships, B. A man completes a woman. Now mind you, not just any man."

While Virginia droned on about the importance of a woman having a good man, Brenda took in the houses on the cul de sac Virginia pulled into. She also thought about Raymond. She knew she shouldn't have told Virginia about him. She knew Virginia could read a lot into her joy.

Later that day while the earth rotated causing the sun to look like it was going down, Virginia and Brenda ate dinner. Cool, gentle breezes, the kind that made Virginia want to sit on her front porch, came in through the opened living room window.

Virginia ate small bites of baked chicken, seasoned green beans and mashed sweet potatoes. Brenda ate forkfuls of the hot food; she didn't mind when crumbs dribbled down her chin onto the front of her t-shirt. They were different when it came to their conversation too; Virginia did nearly all the talking.

She pushed a piece of biscuit inside her mouth, something to mix her recent bite of green beans up with. "B, how long have you known this man?" She was curled up on the end of her Broyhill living room sofa. Her shoes were on the floor at the sofa's edge. Brenda and she had been at her house for two hours.

Brenda dodged the question by asking a question of her own. "Feeling better?"

"My headache is gone," Virginia answered. "I am fine. I asked how long you have known this man." Her mouth was tight. She was the older sister. She'd spent years at the lead. It started when Brenda and she were small, not even tall enough to reach their father's knees.

"I've known Raymond a few months."

Virginia stretched out across the sofa. The ends of her feet brushed Brenda's thigh. "You cannot do this." She spoke as if she was talking about her own life, as if she had the right to make decisions for Brenda. "A cheating woman is a bad woman." She shook her head. "It is not right for a woman to cheat on a man. It is not natural," she said. "It's wrong, and if there is one thing I know about you," she smiled and said, "You are not an evil woman."

"Are you telling me it's wrong to believe in my dreams?"

"I am telling you that Byron is your dream. Byron is from good people." She peered at Brenda. "For goodness sake, Mama went to school with Byron's mother. You know that. Open your eyes, B. Relationships take work, hard work," she added before she said, "You are going to get hurt if you do not open your eyes."

"Maybe you're the one who has her eyes closed," Brenda offered. She almost regretted saying the words; she'd long been familiar with Virginia's temper.

"I see your mind is made up," Virginia declared. She waved her hand through the air. "When this does not-know-how-to-have-fun-serious man breaks your heart, don't come crying to me." She pursed her lips. "You and Byron have been together for three years. And, what do you know about this Raymond's family? Have you met his mother? Have you met his father? Does he have any siblings?"

"I haven't met them. I told you I've only known Raymond a few months."

"And you know he's good enough to leave Byron for?"

Brenda was silent.

"I remember the day you came home from school and told me you met Byron," Virginia grinned. She relaxed her shoulders into the sofa pillows. "You were so happy, you even told Mama before you told me. Byron is the one who loved you first." She looked right at Brenda.

Images of Virginia crying on her shoulder after she discovered her first romantic love -- a fifteen year old boy -- cared for another girl flashed across Brenda's mind. Out of breath and distraught all those years ago, Virginia had told Brenda about the incident as soon as she raced through their parents' front door.

Back then leaves hung, like long ornaments, from the weeping willows spread about their parents' estate. On that afternoon, an ice cream truck rang its way up the street. Virginia had walked to the boy's house to pay him a visit. She gazed through the boy's front bay window when she neared the porch. The boy was sitting on the sofa with a curvy sophomore. The girl's hair was styled in tight cornrows. The boy Virginia swore she loved and would spend the rest of her life with had his arms around the girl. Their mouths were pressed together. Their eyes were closed. They looked like they were soaking up a dream, its sweet juice going down-down deep inside of them. While the couple kissed, Virginia raced away from the house. She ran until her sneakers echoed against the sidewalk and her breath caught, like a dry cough, in her throat. By the time she reached her own home four blocks away she was sobbing.

"What's wrong?" Brenda had asked from her place on the living room sofa as soon as Virginia burst through the front door. "What's wrong?" she asked again while she wrapped her arms around Virginia the way the boy had wrapped his arms around the girl. She held her sister as if her arms were paper and she was covering a gift. She rocked Virginia until her sobs and cries of unfairness subsided.

After she washed a forkful of mixed vegetables down with ice water, Brenda snapped, "I'm not Eugene. I'm not your first boyfriend, so you don't need to try to make me pay for what he did. Even if you think I don't have enough moral fiber not to sleep around, you don't have to look down on me."

"Forget Eugene," Virginia said. "This guy's father is probably some bootlegger. His mother probably didn't even finish high school."

"You don't know them, Virginia. You have no right to talk about people like this. We weren't brought up like that and you know it."

"What if this guy is into some trouble?" She sat up and examined Brenda's face. "Remember Rochelle?"

"Yes."

"She was one of the coolest, most had-it-together women in the neighborhood. She left her boyfriend of five years, took up with this guy she barely knew from her job and now she's a statistic."

Brenda turned away from her. "I'm not like that and you know it."

"He beats the life out of her two, three times a week. But, oh," Virginia grinned, "He started out like a prince."

Brenda rolled her eyes. She loved her sister. They'd always been honest with each other, even to the point where what they said cut, like it was doing now. But they always mended their wounds and went on like they were thick as thieves. Yet, Virginia's attacks on Raymond were going too deep.

"Oh, and Morgan. Remember her?"

"Yes," Brenda said in a lazy see-saw kind of way.

"Smart as a whip. Model-looking pretty. Feisty too. Morgan had fire in her. She and Darrell started dating in what, the eleventh grade?"

"Yes," Brenda nodded sloppily. "The eleventh grade."

"What did she do? She went to college, met this smooth talking guy, dropped Darrell like a hot potato, and moved in with this other man. Three kids and four years later, Morgan found out this jerk's a raging alcoholic. Those social drinks turned into one too many. Morgan and her kids have been down to the Woman's Shelter twice in the last year. But, oh," Virginia sang, "It started out like a dream."

"Okay," Brenda shouted. "I'll ask Raymond about his folks. I bet they're good, loving people. Raymond's that way. He goes to church on Sunday and Wednesday. He's the reason I started going to church again. And you know Mama always told us, find a man who loves the Lord and you've found a good man." She purposefully avoided telling Virginia about recent changes she'd noticed in Raymond, his sudden increased religious loyalties and his insistence that they avoid being too intimate – thus tempting him with sex, advice she'd overheard Bishop Moore give Raymond the Sunday after she met him. As she traveled down the highway with Virginia, Brenda hid her concern behind a wide grin. "You know what they say. The apple doesn't fall far from the tree."

Virginia smirked. "That is what I am scared of. What if his father has a criminal record? What if his mother is on drugs? You know how bad that crack has spread."

"First his dad was a bootlegger and now—"

"Has this man even offered to have you meet his family?"

Brenda's tongue caught in her mouth.

"He hasn't," Virginia said, answering her own question. "And you have not even thought about it. Isn't it odd to you that this man has not offered to introduce you to his family?"

"We just met," Brenda stammered.

"Okay. I will give you that," Virginia said. "But let me ask you this. What are his parents' names? After two months a man would tell you that unless something is wrong back home." She didn't give Brenda time to respond. "For all you know, he came to Philadelphia to escape a dark past."

"Glad to hear you be so positive," Brenda remarked derisively. "Since we're not going to agree on this, why don't we just watch some TV then get to the Smoky Mountains tomorrow? We can go shopping in Pigeon Forge." Her gaze went up and across the room.

A flock of birds lifted off a tree and flew in front of Virginia's living room window. Then the birds flew further up across the sky. Brenda followed them with her gaze for as far as she could, which was the start of Virginia's neighbor's front yard.

Three days later when Virginia drove Brenda back to McGhee Tyson Airport she surprised her with a yellow and pink dress. Brenda's face lit up as soon as she saw the garment. For the next several minutes she lavished Virginia with thank yous, until Virginia announced, "When you come back, Scott wants to take you some place special." She switched to the fast lane and whizzed past a black Ford Mustang. "He gave us space to enjoy each other this time. Plus, and you will not believe this," she continued, "Scott's baby brother Michael came home to Tennessee this week. He said he needed to take a break from Philadelphia for awhile."

"Does Scott's brother attend UPemb?"

"No. He lives in Philadelphia with friends. Scott said Michael got into a scuffle with some nuts at UPemb and came home to relax." She laughed. "You know how dumb some college fellas get? Well, Scott's brother ran into some dumb brats from UPemb, but he kept his wits. He is home now. Scott will help him get his head straight. In fact," she said flipping on her right blinker, "I gotta stop by Scott's on the way to the airport to pick up some papers he wants me to fax to an attorney in Philly."

When they pulled in front of a three story, red brick house sitting on two acres of lush grass, Virginia turned to Brenda and said, "I'm just gonna run in and grab the papers. I'll be right back."

"Cool," Brenda nodded.

Moments later as Virginia exited the house's front screen door, two German Shepherds ran onto the lawn.

A tall, ebony skinned man with a muscular build stuck his head out the house door. "Roger and Ricky, come back!" he called. When the dogs didn't turn back, the man stepped onto the wrap around front porch. As soon as the man saw Brenda sitting in the passenger seat, he smiled and hurried off the porch. He wasn't halfway down the expansive lawn, when another man came and stood in the doorway.

"Hi," the first man said when he reached Virginia's car. He wore a pair of black silk dress pants and a yellow knit shirt. He extended his hand through the lowered window. "I'm Scott."

Brenda leaned across the seat and shook Scott's hand. "Nice to meet you. Virginia's told me nothing but good things about you."

"Next time you're in town, we'll all go someplace fun," Scott told her.

"I'd like that," Brenda said, sitting erect.

Brenda squinted and looked toward the porch, trying to make out who was standing behind the screen door.

Scott followed her gaze. "Mike!" he waved and hollered. "Come meet Virginia's baby sister."

Michael pushed the screen door open, released an exasperated breath, and walked down the porch steps. He wore a white sleeveless t-shirt, showing off his powerfully built torso. He walked, one hand jammed in his pant pocket, down the lawn.

"This is Brenda," Scott said as soon as Michael reached the car.

Brenda leaned across the seat again. Michael nodded at her and shook her hand loosely. "Pleasure," he said, stepping back.

Virginia opened the driver side car door, and Scott circled her lower back with one arm, pulled her close and kissed her fully on the mouth.

A few feet behind Scott, Michael eyeballed Brenda.

After several seconds, Brenda turned away from him, but not before taking note of the facial scar.

With one last kiss and wave to Scott, Virginia climbed inside the BMW. She shoved the papers she'd gotten from Scott in her purse.

As Virginia put the car in reverse and backed it out of the long driveway, Brenda scanned the legal document. *Michael Lowry vs. The City of Philadelphia* was printed across the top page; it was the only part of the document Brenda could make out from where she sat in the car.

Scott and Michael stood side by side on the lawn next to the dogs watching the car back away from the house.

Soon Virginia and Brenda were on Alcoa Highway again. "Do you see Scott every day?" Brenda asked.

"We're a couple," Virginia laughed. "Yes. We see each other every day."

Brenda gazed out the windshield. "That's good. Gotta make sure you know a person." She watched a car zip passed the BMW. "But sometimes I guess you want a break."

"A break?"

"I'm just saying that after spending a lot of time together sometimes couples want to be with other people. And from the sounds of it, Scott might need to spend more time with his brother. Philadelphia is not the city to go wrong in."

Virginia paused. "You don't like Michael?"

"I don't know him," Brenda said. "Never seen him before."

Virginia glanced at Brenda out of the corners of her eyes then pressed the accelerator. "Michael will be fine," she said. "Scott is a great communicator. He'll get Michael straight. And Scott is not going to spend less time with me. We love being together."

"Scott feels the same way?"

"About what?"

"About you two being together so much." Brenda chuckled. "I wasn't talking about Michael. He's Scott's brother. I know Scott ain't gonna leave his side."

"Yes, Scott feels the same way," Virginia answered convincingly. "Absolutely."

"How do you know? Did he tell you?"

"Yes and he shows it. It is not so much what a man says. It is what a man does. A man can say anything. It does not mean you believe it." She paused. "I love that man more than I thought I would ever love anyone. The more Scott and I get to know each other, the deeper we want to go."

Brenda turned away from Virginia. Tears pooled in her eyes. Not once had she spoken it during her visit, but deep down she wanted what Virginia had with Scott. She wanted to be loved by a man. It was a yet unlived experience for her and because of that she found it hard to believe Virginia when she talked about the joys of Scott and her love. So far in her life, when it came to men, all Brenda had was time – three years with Byron. And the more Byron got to know her, the less he wanted to be with her.

She hoped it would be different with Raymond, but after talking with Virginia the last three days she was beginning to have doubts. She didn't want to get her hopes up. She didn't want to get hurt.

A Ford Expedition sped by. Orange and white Lady Vol basketball stickers clung to the truck's rear bumper. Brenda looked at the truck then she turned away from the window and faced her sister. "Scott seems cool. But then, you don't roll with guys who don't know how to love you." She glanced out the window again. The truck was long gone down the road. It looked more like a dot than a truck now. "I like that," she said. "I need to be more like that."

They drove over bumps in the road; the car shook and static filled the radio. Virginia turned the volume up and scanned the dial. *Brick*'s hit song, "Dazz" filled the car.

"This is my jam," Virginia smiled.

"Those brothers play with heart," Brenda declared. "It takes heart to play good live band music. You can't just press buttons on a machine. You gotta put your heart into every note."

"What do you know about making music?" Virginia teased while they sped down Alcoa Highway toward McGhee Tyson Airport. "And speaking of heart," she added. "Why don't you follow your heart this time? See where things go with whoever you decide to get with?" She twisted her mouth as if she'd swallowed a bad lemon. "Even if it turns out to be this man Raymond."

Suddenly and as if she was in the car alone, a memory nipped at Brenda's thoughts and she smiled. Her voice was wispy, her mind far away – back at the stadium. "The first time I spoke to Raymond we were at a football game."

Virginia shot her a quick glance.

"Maybe it's time you dated more. Give Byron some space and do not get stuck on this man

Raymond." She glanced into the rearview mirror. "If you date more, you will know for sure if you want to be with Byron or Raymond or whoever. But if you only date one or two men, you might not ever be sure that you are with the man you want to be with."

Brenda gave a slow nod. Sloppily, with the back of her hand and after she was certain that Virginia wasn't looking at her, she wiped tears away from her face.

They pulled into the airport's short term parking lot, the one right across the street from the main terminal. A string of taxis, lined three rows deep, honked their horns and let out chatty passengers making the area loud with noise.

It took Virginia and Brenda a long time to part. They embraced, patted each other's backs and rocked inside one another's arms. Just before they let each other go, Virginia kissed Brenda's face and squeezed her shoulders tightly. "I love you," she avowed. With her free hand she clipped a pendant around Brenda's neck.

"I love you too," Brenda said. A second later, she leaned back on the car seat and gasped. "Grandma's pendant," she murmured while she fingered the large pearl. "Grandma gave this to you as a keepsake." As slowly as the homemade molasses Virginia gave her two days ago had poured into the empty canning jar, she looked up and met Virginia's glance.

"I want you to have it," Virginia told her. She kissed Brenda's forehead. "It will bring you good luck. Keep it close to your heart."

"I love you," Brenda called out again after she climbed out of the car and walked toward the terminal. Twice she looked back at Virginia and waved. The brittleness in Virginia's conversation the day she first arrived in town had been forgiven. Uncertainty hung in the air, and because it did, Brenda wanted to hold onto what was familiar to her.

She couldn't explain it. With each forward step she took, she had no evidence for it, but she felt certain that when she saw her sister again she would be deeply changed – forever.

Chapter Thirteen

Outside Roddin House, scent of recently mowed grass hung in the air. At the edges of wide campus lawns near the residence hall, children chewed and popped bubble gum while they walked next to their parents. In the distance, old cars coughed and clanged their way down the street.

It was May 20, 1985. Brenda had been back on campus for two days. Raymond picked her up from the airport and drove her to Red Lobster on Roosevelt Boulevard where they dined on flounder, stuffed mushrooms and coconut shrimp with spare money Raymond earned from a two day work-study job Coach Carter helped him get. Brenda hadn't told Byron she was back in town, preferring to wait a few more days before she saw him again.

She and Raymond sat at a semi-private table at the restaurant, filling each other in on recent events in their lives. They talked fast and ate slowly, not wanting to part. Halfway through their meal, Raymond stood and leaned slowly, deliberately across the table and kissed Brenda tenderly on the mouth. They closed their eyes against rising emotion, reached out and clasped each other's hands and parting their lips slightly, enjoyed the taste, the touch, the pull of each other's tongues. "It's so good to see you again," Raymond told Brenda as he sat back down. She sat across from him taking in deep breaths while she gazed into his brown eyes, hungry for more.

That was two days ago. Presently, Raymond stood alone in Patrick and his apartment talking in hushed tones on the telephone. Less than an hour ago, he finished a brisk six mile run during practice in preparation for Saturday's, Penn Relays. There was a message on his answering machine. It was from Anthony. "I need to tell you something important," Anthony said, his voice hurrying across the wire. Raymond listened to the message twice but he hadn't returned Anthony's telephone call.

Instead he pressed the telephone receiver so hard against the side of his head, his ear sweat. "You've got to stop calling here." He looked at the crack at the bottom of the front door. A second later, he leaned back on the sofa, closed his eyes and let out a long, deep breath. No one was coming. "Dad," he begged, "Don't call Student Affairs anymore. Stop," he demanded. As he pressured his father to meet his demands, sermons Bishop Moore preached at Arch Street started to dominate his thoughts. Despite Anthony's efforts not to notice it, Raymond heard Bishop Moore preach about forgiveness. *"We've all made mistakes,"* Bishop Moore told the congregation from the pulpit. *"When we forgive others, it's as if we're also forgiving ourselves."*

Raymond stood in the silence, looking toward the ceiling; the telephone receiver dangled in his hand. He begged for Malcolm and his relationship to change, to stop shifting from hate to hurt to anger to rage back to hate again.

"Ohio State—" Malcolm tried, his voice that of a defeated man, no longer the angry father in search of a son to abuse.

"Ohio State hasn't called for me," Raymond said, pulling the receiver to the side of his head again. He recited scripture verses to himself and released three quick breaths, but childhood memories would not release him. He clenched his teeth and told Malcolm, "I've been here for a year. This is where I'm at school. Happy now?" he scoffed. "Now you know."

"You just up and left," Malcolm complained. The Steel Fervor he flooded his hurt with caused his words to sound like they were being dragged out of his mouth.

"No," Raymond tried. He bit down on his bottom lip and pushed images of Bishop Moore's sermons out of his mind. "I escaped. I escaped you."

"Glad you called, Son," Malcolm offered in a change of tone. "You going to keep in touch?" He sat alone at the kitchen table in Dayton. A cockroach raced across the floor then under the refrigerator. Dirty dishes were piled in the sink. On the other side of the refrigerator Malcolm could hear a raccoon gnawing at the floorboard. The house hadn't been swept in months. Malcolm had taken to sleeping on the sofa, his dark thoughts that once attacked Raymond, now turning on him. He kept a gun nearby, in case burglars came for his valuables, chief amongst them being the eleven year old 18-inch color television set that barely worked anymore.

"You going to stop calling me?" Raymond asked in mock amusement. He laughed dryly and with aim; he wanted to hurt his father.

Malcolm strangled the neck of the Steel Fervor bottle. "If that's the way you want it. But, I looked all over for you," he added, the hardness Raymond had grown up hearing in his voice near gone. "And I want you to know."

"Don't make yourself out to be a hero."

"That ain't what I'm trying to do—"

"Look," Raymond said flatly, glad to, for once, be the one causing the hurt in Malcolm and his relationship, remorseful that his religious practices, his church going, had been unable to cleanse him of blame. "I only called you so you'd stop calling here. I'm a man of my word. I told Student Affairs I'd get in touch with you and that's what I'm doing. It didn't have to come to this, but you had to have things go your way--"

"I got your message," Malcolm interjected, the volume in his voice lowering, a hint of appreciation in its tone.

"What message?" Raymond asked, careful to look beneath the door again.

"You called here and wished me a Merry Christmas." Malcolm took another swig of the Steel Fervor then he raised his free hand and wiped tears from his eyes. "I just wanted to hear from my boy."

Raymond shut his eyes and blew out several bursts of air. He fought not to become as angry as he'd grown up watching his father be, but he was starting to lose that battle. Malcolm had a way of pushing up the grit in him. "I am not a boy," he said. He released a noisy breath. "Are you finished? Do you want anything else or can I hang up now?"

Malcolm let go of the liquor bottle and leaned back in the kitchen chair. His voice bellowed across the wire, tears nearly breaking his words up. "Said I looked all over for you."

"I didn't ask you to." Raymond said while he glanced toward the front door then at his watch. He could easily see that he'd done the right thing to skip his Advanced Chemistry class after he finished track practice so he could call his father without fear of Patrick coming in on him.

"But I did look all over for you," Malcolm said. He spoke with such force, his body shook. "I did," he repeated, a string of expletives rushing out of his mouth.

Shame over Malcolm's alcoholism stirred up rage deep within Raymond and sent crimson rushing to his face. "Okay, Dad," he argued. "What do you want from me?" He didn't give Malcolm time to answer. He jabbed his finger against his chest. "You've already taken blood from me." He stared up at the wall and blinked. "Can't count how many times you beat me when I was a kid." He shook his head. "But not anymore," he declared. "You'll never hit me again."

Malcolm sat up in the chair. Although he was alone in the house, he shifted and adjusted his position until he felt professional, like a man worthy of another man's respect. "When're you coming home?"

"When are you going to die?"

Once spoken, the words sounded too hard. Apology hovered on Raymond's tongue, pulled and tugged at it, but he pushed the apology back. "I gotta go," he said. The question he'd asked his father stabbed his conscience, made it hard for him to stay on the phone.

"Stanley and Joey asked about you," Malcolm said in effort to extend their conversation.

"Yea," Raymond said. "Tell them I said hi when you see them. Look, Dad," he began. "I didn't mean what I said earlier."

"Ahh," Malcolm waved off. "I know you didn't. We got history and all, you and me. We don't mean half the crap we say to anybody."

"Nah," Raymond responded. He listened to approaching footsteps outside in the hallway. "I mean what I say every other time. I just didn't mean that." A part of him didn't want to, but he said it anyway. "I apologize. I was wrong. I shouldn't have said that. It wasn't cool."

"Well, now," Malcolm laughed. He leaned forward and hugged the bottle of Steel Fervor like it was an old, trusty friend. "When have you ever been cool?"

"All right, Dad. I have to go."

"Met anybody while you've been up there in Phi-la-del-ph-ia is it?" He didn't give Raymond time to respond. "I would come up there but the ol' Mustang won't make it that far. Drug your ass around a lot of miles in that car. Tore it up after awhile."

"Yea, Dad," Raymond nodded. He glanced beneath the front door. Beads of sweat dotted his forehead. He listened while Joe Joe across the hall, opened and closed his door, then he leaned back on the sofa and sighed.

"You're one friendless mothafuka," Malcolm said. "You—"

"Dad, why are you talking like this? You don't sound like yourself. Your English is all broken. What's going on?"

"Don't you go correcting me, boy," Malcolm ordered. "I asked you if you met anybody up there in that useless town."

Raymond paused for a long time. He brought Brenda's soft smile and her clear brown eyes into his mind's view, but he didn't utter her name.

"Ray?"

"I haven't met anybody since I came here," he lied. "I'm focused on track, you know that."

"Why didn't you take up football or weight lifting or some sport like that?"

Raymond glanced out the window and watched a red bird fly across the sky. The bird flapped its wings and soared higher, to the edge of the building then above it. "I won the indoor nationals earlier this year."

"You're such a queer," Malcolm bellowed for no reason other than that he'd said it so many times before, the accusation seemed to be waiting for him to make good use of it.

"Yea, Dad."

"I got locked up on account of you." The liquor was doing its work. Malcolm was getting drowsier by the minute. "Went all over this town looking for you. You couldn't even leave me a note, you sorry bastard. You just up and walked out. I remember," Malcolm told him. His arm went up then slowly swung back down like it didn't have bone in it anymore. "I had gone out to the store to get you something to eat. You said you'd be here when I got back. Oh," Malcolm droned. "But you were gone. I dropped those groceries and went all over this house looking for you. I asked Stanley and Joey if they'd seen you. They said 'no'. Then I called the police. I called that school in O-hi-o."

Raymond listened in silence. He thought about turning on the television to drown out his father's voice. Despite the cursing and put downs, Malcolm seemed different to Raymond, broken, desperate to feel powerful and in charge. His dejectedness made Raymond feel uneasy, responsible for his pain.

"They locked me up on account of my looking for you." And there were tears in Malcolm's voice. It was the first time Raymond had heard the emotion hemmed in his father's throat. He felt sympathy for his father but not enough to wash away the hate that Malcolm had birthed in him when he was just a kid. His ears started to hurt as he remembered the times his father dug his fingernails so hard into his earlobes when he was a little boy they would start to bleed. It was his punishment for interrupting Malcolm when he got excited listening in on grown people's conversation to the point where he joined the conversation. After each punishment Raymond tried to keep quiet when grown people were around, but sometimes their conversations sounded fun and he got so excited he couldn't hedge off the urge to belong.

"Sorry you got locked up on account of looking for me," Raymond offered.

"No, you're not. You're not," Malcolm shouted, the alcohol strengthening in effect, tears going down his face. "I took care of you, boy."

"I know."

"I took care of you," Malcolm avowed. "And I don't care what you think. I wasn't drinking when your mom left. I was sober," he shouted. "I didn't start drinking until she left."

"Want me to hate my mother now?" Raymond asked while he turned and looked toward the window. Talking to his father had always been hard. It was the reason he avoided making this phone call for nearly a year. But he couldn't afford for Malcolm to call Student Affairs again and have Dr. Davis put him in a spot where he was forced to call Malcolm right there in front of him.

Malcolm sat up in the kitchen chair. He kicked his work boots off. They swung across the floor, close to the humming refrigerator. "I don't want you to hate her," he said. "I just want you to know. I want you to know," he repeated. "I don't know why she left." Hot tears went faster down his face. He drew them away sloppily with the back of his hand. "I was good to her," he said. "That use-less—" He stopped himself before he swore at her. "She just walked off and left me with one more bur-den to bear."

"All right, Dad," Raymond tried. He thought of things he could say to get his father to hang up. "It was good to talk to you—"

"She never even called back here looking for you. I sent you those birth-day cards you think she sent you when you were a kid. I sent those stupid cards," Malcolm shouted. "Me," he said. "I wanted you to think you had a mother who gave two cents about you so that's what I did."

"Maybe it all worked out the way it was supposed to," Raymond said. He looked beneath the living room door. "Dad, I gotta go. I might call you back sometime." His chin quivered. He wished Malcolm and his relationship was different, more like the relationships his friends had with their fathers.

"What's her name?" Malcolm demanded to know. "What's her name?" He teeter-tottered on the chair then he sat straight up. "You've been humping some-bo-dy. I hear it in your voice. Some slimy girl has been chewing up your time. It's the reason you haven't called your old man in so long."

"Dad, I'm good," Raymond said. He stood and hurried across the floor. He listened to the front door unlock then watched the door open. "I gotta go," he rushed out while he watched Patrick walk through the front door. What he didn't plan on seeing was Brenda on Patrick's heels, smiling and laughing like she didn't have a care in the world.

Raymond had talked with Virginia yesterday when she called Brenda's dorm while Cynthia was out. Since Brenda had been in the bathroom when the telephone rang, Raymond answered the call. During the conversation, Virginia sized him up good. She examined him so intensely he wished he were standing in front of an x-ray machine instead of talking on the telephone. He tried to hand the receiver to Brenda when she exited the bathroom, but Virginia kept him on the line, refusing to let him go.

She didn't come right out and say it, but Raymond knew. He heard it in the hardness in her voice; she didn't think he was good enough for Brenda. Her judgments hurt, but he kept it to himself.

Virginia mentioned Byron's name at least half a dozen times while Raymond was on the telephone. He overlooked each instance, tried to move on to another subject.

After they bid each other farewell, Raymond came away with a certainty. If Brenda knew about Malcolm, she'd leave him. That much he knew for sure. She wouldn't even think about it, Raymond told himself. She'd just be gone.

"Ray, who are you talking to?" Brenda asked while she walked passed Patrick and neared Raymond's side.

"Is that her?" Malcolm shouted through the phone.

Raymond slammed the receiver into the cradle. He hurried beyond Brenda and Patrick and headed toward his bedroom.

"Ray?" Brenda asked. She tugged on his hand. "Sweetheart?" she tried.

Raymond eyeballed Patrick. He needed one of them to believe him, even if just for this second. "I was talking to that guy from the apartment complex in Bensalem." He looked over the top of Brenda's head at Patrick. "You know that apartment Anthony and we are trying to get?"

Patrick noted the urgency in Raymond's eyes. "Yea," he nodded. He glanced from Raymond to Brenda. "Yea," he repeated. "Did we get the place?"

"Dude said he'll call us back tomorrow," Raymond told him. A smile tugged at his mouth. "We've got a good chance."

Brenda looked from Raymond to Patrick. She examined their faces, the questions in their wide eyes, the mockery in the curl of their mouths. "That wasn't a landlord," she said. "Not the way that guy was talking to you." She waited a second then she waved her hand and said, "Never mind. I'm glad I ran into Patrick when I was coming up here. Some of the guys in this hall hit on a woman every chance they get." A second later, she smiled at Raymond.

"You want to hang out, go see *Rambo* at the movies?"

"Yea. Let me get my jacket and we can grab a bite then head to the movie."

"Is Sandra coming over?" Brenda turned and asked Patrick while Raymond disappeared into his bedroom.

"Later," Patrick told her. "I gotta study for now. This African Literature course I'm take kicking my butt."

Brenda laughed until Patrick left for his bedroom. Alone in the living room, she turned and stared at the telephone. She glanced over her shoulder. Both Raymond and Patrick were still in their separate rooms. She inched closer to the telephone. She stared down at the dial. *"Star sixty-nine,"* she told herself. *"Star sixty-nine and get the number."*

That night as Raymond drove back to campus from the movie, he told Brenda, "I'm gonna run by Anthony's. He called and left me a message earlier and I forgot to call him back."

Moments later, when they pulled in front of Anthony's apartment Raymond asked her, "You want to come up or are you going to sit in the car?"

"I would come up," she said, leaning forward and squinting. "But," she continued, pointing toward the sidewalk across from where they were parked on the street, "Isn't that Anthony and Aretha?"

Raymond and Brenda hurried out of the car, waving to Anthony and Aretha who walked, their fingers entwined, toward Anthony's car.

Aretha wore a pair of diamond studded, looped earrings, hip hugging jeans and a pink cashmere blouse. Anthony wore a pair of white cotton shorts and a black knit shirt.

"Hey, Aretha," Brenda called out as Raymond and she crossed the street. "Where are you two headed?"

Aretha eyeballed Brenda, angry that someone had intruded upon her quiet time with Anthony. "To the movies." She looked down the bridge of her nose at Brenda, a woman she considered to be far too plain and unsophisticated, someone who, although friendly, would never earn her way into her inner circle.

Raymond and Anthony slapped palms. "What you two going to see?" Raymond asked his good friend.

"*Rambo.*"

"You're gonna like it," Brenda exclaimed. "Raymond and I just came from seeing it."

"Oh," Aretha said, disappointment filling her voice.

"We won't give it away," Brenda assured her. "We won't tell you what happened."

"Anthony," Raymond said, stepping within inches of his friend. He lowered his voice. "You called earlier."

"Oh, yeah," Anthony said. He tapped Aretha's shoulder. "Me and Ray are gonna step to the side. We'll be right back."

"Okay, Baby," Aretha said, leaning forward and kissing Anthony's mouth hungrily, as if he was going on a week-long trip, rather than merely stepping away from her for a few moments.

As Raymond and Anthony walked down the sidewalk, out of Brenda and Aretha's earshot, the two women exchanged conversation, Aretha doing most of the talking. Her long, polished acrylic fingernails waved through the air as she clued Brenda in on her previous weekend shopping spree.

Brenda smiled and nodded while Aretha talked fast, as if there wasn't enough time to express all that was on her mind.

Not once did Aretha ask Brenda how she was doing or what her plans were for the summer. She simply continued their one-sided discourse, as if, of the two of them, she was the only one that mattered.

Several yards from where they stood, Anthony stepped in front of Raymond, allowing Aretha and Brenda to only see his back. "Glad you came by, Man," Anthony told Raymond. "Thanks. That dude," he whispered, "Michael." He scanned Raymond's face. "His brother got him cleared, worked with some high priced attorney."

"His brother's got money? I heard Mike slings dope. You're telling me his brother's got paper?"

"Heard through the grapevine his brother owns several sweet pieces of real estate down south." He shook his head. "Somewhere in Tennessee."

Raymond looked over Anthony's shoulder at Brenda. A second later, he waved the idea that Brenda might know Michael's brother out of his head. He also remembered that Anthony was from Tennessee. "You don't know this dude, do you, being that you're from Tennessee?"

"Nah," Anthony said. He chuckled. "Brenda's from Tennessee and I didn't know her until you started dating her."

"Yea," Raymond nodded, glancing at Brenda again. After he returned his attention to Anthony, he asked, "So?"

"So," Anthony said waving his hands. "The investigation around the car chase we were involved in was dropped. Cops only went after Michael about that shoot out and chase because of his long record." He shrugged. "Cops don't have anything material about that chase."

Raymond's shoulders dropped, his mind retracing the night of the car chase. "Glad I called a tow truck and got my car out of that ditch before anyone called my license plate number into the police."

Anthony stared at Raymond in silence before he nodded somberly and said, "Word."

"What about the club shooting?"

"I think that's done too." Anthony shook his head. "There's not going to be a trial. DA's ruling it an accident."

"Wait a minute," Raymond said, peering over Anthony's shoulder. Seeing Aretha talking and Brenda listening, he looked at Anthony and said, "A dude got shot and it's ruled an accident?"

"Looks like Michael's brother's got some real pull." He spread his hands. "Like I keep telling you, people's stories never added up." He pressed his hands against his chest. "All I know is, I was in the club having a good time. An argument breaks out, I go to leave and next thing I know, I hear gun shots ring out." He raised his hand and counted off facts. "I didn't have a gun on me. You know me," he said, tapping Raymond's shoulder. "I don't carry a gun. I'm an easy going dude. I stayed at the scene of the crime until the cops got there. I didn't run. I didn't lie. I didn't hide." He arched his shoulders. "There was nothing to hide." He paused. "At least not on my part."

"They didn't get DNA or nothing?"

"Nothing pointed back to me," he told him.

"All right," Raymond said. "Thanks for telling me." Shaking his head, he said, "I'd been praying about this. God worked it out," he nodded matter-of-factly. Seconds later, he examined Anthony's face. "You good?"

"I'm good," Anthony smiled. "And hey, yo, Man, thanks for helping me study for my English Composition final. Got my grades back. I got three Bs and one C, and one of those Bs was in English. That class was kicking my butt, Man. You were a big help," he smiled. "I appreciate you."

They joined hands as an expression of solidarity. "Good job," Raymond grinned and told Anthony.

As they walked back toward Brenda and Aretha, Anthony told Raymond, "I'm gonna study even harder next semester. Watch," he said, raising a finger. "I'm gonna make the dean's list next time."

They laughed, gave each other a one armed hug, climbed inside their cars and sped off into the night, a mirage of innocence trailing them.

Chapter Fourteen

A month later, and as if he had never meant to stay at Roddin until graduation, Raymond drove away from a year of memories. He drove away from Malcolm's only connection to him, his campus telephone number. He drove away from lingering memories of the shoot out, the living room window he'd looked out of as soon as Anthony and he sprinted all the way back to Roddin, the place from which he learned that Walter's disturbing habits extended beyond gossip.

While he pushed the last box of his belongings, track shoes, school jerseys, jeans and sweaters, onto the back seat of his car, recollections from the night he asked for directions to the residence house bubbled up in his consciousness. He saw Roddin's lights reflecting across campus on that later summer's evening, beckoning to him like a guide. He'd just left downtown Philadelphia and the Greyhound bus station. Over time, he'd made friends and met the woman he believed to be his soul mate. He earned himself the title "America's top collegiate middle distance runner." And thanks to Anthony, he found a church home, a place where he could lay his burdens down, a place where he could steep himself in religious beliefs and traditions until, like magic, his troubled childhood no longer stung.

The Excel was halfway down the street, putting Roddin further into the background, when, through the rearview mirror, Raymond spotted Walter. When Raymond pressed the accelerator harder, Walter shouted and ran that much faster behind the car. His arms flailed wildly through the air.

"Ray," Walter screamed. He sprinted after the Excel. His eyes were as wide as he kept his ears and just as hungry, eager for information.

Raymond let up on the accelerator and the car crawled to a stop. "What?" he asked through the closed car window.

"You forgot to turn in your key."

"Nah," Raymond said with a shake of his head. "Patrick turned it in half an hour ago after he packed up the last of his things and moved out. All I had to do was shut the door."

Walter stepped back and grinned. "A'right," he said.

To prevent Walter from reading his lips, Raymond turned away from the window. Then he stammered, "Why're you messing with me?" Seconds later he recalled a sermon he heard in church and he retreated. He also didn't want Walter to know he was on to him. He had more digging to do, people to talk to in order to find out Walter's involvement in the car chase and shootout. "Yo, Walt, we're good?" he rolled the window down and asked.

Walter folded his arms and leaned his elbows atop the window's edge. "Where you moving to? Word on the street is you, Anthony and Patrick got an apartment in the suburbs."

Raymond sat back on the seat. He glanced into his lap, anywhere but at Walter. Then he faced the window again. "Something like that."

Walter laughed so hard spit flew out of his mouth. Bits of it landed on Raymond's shoulder. "A'right," he nodded after his laughter subsided. "I see you're a man who wants to have secrets."

"And you're a conniving, twisted, nosy mother —" Raymond thought while he brushed his hand across his shoulder. Religious lessons nipped at the words, kept them from spilling out of his mouth. "I'm outta here," Raymond waved. He pressed the accelerator and sped to the end of the street. The further he got away from Walter, the better he felt. A switch of his blinkers, a turn of his car and he drove closer to his new residence – Parksouth Apartments, a large complex located in Bensalem, a suburb twenty minutes north of center city Philadelphia.

Walter stood next to a parked car and watched Raymond go. "And I ain't messing with you," he grinned, the two sets of keys to Apartment 712 now jiggling in his hand. "Not yet."

Less than a mile away from where Walter stood watching the Excel speed off campus, Brenda sat across from Byron at a table at the back of the Student Center cafeteria. Waitresses washed recently used tables near where Brenda and Byron sat. At the front of the cafeteria, students stood in line waiting to order hot sandwiches, salads, snacks and juice.

Brenda's hands were folded in her lap. She looked across the cafeteria, away from Byron. As she did, she met Aretha and Sandra's gazes, the two having just exited the bookstore across the hall.

Brenda turned away, but not in time.

Within seconds Aretha had sashayed into the cafeteria, approaching the table Brenda and Byron sat at. "Hi," she said, smiling glumly and extending her hand toward Byron.

"How're you doing?" Byron asked, out of habit and politeness, not genuine interest.

Aretha turned and faced Brenda. "Hey," she said coyly.

"Hi," Brenda responded, smiling nervously.

"Is this your brother?" Aretha asked, flipping a thumb over her shoulder, toward Byron.

Brenda looked up at Aretha, her *perfect* size six figure, her arched, pencil lined eyebrows and her diamond studded earrings. If Aretha respected her, she'd remind Brenda of Virginia, both women being so well put together.

"No," Brenda said, shaking her head.

"You get around for a plain girl," Aretha mouthed. She smiled at Brenda, her back to Byron. "Think Raymond—"

"He knows," Brenda told her in a hushed tone.

"Come on, Aretha," Sandra called out, continuing to stand outside the bookstore, not wanting to eavesdrop on Brenda and Byron's conversation.

Glancing silently across the hall at Sandra then again at Brenda, Aretha rolled her eyes and walked away from the table.

Brenda glanced over her shoulder at Sandra. "Brenda's cool. Don't go blabbing about her around campus," was the last thing she heard Sandra say seconds before she exited the student center alongside Aretha.

"It wasn't enough that you came home from Tennessee nearly a week earlier than you said you would," Byron told Brenda.

Facing him, Brenda said, "I wanted to take some time to think—"

He raised a hand, silencing her. "Everybody on campus has seen you gallivanting around with—" He paused. "What's his name?" He answered his own question. "Ray-mond." He leaned back in his chair. "Your own sister thinks this guy is a loser."

Her eyes expanded; her gaze roved. She wondered if Virginia had actually spoken to Byron without her being present.

As if he was reading her mind, Byron said, "I went home a few days ago to check on my grandmother. She hasn't been feeling well." He smiled quaintly. "You remember her, don't you?"

"Yes," Brenda whispered.

"They all remember you," he told her. "My mother, my father, my brothers and sisters, my grandparents, everybody."

She glanced at him. "Is your grandmother okay?"

He nodded. "Her blood pressure was way up. Mom and dad put her in the hospital for two days and now she's stabilized. She's doing better," he added.

"Glad to hear it," Brenda responded.

"She asked about you." He paused. "Everybody did."

"You have a wonderful family, Byron. You know how much I love your family." Before she spoke again, she shook her head. "I didn't mean for it to happen this way."

He leaned across the table, closer to her. "You didn't mean for what to happen?"

"For—" She sat back in her chair, creating more space between them. She examined him, the arch in his brow, how his eyes had narrowed since she joined him at the table.

"You're gonna take a guy whose family doesn't even support him? You're gonna take that guy over me?" he jabbed his finger into the center of his chest.

"It's not about choosing--"

He laughed. "I'm an honor student majoring in neurosurgery and you dare to step out on me with that boy?"

"It's not—"

"I knew something was up when I saw him at that football game last winter. He didn't just show up, did he?"

"I didn't even know he was at the game until I went to get something to eat."

Glaring at her, he said, "Just like you didn't know I'd be sitting here."

"Oh, Byron," she waved. "I was walking through the student center and you call me over here. What's the big deal? Besides, we haven't had a good conversation in what, weeks . . . months? Nothing we do or say is deep. Goodness," she sighed. "You went home for a few days and you didn't even tell me."

"Funny how you think we don't have anything deep, but you still sleep with me." A question popped into his mind, and he blurted, "Have you slept with him?"

She rolled her eyes and turned away from him.

"Have you slept with him?" he pounded the table and demanded to know, not caring who overheard him.

"No," she finally answered. "And you and me, we haven't slept together in weeks, and you know it. We hardly see each other anymore."

"I've been busy," he leaned back and said.

"This past year you've always been busy," she told him, shaking her head. "I can't believe I held on this long. Sometimes," she said with exasperation, "I wonder if I stayed for our families more than I did for us." Biting back tears she added, "They wanted us to work so badly."

"That's a cop out," Byron told her. He didn't mince words. "What you're doing is wrong," he said, shaking his head. "That boy Raymond's too much like his good friend Anthony." He sat back and pointed sharply at her. "You better watch yourself. Anthony gets around as far as women are concerned, and as much as you might not want to admit it, birds of a feather do flock together."

Brenda's spine stiffened. She sat erect in the chair. "Reminds me of you."

"What?" he chuckled. Before she could respond, he added, "Trust me. If I really wanted to fool around on you, I could have done it a whole lot more—"

"Exactly," she stood and said. "You know, as long as we've been marking time, I imagined that we'd do this intelligently."

He spread his hands and arched his shoulders. "Do what?"

"Say good-bye to each other."

"What?" he asked in a raised voice, now standing too.

She chuckled. "Are you going to stand over there and tell me that you think we still—" She lowered then shook her head. When she looked up again, she continued asking him, "have something to work for?" She looked right at him. "You never respected me. You never saw me as your equal." She shook her head. "Sure, you think I'm intelligent and well put together, but there's nothing, absolutely nothing, about me that you love. There's nothing about me that would make you choose me over another woman who carried herself the same way I do." She turned away from him, looking down at the floor as tears pooled in her eyes. "You don't even know me," she said when she looked up at him again.

He stepped towards her, close enough to feel her breath against his skin. "After all this time you're telling me I don't know you?"

She laughed. "People stay married for fifty years and don't even know each other."

"Okay, so you're telling me I'm in love with an ideal?"

"In love," she laughed. "Byron, I've spent my share of nights begging you to spend time with me. And I've certainly spent my share of mornings asking you where you were the previous night while I sat alone in my dorm room waiting for you to call just once." She sighed. "I'm telling you that I fulfilled the image of a woman you wanted." She tossed her hands up. "Somehow I did, but I'm not that woman anymore."

One of his eyebrows rose.

"I worked hard to be the woman you imagined, so you'd stay with me," she told him. "You never gave me permission to be who I really am."

"Which is a two timing woman—"

"—Who was terrified of what you thought of her."

He waved his hand. "Brenda, we're talking three years here, and I didn't do anything to make you afraid of me."

As they continued to talk, she looked over her shoulders to see if other students were eavesdropping on their conversation. Fearing that someone might be watching them, even from across the room, she pulled loose strands of hair behind her ears and smiled at him. Her facial expressions, her smile and her wide opened eyes, betrayed the words she spoke. "You've pushed me. You've grabbed me and jerked on my hands and shoulders." Her brow narrowed; she was no longer smiling. "From the beginning you did, and I put up with it. I walk around here scared to say a simple 'hello' to another guy, fearing it would get back to you and you'd get mad. You've shouted at me.

You've made me the butt of your jokes in front of your friends. You've actually told me that I was a good business investment because I was pretty and smart."

He rolled his eyes, obviously fatigued with her charges. "You're a simple woman." He leaned forward and enunciated his words. "You're plain, Brenda. What more do you want me to say?"

She stepped back, away from him. "It doesn't matter anymore," she said, shaking her head. "There's nothing left to work for. It's over," she told him. "I don't want to do this anymore."

He moved to within inches of her. His hands were balled into tight fists. "Are you just going to walk out on me?"

"Is there anything left to stay for?" she asked him. "Okay," he told her, pacing the floor. "All right. Go ahead and get all tangled up with this Raymond." He stopped pacing and leaned so close to her that his nose grazed hers. "A guy you don't even know. Virginia told me," he revealed. "She said you don't even know this guy."

Brenda sighed. "My sister believes in fairy tales. She's probably going to spend the rest of her life trying to see if she can make one come true. Me," she shook her head and told him, pulling the small diamond friendship ring he gave her early in their relationship off her right index finger and placing it on the table. She'd worn the ring for nearly three years, but the last several months she'd spent more time twirling it nervously in circles on her finger than she did appreciating it. "I don't believe in fairy tales," she told him. "I want the real thing."

He stood next to the table watching her walk away from him, struck with regret, sensing the finality of their relationship.

Chapter Fifteen

It was the last week of June 1985. Except for clothes hung in the closet, a queen size bed, and a nightstand, Raymond's room was empty. He'd been living at the apartment in Bensalem less than a week.

The day after he moved in he drove to the CVS on Bustleton Avenue and bought a journal. Any other day he would have kept the journal tucked in the top drawer of his nightstand. But this morning he woke late and ran out of the apartment to his English Composition class without checking that the journal was put away.

Haste. Today it revealed a lot about Raymond.

The journal – its paper thick and un-ruled -- fit in Brenda's hands perfectly. Like a professional book binder, she ran her hand across the journal's spine. Its smooth brown leather covering made it look like it belonged to a businessman.

She re-opened the journal and stared at the handwriting. The cursive 'Is' had big loops at the top. The 'ms' and the 'rs' were small, as if Raymond wanted to hide them. *"I'm sorry to disappoint you,"* the first entry began. *"I've been a mishap, a tragedy waiting to happen, from the start. Please forgive me."*

Again and again the words were scribed.

Brenda ogled the words. A sunken feeling washed over her. She wished she could repair Raymond's wound; the fear that she wouldn't be able to caused sadness to rise within her. "What unforgivable wrong," she asked herself, "could Raymond have committed."

As if to provide an interlude to her worry, the apartment's front door opened then closed with a hush. It was an unexpected change, an unwanted shift.

Brenda took in a deep breath and held it.

A man's raspy voice called out, "Hey, yo!"

It was Anthony.

Brenda let out the long, slow breath she'd been holding. The tightness in her chest loosened. She wasn't born for hiding, for tiptoeing. She was an honest woman. She wasn't a sneak and yet here she was forcing herself not to move, forcing herself to breathe gently while she stood in her boyfriend's bedroom.

"Patrick? Ray," Anthony called out. His voice grew nearer as he made his way toward Raymond's bedroom.

Brenda searched the room for a place to hide.

"Ray?"

"The closet" Brenda's mind demanded, but her feet stayed planted by Raymond's bed. She couldn't figure why she was hiding except that she'd read Raymond's private thoughts without his consent. She'd also dialed the phone number of the last person she'd heard Raymond shout at, a man Raymond wanted to disguise behind polite conversation – his father. She'd found the phone number in Raymond's wallet after he asked her, a pizza man standing at his apartment door holding a medium deluxe pizza, to grab ten dollars out of his wallet. The phone number was written on the back of a Gunnex Motors auto plant business card; it followed the word, *Dad*.

Malcolm's voice had come out gruff, uncertain, when Brenda dialed the number days ago. "Who is it?" Malcolm had asked. His words sounded sleepy; they took a long time coming out of his mouth.

"Who is it?" Malcolm had asked again. This time his voice was louder, mean. Mixed in with the new edge in Malcolm's voice Brenda heard sorrow, a touch of loneliness. She didn't know who the man on the other line was, not yet, but the sound of his voice made her want to flee.

"Who is it?" Malcolm asked a third time to which Brenda responded by hanging up the telephone.

She never did tell Raymond that she dialed the telephone number and here she was again, spying on the man she swore she loved.

Anthony's footsteps echoed against the floor. They sounded like tom-tom drums beating in the distance.

Brenda had no more time to think. She went to her toes and dashed inside the closet. She shut the closet door in quick tugs. Then she kneeled toward the floor and peered between the slit in the door. *"Why had it come to this?"* she wondered, *"to hiding."* She knew Anthony. She trusted him. She had done nothing to be ashamed of, but she felt wrong and that feeling had grown until here she was, crouched down in the closet.

She grimaced when she gazed at the closet floor. The journal – it lay between her feet.

"Ray?" Anthony called from the edge of Raymond's bedroom. Anthony finally gave up and walked away from Raymond's door toward his own bedroom.

Brenda tiptoed, one quiet step after another, across the floor to Raymond's bed. She stared down at the journal. *"Put it back,"* she told herself. But she wanted to keep it.

If the journal had been shut, she wouldn't have read it. She imagined that Raymond usually kept the journal, the book that housed his private thoughts, hidden inside his nightstand drawer. But even if she had merely seen the journal, she would never have read it. She would not have read from the journal even if Raymond had begged her to. It was the fact that the journal was open atop Raymond's nightstand when she entered the room.

She believed the thoughts inside the journal to be sacred. After all, she herself was private. She valued the keeping, the shrouding, of privileged information. Everyone who knew her knew that. She wasn't given to prying.

She was like a closed book except when she was alone with Raymond. Only then did she share her deepest desires and longings. Raymond knew her better than her parents or Virginia. Raymond was her journal. He carried the deep parts of her around with him wherever he went.

Yet, she'd done too much. Now she knew too much.

From reading the journal, it was clear to her that Raymond kept profound experiences from her. He didn't open up to her. She'd suspected that from the start. Even when she visited with Virginia weeks ago and especially while Virginia talked about Scott, the fear that Raymond hid his core from her nagged at her, but she pushed the suspicion down.

However, the misgiving wouldn't vanish. Not now. Not anymore. Brenda couldn't rid herself of it.

Her guilt about what she should do with the journal turned into anger, then rage. She dropped the journal inside the mouth of her hand bag. Then she waited.

It didn't take long. Within moments she heard Anthony exit the apartment. To ensure she was alone she went to Raymond's bedroom window. She pushed the sheer curtains apart and watched Anthony climb inside his sports car and speed away from the building. "Football practice," she said while she peered outside.

When she turned her back to the window she nibbled her lip. She'd come to the apartment to surprise Raymond with a gift. Since the Saturday she saw him eyeing a single diamond earring at the Neshaminy Mall, she'd saved a portion of her work/study check so she could afford to buy him the jewelry. Her roommate Cynthia, a gregarious woman who rarely minced words and someone who Brenda had hit it off with from the start, drove her to the mall yesterday so she could pick the diamond up and have it gift wrapped. She was going to place it beneath Raymond's pillow with a note that read, *"I love you, Raymond. I love you from the bottom of my heart. I love you with all my might. I'm so glad you're in my life. You're wonderful. Love – Brenda."*

That's what she meant to do.

But she didn't. Instead she grabbed her shoulder bag and, resolve in her stride, she headed for the door. Then she stopped. Love and respect for Raymond broke her determination. She turned back and hurried around Raymond's bed and placed the journal back on the nightstand, careful to lay it just as she'd found it. Then she headed out of the bedroom. The only thing that stopped her was the sound of another key turning in the front door lock.

She froze. She waited.

A grueling day of engineering classes followed by four hours of work/study at the campus traffic ticket office exhausted Patrick. He pushed the apartment's front door open. "*Bueno estar en casa,*" he sighed to himself.

He went straight into his bedroom. After he kicked off his brown Timberlands, he hurried into a pair of long blue and gold University of North Mexico basketball shorts.

"Been standing all day," he moaned while he unbuttoned then raised the hem to his Guayabera shirt above his waist and prepared to pull on a Nike t-shirt.

Further into the apartment, Brenda shifted her weight from foot to foot. The bag, filled with four thick novels, grew heavy; she hoisted it onto her left shoulder. When she did, the books bumped Raymond's bedroom wall. It sounded like a shoe falling to the floor.

"*Hola?*" Patrick shouted. He knew Anthony wasn't home. He'd passed him on his drive into the apartment complex. And he remembered Raymond telling him that he was working late and wouldn't be home until eleven o'clock.

"Yo?" Patrick shouted again as he emerged from his bedroom. At the edge of the living room, he reached for the baseball bat Anthony had autographed by Rickey Henderson late last year.

He tiptoed through the apartment. His hands gripped the base of the bat tightly. He went in and out of the kitchen, the bathroom and Anthony's bedroom. He raised the bat to his shoulder and checked the living room closet. Then he moved toward Raymond's bedroom which was in the furthest corner of the apartment.

"Hello?" he called. He didn't want to bash anyone's skull, but he told himself that's what he'd do if he came upon an intruder.

He raised the bat until the hard wood handle was inches above his right ear. One more step and he swung at the shadow in the doorway.

Brenda let out a long, piercing scream.

Slowly Patrick lowered the bat. "You all right?" he asked while he looked at her.

Brenda braced her hand against her chest. "I'm okay."

"*Siento*," he told her. "Sorry," he repeated in English. "I thought a thief was here." He watched her press her hand on her chest. "You sure you all right?" he asked. After she assured him with a nod, he wondered aloud, "Is Raymond here?" He peered around her shoulder and looked inside the bedroom.

She looked at Patrick's shoeless feet then she looked up into his eyes. She tugged on her shoulder bag. "No," she answered with a stutter. She shook her head and said, "Raymond's not here."

An idea came to her like a prize and she smiled. She'd read Raymond's journal, but her intentions for coming to the apartment were honorable, and it was that intent upon which she hung her guilt. "I came here to surprise him." She said flatly. "I wanted to do something special for him. You know he's wonderful," she added, her smile now wider.

She dug inside the shoulder bag and pulled out a small jewelry box. She moved the box beneath Patrick's nose. "I saw Raymond eyeing a gorgeous diamond earring last weekend when we were at the Neshaminy Mall. He'd been talking about getting a earring, but I didn't think he'd get his ear pierced." She softened her smile. "Not without a good reason anyway." She dropped the box inside the shoulder bag again. "You know Raymond. Two days ago when we were having lunch, what do I see he'd gone and done?" She chuckled. "Got his ear pierced."

Patrick laughed.

"I was shocked. That is so unlike him." She looked closely at Patrick. She examined him as if in his eyes she could see a secret about Raymond, something that wasn't in the journal, something men only shared with each other, but she saw nothing.

"He'll like the earring," Patrick said with a nod. Then he turned and walked away from her.

She tried to cover her tracks further, bury facts beneath long conversation. "Do you know where Raymond is?"

Patrick was halfway across the living room when he answered, "He said he was working late." He glanced over his shoulder at her. "Surprised he didn't tell you that."

Nothing in Patrick's tone hinted at distrust, yet Brenda felt her shoulders stiffen. "He may have told me," she said. Her pace quickened. She almost jogged across the floor. Soon she was ahead of Patrick.

Patrick watched her hurry away from him with raised brows.

She continued to walk fast. "But if he did tell me, I forgot." And for a moment she had forgotten. In fact, mixed in with anxiety, was much of her memory. Just now she didn't recall Raymond mentioning that he was working late, and they'd spoken three times yesterday.

Near the front door, she turned. "Don't tell Raymond I was here. Please," she added gently. Her tone was pleading, like a trapped butterfly's wings.

The front door swung open.

Raymond stood in the space between the door and the walkway. His keys dangled in his hand. He stared at Brenda then he turned and looked at Patrick. He didn't see the bat resting against the back of Patrick's thigh.

He did see his lady and one of his best friends standing alone in the apartment. He saw the hem of

Patrick's Guayabera shirt pulled away from the blue and gold University of North Mexico shorts he wore. He saw Patrick's bare chest and his naked feet. And before he unlocked the door he knew he'd heard Brenda ask Patrick not to tell him that she had been to the apartment.

The trio stood in the room in frozen silence. An icy, mental wind passed between them. It was as though it was not June in Philadelphia. It was as though flowers and trees were not in bloom, their white buds exploding with color, their shoots dancing and swaying beneath the warm mid-day sun, bursting with delicious scents.

The icy, mental wind sucked the heat out of the living room. Everything felt cold.

Chapter Sixteen

"Ray," Coach Carter called out as he jogged across the parking lot outside UPemb's track and field stadium.

Raymond reached out and embraced his coach. "Thought you'd have started fishing by now," he said teasingly as he tapped Coach Carter on the shoulder.

"Wanted to check with you and see if you want to race in next month's Westfield Invitational." He talked fast, searching Raymond's face. "It's in Oregon. The school'll pay for your transportation, food and hotel," he assured Raymond.

"Who's signed up so far?"

"Well," Coach Carter began, tiling his head to the side, "Dwight Gooding's gonna be there. I found that out this morning."

Raymond laughed. "You want me to beat him again about as much as I want to."

"I don't like how he and the rabbit had you penned in at the start of the eight hundred meters at the Penn Relays." His brow narrowed. "They need to make that crap a rule breaker."

"Yeah," Raymond said, glancing over his shoulder across the parking lot. Only one vehicle was in the lot, Coach Carter's Ford pick-up. "But," he added as he faced his coach again. "God worked it out. I won the eight hundred and fifteen hundred meter runs and as a team we won the two mile relay. It was a sweet two days, Coach," he smiled.

"It was," Coach Carter nodded. Not squandering time, he quickly added, "Westfield's big, Ray. A lot of legends got their big break there." He placed a hand on Raymond's shoulder. "You've got a real good chance of making the Olympic team, Ray." He nodded once. "A real good chance. Westfield is that first step."

Raymond looked hard into Coach Carter's eyes then he stepped back and told him to, "I feel like God wants me to do this. Sign me up."

After Raymond got back to his apartment he showered, the scent of lavender soap filling the bathroom as he scrubbed sweat and dirt off his muscular shoulders, taut stomach and thick, chiseled legs. Moments later, he sat on his bed gazing up at the ceiling. He wore a pair of tan khaki shorts, a red sleeveless knit shirt and a pair of red and white Tiger Asics. Thanks to Coach Carter, the biggest track and field invitational of his life was a month ahead of him, and all he thought about was Brenda. He wondered why he hadn't thought of it before. She was with Byron when he first met her. He wanted her so badly he was blind to the fact that in order to be with him, she had to be unfaithful to Byron.

He hadn't talked with Brenda since yesterday, the day he came home from work and found her alone in the apartment with Patrick. She became angry when he asked her what she was doing at the apartment. She looked guilty, like she'd stolen something.

Outside a car bumped its way inside the apartment complex parking lot. When it did a flash of light went across Raymond's bedroom ceiling. Scent of fried pork chops covered with onions came into the apartment from a neighboring home as he paused and looked out the window. In the distance another neighbor's television blasted a *What's Happening* re-run.

Raymond sat on the bed wondering if he should have dismissed his newfound, yet deepening, religious beliefs and made love to Brenda weeks ago, soon after they started dating. He told himself she wouldn't have an appetite for another man if he had.

He leaned across the bed and picked up the telephone. He dialed Brenda's number.

"Hello?" Brenda answered. She turned away from the telephone and mouthed, "Just a sec," to Cynthia.

"You sound like you're in a hurry," Raymond said.

"Cynthia and I are running out to the mall. What's up?"

He was direct. "I want to see you. Call me when you get back from the mall and I'll come pick you up."

"Sure," she beamed. "Especially if you understand about my being at the apartment yesterday when you thought—" She laughed. "--Something was going on between Pat and me."

Raymond ran the vacuum cleaner, dusted furniture and washed the dishes after he hung up with Brenda. Then he went outside and leaned across the railing lining the front of the apartment building's narrow balcony, waving at neighbors as they went in and out of their apartments. Half an hour later, he was sitting on the living room sofa watching the Phillies play the Mets on ABC. He waited for Brenda's telephone call.

At eight o'clock the telephone rang. "Come get me, Sweetheart," Brenda told him.

He drove her to Fairmont Park where they linked fingers and walked along the edge of the Schuylkill River. They talked for two hours, cool air lapping off the river and across their skin. They talked about a movie Brenda recently watched with Cynthia on television. They talked about their plans for the summer.

"Coach is registering me for the Westfield Invitational," Raymond told her. "It's in Oregon. And yes," he nodded, "I want you there."

She moved closer to him, leaning her hand atop his shoulder as they walked slowly through the park.

"Are your parents coming?" she asked.

"I already told you, my mother lives her own life. I haven't seen her since I was a kid."

"I'm so sorry," she said. "What happened?"

"She fell in love with someone else," he told her plainly, not feeling a need to keep his mother's long absence a secret from her now that she'd asked. "I don't know a lot about it. I only know one day she packed her bags and left."

Seconds later, recalling entries she read in his journal and the way he'd abruptly ended his conversation with Malcolm several weeks ago, she asked, "What about your father?"

"He's not coming," Raymond answered, quickly shaking his head.

"Are you going home to visit him this summer?"

He shrugged. "I might."

She squeezed his hand and kissed the side of his face. "I'll go with you if you want me to."

He stopped walking, turned and looked into her eyes. "Thanks, Baby. That means a lot to me."

A couple rowed a boat down the calm river water beside them, talking and laughing gaily.

Brenda and Raymond started walking again, their arms beginning to swing back and forth, their fingers still joined. "Do you talk with your father a lot, Raymond?" she asked.

"We talk," he replied somberly.

"What's your mother's name?" she asked.

"Jennifer," he told her, recalling the inscription on the back of the picture he'd found in the basement when he was a boy.

"That's a pretty name," Brenda smiled, trying to create an image of Raymond's mother. Soon she asked, "What's your father's name?"

Raymond slowed. "I didn't come out here to talk about my father," he told her.

"But I've never met him," she said.

"I haven't met your parents yet either," he told her.

"You talked with Virginia," she quickly interjected.

"And she doesn't like me."

"In her own way she does," Brenda tried.

Raymond laughed. "Your sister doesn't like me."

"She's got her views, her perceptions and her beliefs."

"We all do," he said.

"But Virginia likes you," Brenda said. "I told her how happy I am with you and that did it. She just wants me to be happy. She wants me to be with a guy who loves me and who's from a great family."

He stopped walking, "Like Byron?"

"No," she said, shaking her head against his shoulder. "Virginia really does want me to be happy."

"She mentioned Byron's name I don't know how many times when I talked with her, and I was only on the phone with her for a few minutes."

"My mom and Byron's mom went to high school together. Our families know each other; our families are close."

"So your mom thinks you should still be with Byron too? Not some guy whose father is an--"

She stopped walking, gently pulled his hand. "Is what?"

He looked away from her.

"Whose father is what?" she asked him again.

"Nothing," he told her. "My family's not as perfect as Byron's is."

"Your family can't be all bad," she smiled and told him, pushing aside facts she'd read in Raymond's journal, not wanting him to know she'd pried. "You're a champion. You're a winner, and I'm not talking about your running." She stopped walking, turned and faced him. "You're a good man, Raymond. You got that way somehow." She nodded. "You had help getting to the man you are. Somebody helped you," she told him.

He wrapped his arms around her, pulling her close, tight against his chest. His hands went down around her lower back, pulling her up. He looked into her eyes, smiling at her. "I love you," he told her. He kissed her forehead. "I love you so much."

She caressed his back, kissed him on the nose then gently on the mouth. "I love you too. And," she added, "I'm glad you're loosening up and not spending so much of your free time at church. You

187

don't want to overdue religion," she advised. "People have gone insane behind religion."

He looked at her, enjoying the feel of her body against his, questioning her advice, her guidance.

Chapter Seventeen

Raymond lay in his bed and listened to a Rottweiler bark and yelp in the back yard of a house a block away on Knights Road -- a four-lane thoroughfare bordered with brick homes, apartments and shops. It was two o'clock in the morning. Sidewalks were clear of pedestrians. Few cars went down the street.

Next to him, Brenda, her sleep sweet and gentle, let out a noisy breath, then squirmed and pressed her head deeper against his chest. The strength in his body softened to her touch. Her bare legs and arms were crossed over and looped through his until their limbs twisted like pretzel threads.

Scent of Victoria's Secret vanilla body lotion, mixed with dried sex, pushed off her body and wafted through the air. As he breathed in deeply and savored the scent of her body, passion burned like fire within Raymond. He pulled himself down over Brenda's sleeping body. Tendons in his shoulders stretched then grew taut, causing his muscles to bulge. He kissed her so full on her forehead his warm lips left a wet mark. But that was not enough, so he pulled her closer to him, massaging her arms in long, slow, sensuous strokes. When her breasts merged with his and pulsed against his chest, he closed his eyes and exhaled.

Soon he was stroking, not only her arms, but her back and her lower spine. Using the tips of his fingers, he worked circular motions into the fleshy part of her lower spine. It wasn't long before the thickness of her backside beckoned to him and he lowered his fingers, and filling his hands with her flesh, he squeezed down on her buttocks then pulled his hands up again and resumed stroking her back.

She squirmed and moaned softly into the night.

A soft jazz cut by Gerald Albright played on the radio. For hours they had swayed, rocked and tasted the energy that connected them, calling them forth from their separate lives to unite. Their bodies had joined, tugged, pulled and exploded into ecstasy so many times they didn't want to let go.

Light from the street lamp made its way inside the bedroom; Raymond used the light to gaze at Brenda. He smiled at her and tucked her shoulder beneath his. "You're an angel," he cooed. The words echoed back to him and emotion swelled in his heart like delicious fruit.

On his nightstand was a small opened box. It was filled with the diamond earring Brenda bought for him days ago. "I love my surprise," he'd told her during a pause in their wild lovemaking.

Two empty boxes of African cuisine from Marrakesh's in Philadelphia – take out – were on the floor next to the bed. Ash from the cinnamon incense Raymond lit at the start of the evening was spilled into an old glass next to the empty cartons.

"I love you," Raymond whispered while he stroked Brenda's hair. He swallowed hard, but the emotion would not go down. "I love you," he whispered again. "Your love sets me free."

"I can't believe," he continued, "that I wondered whether the work I put into our relationship would pay off, would yield a reward." He listened to her breathe. He watched her chest rise and lower. "Why did I doubt your affection?"

As if the light from the street lamp held further truths than those birthed in his recent observations, he looked at her closed eyes through the streaming light and realized that she was his reward. He wrapped his strong arms around her waist and pulled her sleeping body even closer to him. Then he leaned over, and with quick, butterfly touches, he kissed her neck and shoulders. "I love you," he whispered so as not to awaken her. "I love you."

She squirmed. When she did, her breath tickled his chest then went up and across his shoulder.

A peace, somewhat like a weightless cloud, hovered, no longer in the distance as it had been so many years before, but deep within him. The opened bedroom window, air breezing into the room between the curtains, swept the stale, sticky scent of sex outdoors, breeze by cool breeze.

He lay with his back against the moist mattress and his chest against Brenda's breasts. A water bug scurried across the floor toward his closet. Through the window, two male voices broke up the night's intermittent silence.

"Yo, Theo, let's go to the courts in the morning."

Theo laughed. "Sure. As soon as I sleep off this hangover. Man, I ain't like you. I can't go all night then wake up in the morning like I ain't been nowhere."

A second later, Raymond heard separate apartment doors open and close. The voices were gone. Silence filled the night again.

"This is a good night," Raymond said. He listened. "Not one siren. People partied and had fun and nobody got shot." He squeezed Brenda's shoulders. "Nobody made the news tonight. Thank God."

Brenda ran her hand to the top of his shoulder. She circled her mouth with her tongue then she opened her eyes, and, sleep heavy upon her, she quickly closed them again.

"*I don't care what Bishop Moore and people at church say,*" he thought after Brenda stilled against his chest. "*We didn't do anything wrong. Nothing can shackle romantic love.*" He didn't feel the way he'd felt the few times he'd had sex with teenage girls in high school, his body, particularly his male organ, tingling with erotic energy as he thrust himself between the girls' thighs, his heart unyielding, far away. He knew the teenagers only opened themselves up to him sexually out of admiration for his athletic prowess. Brenda, he knew, truly loved him.

He looked at her. He saw it clearly. "Some people come into our lives and change us forever." He kissed her forehead. "For me, you're that person."

The curtains swayed against the window then blew further inside the room on the cooling wind. When the curtain's hem swayed and shimmied outside the room again, it carried his words.

"I can't believe," he whispered in reflection so as not to awaken her, "that I thought loving a woman this way was wrong." Stillness came over him. "I've never felt so right."

A moth flew into the room, riding on a stream of light from the street lamp. "I don't feel shame, guilt or regret. My conscience is clear."

He glanced at Brenda. Wind blew the ends of her hair against his chest. It tickled and he smiled.

"No," he asserted, "I don't have an ounce of regret." And he didn't. He told himself that everything they did that night, as the moon hung in the sky like a fattened melon, had been right. Even now when he thought about how they had savored each other's bodies, releasing pent-up sexual energy, his male organ tightened and lengthened. He lay against the bed like the whole mattress was a pillow. He thought about how he had licked and suckled Brenda's erect nipples. They had moaned and sung a delicious, erotic song that went on long after Miles Davis' *Somethin' Else* stopped playing on the radio. While crickets chirped on the other side of the window, their bodies had constricted then exploded and filled with delight.

He peered at her. His stiffened male organ brushed against her thigh and stayed there. "We belong together," he whispered to the quiet room.

He placed his head against the top of hers. "We belong together." As he lay with her, he contemplated distancing himself from the dictates of church. In Brenda's love, he'd found the courage to navigate life absent the quest to cling to religious rules, the effort to make himself feel safe, loved by Source simply because, like a child gazing into the face of a parent who could be both loving and cruel, he'd behaved. Now that he'd tasted loves delicious fruit in one form, he longed to be loved, more fully, more often, simply because he existed. As Anthony had done months ago, he started to question what he was hearing in church.

Chapter Eighteen

It was Sunday morning, June 16, 1985. Although Arch Street AME's central air was on, parishioners waved themselves with hand fans, heat from the noonday sun creeping inside the building. Raymond sat on the last pew. Three weeks had passed since he spoke with Bishop Moore, guilt over embracing sexual intimacy with Brenda beckoning him to distance himself from the church.

At the end of morning worship, Bishop Moore rounded the corner of the last pew. His long burgundy and white minister's robe set him apart from the congregation, drew glances from several church goers. He reached out and tapped Raymond's shoulder. He didn't say a word. He didn't have to. Raymond knew. This tap was more than a greeting.

Raymond sat forward on the pew. He recalled a two day old conversation with Anthony and Doug. "Be careful of everyone around you at church," they cautioned him. "You're not a visitor anymore."

Raymond couldn't count the times Anthony told him to watch himself, and if anyone knew people, Anthony did. He told Raymond, "If you do something they don't like, they'll get you. It happens in religion. It happens in schools. It happens in business. It happens in families. It happens."

"Listen, my friend," Doug nodded in accord. Patrick was at work that day, and in a welcomed respite, Doug had stopped over for a visit. They were sitting in the apartment living room with the television on. Michael Jackson's video *Wanna Be Startin' Somethin'* aired on BET. "You really get to know people after you break one of their edicts." Glancing at Anthony and seeing him nod, he added, "Break some social rule and watch what happens to you."

Raymond sat on the back pew and waited for the service to end. For the first time since he attended Arch Street AME he told himself he was going to leave as soon as the altar call invitation was given. He wasn't going to stay for the closing prayer. He'd duck out before anyone could catch up to him.

Seconds later, Reverend Ike Hughes, a senior associate minister, stood and, with raised arms, he said, "Let us come to the altar and lay our burdens down. Let us bring our petitions to a wise and loving God."

Raymond stood. His head was bowed; his shoulders curled. He made his way around the back pew, a place he had not occupied since the first Sunday he visited the church. As he neared the church's exit doors, he heard a familiar voice.

"Surprised you're not staying for altar call," Bishop Moore said. His tone was firm.

If Raymond hadn't known better, he would have thought an Army general had spoken to him. He hardly looked at Bishop Moore, and he talked fast. The sound of Raymond's own words shocked him. "You're not at the front of the church for altar call either. But," he added to his own astonishment, "Maybe pastors don't need to pray."

Bishop Moore gawked. Regret snipped at him. He saw it now. He heard it in Raymond's voice. He had been too hard on Raymond this morning, making inferences to backsliders and fornicators in his sermon. As he preached, he had wanted to scold Raymond with firm, frosty glances because he had heard congregants, some who attended UPemb, whisper beneath the guise of concern that Raymond and Brenda had started to behave differently toward one another and that they gave off the impression of a couple not only in love but also of a couple who had consummated their relationship. All of Bishop Moore's religious training told him that sexual intercourse absent a marriage license was sin and, on that point, for Raymond, one of his beloved members, he would not allow for error.

From the first day they met, he knew Raymond felt small, and in that smallness he saw Raymond relinquish his power to men of great authority, to men like him. But he had not intended to make Raymond feel diminutive. And he certainly had not believed that Raymond would, in any way, fight back.

"Can I see you in my office?" Bishop Moore asked with raised brows.

Raymond followed him somberly. Despite his intentions to appear strong and unconcerned, his head was slightly bowed. He wished he had listened to Brenda and stayed away from Arch Street. He could have gone to Liconia Baptist Church on Broad Street with Cynthia and her, but he'd felt a pull to be loyal to Bishop Moore. After all, Bishop Moore had taken him in, accepted him right from the start. Over the last several months, Bishop Moore had made time for him whatever the request: counseling, advice, an older man's open ear. Other than Coach Carter, Bishop Moore was the only older man Raymond trusted, felt he could let his guard down with.

Recent turn of events threatened to change that.

"Have a seat," Bishop Moore offered with a wave of his hand.

Raymond eased down into a soft burgundy leather chair.

"You don't mind if I close the door, do you?" Bishop Moore asked. He moved toward the door which was a few feet behind the chair Raymond sat in. He didn't wait for Raymond to answer.

The next sound Raymond heard was the noise of the door catching in the lock.

"Raymond," Bishop Moore began, sitting in his desk chair. "Is there something you want to talk about?"

"No," Raymond answered flatly. "I'm fine. I'm cool. What makes you ask me that?"

"Well, to start," Bishop Moore said while he rubbed his hands together. "You've missed weekday services." He paused. "I also haven't seen your lady friend at church."

"You travel a lot, Pastor. You're hardly here yourself." He almost turned and looked over his shoulder, back at the door. "How would you know who was and who wasn't here?" He had never told Bishop Moore how much he admired him, so he felt he had nothing to lose by being flippant.

"We have associate ministers." A slow smile widened Bishop Moore's face. "You know that."

"That doesn't mean I'm being watched, does –"

"Raymond," Bishop Moore's brows rose then narrowed. He placed his elbows atop his shiny mahogany desk and leaned forward. He looked Raymond squarely in the eyes.

It surprised him when Raymond stared back at him. He almost leaned back in his chair. "Nobody's spying on you."

Raymond swallowed hard. "I didn't say anyone was."

"Then why are you looking over your shoulder?"

"I'm looking right at you."

"It's as if you're hiding something. I want to make sure you're okay."

Although he couldn't explain it -- he had no evidence for it -- Raymond felt Bishop Moore knew undisclosed details of how he spent his days, details he shouldn't be privy to. Despite the long hours he'd spent with the older man -- except for what he shared about Malcolm -- not once had he divulged his inner life to Bishop Moore, particularly the intricacies of Brenda's and his relationship.

The longer he looked at Bishop Moore, the more he wondered if the pastor was telepathic. A second later he almost laughed at the thought. He told himself that Bishop Moore knew no more about him than what he'd told him.

"I'm not hiding anything." He shrugged. "I wanted to take it easy. I wanted to enjoy life more, go to the beach, to the park, down by the lake." He shrugged. "You know. Soon I'll be working full-time. That is, if I don't strike it rich first. I don't want to lose this chance to relax before I get into the grind."

Youth. A season in Bishop Moore's own life when he wished that time had not moved so fast.

He ate up his youth contemplating the future. He never had a lot of friends, and even with the two to three friends he did have, his mind was always elsewhere. He was never totally present, even while he was with his buddies.

He spent his youth mulling over how to save the world. He didn't laugh or play enough. He didn't value friendships. He hadn't enjoyed being young and now his body, arthritis and poor eyesight constant companions for the last five years, seemed to rob him of a second chance. He regretted that he had not been more like Raymond when he was younger. If he had been more like Raymond, he told himself that he would have escaped a loveless marriage.

He was jealous of Raymond. He envied the way Brenda doted upon him. She was unlike Leann, his tall, wiry wife of thirty-eight years, an emotionally steely woman with a frozen heart.

Leann and he were tucked inside the walls of a dead union that not even all his preaching could revive. Yet somehow they found the energy to play the role of a happy, spiritual couple. Even their families thought love, not communal concern, kept them together.

He saw that Brenda didn't stay with Raymond out of duty and religious obligation, out of fear of what people would say if she walked away. Brenda loved Raymond with passion. She was a woman in love.

Notwithstanding, recent events wouldn't permit him to think further about the state of his marriage. He had parishioners' lives to tend to.

"Raymond, I want to make sure your spiritual growth remains on track. You don't want to skip services, especially bible study and prayer meeting. A little here and a little there and before you know it, you're relationship with God will have wilted to nothing."

"If it's God who's keeping me alive, then how could coming to church—"

Bishop More pulled down on his shirt. Its blue and white cotton stripes went over the fat of his stomach, fat that had built up, one fried chicken dinner after another, to more than forty pounds over the forty-two years he had served as pastor at Arch Street AME. "It takes effort to make a relationship good."

Raymond sighed. "I want to go back to the days when God spoke to us in our hearts and we followed God rather than what others told us God told them to tell us." With a shake of his head, he added, "Sure think life would be simpler that way."

"God does speak to us."

"But only through certain special people?"

"No," Bishop Moore smiled and said.

"Then why is it such a crime to miss a mid-week church service? How does that destroy my relationship with God?" He paused. "Have you ever wondered how a building, brick and mortar, has changed billions of people's perception of God? Does that ever concern you?"

"You're right," Bishop Moore nodded. "It is an error to think humans can change God in any way. Our edifices, our human made temples, do not draw us nearer to God nor do they define, in any way, who or what God is. That's not what I'm saying. I'm not implying that at all. I agree with you."

Raymond continued, "And there are questions none of us, not one of us, has the full answers to. None of us knows everything. None of us has seen God face to face; at least I don't think so."

"Ray—"

Raymond talked fast; his words seemed jumbled. He felt like he was defending himself against Malcolm rather than having a discussion with the man he'd admired for the past several months, the man he often wished was his father.

Yet, he was willing to argue, to put Bishop Moore and his relationship at risk, to continue to feel safe in Brenda's love, the very life line he thought Bishop Moore was trying to take from him.

Bishop Moore sat back. He pulled down on his shirt again. This time buttons at the middle of the shirt protruded; their holes spread against the girth of his stomach. "Raymond," He clasped his fingers together and said, "This is not what I called you in the office about."

"You asked me if anything was wrong with me. Not sure why you wouldn't assume something was right, but –"

"Okay. Okay," Bishop Moore nodded. "I was thinking negatively. Thanks for pulling my coat. I'll watch that." He sighed. "Raymond, it's not so much about you coming to church every time the doors open. People are concerned about you. I don't see that young lady you were with like I used to."

"You're hardly here and that's the second time you've mentioned her. Do you have some special interest in her?"

"Why are you being defensive? You've known me how long now?"

He recalled the scared look on Raymond's face the first time he saw him five months ago. He'd been with Anthony, a man who no longer frequented the church. Bishop Moore never mentioned it, not once, but he saw it in both their faces. Raymond and Anthony had come to Arch Street because they were running. Bishop Moore wondered at what they had done, but he never asked them or let on that he knew fear of being caught had brought them here.

Raymond lowered his shoulders. "I'm trying to really get to know God and move away from religion." He shook his head. "Religion is costing me too much. Coming to church doesn't make me close to God. There's a double message delivered. It's almost like a health club that doesn't want to see its membership drop."

Bishop Moore chuckled. "You're not saying anything I didn't say to myself time and again when I entered the ministry. After all these years I know I don't have all the answers, and I don't think I need to. As I told you before, I agree with you that being in a building doesn't make one closer to a loving God. Yet, this church is the place many people throughout Philadelphia come to when they hurt, when they are confused, when they want to feel loved. Now if the bill collectors didn't come around, there would be no need to support the building, but every month PECO Energy and Verizon come a calling like clock work." He laughed.

After an awkward pause, Raymond started to laugh too. The mirth allowed the former tension in the office a brief interlude.

"And you know," Bishop Moore said after he tapped Raymond's forearm, "How good it feels to be around people who have a shared vision." He smiled. "It's encouraging. If church didn't exist," he added, "People would start a fellowship group somewhere. It happens all over the world, even in places where no one has heard the word 'church'. As humans we long to unite." He laughed. "We unite in so many ways. We unite in marriage. We unite in friendships. We unite by race, nationality, gender, age, economics, etc. We even unite based on where we work." He laughed. "It's not a complete joining. It's partial which gives evidence that there's a better way, another joining – a complete coming together."

Raymond was silent.

He shook his head. "We long to unite to the point where we'll create a gang to have people we deem to be like us to join with. But the right joining," he said, "That's what Christ came to do. And one day there will be a return or a coming together – us one to another absent any separation, as well as us to our Creator. Christ did that good work."

He searched Raymond's face for a response. There was none.

He leaned back in his chair. "Raymond, you're not looking at a preacher who climbs into bed with politicians or who runs around on his wife. You can shake out all the closets in my life. Ain't nothing in them. Do we take up collection here? Yes. But we pour the money right back into the community. Each and every week we do. You know what we do in the community."

At that Raymond had no rebuttal.

"Unless we want to run this church like a public hospital, we had best continue to take up a collection. And in order to provide a love service, the doors stay open and that doesn't come free. It's not just money; it takes dedication, time, effort, love and a passion for people. Think about it," he continued, "You came here seeking something. Whether you found what you sought or not, I don't know. But I feel you've missed church not because it's cramping you or taking freedoms from you, but because you're—" He paused. He chose his words carefully. "Avoiding something."

Raymond nodded. "I see what you're saying," he acquiesced. "And I didn't say you preach for money."

Bishop Moore smiled. "I know that." He shook his head. "Man, you sure remind me of myself when I was your age."

Surprise showed in Raymond's wide eyes.

Bishop Moore chuckled. "I wasn't born fifty-nine years old." He laughed. "All of us old cats used to be young." He smiled. "I used to be a young man. I have questions just like you do." He paused. "I don't know it all, and I don't have a problem saying so. I do know I don't want to see another person fall through any cracks. Raymond," he said, "If you're at peace with not coming to church as often as you used to, then so be it. I just don't want there to be something that recently happened in your life, even here at church, that's caused you to make this decision. That's why I called you in the office, and the reason I asked you about your lady friend was because sometimes—" He raised a hand. "Now I'm not saying anything amiss about your lady friend. What I'm saying, and please hear me out, is that sometimes a woman or anyone close to us can cause us to move in a direction we may come to regret years later. Life consists of more—"

"Brenda's not talking me into anything." He paused. When he spoke again, his voice was raised. "Her name's Brenda. I introduced her to you before. She came to church with me for weeks. You know her. You know her name's Brenda," he repeated with a clenched jaw. "And," he shrugged, "she's not trying to get me to do or not do anything. In fact, she went to church today with her roommate, Cynthia. They went to Liconia Baptist, a church Cynthia visits from time to time," he added. "Brenda has nothing to do with my decision. I made this decision on my own."

"Raymond, I want you to continue to diligently seek the Lord and the kingdom of heaven, and you can't get there without keeping the lines of communication open with God. That's what I want to see you do, Raymond. Keep asking questions. Don't take things, even things spoken in this church or any church, at face value. Seek. Dig deep. Ask questions. Continue to grow." He gave a slow smile that widened the longer he looked at Raymond. "Do you understand?"

Raymond returned his smile. "I do," he nodded. "And thanks." He stood.

"Good. Don't let others make decisions for you, not even that pretty lady you're getting so close to."

Raymond was at the door. "I love Brenda." He turned slowly. "She's a good woman. She wouldn't steer anyone wrong. If anything, she's pulling me toward love."

Bishop Moore gave a tight lipped grin.

Raymond turned. His mind was clear. Not a bit of regret was upon him when he exited the office. "Thanks, Pastor," he said when he reached the center of the hallway.

Bishop Moore followed him into the hall like a shadow, caught up in the uncanny feeling of how much Raymond seemed like a younger, albeit less serious, version of himself. In Raymond he saw the chance to redeem his life and live it right this time. Just before Raymond pushed the large church doors apart, Bishop Moore patted him between the shoulders.

A gust of cool air blew up as soon as Raymond stepped outside. His thoughts volleyed from Bishop Moore to Brenda while he walked to his car.

Although the pastor hit a raw nerve during their conversation, Raymond continued to admire him. Except for Coach Carter, he had never met a man who gave of himself so fully to others. Bishop Moore was always in service. To promote peace, he preached for balanced justice. To eradicate crime and usher in healing, regularly he met with the mayor, members of city council and, his unorthodox methods in full swing, he also met with the city's most notorious gang members.

On Saturdays, just like clockwork, Bishop Moore could be found at Philadelphia's House of Correction. "You young men best be glad they closed down Eastern State Penitentiary in '71," he could often be heard preaching to the men housed in the Correction's thick, chilly walls, surveillance cameras and security guards always on look-out. He'd make note of the drawn down faces of the men he spoke to, all their pants and shirts the same drab blue color. "Its old solitary confinement system didn't rehabilitate. It didn't break men's wrong thinking or men's ill habits. Instead it broke men's spirits, tore at men's souls. You didn't belong there," Bishop Moore would continue to preach. "No one belonged at ESP. And," Bishop Moore would pause for effect and say, "You don't belong here either, so start living like it," he would shout. "Start thinking, start talking and start living out your truth. Stop being an inmate, and start being the good man that you truly are."

That wasn't all. Arch Street AME sent a monthly check to A Woman's Place, an area Bucks County women's shelter, a safe haven for women seeking refuge from abusive men in their lives. Bishop Moore spoke out against domestic violence right from the pulpit. He didn't mince words and he refused to allow Arch Street members involved in violent behavior to hide, didn't matter if the member was an abuser or the one being abused.

Thus, despite differences in their religious inclinations, a gap that had widened during their meeting, Raymond held Bishop Moore in high regard. But his spirit didn't lift until he thought about Brenda.

Tall poplar and oak trees, their limbs long and curvy, lined the sidewalk. Cool breezes lapped off the foliage and blew across Raymond's scalp. After he took off his suit jacket and tossed it onto the back seat, he climbed inside his car and pulled away from the curb.

Outside his car window, tree leaves swirled and tossed. If not for the glaring sunlight, Raymond would have sworn that a storm was brewing. Across the street from his car, except for parishioners chatting and laughing on the church's front porch, the street was quiet, serene.

His foot became heavy on the accelerator; soon he was at the end of the street. He glanced into his rearview mirror and rounded the corner. Then he saw it -- a Toyota Nissan with tinted windows headed toward him.

It was too late. The car darted, like a burst of blinding light, in front of him. "Watch your step," the driver shouted out the window.

Raymond slammed on his brakes. His tires burned into the road and screeched so loudly, people stood from their porches and looked out onto the street.

The impact of the stop forced Raymond forward. His chest hammered the steering wheel. "Agh," he moaned. When he pulled his hand away from his shoulder, he stared at a small spot of blood.

He looked onto the street as he unbuttoned his shirt and stuck his hand over his shoulder, wiping it free of blood.

The Nissan was gone to the end of the block, but Raymond had seen the logo at the top of the car's back window and the sticker on the rear bumper. "Walter," he mouthed.

Fatigued with close calls, hard religious conversations and dodging cars operated by men he scarcely knew and had done nothing worth revenge to, Raymond leaned forward and gasped. Moments later he buttoned his shirt and pulled his car to the curb.

Cars honked when he opened his door and stepped out. The drivers waved angrily and shouted, "Get out of the way."

While the cars whizzed by, thick exhaust smoke puffing out of some of their tail pipes, Raymond stood in front of his Excel. He stared at the crater-shaped dent in his bumper and the chipped paint on his hood.

Then he started pacing. Seconds later, pain pierced his shoulder, sending him back inside the car. He sat briefly with the driver door ajar then, fearing Walter might reappear, he exited the car and glanced down one end of the street, looking for Walter. Turning, he looked down the other end of the street. His heart raced when he saw the Nissan parked at the corner.

Anger overtook fear, sent Raymond's hands into tight fists. His gaze fixed on Walter; he started walking across the street, the heels of his shoes hitting the ground hard. Several steps into his anger-fueled walk, a knifing pain shot through his torso, causing him to slow down and grab his shoulder.

Walter pressed the Nissan's accelerator, revving the car's engine. One end of his mouth turned up into a sinister grin.

Raymond clenched his teeth, eyeballed Walter and started to run toward the Nissan. In the middle of the street, he pointed at Walter. "What have I done to you—"

Walter shifted the Nissan into drive and sent the car speeding around the corner, toward the middle of the street.

Raymond turned and sprinted back toward his Excel. As he rolled his injured shoulder forward and reached for the door handle, the Nissan grazed the back of his thighs, sending him spinning toward the center of the street.

A woman stood off her front porch chair, waved and hollered, "Stop!" as if doing so would stop Walter from using his car as a weapon. Two houses down, an elderly ebony skinned man stood from his porch chair and, leaning heavily on a cane, made his way toward his house door, determined to call the police.

As Walter put the Nissan in reverse, aiming to back the car into Raymond, Raymond lunged toward the Excel. Just as he did, a Chevy Impala drove around the corner.

Raymond recognized the driver. She was a middle-aged woman who attended Arch Street AME. Her passenger was an associate minister at the church. "Hey," Raymond waved.

The woman stopped.

While Raymond leaned into her window, he glanced over his shoulder. The Nissan was gone, Walter having put the car in drive, was speeding down the street, closer to the heart of the city.

"You all right, Ray?" the woman and minister asked.

The woman looked over her shoulder at the Excel's banged-up bumper. "Before we came around the corner, we heard brakes squealing then we heard a loud noise. But we didn't know it was you."

"Yea. Got myself into a fender bender. But I'm all right."

The woman and the minister gave each other a telling glance.

"Hop in your car," the minister said. "We'll follow you back to your place and make sure you get there okay."

"Thanks," Raymond answered, pressing down on his shoulder and grimacing. Seconds later, as he pulled away from the curb, his front bumper clanged.

Thirty minutes later, Raymond pulled into the apartment parking lot. The front bumper shook and clanged when he stopped his car. He waved at the woman and the minister before he headed toward his apartment. Their presence had scared Walter off, Raymond knew.

He clenched his teeth to steel his nerves against the throbbing shoulder pain. "Ant-ne," he called out after the woman and associate minister went down the street.

Chapter Nineteen

Raymond closed his car door until it caught in the latch. Recently mowed grass swayed in the wind. Scent of last night's rain lingered on the lawn. His attention turned to the second floor balcony where Anthony stood with his arms draped over the railing, he stepped back and landed in a patch of wet grass, nearly losing his balance. The grass clung to his shoe. He scraped it off, his foot going down hard then back across each cement step he ascended. He gripped his injured shoulder and walked up the steps.

"You're not gonna believe what happened to me," Raymond said just before Anthony glanced at his shoulder, staring at the spot of blood on his shirt.

"I was driving home from church when that punk a—" He pursed his lips, stopping himself from cursing. "Walter came out of nowhere," he said, his eyes narrowed. "I slammed on the brakes, but still banged into the back of his Nissan." He looked across the parking lot. "Now that I think about it, Walter was probably trying to make the accident look like it was my fault, like I deliberately ran into him."

Anthony looked into the parking lot at the Excel. "Thought I heard your car rattling when you parked." Together they walked down the stairs and examined the Excel. "Looks like he only got the front of your car," Anthony said. He turned and looked at Raymond. "You all right, man?"

"I'm all right," Raymond said. "My shoulder's hurting, but I'm cool." He flipped a hand toward the Excel. "Three more payments and I would have paid this car off."

"Yea," Anthony said leaning toward the car's driver window, checking for damage to the inside of the car.

Seeing none, Raymond and he climbed the stairs to their apartment. Halfway up the stairs Anthony growled, "Walter's gonna get his."

"I'm gonna make sure he does," Raymond echoed decidedly.

"You want to go looking for him?" Anthony asked.

"Nah," Raymond said, turning away from Anthony. "Not now. I gotta figure out what all he knows, why he's coming after me first." He rolled his eyes. "Who knows how this is all gonna turn out." He shook his head. "I don't want to do anything stupid. I gotta think this through, and plus," he added, looking at Anthony. "It ain't like I can just walk in the apartment and call the cops." He sighed. "Nah. I'll deal with Walter later. In the meantime, I'll just take it easy for a few days, let my shoulder heal." He looked toward their apartment. "Patrick and Doug not around?" He stood stiffly, so as not to aggravate his shoulder.

"Nah. Patrick went out. Doug called and said he was hanging with his lady today. Until you showed up, I was just enjoying this quiet, Man. You know how I don't get time to myself."

Raymond stood next to his friend on the balcony, trying to erase images of Walter sitting in the Nissan from his mind's eye. "How long have you been dealing with crowds?" He leaned gingerly over the railing and peered out across the neighborhood, searching for something that would help him forget the day's earlier events.

Six pig-tailed girls double-dutched across the street. "Going downtown in my brand new ride, top turned down, stereo jamming. . . ." the girls sang while they turned and jumped the rope.

"Kids grow up fast these days," Raymond said. He peered across the street at the girls. He listened to them sing until Anthony spoke.

"Yea," Anthony murmured. "I grew up fast myself."

Raymond turned away from the street and looked at the side of Anthony's head. "How so?"

"Like you said," he chuckled, "Fans. Man it started when I was in middle school."

"You've been doing your thing for that long?" Raymond asked.

"I started running over dudes when I was just a kid." Anthony glanced across the street. "About the same age as those little girls." He paused and recalled those days, bitter-sweet moments from the past. "It was all good when I was in middle school. When I got into junior high and especially high school," he said, "things started to change."

"Yea?"

"Yea. Coaches started pulling me to the side and telling me how much the whole team, the whole school and then the whole town was counting on me to win."

"And you came through?"

"Straight up, I did. There wasn't one guy in all of Tennessee who could hang with me. Nobody ran like I did."

Raymond wondered at how differently track stars and football running backs were received by the public. When it came to running, he was as talented as Anthony. They both knew that. Everyone at UPemb who had an interest in sports knew that. But it was Anthony who got the accolades while he got a head nod every now and then. On the other hand, that's the way he wanted it.

"My mom saw how the pressure to win started to get to me." Anthony said somberly. "She saw it before I did. She has this," he shrugged, "What do they call it?" He paused. "Sixth sense."

"Oh, yea?"

"When I was a kid she watched me. She tried to be slick about it, but I saw her."

"You told me before but I forgot. How many of you are there?"

"I'm the youngest of two brothers, Mike and Everett. But I'm older than my sisters Rachel and Alyssa. Anyhow, when my mom sensed I was uncomfortable, she'd crack a joke and get the press and fans to back away from me." He looked across the street at the girls. "She was good at that. That's how I learned how to handle myself in crowds," he added. "From her."

"Good thing you did, man, because you're not a kid at home anymore. You're up here in Philly at big ol' UPemb."

They worked at laughter.

"Balling is the easy part," Anthony said. "I was born for this. It's nothing for me to dodge defenders while they rush at me full force, all three hundred pounds of them. Man, I sidestep those big dudes like I was born to escape trouble." He sighed. "I can avoid an opponent the same way on a soccer field. Doesn't matter what the sport is. I can get you a score. What I'm trying to learn how to do--" he paused, "Is how to live off the field."

"Every now and then tell people you want to chill. Know what I'm saying? Stay in sometimes." Although he knew Anthony wasn't going to listen, he said it anyway. "Stop partying so much."

"It ain't that easy."

They looked across the parking lot and waved to their neighbor, Nelson. "What's going on, Nelson?" Anthony hollered.

Nelson, recently come outdoors from a late afternoon of sleeping, followed the sound of Anthony's voice to the second floor balcony. "Nothing much, Ant-ne and Ray. What are you two up to?"

"Just chilling," Raymond answered.

"Yea. Just chilling, man," Anthony echoed.

They waved a second time and watched Nelson climb inside his Pontiac Skylark, fire up the engine then peel his way out of the parking lot.

Nelson gone blazing down the street, Raymond turned to Anthony and asked, "Why not?"

"Why not, what?"

"Why can't you tell folks you want to chill—"

"Man, you don't know football fans and the press. They're like a swarm of bees. They get pissed off when I tell them I'll sign an autograph, a poster or take a photo later. Not right now, but later." He shrugged. "Sometimes I feel bad about it. You know. The press and fans are a big reason for my success—"

"I don't see it that way, and you've let your fans get you in enough trouble already."

Anthony squinted. "What?" He asked as he turned and entered the apartment.

"The club, man," Raymond said, following Anthony. "I told you Walter darted out in front of me after church with that raggedy car of his."

Anthony clenched his teeth, lowered and shook his head. Then he shrugged. "You said you were okay, right?" he asked glancing at Raymond's injured shoulder.

Raymond turned away from him.

Anthony shrugged again. He lived his life the way he kept his room, wild and carefree. Of the three bedrooms in the apartment, only Anthony's had dirty socks balled up and thrown across the floor. His clothes were shoved inside his dresser drawers; he didn't bother to fold them. When he did laundry, he dumped his clean clothes atop his bed and left them there until three to four days later, when he got in the mood to put them away. Empty Gatorade bottles lined the tops of his dressers and his bed was never made – never.

"Exactly what happened that night at the club," Raymond turned at the edge of the kitchen and asked. He'd never been this direct with Anthony about his involvement in the shooting before, but it kept coming up. Desire to be rid of the shooting and all its history once and for all pushed Raymond. He had to know.

Anthony sighed like he was exhausted. "I was at Club Zone when a dude steps to me, right?"

"Right."

"And ask me to sign a jersey for his lady."

"Right."

"Man, I was clubbing. I didn't go there to sign autographs, and you know me. I'll sign an autograph in a minute. But on this rare night, I didn't feel like being bothered, so I told dude no and he got greasy with me, downright greasy."

"Yea."

"I didn't want a hassle, so I stood to leave. Guy leaned forward or," he shrugged. "Maybe I accidentally bumped him." He pursed his lips. "I don't remember. Next thing I know, dude has his finger in my face. He's shouting at me and calling me everything but the name my mama and dad gave me. And I still tried to walk around the dude. I wasn't ready to leave the club, but I was going to leave to avoid a fight." He looked at Raymond for support. All he got was a blank stare.

He resumed his talk slowly, carefully. "Before I knew it that mouthy dude Mike was pushing on me. Walter must--"

"Walter," Raymond interrupted. "Walter was there?"

Silence filled the room. When it started to feel too uneasy, Anthony started talking again. "Walter was there, your boy from Roddin."

"He's not hardly my boy," Raymond let it be known. "I thought Walter was cool the first night I got to campus. But that next morning and like I told you months ago, he started asking me questions, saying he heard I was supposed to be at Ohio State. Now that might have aired on ESPN because OSU did recruit me, but in all this time Walter's the only person on campus who ever asked me that. I should have known then that he was a nosy dude. And--" He bit his tongue and stopped himself from telling Anthony about the time he looked out of his apartment window and saw Walter talking with Michael the night of the car chase.

"You trusted him." Anthony's mouth curled on its ends. It stayed that way until Raymond responded.

"I didn't know him. Damn," he moaned. "I had just got here. I also didn't know I'd become good friends with a football star who knows how to keep all of his troubles out of the press. And," he added. "I still don't know why Walter was checking up on me before he even met me."

Anthony flashed his famous, toothy grin. Raymond had seen the grin so many times before it lost its impact. "Believe it or not, I heard he does that with everybody." He waved. "Walter was just being Walter, digging for information he could use to cover his tracks in case you found out about some wrong he was mixed up in."

"Maybe," Raymond said. "Go on about the club."

"I was trying to get out of the club," Anthony said, his tone edgy.

"All I know," Raymond added while he looked at Anthony, "Is that a man got shot and killed."

"Why do you have to say it like that?" He walked around Raymond. He went into the kitchen and leaned over the counter.

"My fault, man. Go on about what happened that night. I know you want to forget it but it keeps coming up. And with Walter darting out in front of me today after church. Man," he raised his voice and said, "Walter even tried to back into me." He glanced up at the clock on the wall. "Not even an hour ago. Well," he added. "I need to know. I really need to know what happened that night." He locked gazes with Anthony. "I know you're a good Brother, man. I just need to know."

"A'right." Anthony didn't waste time. "I had to push my way out of the club. People followed me. Comes with being a baller. Truth be told, sometimes it seems like no matter what I do, somebody always wants me to do more." He tossed up his hand. "I just wanted to get out of there. Your boy Walt—"

"He's not my boy," Raymond shouted.

"I forgot," Anthony laughed. The next second he turned away from Raymond and, his head bowed and shaking, he said, "I don't want to talk about this."

Raymond hurried across the kitchen floor. "I have to know," he demanded.

"Walter came up behind Mike," Anthony slowly began. "They both pushed me. Later Walter said he slipped, but," he shook his head. "He didn't slip. They were trying to knock me off balance. I almost fell, but I caught myself in time. Long story short, Mike and I got to yakking and before I knew it, Mike pulled out his gun and shoved it in my stomach. You know. So nobody would see he had a piece."

Raymond stared at Anthony. He didn't speak.

"I knocked Mike's hand down and snatched the gun away from him. Things got so fast after that, I hardly remember what happened next. Before I knew it we were all out in the street. A gun went off. Then three other dudes started shooting. Then a dude was laying on the ground."

"Who shot who? Did you know the guy who got shot?"

"Nah, I didn't know the dude," Anthony said. His voice went up. "I was just at the club." He shook his hands, longing for Raymond to understand him. "I'm telling you the truth. This is what I remember."

"All right," Raymond said in effort to calm his friend.

"Later I found out the dude and Mike had some beef. But I didn't know that at the time."

"Let me get this straight. You're in Club Zone, Walter and Mike start giving you trouble, jaw jacking. Then gun loving Mike pulls a piece on you. You all go outside, and a guy who Mike was fighting with gets shot?" More questions than answers filled his eyes when he looked at Anthony.

"Who shot the dude first?" Raymond asked. "That's what I'm trying to figure out."

The burden of carrying a secret weighed down upon Anthony. It twisted his stomach into knots and made him nauseous. It stole his equilibrium. Soon he was standing next to Raymond with his elbows pressing hard against the kitchen counter. He appeared to be another man, no longer free-spirited Anthony Thompson. "I shot him," he said. His once firm voice cracked. "I shot him," he added as he looked at Raymond. "I thought he was Mike." He noted the sweat breaking out on Raymond's forehead. He watched Raymond's eyes dart, shift and rove. "I shot the wrong dude."

"Every man was the wrong dude," Raymond told him. "Nobody should have got shot."

Anthony's hands started to shake again. "I didn't mean to shoot anybody. I didn't want to beef. It all happened so fast. I was sitting there minding my business. I would have signed that dude's autograph, but not right then and there. People don't want to wait," he frowned.

"Okay. Okay," Raymond said. "What were you thinking when you went to shoot Mike?"

"You ever have a dude point a gun at you?" he narrowed his brow. A second later he answered his own question. "Never mind."

"All right," Raymond said. "I get it. I get it now. Adrenalin was pumping. Guy just pulled a gun on you and before you know it things are spinning too fast, things are way out of control."

"Yea," Anthony nodded.

"How do you know Mike?"

"You have a lot of questions?"

"I don't need to carry anything else around with me. It's starting to get heavy."

"I saw Mike around campus a time or two. He doesn't even go to UPemb. He reminds me of those punks who terrorize a high school years after they've graduated. Dudes who don't have anything better to do." His knotty shoulders lowered. When they did the tension in the back of his neck let go. In all their conversation, Raymond hadn't said it, not once. He didn't need to. Anthony knew. Raymond was going to continue to carry his secret.

"It wouldn't have happened if I was just another dude," Anthony said, breaking up Raymond's concentration.

Raymond shot him a glance. "Maybe not."

"I've been dealing with this since high school," Anthony told him. "People thinking they own me. It's how this kinda stuff gets started. People get pissed off because I don't do what they want me to right when they want me to." He scowled. "Like I don't have a life of my own." He shook his head. "Ball's been in motion a long time now. But," he tapped Raymond's forearm and added. "I have a few good partners. I do have some good friends."

Raymond worked at a smile. All this time he thought he wanted to know the details of the Club Zone shooting; now he wasn't so sure. It was as if he'd heard too much. He found it hard to look at Anthony the same way. Then again he knew Anthony had finally come clean, and he knew Anthony wouldn't have done so if he didn't trust him. It created an awkward bond between them, a lifetime bond forged with a dark secret.

The revelation out, suddenly Anthony bumped Raymond's elbow. "And what are you doing home now? Not going to work today?"

They talked as if a man had not been shot and killed a year ago. They talked as if their lives bore no scars, knew no trouble.

Then suddenly Anthony said, "And don't worry about Walter. He thinks you know more than you do. He thinks you knew all this time. I'll talk to Walter." He squinted. "I'll get him to back off and see reason."

"Why would Walter listen to you?"

"Because he, Mike and another dude I don't know and never saw again after that night are the ones who killed the guy. I accidentally shot the guy once. They shot the guy like nine or ten times, until he died. I know that. Walter knows that. I'll tell him you don't know what happened and he'll back off."

"And why did Mike try to kill us that night?"

Anthony shrugged. "Don't know." He looked at Raymond. "But I think, with talk about the club shooting surfacing again, he thought one of us was gonna talk to the cops."

Raymond pointed at his chest. "Me?" His brow went up. "I didn't know anything about that shooting."

"We both know that," Anthony told him. "But Walter and Mike don't."

"And," Raymond wanted to know. "I thought you said this was all over? Didn't you tell me a few weeks ago when we were both out with our ladies that Mike's brother talked to some lawyer and fixed things?"

"Man," Anthony nearly hollered, "Mike and Walter are dirty living dudes." He pointed. "That club shooting ain't all the trouble they've ever been in. One slip up on either of their parts and any DA will pull out every charge that's ever been posted against their record. Shit," he said, tossing his hand over his shoulder "The only reason Walter's probably working as a resident hall director at Roddin is too appear clean." He shook his head. "It's all smoke."

Raymond looked at Anthony, his gaze roving, trying to put the pieces together.

"Walter and Mike probably got in new dirt," Anthony said, "and now they're scared again." He shook his head. "We're probably not the only dudes in town they're trying to scare off for one reason or another." He scowled. "That's what living dirty will get you," he shouted, "a life on the fucking run."

Raymond shook his head, working to digest the facts, memories of Stanley and Joey surfacing. "Damn," Raymond said, shaking his head again. "The first few weeks I was here I thought Walter was cool, nosey as an old woman, but okay. I never saw him trying to start a fight with anyone. He seemed to just be doing his job," Raymond snarled. "Come to find out he was just keeping close tabs on me."

Anthony shrugged. "That's how it goes sometimes, Man."

After he propped his head in his hand, Raymond sighed. "Damn," he moaned. He sighed again then looked up. "And," he said, "I'm not working today. One of the store managers called last night and asked me to come in, but I promised Brenda we'd chill this afternoon."

Anthony nodded. He was relieved to have told Raymond, the only person he fully trusted, about his complete involvement in the shooting, and now he never wanted to talk about it again. His parents didn't even know about the shooting; they definitely didn't know he'd been caught up in trouble since he arrived on campus. He began to bury the killing in his subconscious; he vowed to keep it there – forever.

It took Raymond longer to adjust to the news. It fit him like a two ton suit made for an elephant. It jammed its way inside his head and made it hard for him to think. He spun the story in his mind. He worried.

On the outside he chuckled and patted Anthony's shoulder. "I gotta find someone who can fix the bumper on my car."

"Call Keith," Anthony told him. "He's a friend of mine. He loves fooling around with cars. He can get you straight." He smiled. "That dude knows cars."

"Think he's around today? Does he live on campus?"

"He lives in the same hall you used to live in. He's on the third floor, but I'm not sure if he's around today. He was talking about going home to visit his folks in Detroit this weekend."

"So, you got his number?"

"Yea," Anthony said. He crossed the floor and went into his bedroom. "Let me get it," he hollered back into the living room from where he stood in front of his dresser turning over bits of paper.

"Here it is," he said when he came out of his bedroom with his arm extended and a piece of paper in his hand. He waited while Raymond dialed Keith's phone number.

The phone rang four times then the answering machine picked up. "Hello, Keith. My name is Raymond. I'm a friend of Anthony Thompson's. Anthony gave me your number and said you knew a lot about cars. I had a fender bender this morning and need to have someone look at my ride. I'd really appreciate your help getting my ride straight. My number is 555-6237. If I'm not here, please just leave a message. Thanks, Man. Really appreciate it. Have a cool weekend."

"Thanks, Man," Raymond told Anthony when he hung the telephone receiver in its cradle. He returned Anthony the sheet of paper that had Keith's phone number written on it. "You're probably right. Your friend probably went home to see his folks. I'm gonna chill."

"You and Brenda going somewhere?"

"Not now. My car's messed up," Raymond answered. It was odd to him while he listened to himself speak, but somehow, someway, with each passing moment, final details of the club shooting drifted away, as if the discussion had never happened, as if an innocent man had not died.

"You want to borrow my ride?"

"Nah." A second later, Raymond asked, "And you? Are you going anywhere or are you just going to lay low around here for the rest of the day?"

"I might play some round ball."

"Sounds like a winner," Raymond said. He poured himself a tall glass of grape juice. Then he went into the living room and sat on the sofa next to Anthony.

The front door opened and Patrick entered the apartment.

Patrick went straight to the television, punched the power button then headed into the kitchen. "Anymore lasagna Aretha made yesterday left?"

Anthony laughed. "What do you think?"

"Aw, Dude," Patrick said while he pulled his head out of the refrigerator. He walked to the counter and pulled down a loaf of wheat bread and jars of peanut butter and jelly. "Guess it's the old faithful peanut butter and jelly sandwiches."

"Unless you want to cook," Anthony hollered from his place on the sofa. He glanced at the television and watched a woman run around third base to home plate in a championship softball game.

"No," Patrick said while he spread a thick layer of peanut butter across one slice of the wheat bread.

"I think I'm going stop by White Castle later. I'm not trying cook anything, *Amigo*. You heard?"

"I got you," Raymond chuckled.

"Are you dudes staying in?" Patrick asked while he leaned against the kitchen archway and chewed on the peanut butter and jelly sandwich.

"I might shoot some ball and play pool with Doug and my friend, Charles, later," Anthony said. He crossed his legs at the ankles and propped them atop the coffee table. "How about you?" he asked while he looked up at Patrick.

Now, for Anthony, the day felt perfect. Except for Doug, he was with his best friends. He didn't have football practice. There was nothing for him to do except to lean back on the sofa and relax.

"I think I'll catch a movie with Sandra." Patrick told Anthony after he bit into the sandwich again.

"I feel you, Man," Anthony nodded.

"Yea. I'm with that," Raymond said. "Plus, I heard it's supposed to rain hard later today." Raymond got an idea. "Let's go to the beach next weekend," he blurted, guilt over his decision to forego church stabbing his conscience.

"Let's," Patrick agreed. "We're always going and coming. It seems like when one of us is here, another one of us is at work, practice or a game. Let's hang out next weekend down at Jersey Shore."

Raymond was glad his friends agreed to visit the shore. He hoped the trip would help rid him of thoughts that Anthony was conning and using him as much as Walter was.

Chapter Twenty

The following Sunday at one o'clock in the afternoon -- the time of day when children grow restless while they sit on their grandmothers' laps in church – the guys left for Belmar, a popular beach on the Jersey shore. Raymond drove.

Paint at the front of his car was still chipped, lingering evidence of the week old accident. But his bumper was fixed. Anthony's friend, Keith, only charged him $50 to repair the bumper. The Excel rode as smoothly as a whistle all the way to Belmar.

"Yo," Anthony said after they pulled onto Route 29 South. "Have you dudes seen that brand new Maserati on campus?"

"Yes," Doug answered, tapping Anthony's forearm. "I've seen that beauty around campus. Whose is it?"

Anthony twisted his mouth. "Some fat dude who lives across campus from Roddin." he laughed. "His parents must have some serious cash, but," Anthony joked, "you know a big greasy dude like that doesn't need to be in a nice ride."

"Probably thinks he can catch some *manifica ragazza* or gorgeous women with that ride," Doug joked, glancing at Anthony. Leaning against the car seat, he laughed, "*Come sei bella.*"

"*Amigos,*" Patrick waved his hand and said, "Forget chase women. Get one good woman and appreciate her. That's what I say."

"Raymond's got a woman like that," Doug teased.

"And you wish you did," Raymond responded.

"Hey, anybody driving up to Rucker next weekend to catch the outdoor b-ball tournaments?" Doug asked, the ends of his long blonde dreads blowing out the window as the Excel sped down the highway. "Those Brothers play real basketball up at NYC's Rucker Park. Reminds me of games I watched with my older brothers at parks in Siena when I was just a kid."

"Not me," Patrick said. "I'm doing presentation at Franklin Institute next Saturday."

Anthony slapped palms with Patrick. "That's cool." He sat back on the seat. "You're going to be the next big inventor."

"Hey," Raymond said, "One day we're going to open up the newspaper and see Patrick's name splashed across the front page with some life saving apparatus he created." He smiled approvingly.

"And Doug going have home design business," Patrick chimed in. "He's always upgrading somebody's place. It's the reason he can stand living the dorm. When Doug moves out of residence hall, his dorm's going to be so well put together, school's going pay him just for staying there and fixing the place up."

"Those stainless steel countertops he put in his kitchen," Anthony joked.

"And those colored venetian blinds he hung in his living room," Raymond added.

"Not to mention that leather sofa," Patrick said. He bumped Doug's elbow. "No wonder you're always up crack of dawn on Saturday catching a flea market."

"Forget his dorm, if not for Doug we wouldn't be able to stand our apartment," Raymond said. "Doug, you hooked us up with that discount furniture you got from Irok. Even with Anthony living like a slob, the apartment looks good."

The guys joked the rest of the way to Belmar like they'd always been happy, had not once experienced or felt an ounce of melancholy. Outside the wind whipped up around the car as it sped down the highway, closer to the ocean.

An hour and a half later, as soon as Raymond parked his Excel, the guys' stepped on the sand. Its color was grey; its temperature was hot. Eager to retreat from the looming heat beneath the solace of the cool, inviting rolling waves, they tore off their clothes – down to their swimming trunks -- and then they rented scuba masks, fins and snorkels and dived into the ocean. They explored the deep for more than an hour. They swam and surveyed the water, their gazes darting as quickly as the fish swam back and forth in front of them as they marveled the cod, herring, starfish, squid and jelly fish.

Patrick, the real explorer of the quartet, stayed in the water the longest. He studied the deep long enough to gain the trust of a dolphin which let him cling to its fin while it pulled him across the water.

Half an hour later, from the ocean's edge, Raymond cupped his hands around his mouth and hollered, "Come on, Patrick. Stop living like a fish. Let's get a good volleyball game going."

Water beads clung to Patrick when he came up out of the ocean. "We should have done this sooner," he told Raymond moments later while they washed off in the public showers.

"For real," Raymond agreed. "Did you see that orange angelfish?"

"I saw two porpoises," Doug interjected while he stepped from beneath the shower spigot and dried off. "They were about a quarter mile ahead of where we were." He looked from Anthony to Raymond to Patrick. "I saw them when we were way out, in the deeper part."

"I believe you," Raymond said. He grabbed his towel, the one with the bright red buckeye stretched across its center, and wrapped it around his waist. "Really. I do," he added while he chuckled and bumped Patrick's shoulder.

"Aw," Doug stomped his foot and waved. "Later for you, Pal." He pushed his feet inside his Adidas sneakers. "I know you're not being truthful. I know you don't believe me."

"Forget all that," Anthony said with a swing of his arm. "Let's go play some volleyball." He looked over his shoulder at his friends. "Did you see that mean game they had going when we were on our way up here to shower off?"

"Homeboys, you all can play volleyball," Patrick said. "I'm going hop on jet skis."

225

Raymond watched Patrick go. "And you came up here and showered off because?"

"I don't want my skin get ashy and dry," Patrick called back. He kept running toward the ocean.

He left so quickly, to his friends it seemed as if he had been riding the jet skis for as long as they'd been at the beach. For the next hour while Patrick sped over the water and zipped up white foamy waves, Raymond, Doug and Anthony lobbed a Spalding Top Flite volleyball across a tall, wide net and dove into the sand after spiked serves.

More than an hour later and Patrick out of the ocean, all four friends were sucking on wind when they left their play and found their way to a table.

"Where are you going?" Anthony asked while he watched Raymond hurry away from the table.

"To rent a grill," Raymond exclaimed. "What else? It's time to cook up some grub."

Patrick was first to clean, season and throw chicken and corn on the cob on the grill. "Ewwwweee," he shouted when he stepped back and eyeballed smoke, thick with spicy barbecue sauce, swirl away from the grill. "I'd put my chicken and corn on here if I was you," he added while he gave his friends a telling glance. He grinned. "If anybody knows how burn up barbecue, I do."

"Well do something then, Patrick," Raymond said while he plopped two thighs on the grill. He jumped back when heat from the fire rolled across his forearm.

"Might as well let you practice your cooking skills," Doug laughed as he pulled his long blonde dreads behind his ears and placed two thighs and two breasts on the grill. "We don't mind you cooking for us."

The sun was starting to lower, the wind warm and balmy. Heat from the sand carpeted the guys' feet. They kept their chests free of the shirts they wore on the drive to the shore, a choice that turned women's heads. If perfection existed, it was in this

Love Pour Over Me

day. Crystal blue was everywhere. It was in the sky; it was in the water.

The guys weren't at the grill five minutes when friends from campus called out their names. Anthony turned first.

"What's up?" Tyrone, leader of the campus pack, called out as soon as he saw Anthony.

Anthony slapped palms with Tyrone. Then he looked over Tyrone's shoulder and said, "Yo, Bradley. Yo, James."

"What 'cha'll doing down here," James said in his Birmingham, Alabama drawl. "Got any more grub?"

"We're cooking up delicious foods," Doug answered.

Bradley reached inside his pants pocket with such haste the lining to his pocket turned inside out. "Hey, yo," he said when he pulled out his trusty red and white box of Bicycle cards. "Want to get a game going?"

"As soon as we finish grilling," Patrick said. "But make sure you know what you asking." His grin turned lopsided. "I play mean game of cards, *Amigo*. No way you can beat me."

Bradley laughed. He was a card shark if ever there was one. He never left home without a deck of cards in his pocket. "We're playing Spades. Teams. We'll see what you've got."

Two sleek women -- their skin was the color of dark copper -- sauntered by. The bikini bottoms they wore pinched their thick buttocks and showed the guys where the center of their backsides were.

Anthony turned and, with a wink, he watched the women pass. The swing of their broad hips nearly put him in a happy trance. After they went further down the shore and out of his sight, he shifted his gaze and looked out over the coast. He listened to the water roll back and forth against the sand.

Temperatures were cooling. The time, eight o'clock in the evening, was sweet, just like the smell of the food coming off the grill.

By the time Patrick finished cooking then tossed a bucket of water over the grill's hot coals, sundown had turned the sky burnt orange. The fire went out with a hiss.

"All done," Patrick announced while he lifted a plate stacked high with barbecued chicken and grilled corn. "Dig in, homeboys."

The guys ate fast, sloppily. They wiped grease off their mouths with the backs of their hands. The chicken was tender, its spicy barbecue sauce stung their tongues and brought water to their eyes. The saucier their mouths became the more they ripped at the chicken until it came away from the bone. Their stomachs begged for more, but there were only two pieces for each of them, so they washed the food down with several glasses of fruit juice.

Doug leaned back, patted his expanded stomach and belched. "Hit the spot," he told Patrick. "You weren't lying. You do know how to burn up a grill."

Patrick nodded. "True, *Amigo*."

"So," Tyrone stood and said. "How about those card games?" He looked at Bradley. "Got that trusty pack?"

Raymond walked around the picnic table and snatched the deck of cards out of Bradley's hand. Trouble was gone away from the guys, especially Anthony and Raymond; it was seemingly burned up in the hot grill coals. All there was to do now was to have fun.

"We're not hardly playing with this deck, Bradley." Raymond snapped while he examined the bent ends of the cards. "No wonder you always win," he laughed. "These cards are probably so marked up, it's not even funny." He reached inside the sports bag he'd carried to the beach. "I bought a brand new deck this morning. We'll play with these," he told his friends while he unwrapped the new deck of cards and waved aside guilty feelings that he'd bought the cards at the time of day when he'd normally have been in church.

Laughter echoed around the table. Bradley laughed too, but his laughter was forced.

"I never cheat," Bradley said with finality. He looked around the table. "I don't have to." He could read, almost to the card, what each opponent had in his hand. He was that good.

"Well," Raymond said, "let's get to it."

"Let's do it," James agreed.

For more than ninety minutes, they played hard, until the orange colored sun turned dark red then dipped behind the ocean. Temperatures dropped; yet it was still warm enough to walk down the shore in nothing more than shorts and a t-shirt.

The ocean looked peaceful, like a wet carpet. When the guys stopped tossing out empty threats to each other and listened, they heard the swooshing sound the ocean made as it rolled to and from the shore in long, slow waves.

Other than the rolling waves, silence swept over the water. Not even children played in the water. In the distance a pair of dolphins frolicked in the deep. The water gave off a fresh scent that reminded Raymond of dawn. Many of the beaches' visitors had packed their coolers, towels and sunscreen and traveled back to their nearby hotels or to their homes in New Jersey or Philadelphia.

Seagulls flew across the sky in bobbing motions. They swooped down and pecked at crumbs and chunks of food. The birds loved summer as much as the town's shop owners. For both, summer, with its thousands of beach dwellers whose stomachs asked for food that guaranteed crumbs to the ocean and whose pockets asked for trinkets and t-shirts that guaranteed currency to cash registers, came like a feast. What summer brought to Belmar lasted for months, long after heat went out of the sky and winter banged like an angry elder at the earth.

No longer playing cards but certainly not silent, Raymond leaned toward Bradley. "I wouldn't cut those cards if I was you. Patrick's gonna settle it if you do."

It was a funny thing when Raymond laughed. The hurts given him at the hand of Malcolm, shame about how he was distancing himself from church and the heaviness of carrying Anthony's secret washed away like sand going out to the ocean when he laughed.

Bradley peered up and studied Tyrone. He didn't want to let on that he was concerned about their hands. Yet, his astute card playing skills told him that Tyrone was sitting on a stack of hearts. He knew that, even if he was on his A Game and played his hand like the pro that he was, he didn't have enough fire power with the cards he'd been dealt to pull out a win.

Tyrone placed a two of hearts on the table. He nibbled his bottom lip then he pulled a card off the top of the deck.

When Tyrone's eyes expanded after he pulled the card in toward his chest, Bradley let out a long breath. "*Maybe there's hope after all,*" he mused while he stared at his own mediocre hand.

"Your turn, Pat," Tyrone said.

Patrick reached for the deck of cards then he paused.

"That's right, Bud-dee," Bradley said, "You have to put something down before you pull a card."

While he listened to his friends take jabs at each other, Tyrone laughed dryly. "Don't go cheating, Pat," he mumbled.

Patrick studied his hand. He savored the cards; his hand was that good.

"Come on, Pat," Bradley whined. "Don't take all night. We have to get on in a few minutes." He looked up at the sky. "You see it's getting dark out here."

Patrick gave Anthony a sneaky nod then he placed a queen of spades on the table. He pulled a king of spades off the top of the deck. When he sat back and perused his hand, he almost laughed out loud.

"Now you know, Tyrone and Bradley," Raymond boomed, "That Patrick alone, all by himself, can beat you two."

James leaned forward. "Bradley, show 'em how a pro wins a game."

And so it went for the remainder of the game. Patrick kept pulling and laying down unbeatable spades. For a last show of finesse, he laid the king of spades down and that was that. By then it was nine-thirty.

The guys stood from the picnic table, grabbed their belongings and headed for their cars. They talked and joked their way up the short incline to the parking lot.

"Who drove?" James asked while he carried the cooler he brought to the beach.

"I did," Raymond answered. He stood across from Doug. They each held a handle to their own water cooler which they carried to the parking lot.

"I have a question for Bradley," Patrick interjected while he walked between the two coolers that swung from side to side while the guys carried them.

"Go ahead," Bradley said.

Patrick went into a semi-trot, until he was walking shoulder to shoulder with Bradley. He bumped Bradley's shoulder and grinned like a fox. "Who won last card game?"

"Bradley, you know this is never going to end," Raymond said. "You'll be one hundred years old, minding your own business, sitting at a park feeding birds. Then all of a sudden you'll look up and see another hundred year old man coming toward you with a familiar look in his eye. He'll sit down next to you. Won't be long before he'll tap you on the shoulder. He'll lean close to your ear so you can hear him, then he'll say, 'aren't you the guy who lost that card game at Belmar in 1985?'"

"Now you're a storyteller, huh?" Bradley laughed. "Your sense of humor is coming out strong today." His brows arched. "Don't tell me you've been drinking."

"Nobody been drinking," Patrick said. He gave Raymond a slow once up – once down nod.

"Don't try to deflect what we were talking about," Raymond waved. "Patrick asked Bradley who lost and you're trying to change the subject because your boy who's not supposed to be able to be beaten at cards lost today."

James said, "Y'all lost every game 'cept one. The real question is who lost game after game after game."

"*Basta*," Doug piped in his native Italian tongue. "Enough," he said, repeating the word in English. "We know how the game ended, and that's what matters, my friends."

"*Si*," Patrick nodded, reverting to Spanish.

"What's everybody doing later tonight?" Tyrone asked to shift the conversation. He tapped Anthony's shoulder.

"We're heading back to campus," Anthony said. "You know there aren't any good clubs around here."

"Why don't we go to Zanzabar Gold?" Raymond said, pushing aside humiliation that he hadn't read scriptures or prayed all day. Far too much time had passed since he last hung out with his friends. This day at the beach was like medicine for his soul. "They have good live jazz and," he added while he rubbed his stomach," Some slamming food."

"That settles it," James said. "Let's go back an' hang out at Zanzabar Gold." He turned to Anthony then Raymond.

"So, what time do we want to meet at the club?" Doug asked. He turned his wrist over and looked at his watch. "It's almost ten o'clock now."

"Well, it's gonna take us about an hour and a half to get home. Why don't we meet at the club at midnight?" Raymond said.

"Sounds good," James agreed. "It'll give us time to get home and hook up a shower and put on some fly clothes."

As if to bid the guys farewell, a cool breeze blew across the ocean. Stars hung brightly in the sky.

Doug released a deep breath then he turned and looked at Raymond. "And, Ray, I'll drive. I know it's your car, but you don't have to drive us here and then back home too."

"Yea," Anthony agreed. He shook sand off his shorts. "And yo," he added, "This was the kind of weekend I thought I'd have when I came to college."

"To get more free time, a friend told me to schedule all my classes on two days," Doug advised. "I tried, but there was one problem."

"What's that?" Raymond asked.

"I had to work. I mean work," he stressed. "My folks didn't have the kind of money for me to come to school on a free ride as an international student."

Raymond chuckled. "Doug, did you know how much university was gonna cost coming in or were you surprised?"

"I knew what the tuition was going to be, but the books and other stuff." He walked toward the driver side of Raymond's car. "I didn't have a clue how much the other stuff was going to run me. Coming from Italy, I thought the books would be ten or twenty dollars each. Like so many other college students I didn't do enough research on cost of living expenses before I took the plunge and came to the States for school. I had this odd thought—" He shook his head. "Don't ask me why, but I thought things would be less expensive here."

The guys laughed.

Doug's gaze circled the car, setting on Anthony then Patrick and finally Raymond. "I also didn't expect to meet three of the coolest dudes on the planet once I got to UPemb."

Doug looked over his shoulder at Raymond. "And what are you doing?" he asked with raised brows. "I said I was going to drive." He wore a lopsided grin as he draped his arm across Raymond's shoulder. "I won't crash."

"It's not that," Raymond said. "I just want to drive. Plus I had a small accident. And," he teased,

"There aren't too many people as good behind the wheel as I am."

"You had an accident?" Tyrone asked, standing several feet from the Excel and closer to Bradley's car. "What happened?"

"I was turning a corner by the church. Another car hit me. It wasn't bad, a fender bender." He didn't mention Walter.

"All right," Doug acquiesced. He stepped away from the driver side door and gave Raymond room to enter. "You just had a fender bender. I know how important it is to re-build confidence. I totaled my first car when I was in senior cycle at high school in Italy."

"Hey," Raymond called out to Bradley, James and Tyrone. "See you guys at Zanzabar Gold in a few."

"Cool," Tyrone nodded.

With that the guys climbed into their separate cars.

Talk about all the cars they'd driven and crashed, young women they'd dated and hangouts they'd frequented in high school passed like popcorn between Anthony, Doug and Patrick. Raymond didn't join in the discussions; his mind was crammed with yesteryear's ache. While his friends chattered loudly, he sat at the steering wheel and turned the key in the ignition. He listened to his friends talk and laugh.

The engine hummed. Raymond stared out the front windshield until his eyes felt glazed. Buried in the sound of the engine, he heard his father scream at him to "walk your sorry ass to the mall with your friends, you bastard. I don't care if you do have your driver's license. I'm not letting you drive my car."

There always seemed to be a potent memory to separate him from his friends. Each memory, each gap, stretched and widened and threatened to tear at his sanity each time he listened to stories about the love and warmth his friends shared with their parents. As if that was not enough, he had to steady himself beneath the fact that he hadn't heard from his mother in nearly twenty years.

Most times Raymond couldn't put his finger on it, but he felt empty, lacking, when he witnessed a mother loving her baby, soft cotton blankets insulating the infant with tenderness and the mother's arms rocking the child. When he saw a mother coo at her infant or hug her teenage son, he stared on in disbelief. He wondered if the children would have become like him, afraid to let someone get close to them, afraid to love, afraid of love, if their mothers had abandoned them when they were only two years old.

He backed out of the gravel parking lot and pulled onto the main road. Bradley followed not far behind him.

After forty minutes, so few cars were on the highway, the drive from Belmar to Philly nearly lulled Raymond to sleep. Twice he rolled down his window to let cool air brush his face and push him to wakefulness.

"Ray, *Amigo*" Patrick said from the front passenger seat. "You want me drive, all you have do is pull over." He looked out the side window. "Nobody's behind us for miles. Just pull to side of road and we'll switch seats."

Raymond shook his head and opened his eyes wide, but he refused the help. "I got it," he told Patrick.

"I don't blame you for not trusting Patrick to drive your hog, man," Anthony teased. "I'll take the wheel if you want me to."

"Nah," Raymond responded. Just to prove he was in control he reached for the radio and turned the volume up. Aretha Franklin sang the lead soundtrack to *Sparkle*. Her rich alto voice filled the car with a sweetness the guys appreciated. Moments later they bobbed their heads to the beat of Run DMC's *It's Like That*.

"Now that's my jam," Raymond said when the Run DMC song went off and Earth, Wind and Fire's

Reasons started to play. He turned the radio up louder.

"That's a band," Doug said.

"Fellas," Doug shouted, "Did you all catch that thick brown skinned beauty on the beach, the one wearing the black and red swimsuit?"

The guys laughed.

"Aw, homeboy," Patrick said with a wave of his hand. "There were so many beautiful women on beach today you know we don't remember the color of bathing suit."

"It's like a mating scene," Raymond chuckled. He glanced into the rearview mirror.

Beside him, Patrick lunged forward. His fingers dug into the dashboard. "Watch out! Patrick screamed, his neck veins bulging, his heart racing.

A Pontiac Sunbird, its high beams on, Metallica's *Nothing Else Matters* blaring on the radio, fishtailed and swerved across the divided highway. The car came, tires spinning out of control, right at the Hyundai Excel.

Raymond tried to shield his face with his right hand while he kept his left hand on the steering wheel. He turned the wheel sharply to the right, away from the Sunbird, but the Sunbird came like a crazed hunter at him.

The Excel's front windshield shattered. Jagged chunks of the glass went into Raymond's forehead, face and neck.

Blood oozed down his face and dripped into his eyes.

Next to him, Patrick's head leaned to the side, against the passenger window. Anthony and Doug sat in the back seat kicking at the door that wouldn't open. They screamed for help.

The Hyundai was mangled. Keith couldn't fix it this time. No one could fix the car this time. Its entire front, from the bumper to the steering wheel, was smashed. The driver's side was sunken.

The door was sealed, as if it had been seared to the front and back hinges. The front axle was bent; the tire leaned in toward the body of the car.

The Sunbird spun around on the highway, and stopped in front of the Excel.

It took the four women who rode in the Pontiac only moments to come to. When they did, they opened the Pontiac's doors and stepped out. As they walked across the highway, they swerved and wobbled to the center of the lane the same way their car had swerved across the road to the wrong side of the highway. Two empty Steel Fervor bottles lay on the Sunbird's back seat. Two half empty bottles of bourbon were beneath the front seats where they had rolled after the collision.

Cars and trucks began to back up. On the opposite side of the highway, people craned their necks and tried to see how bad the accident was and what might have caused the collision. No one stopped to help the injured.

Following several minutes behind, Bradley saw the crash and even though he was yet to know that his friends were involved, he picked up his walkie talkie and radioed the police. "There's been a major accident on I-95," he told the cops when they picked up the line. "It's bad, real bad. Please get here soon."

It took half an hour to pry Raymond out of the car.

While police and fire station crews worked to free Raymond from the Excel, two ambulances rushed Anthony, Doug and Patrick to the nearest hospital, Trenton, New Jersey's Mercer Medical Center.

Raymond's mangled body was soaked with blood from head to waist when the police, firemen and ambulance technicians finally got him out of the car and onto an ambulance gurney. They raised him into the back of a screaming ambulance.

Down the highway, the ambulance went. Cars pulled to the side of the road and occupants stared as the emergency vehicle passed. The ambulance carrying Raymond sped, its horn honking when cars were slow to create a clear path, down I-95 to Mercer Medical Center. Further back on I-95 the police officers cuffed the four women who'd been in the Pontiac Sunbird and drove them, uninjured and intoxicated, to the nearest police station.

Chapter Twenty-One

At Mercer Medical Center, nurses and ambulance technicians raced alongside the gurney Raymond lie on. "More oxygen," a registered nurse shouted seconds after she pointed to the clear mask that covered Raymond's nose and mouth.

"Hurry," another nurse shouted. "We're losing him. His vital signs are dropping fast." The pace of her heart quickened. Death upon the human body was the thing she worked feverously to ward off and yet it was right upon her. She almost turned away from watching Raymond's body jerk and convulse on the gurney. His body shook so violently she feared he'd fall onto the floor.

A doctor sprinted around the corner. "Get him in op. We have to get him stabilized. Now. Now," he demanded.

Three other doctors rushed to get Raymond inside the nearest empty operating room. It took two defibrillator applications to pull Raymond back from cardiac arrest. The surgical lights above the table where he lay were sharply bright. He was hooked to a respiratory ventilator and two vital sign monitors. Thick chunks of jagged glass were removed from his face. To stop the bleeding, his neck and arms were covered with gauze over which two nurses applied pressure. Then he was given a brain scan at which time the head surgeon announced, "He's suffered a traumatic brain injury. Cerebral contusion to the front lobe. Deep sec in the cervic and upper torso."

"Clear," the surgeon said after he investigated the extent of Raymond's open wounds. "I'm going to do vertical mattress sutures to close the deepest wounds."

At the end of the exhaustive surgery, he nodded at the head nurse and said, "Clean him up." Then he released a long, slow breath. "Admit him to a room for non-stables. Keep him there over night. If he remains stable through morning, we'll discuss next steps."

Raymond lay unconscious. The peace he had longed for since he was two years old was upon him. It started with hours of laughter shared with his best friends at the beach.

At the beach, he'd opened up in ways he hadn't in months. He hadn't spoken a word about it, but he hadn't wanted the day to end. He hadn't wanted to watch the earth move around the sun and turn the sky red-orange. He hadn't wanted children to stop running, giggling and splashing in the water as they played at the edge of the shore. He hadn't wanted the sweet smell of spicy barbecue to go away. He had wanted to hang out with his friends forever.

Now medical equipment engulfed him like cold, metal companions. "Let Patrick, Doug and Anthony be okay." That was the last thought he had before the force of the collision threw his body back then powered his upper torso forward. By the time his neck jolted and his head slammed again into the headrest he was unconscious.

As soon as word of the accident reached UPemb, Anthony's head and offensive line football coaches got on the phone. They called Mercer Medical Center and requested the details of Anthony's condition.

"Let me speak with him," the head coach demanded. "Put Anthony Thompson on the phone."

After several whispers from the resident nurse with "Come get the phone. It's your coach," Anthony left his place in the waiting room and took the phone.

"Really. I'm fine," he kept saying. "They rushed me, Patrick and Doug to the hospital as a precaution, to check us out and make sure we were okay." He paused. "It was a really bad accident, but," he repeated. "Except for two broken fingers and a cracked tooth, I'm okay. I'm a little sore, but I've felt worse after a beat-up football game," he said. And it was the truth.

The back of the car protected Anthony and Doug from much of the collision's impact. They had minor contusions, but no major broken limbs or torn ligaments.

As soon as they received news of the accident, Patrick and Anthony's girlfriends, Sandra and Aretha, jumped into cars they bummed off campus friends. Their friends turned over the keys to their cars without hesitation. Once in their friends' cars the pair hurried across the Morrisville, Pennsylvania free bridge to Trenton.

"Oh, baby," Aretha cried as soon as she saw Anthony in the waiting room. She walked so fast, she practically slid across the floor. She leaped into Anthony's arms and clung to him as if her life depended on it. "Oh, baby," she cried, "I'm so glad you're okay. Thank God you're alive." She looked at Patrick and Doug. Each of them wore a cast on his right arm. Cloth bandages were wrapped around Patrick's head. "Bradley, Tyrone and James said they were about five cars behind you." She faced Anthony again. "They saw the accident," she stammered. Her voice was loud, reeling with nervous energy. Her hands shook. She'd done a lot of things since she graduated from high school; imagining life without Anthony had not been one of them.

Sandra ran into the waiting room before Aretha finished her story. "I'm glad you all are okay," she said when she passed Doug who sat closest to the entrance. She kissed Patrick full on the mouth. "I love you, Sweetheart," she told him while she pulled him close. His chest warmed hers. It wasn't long before she felt the beat of his heart. It made her feel alive, blessed.

"We're all right, Honey," Patrick assured her. He took her hand inside his and walked her to the waiting room sofa. They sat next to Doug. In between discussing what they recalled about the accident, the guys stared across the room at the blank wall.

Aretha never did stop talking. Her voice droned on like an endless monologue. Her polished acrylic fingernails soared through the air when she waved her hands, which was often. She chewed a wad of spearmint gum until it popped -- loudly. The more she talked, the louder she popped the gum. She talked about the accident, classes, football, relationships, Trenton, home, life after college, bills, cars, beaches, shopping, food, parties, movies, songs, TV shows, other women on campus, marriage and family.

Sandra sat mute next to Patrick. Every few seconds she tightened her grip on his left hand. She ran her fingers over the tops of his as much for herself as for him. She needed to feel him, breath in the same air that he did. She needed to be close to him. She needed to believe that nothing – not even death – could rip them apart.

In between stroking Patrick's hand, she stared at Anthony and Doug gape-eyed. She prayed a repetitious, anxiety-laden prayer that went, "Dear God help us. Help us. Help us."

Fear rushed at her in waves; she didn't know why. Each time she looked at the guys, except for Patrick's head bandages, Anthony's two fingers enclosed in casts and Patrick and Doug's broken arms, the guys looked the same as they did before they left for the beach earlier in the day. Yet, she couldn't forget the terror she felt when she entered the hospital and stopped at the emergency room desk to ascertain Patrick's whereabouts, and the attendant confirmed the stories she'd heard on campus. Patrick and his friends had indeed been pulled out of a mangled car and rushed to the hospital in ambulances.

She refused to think about Raymond. His absence was like a hole in a wall. It was like there was a tear in their lives.

She thought about Brenda and bit down on her lip. *"Why didn't I stop by Brenda's dorm on my way over here?"* she thought. A second later she told herself, *"Because I was in a panic, that's why. And,"* she added, *"certainly Aretha told her. She left campus after I did."*

Emergency and dread excused everything. It made thoughtlessness forgivable, even amongst friends. Notwithstanding, she knew she hadn't forgotten Aretha. She called Aretha as soon as she got news of the crash. But she hadn't thought of Brenda then, not once.

She breathed in full, deep breaths. She placed a hand against her chest before she interrupted Aretha's choppy monologue. To no one in particular and to everyone in the room, she shared, "Bradley said he saw Ray drive toward the guard rail. Then he heard a loud bang."

Aretha leaned forward. She rocked her crossed legs and popped her gum. "That's not what Bradley said," she advised. "James and Tyrone too, they all said Raymond lost control of the wheel and drove across the highway. They said Raymond ran head-on into another car." She sat back and chewed her gum. She was satisfied. For Aretha, only sugar straight from the cane was sweeter than gossip. "I hope you all don't go to court over this," she added. "We all have other things to do. Nobody has time to spend all day in court."

Patrick frowned. "Ray didn't drive across road." He glanced at Anthony then he glared at Aretha. "He veered away from other car. The other car drove across the road."

Aretha shrugged. She glanced at Anthony but he didn't offer her support. "I only know what Bradley told me," she said.

"Bradley's my amigo," Patrick said. "But he's got it wrong." He waved his hand. "Don't spread rumors that this Ray's fault. It didn't happen like that. I don't care what Bradley, Tyrone or anybody else said. We were in the car—"

"Aretha, I don't know what Bradley saw," Anthony interjected. He took his arm down from around her shoulders. He folded his hands and placed them in his lap. He glanced up at the clock. They'd been in the waiting room for fifteen minutes and Raymond still hadn't come out. "Ray didn't do anything wrong. Doug and I were sitting in the back seat. I remember seeing a car come racing across the road on the wrong side of the highway. Next thing I knew—" He brought his hands together; they clapped like thunder. "We were hit and I went out."

He looked at Doug. He wanted to take the focus off of Aretha. "So where's your lady Linda, man?"

"Linda's out of the country at her parents," Doug said matter-of-factly. Concern etched across his face. "More importantly," he added, "I wonder where Brenda is."

Aretha stopped popping her gum and clasped a hand over her mouth. "Oh, no." She glanced at Sandra. "We forgot to tell Brenda."

"Go call her now," Doug directed. "Or give me her number and I'll call her. She has to know."

Sandra looked at Aretha. "You didn't tell her before you left campus? You left after I did." She stood and jogged out of the waiting room. She cursed while she ran around the corner to the nearest pay phone.

Back in the waiting room, Aretha grabbed Anthony's hand. "I'm so glad you're all right." She leaned her head against his shoulder and closed her eyes.

Anthony smiled. It was an old habit. He'd smiled as a little boy when he came home with a sports injury and his mother asked him if he was okay. His soft smile never failed to calm his mother's nerves. He almost laughed while he sat next to Aretha. Her head was light against the strength of his shoulder. Even now it was obvious that his soft smile hadn't lost its impact on women.

Aretha's shoulders lowered and Anthony kissed the top of her forehead. "I'm okay," he whispered in her ear. She snuggled closer to him and he looked up at the clock on the wall. Then he looked at the door and wondered what was taking Raymond so long to come down the hall.

Patrick leaned against the wall outside the waiting room. He shifted his gaze to the long corridor that seemed to darken at the end. He waited for Sandra; he waited for Raymond. To him it seemed as if Raymond was caught somewhere at the end of the dark corridor and unable to come to them.

"Brenda's on her way," Sandra said as soon as she saw Patrick. Words spewed out of her mouth. "I should have told her earlier. I should have picked her up on my way here. I don't know why I thought she knew." She shook her head. "I know how much she loves Ray. Those two are inseparable. I don't know why I didn't tell her earlier."

"Come here, Honey," Patrick said. He draped his arms around her shoulders. "You all right?"

"Yes," she nodded. "A little shaken up, but I'm okay." Silence passed between them. "I just don't understand why Ray's not out here with everyone else. You all were in the same car—"

Mental relaxation techniques she learned in psychology courses, things like deep breathing, counting and drawing up pleasant memories, failed her. She was scared. Worry etched deep into and across her forehead in three straight lines. Emotion started to choke in her throat. She wanted to flee what to her, hidden behind polite smiles and routine headshakes, looked like a crisis.

Patrick kissed the sides of her face. "The accident happened on Ray's side," he gently revealed. "When do you think Brenda will be here?"

"She was running out the door when I hung up. Cynthia let her drive her car. She should be here in half an hour. I wish Aretha and I had remembered to pick her up on our way here. I don't want Brenda to drive to the hospital alone." She lowered her head. "She was shocked when I told her Ray was hurt. She was grabbing the car keys and her purse while I was on the phone with her. I told her to be careful." She paused. "She said she would."

Patrick pulled Sandra close as he leaned over the front desk at the attendant's station. "Can you tell me how Raymond Clarke is doing?"

The attendant shuffled a stack of papers, scarcely looking up. "A doctor will be out shortly to meet with you." She tilted her head toward the waiting room door. "Have a seat in the waiting room. As soon as they get Raymond stabilized, someone will be in."

"*Gra-gra-gracious*," Patrick stammered. He tugged on Sandra's shoulder. "Come on."

Forty minutes passed before they heard Brenda rattling off a string of questions to the attendant at the front desk. As soon as she heard Brenda's deep alto voice, Sandra released Patrick's hand and sprang from her chair in the waiting room. "Brenda," she called while she ran to the front desk. "It's Sandra."

The weight of the crisis mounted for Brenda. She didn't like the look of uncertainty in Sandra's eyes. As it was, she had driven all the way to the hospital in absolute dread, her hands sweaty and quaking. The glazed look in Sandra's eyes caused her knees to buckle. Her purse slid out of her hands. It landed on the floor. She grabbed the strap, dragged the purse across the floor and rushed to Sandra's side. They fell into each other's arms. "Where's Ray—"

"I'm so glad you're here," Sandra stammered. "I was so confused. I was so out of it I forgot to stop by your dorm." She cupped Brenda's hands inside her own. "I apologize for not stopping by and getting you."

They walked on in silence.

Finally Brenda asked, "Where are the guys? I know Raymond drove them all to the beach. Where are they?"

For all of Sandra's angst, she knew she couldn't keep Brenda from finding out the truth – that of the four friends who were in the car, only Raymond suffered major injuries. She had no idea why Bradley and other students who had driven behind Raymond's car blazed back to campus after they saw the accident and reported that it had been Anthony, the school's star football player and not Raymond, who was seriously injured.

In the waiting room, Aretha glanced at the empty chair Sandra once occupied. She didn't leave her seat. She refused to depart Anthony's side.

A Moet painting hung on the wall several inches below a battery operated clock. Aretha stared at the flowers in the painting. Their pastel colors -- streams of pink, lemon, powder purple and soft green -- went up and out like jets of tinted water. Center of the flowers was a country cottage. Everything seemed simple in the painting, like every flower, every stone in the cottage, was where it was supposed to be.

"Maybe I'm jealous of Brenda and Ray's relationship," Aretha thought. She glanced at Anthony. His jaw was square – strong – just like the rest of his body. His wide, dark brown eyes, his smooth, thick lashes and his full supple mouth made him gorgeous. She often wondered how she had managed to hold onto him for four years.

She swallowed hard and worked at a story, a back drop she could create that would explain why Anthony had barely spoken to her since she came to the hospital. She struggled to invent a tale her inner woman would believe.

Months ago she made Anthony sweat. She knew he wasn't ready to be a father. Yet, she lied and told him she was pregnant. What he didn't understand was that it was all she could do. After rumors of him stepping out on her circulated around campus, she had to tell the lie. And it worked. She lost Anthony for awhile, but she knew he'd come back to her. The idea of marriage and family later in life, a few years after he graduated from university, appealed to him; Aretha knew. And yet long before she changed her story, molded it into another lie, and told him she'd miscarried, he hurt her.

She would never forget the expression on his face when she told him that she was pregnant with his child. She watched color go out of his face. She watched his mouth swing open. She didn't blink or turn from studying him. What she saw pushed her to tears. She wept and heaved uncontrollably. Yet, each time she looked up, Anthony looked shocked, like he didn't want their child – like he didn't want her.

Now while she sat in the waiting room thoughts and questions merged until a chill raced up her spine. She leaned closer to Anthony. She would never let him go. Ever. If pushed, she'd create other lies years down the road, but she'd always find a way to keep him with her.

"It'll be all right," she heard Sandra comfort Brenda.

Aretha pursed her lips. Deep down, she knew the truth. Hers was the burden of performing tricks. She had to keep her hair styled right. She had to wear make-up absent a smudge. She had to frequent the gym for two to three hours a day and power pedal, pump iron, swim laps, do aerobics and sit in the sauna to keep her body petite and tight.

Right away she liked Anthony. He had charisma. His was a magnetic vibe. It's what drew people at high school, university and around the country to him. It's what pulled her inside his sphere, close, like a shadow.

From the start of their relationship in high school she performed sexual tricks on Anthony that brought him to intense climaxes. This at a time when her parents thought she was still a virgin.

When her parents were away from home she would mount Anthony. More times than not she ripped off her blouse before the thought had chance to cross Anthony's mind. She kissed him full and hard on the mouth, smearing his face with her scented lipstick. Each thrust of her hips, each stroke of her tongue, every suckle of her mouth worked together like a key. It allowed her constant entrance to Anthony's life. It made her 'his woman'.

She was the pursuer in their relationship. She'd gone after Anthony in her tight Guess jeans and lace blouse the day she spotted him shooting pool across the room from her and two of her good high school friends. She gave him her body like it wasn't attached to her psyche or her soul. She gave him her body like she was merely giving him a hot plate of down home cooking.

She loved to share the spotlight with him. What she hated was the need to perform, to be perfect, in order to remain 'his woman'. She didn't kid herself. She knew he had his pick of glamorous females, and yet he'd chosen her. For that, she felt honored and burdened at the same time.

Aretha looked up. She stared at Sandra's shadow filling the doorway. She tilted her head and looked around Sandra for Brenda, but she only saw Sandra.

"Where's Brenda?" Anthony asked. He started to stand.

"She went to the ladies' room," Sandra answered. She crossed her arms and raised her shoulders. She looked like she was cold.

Doug moved to the edge of his seat. "She's upset?" Before Sandra could answer, he asked, "Is she okay?"

"As best as can be expected." Sandra paused then said. "Brenda's strong." Her gaze went up and across the room. "She wanted to know why Ray was the only one in the car who was injured. I told her what I knew and that is that the collision happened on the driver's side of the car and that Ray had been driving."

"Is she coming in here?" Aretha asked.

"Sure," Sandra nodded. "Said she's not going to budge until she sees Ray."

Moments later Brenda entered the waiting room and walked to the first empty seat she saw and sat next to Aretha.

Aretha sat still for a long time. The clock on the wall turned three whole minutes, then and as if something had nudged her, she reached out and took Brenda's hand inside her free hand, the one not clutching Anthony.

Chapter Twenty-Two

A white cotton coat hung off the doctor's square shoulders. His salt and pepper afro was thin at the front. His hands were shoved to the bottoms of the coat pockets. He stood, rigid and straight faced, at the edge of the waiting room. Although he'd never seen her before, he looked right at Brenda.

Brenda's mouth swung into a round 'O'.

"Now. Now," the doctor said with a raised hand. He examined her with tight, sweeping gazes. "No need to get worked up."

Brenda stared at him so intently she felt she could bore a hole through his forehead.

"Are you Ray's wife?"

They locked gazes before Brenda said, "I'm his girlfriend." She glanced at the name tag penned to his white coat. "Dr. Kelly". A second later she asked, "How is he?"

Dr. Kelly lowered his voice. "Step into the hall please."

Brenda looked back at her friends as she left the room.

"We contacted school administration and we've tried to contact your boyfriend's parents, but—"

She shook her head. "Raymond hardly talks to his father."

Dr. Kelly nodded. "Okay," he said. "But if you can reach his father, please do." He paused. "He should know."

"Of course."

"I can tell you so much, but I really need to reach his family. Grandparents, someone."

"There is no one else," she assured him.

Dr. Kelly's gaze lowered then he looked up at her again. "That's what the school told us." He spoke matter-of-factly. "Very well." Time was wasting and there was only one person nearby who was close to his patient and she was standing in front of him.

"Ray's in stable condition," he slowly began. "But he's not out of the woods yet." He paused. "He's suffered serious injuries. He's fortunate to be alive." Quickly, he added. "There was no alcohol in his system."

"Raymond has never taken a drink—"

He raised his hand. "We had to do it. It's normal procedure. But," Dr. Kelly searched her face. "There is absolutely no alcohol or drugs in his system. Now, I can't say what will happen beyond that. He has insurance, so that's good. After he rest here tonight, we are going to check him thoroughly again tomorrow. Then," his next words came out slowly, like he didn't want to utter them, "We're going to have to operate."

"Why?" She looked up at him, a man more than a foot taller than she was. Love and empathy gushed out of her heart like fresh water. She refused to allow herself to think that Raymond might not pull through.

"Your boyfriend," Dr. Kelly said, "has suffered significant internal damage. One of his lungs is collapsed. He broke his left arm in three places. His left foot is broken and his right ankle has suffered a severe rupture. It looks as if his right foot got stuck beneath the gas pedal upon impact. In addition, he has a fractured skull. The good news is that he was in excellent condition before the accident. His vital signs are strong--."

"When can I see him? Which room is he in?"

"He's in intensive care. I may allow one person to see him tonight, but only one, if that."

"When will you decide whether or not he can have a visitor tonight?" Her face was set. "I'm not leaving until he walks out of this hospital with me." Then she held her breath.

"Your boyfriend's in a coma." He waited for her to react. "We expect him to make a full recovery. It's going to take some time, but we expect him to completely recover. Ma'am," he continued, "We're going to do all we can to help Ray heal." He placed his hand gently atop her shoulder.

She nodded several times. Because she didn't want Dr. Kelly to worry that the news may have been too much for her, she smiled.

He returned her the smile. Then he stuck his hands in his coat pockets and prepared to walk back down the hall, away from her. Just before he turned on his heels, he stopped. "Ma'am," he said, "You can go see your boyfriend in fifteen minutes." He gave her an assuring nod then he turned and walked down the long corridor.

"They're going to let me go see Raymond in fifteen minutes," Brenda announced when she returned to the waiting room.

"It's about time," Anthony made clear.

Aretha shot him a chilly glance. She felt like he'd talked more with Brenda since she'd arrived at the hospital than he'd spoken to her all day. Jealousy turned to anger; it boiled beneath her skin. It wasn't long before she sat erect and folded her arms. She didn't want any part of her body to touch Anthony's – not now.

"So," Brenda started slowly, cautiously, "How was the day at the beach?"

"It was all right." Patrick shrugged. He glanced at Anthony then at Doug. He knew what Brenda was trying to do. He'd done the same thing himself when he was twelve years old sitting at the edge of his grandfather's hospital bed. He kept asking his grandfather, an animal lover and for thirty years the town's most beloved veterinarian, questions about big cats – to keep himself from picking up the scent of death that hung like rotten pine in the hospital room.

"We played volleyball, surfed and got in several good hands cards before we left—"

"It was cool," Anthony said in effort to intercept Patrick. No way was he going to let the conversation move toward the highway. "We had fun. It was a good day."

"Raymond's *forte* or strong," Doug said, nodding emphatically. "He's going to get through this," He kept nodding. "Ray's *forte*. He's a stand up guy." He bit down on his bottom lip. "There isn't an ounce of quit in Ray." He smiled. "Not an ounce."

"*Si*," Patrick chuckled. "I remember how tough Ray was when I first met him. I think he was warming up to thought of having apartment to himself." He chuckled again. "And talk about guy who loves to run. I wonder what Coach Carter is going say soon as he finds out about—" A cough preceded his next words. He glanced at Brenda. He'd said too much and he knew it. If he stopped now, Brenda would feel awkward. He wasn't willing to risk that. "The accident. Coach Carter'll be here no time once he finds out. That or he'll be on phone pronto."

"I called him just before I ran out the door," Brenda told them. "Coach Carter is like a father to Raymond. He loves that man. I didn't want him to find out through second hand information."

"What did he say?" Patrick asked.

"He told me to let him know how Raymond's doing and to keep him in the loop. He genuinely cares about Raymond." She smiled. "I think he sees all of the athletes on the track team kind of like they're his children." She fidgeted with the ends of her hair. "Less than three weeks from now Raymond was going to run in the Westfield Invitational in Oregon, giving himself a chance to get more exposure to make the Olympic team."

"Speaking of love, Brenda," Sandra said, "did you call Ray's father and let him know about the accident?"

To hedge off the question, Brenda turned her wrist over and checked her watch for the time. Although it hung as big as a basketball on the wall, not once did she look at the clock on the other side of the room.

It was easy for her to tell strangers like Dr. Kelly that Raymond and his father had a strained relationship, but she hated discussing the strain with people she knew. She tried desperately, but she couldn't recall the older man's telephone number. The older man was like a phantom, like he didn't exist.

She didn't have long to wonder at Raymond's father's telephone number, because a nurse appeared in the doorway. "You can go in now," she told Brenda. "Doctor said it's okay."

Brenda stood. "You all don't have to wait."

"I'm going to stay here until you come back. I want to know how Ray's doing," Sandra said. Her firm tone and raised shoulders made it clear to Brenda that she meant every word she said. Tucked in Sandra's declaration was a familiar thread – deep care -- an emotion that had run between the two women since the day they met.

Brenda smiled. She honestly smiled for the first time since she received news of the accident. Sandra's care and her own smile lifted heaviness from the room.

She inhaled and knew Raymond and she would survive this change somehow . . . she knew somehow they would.

"Thanks, Sandra. Thanks a lot." Brenda said as she and Sandra embraced. "Thank you for staying here as long as you have. But I'll be fine. You can go, and thanks again."

One by one Brenda embraced each of her friends. When she approached Aretha her body stiffened. It both surprised and saddened her when she felt the same inflexibility in Aretha's body. Their torsos felt like two boards leaning against each other. To place a veil over the truth of what had moved like a wall between them, Brenda kissed the side of Aretha's face.

Sandra followed Brenda out of the room. "Are you sure?" she asked. "You don't want us to stay?" Tears hovered in her eyes like large dewdrops.

With one last hug, Brenda stepped away from Sandra and began her walk down the long corridor.

The hall was empty. Brenda felt like she was the only person in the hospital. She passed one room after another. She glanced through a few of the room windows. In those rooms she saw patients sitting up on their beds while a visitor, probably a relative Brenda told herself, sat at the edge of the bed or in a cushioned chair.

The further she went down the corridor, the larger her thoughts became. She imagined Raymond so disfigured she'd turn away from him. She cringed at the thought.

She recalled the first time she saw Raymond. She'd told herself to stay away from him. Her heart raced in uncommon ways when she saw him. It scared her. He scared her. She told herself to avoid him because she feared Byron's reaction and even more, because she knew, she just knew, that if she let Raymond into her life, he would change her in pronounced ways, change her forever.

The closer she got to Room 348, the tighter her mouth became. Her throat was dry and gritty; she felt like she had eaten sand. Her jaw was clenched. Here she was walking down a quiet hospital corridor toward the man who had changed the flow of her life.

Recaps of the accident told by Bradley and other students on campus she couldn't remember seeing before played in her head. Each retelling sounded as if Raymond had been at fault. On top of that Dr. Kelly told her that the police had requested alcohol and drug tests be performed on Raymond. She had to admit that Raymond had changed over the last few weeks. He'd taken a good hard look at his life and decided to loosen up. He'd decided to enjoy life, to stop being so cautious, to stop thinking his way through his days – to live. But drink and take drugs, those two things she could never see Raymond doing. He was too smart for that. Sure, he'd experienced a lot of pain, especially in his childhood and that pain caused him to keep to himself more than he probably should, but he cared about himself enough not to destroy his life with chemicals. He wasn't the type of man to drink or smoke poison. His self-loathing didn't run that deep. At least she didn't think that it did.

She looked at the numbers on the hospital doors. "342," she said in a wispy breath as she looked at the door across from her. "I'm almost there." Seconds later she stared at three silver numbers – 348. She had arrived, but she was not ready to go inside.

Except for the rise and fall of her breathing there was only quiet at the door's edge. Funny. When she had turned away from Sandra, the quiet that enveloped the hall had brought her comfort. Now outside the door, at the place she had longed to be, the quiet chilled her to the bone. She didn't need to be here. Not now. She needed to be on campus walking barefoot on the warm summer grass. She needed to be in the bath tub, her body buried beneath a mound of scented bubbles, while images of Raymond and her happily loving each other moved through her head, images that had abandoned her after she reached the hospital.

Out of habit, she started to tap the door, but stopped. A second later, she turned the knob and gave the door a gentle push.

It yawned open.

Brenda leaned forward and peered inside the white room. The odor of potent antibiotics whisked up her nose.

The door all the way open, revealed the room's contents like a chest unlocked and its lid hanging up. Brenda inched closer. She stared at the clear tubes that dangled out of Raymond's mouth. She inched closer. She looked at the IV stuck in Raymond's arm and the thick bandage, colored with spots of blood, wrapped around his head.

"Extensive injuries," she whispered to the room. Before she knew it, her head was leaning back. Her focus was on the ceiling. In a hushed tone she said, "Thank you, God for taking care of Raymond."

Prayer was her only friend now. It staved off loneliness.

"God, please give me the strength," she begged while she reached out for Raymond's hand.

His skin was soft, like a baby's – not a man's. It startled her how limp his hand was. It felt weightless, as if there was no bone beneath the skin, nothing like it felt the night three weeks ago when their bodies, entwined and folded over each other like pieces of hot candle wax, had exploded in ecstasy.

Everything felt surreal, as if she was imagining it all. She told herself all she had to do was wake up and it would all be over. But the tubes and the crisp, clean white sheets, the monitors, and the name tag fastened loosely about Raymond's wrist – everywhere she turned she saw signs that the man she loved could not remain alive under his own strength.

"Ray—" she began. She scooted across the room and brought the chair, the only piece of furniture in the room other than the twin bed, close and sank into it. Its soft cushion designed in brown, black and orange checkered stitch came up warmly around her hips. For that she was glad. She looked at Raymond again and told herself to settle in for a long stay. Two things she knew for certain. Raymond wasn't leaving the hospital tonight and she wasn't leaving the hospital without him.

An air conditioner was fastened to a ledge at the top corner of the room window. It hummed while it pushed air that felt too cold around the room. Hair on her arms saluted the cool breeze.

She discovered a strange fact about sitting in a room with an unconscious person; she could do or say whatever – anything – and it didn't seem to matter. She crossed her arms and pulled the light jacket she grabbed on her way out of her dorm around her shoulders. Ten minutes later she appreciated that the air conditioner hummed. There was no one to talk to. The steady hum felt like an ally.

She searched the room for a book, a magazine, something to apprehend her attention. There was nothing. She wished she had brought a novel or a newspaper with her. But she hadn't planned on a long stay. In fact, with each mile that she put behind her on the drive to the hospital, not once had it occurred to her that Raymond wouldn't come home tonight. Her endless hope had blinded her.

She glanced at Raymond's still body and choked back tears. In one long, slow stroke, she swiped her face with the back of her hand. Then she pulled the chair closer to the bed and steeled her nerves.

"Raymond, I love you. You won't be here long." She played with the ends of her hair. She patted his hand. "I'm here." She spoke slowly, evenly, as if she thought fast talk would confuse him.

She leaned forward and took his hand again inside hers. "If you hear me, squeeze my hand." She waited. "Let me know you hear me, Raymond."

She took in a deep breath. "Raymond," she tried with urgency. She pulled on the ends of his fingers. "Raymond." Her voice rose. "Raymond." She almost shouted. "Raymond." Tears were in her eyes again.

A knock rattled the door.

She looked up.

A nurse stuck her head inside the room. "Ma'am, visiting hours are over."

"But," Brenda begged while she stood. "I just got here. I want to stay with him longer." She returned to the chair. "Please understand."

"Ma'am."

Brenda sat silently.

"Ma'am."

She looked up at the nurse again. "Please," she begged. "We were together just yesterday. I had no idea." Her lips quivered. She bit down and hid the tears behind a steely face. "I had no idea this was going to happen. I know you've seen this type of thing before, but this is the first time someone I'm close to has been in a coma. I've never even been in this hospital before. I'm not from around here." Her voice cracked. She felt hot, angry. She wanted to leap from the chair and shout at the nurse, a woman who had not harmed her in any way.

"My family isn't from here. They live hundreds of miles away." She glanced toward the bed. Her gaze fell across Raymond's foot which hung outside the wool covers. "My boyfriend's family isn't from here either." She pushed her back against the spine of the chair. She didn't want to give the nurse any hint that she would leave Raymond's side, because she would not. Even if security came and tried to drag her out of the room, she wouldn't leave. She'd scream at the top of her lungs. She'd kick and bang the walls. She'd send alarm throughout the hospital. She was not going to leave.

"Ma'am."

"Please just let me stay."

The nurse twisted her mouth. She stood at the edge of the door. Her hand was still on the knob. Finally she nodded reluctantly. "Let me go ask Dr. Kelly." She went to close the door then she turned back. "How much more time do you need?"

Brenda sat erect. She clasped her hands together. She looked more like a stern school matron than a scared girlfriend. "As long as he's here," she said matter-of-factly, "I'm going to be here." She stiffened her spine. "I'm not leaving until he leaves."

The nurse gawked at her. "Ma'am, he's in a coma. It may be days or weeks before he's released."

Brenda shook her head vigorously. The ends of her braids went against her face like pieces of twine. "I'm not leaving until he leaves, and he won't be here a long time. God's gonna work it out. "

"Ma'am."

"I'm not going to stop praying and I'm not going to leave until Raymond is with me."

And again the nurse yielded to her resolve. "Okay. Let me go speak with the doctor. I think it's best that he come back and talk with you himself. He may let you stay the night, but I doubt you'll be allowed to stay for days on end."

"Weekdays I'll only be here at night. In the daytime, I have school."

"Very well."

The door hissed to a close. Fifteen minutes later, the nurse returned with Dr. Kelly.

Dr. Kelly approached Brenda. He wore a dual head stethoscope around his neck. His Yacht-Master Rolex watch sparkled when bits of light from a nearby street lamp streamed through the window and landed against it.

The nurse checked Raymond's heart rate and oxygen saturation levels. Next she checked his blood pressure, temperature and pupils. She emptied his urine and drainage bags. After she logged his vital signs on the clipboard at the top of the bed, she re-filled the drip bag and rubbed a light anti-bacterial lotion on his skin, concentrating on his leg where the catheter was located.

Her routine work completed, she stood patiently at the door for Dr. Kelly as if "wait" was a part of her job description.

Dr. Kelly looked hard at Brenda. Her resolve intrigued him. She looked too young to feel this great a responsibility for another human being. "So, you want to stay the night, do you?"

"Yes."

"All right." It was her resolve that demanded his agreement. "You'll be on camera. We'll put the room on our security consoles for the entire night."

"I won't climb in bed with him," she teased.

"Okay," Dr. Kelly chuckled awkwardly. He glanced at Brenda, tried to size her up.

Brenda stood and extended her hand. "Thank you for letting me stay the night, Dr. Kelly. Is it okay if I stay every night until he leaves the hospital?"

"Depends on how long he's here," he told her. He walked toward the door. "We're not a long term care hospital. If he's not better in a few weeks, he'll be moved to another care center. But," he smiled. "You can stay for a week." After he smiled at her one last time, he opened the door and walked behind the nurse out into the corridor.

Brenda returned to the chair. She leaned forward and wrapped her arms around her knees. "They're gone now," she told Raymond. "It's just you and me now. I'm not leaving without you. We're walking out of this hospital together."

Silence filled, engulfed, the room.

"I hope my talking doesn't bother you. I don't know if you're trying to sleep or just laying there and are wide awake." Her gaze roamed the room then it landed on Raymond again. "I don't understand a lot about comas. You're body is still there with energy in it, but something's happened to your brain." She folded her hands into her lap. "I miss you. I wish we were sitting on the front lawn outside the Student Center." She took his hand in hers. She needed to touch him. Lavender. It was the scent of the lotion the nurse had massaged his hand with.

It surprised her that his recently moistened hand felt pasty. It was so different than before. Last night when they held hands, his hand was warm, strong. Last night the heat in his hand made her feel alive. Last night and so many days and nights before, his hand had been as hot as an oven. Before on cold winter days, she would reach for his hand the way she watched other people, at similar points in winter's cold, reach for wool or leather gloves.

She twisted her mouth. "You don't even know I'm here." She shook his hand with such force his body rocked on the bed. "Wake up, Raymond. Wake up. I want you here with me. I don't want you wherever you have gone off to. I want you with me. Wake up." At once and in an unexpected step, she chuckled. She laughed as if he had told a joke. "When you wake up, you better tell me where you went while you were in this coma."

She released his hand and moved back in the chair. She crossed and uncrossed her legs. Sitting still for long stretches of time had never been her strength. She had always wanted things to happen quickly; now she was forced to wait. This wait stabbed at her impatience until she felt hurt, because this time she had to wait for what she wanted most – Raymond. She had to wait for his love.

Were she yet a girl, she would have chewed her fingernails until their ends became ragged. It was an old habit she engaged in throughout her childhood and one she didn't stop until she was a teenager.

When she was a child, Victoria would pinch her each time she caught her with her fingers in her mouth. Her mother started to speak her name in a "hard" way when she bit her fingernails. "Bren-da", she would scowl and say. Her father, on the other hand, would grin when he saw her chew her fingernails.

It wasn't until she was grown that her father told her that he'd practiced the same nervous habit as a child. He told her that he knew she would eventually quit the habit.

And she did.

"Odd how hard it is for me to sit here in this quiet, which seems to be getting thicker by the minute when before if it was noisy I'd beg for quiet." She laughed. "Now that I have quiet, I feel like I'm drowning in it."

She scanned the room. She examined the tall ceilings, the off white paint on the walls, the air conditioner that continued to hum, the Venetian blinds and the door that led to the bathroom at the back of the room. "It's too quiet in here."

She wondered why the room didn't have pictures. She looked for a television set. There wasn't one. "Guess this is what a room looks like when you're in intensive care."

She looked at Raymond. "I could swear you're only sleeping." She examined him closely. "You look so peaceful, like you're resting. I hope you are. I hope you're comfortable."

She examined the room again. Nothing had changed. She told herself to create a diversion so she'd lose the urge to stare at Raymond. She turned and stared at the Venetian blinds.

Mere seconds passed before she faced Raymond again. She folded his arm and placed his hand across his abdomen. "It probably wasn't bothering you. But for some reason I kept thinking it was hurting you to have your hand dangling over the edge of the bed like that." She paused. "I was probably wrong."

She crossed her legs at the ankles. "Tomorrow night and for the rest of the week when I stay I'll bring a book with me. That's what I'll do. I'll bring a book with me tomorrow. That way I can read when I'm not chatting with you."

"You already know I'm taking a summer course so I can make up the failing grade I got in chemistry. The class is still kicking my butt, but I'll get through it." She sighed. "I'm going to pass this time."

She leaned forward. "By the way," she continued, "Coach Carter told me to let him know how you're doing. You know how much everybody loves you. You're in so many people's prayers. And I tried," she went on, "To guess at your father's number so I could tell him you're in the hospital, but nothing would come. If he calls or if something comes to me, I'll tell him about the accident and let him know how you're doing. I know he'll want to know. As a matter of fact," she said, "I'll stop by Student Affairs Monday and ask for his number."

Her voice cracked. "You should have heard everyone on campus talking about how much they wanted you to be okay. Bradley, James, Tyrone and some other students from campus were driving behind you from the beach. They saw the accident." She reached down and ran her hand over her shin. "They said your car went across the highway, all the way to the other side of the road." She sighed. "The police and insurance lawyers'll find out what caused the accident." She sighed again. "Everything'll be fine. You didn't do anything wrong." She shook her head. "It was just an accident. Nobody's going to get in any legal trouble," she tried. "You didn't do anything wrong."

Chapter Twenty-Three

It was July 19, 1985, two weeks after the car accident and the day before the Westfield Invitational, the event that would have been Raymond's biggest chance to get recognized on the international track and field circuit. Temperatures rose to record highs. Sun rays scorched the brows of students' taking summer classes and caused them to sweat in the short time it took to walk from their dorms to class. Lecture hall fans offered little relief. Their thick steel blades wobbled in circular motions and blew hot air around the rooms.

One week remained in the summer academic schedule. Brenda wondered if she would last. She walked to and from class and guessed at how other women with broken hearts managed to keep going. While in class, she stared out the window and recalled romantic times she'd shared with Raymond.

Like balloons filled with muddy water, her feet felt heavy. It was as if she had gained fifty pounds since the accident. Everywhere she went, she felt an enormous demand that she stoop and bear up beneath the weight.

Raymond had been in a coma at the hospital for two weeks and already the change had begun to knock the wind out of her. She saw no exit. For hours she replayed conversations she had with Dr. Kelly, conversations that centered on Raymond's condition and when he would awaken from the coma.

With her thoughts pinned to Raymond, Brenda worried that she wouldn't pass her hardest class – Advanced Chemistry. She sat in the Advanced Chemistry lecture hall amid seventy other anxious students. Each of them worried they lacked what it took to pass the final exam Professor Downing, a tight-lipped man with a long, narrow frame, handed out as he moved through the room. When Professor Downing walked down the row she sat in,

Brenda told herself to focus on the test, but it was to no avail. Her thoughts remained on Raymond. Yesterday when she stayed the night at the hospital, Dr. Kelly told her that Raymond would be moved to a regular hospital room. "He's making significant progress," Dr. Kelly told her. "He's starting to show rapid eye movement. His latest x-rays have improved as well. He appears to be on his way out of the coma. We're going to move him to a regular room tomorrow."

It wasn't the first time Dr. Kelly and other hospital staff had relayed "good news" to her, news that hadn't materialized. She was cautious. Yet the bliss of hopefulness kept hovering around her.

Thoughts about Raymond's progress came at her like fast falling water until an interlude arrived. It came in the form of Professor Downing. He stepped next to her and plopped a thick set of stapled papers on her desk.

She waited until he moved away from her then she opened the front flap of the stapled papers. Her heart skipped a beat. Top and center of the second page of the test was a handwritten note. The writing appeared smooth yet hard to read, the mark of a man who wrote often, who wrote fast. The letters were broadly curved at the ends. Space between each letter was wide, as if to leave room for the reader to pause or contemplate what was on the page. There was a pitch of deep sincerity in the note which read: "Even with an ailing loved one, I know you can do it. You've got what it takes to get over the top."

Brenda had seen the handwriting many times before. On those previous occasions, the handwriting had brought her shame with notes like "You know you can do better." "Are you sure this is the best you can do?" "Did you study even once?"

She looked at the note again. Then she looked at Professor Downing. She watched him move down the classroom rows. Then she watched him cross the floor to the front of the room. She stared at him. Their gazes met.

Professor Downing, the man she'd told Raymond was the most stiff and unimaginably unhappy man in the entire world, smiled at her.

She returned him the smile then just as quickly, she turned away from him and returned her attention to the test.

The clock at the front of the room wasn't on her side. Its hands turned faster than she had seen them do before. A minute seemed like thirty seconds. She wrote quickly. She struggled to answer the questions. Nothing she put down sounded right to her. When she wasn't writing, she tapped the end of her pencil against the desk. She did that until the guy sitting next to her gave her a menacing glance.

Forty minutes later she walked to the front of the lecture hall and placed her completed test papers face-down on the top edge of Professor Downing's desk. "Thank you," she whispered.

He stopping browsing the pages of *Science Magazine* and glanced up at her. Neither spoke.

"Thank you," she whispered again.

Seconds later she was outside the lecture hall and on her way to her dorm on the other side of campus.

"Hey, B," a short chatty lady called out.

"Cathy," Brenda said in a raised voice. "Good to see you. Are you taking finals today too?"

"No," Cathy answered in a chirpy voice. "I took my finals yesterday." She rolled her eyes. "It was tough," she added. "I'm here today because Betty and I are going to get bombed as soon as she finishes taking her Advanced Medicine final exam."

"Feels good to be done for the year, doesn't it?"

"For sure," Cathy exclaimed. "Say, Brenda," she quickly added in a somber tone. "How's Ray?" Her face was pulled down, as if she was apologetic for having asked the question.

"He's all right," Brenda said with a slow, even pace that caught Cathy off guard.

Cathy tilted her head slightly downward and peered at Brenda. "You sure?" She quickly added, "I don't mean to pry."

Brenda waved her hand. "It's all right. I don't mind talking about it." She lied. She wanted to keep Raymond's status to herself the way she kept secrets from her mother and Virginia when she was a little girl. She didn't want to talk about it.

"He's a lot better. Doctors performed x-rays on him the other day and," she smiled, "He's coming along."

"Oh, girl," Cathy beamed, "He's gonna be out of that hospital before summer's halfway over."

"I hope so," Brenda offered in a small talk 'I-sure-wish-I-could-get-away-from-you' kinda way.

The Chemistry and Advanced Medicine classes let out and more students poured into the hall. Betty led the way. Her bangs were dyed bright orange and dangled over her eyes.

"Cathy, I'm gonna run," Brenda said. She pulled her book bag to the crest of her shoulder. "I'll see you around."

"Yea," Cathy said. "And give Ray-Ray my best. We all love him here. He knows that."

Wind bursts stroked Brenda's skin as soon as she exited the hall. She peered at the sky and watched dumpling clouds move. Her stride widened. For the first time in a long time, she believed the universe held goodness; it was a new thought, as fresh as the blowing wind.

"I should go shopping," she thought with a tinge of guilt. *"Or,"* she wondered, *"maybe I'll pull out my bike and ride into town."*

She wanted to soak in the sun and the company of good friends. She didn't want to catch the train to the hospital straightaway, a daily ritual that had worked its way into a chain, a binding habit she thought held value because she loved Raymond.

She couldn't explain it. Raymond was in a coma, but she believed that if she spent as little as half an hour at one of her favorite sidewalk cafes, he would hold it against her. The thought seemed locked inside her brain. This despite the fact that she knew Raymond didn't hold grudges.

The closer she got to her dorm, the more she examined the belief; it involved her demand for sacrifice. Forfeit had long stood as a symbol of love to her. The more she sacrificed, the better she felt about herself. It was almost as if she believed that to sacrifice, to do what she least wanted to do, to go where she especially did not want to be, was to earn her place in the universe, akin to a tenant paying rent. Elders taught her that to relinquish her wants for another was the greatest act of love. It's what made mothers good women, they told her.

"Look. See how that woman's going without good shoes?" Her grandmother would say while Brenda and she prepared to enter a store at the mall. "That Sista looks pitiful in those run down heels. But, look there," her grandmother would point to nearby children, their hair thick and curly just like the woman's. "See how nice their shoes are?"

Brenda would watch her grandmother and the woman look up at each other. They'd tug on the straps to their heavy shopping bags and smile a bond of approval at each other.

"She's a good woman," Brenda's grandmother would take hold of Brenda's hand and whisper. "She's going without so her children can wear those pretty shiny shoes."

Sometimes it would be Brenda's mother or her mother's sister, Nancy. "Shame that child doesn't have enough for herself and her four kids," Brenda's aunt Nancy would say while she glanced up at another sacrificing woman's forlorn face. "I know that child's hungry. She sure looks sad," she'd say in reference to the woman while she made her way down a grocery store aisle. "But look at her. She's a good one. She's not going to eat one bite until those kids are full. If there's some left, she'll satisfy herself with that."

Brenda looked across the campus. *"Nah,"* she thought. *"I'm not going bike riding. I don't know why I didn't think of it before. I should drive to the church and let Bishop Moore know how Raymond's doing."*

Bishop Moore was the only person at Arch Street AME she'd told about the accident. A week passed since she updated him about Raymond's condition. She hadn't sought the church's prayers for Raymond. For the most part, she shrouded the status of his health in secrecy.

Reason was the fact that Anthony, Patrick and Doug suffered no major bruises. Even now, she'd look up and see them walking around campus. When she went to athletic hubs, she'd hear jostling about Anthony's recent bicycle mishap with an unsuspecting pedestrian. Students and professors alike still talked about his heroic performance at this year's BCS Bowl where he scored three touchdowns, winning runs that sealed UPemb's victory. Like a hamster in a cage, she couldn't get it out of her mind that it seemed as if Raymond had been alone in the car at the point of the collision.

She couldn't count the times Doug told her that he begged Raymond to let him drive home from the beach that day. When she pulled Dr. Kelly to the side and asked him why only Raymond sustained major injuries, Dr. Kelly told her, "I don't know. It is odd, seeing all the damage to the car." Dr. Kelly shook his head. "For now I'm focused on getting him back on his feet."

"You're right," Brenda nodded. The gesture didn't put her question to rest. She continued to wonder why only Raymond suffered injuries when he hadn't been alone in the car.

She only discussed the accident with Dr. Kelly. For her mental health, she had to pretend nothing had happened. It was the only way she could allow her friendships with Sandra and Doug's girlfriend, Linda, to remain intact. When troubling questions rose in her mind, she silenced them by telling herself that chance had simply chosen Raymond to suffer so that Patrick, Anthony and Doug would not.

Cynthia was standing outside her dorm closet in her panties and bra when Brenda opened the door. "How did your final go?" Cynthia asked when she turned. She held a pair of jeans and a light green blouse in her hand. She'd taken her summer biology final yesterday.

Brenda crossed the floor and plopped down on her bed. "I did all right." She sighed. "I think I passed." She watched Cynthia step inside the jeans. "Where are you going?"

"Right now I'm going to get something to eat. Later I'm going out with friends." She zipped her jeans. "It's ladies night out. Why don't you come? You can always go to the hospital later. If you go tomorrow, Ray'll appreciate that. He's a righteous Brotha. If he was conscious I'm sure he'd tell you to chill. You don't want to fall out of love with him when he wakes up because you feel like you gave too much of yourself while he was down. Know what I mean?" She glanced at Brenda. "Know what I'm saying, B?"

"Yea. I know what you're saying. It's just that," she sighed. "I feel like I should be with him, and I was going to do a few things before I went to the hospital."

"Like what?" She pushed her hips against Brenda's and moved her further down the bed. Then she sat next to her.

"You don't believe me," Brenda chuckled.

"You're right. I don't. So," Cynthia nudged, "What are you gonna do?"

"I might stop by the bookstore."

"Girl," Cynthia teased. "You're only going to the bookstore so you can buy more books to read while you sit next to your man's bed." She paused. "And where do you sleep at the hospital anyway? I thought you said Ray was in a single room."

"He is, but Dr. Kelly put a television, a radio and an extra bed in the room. He thinks my being there is speeding up Raymond's recovery."

"For real?" She paused. "Girl, you and that man love each other."

"We do."

"So, where else are you going?"

"I'm gong to stop by the church."

"AME on Arch Street?"

"Yes."

"So, why are you going over there? Don't tell me it's to work."

"Raymond's the one who worked at the church a lot, not me. I mainly just went to church and came home. Before Raymond got hurt, I think I might have talked with Bishop Moore twice."

"What?"

"Yea. Raymond and he were the ones who were close. I had a few friends around the church, but I mainly kept to myself. Since I told Bishop Moore about the accident, he keeps asking me how Raymond's doing. I hurry out of church on Sundays and head back here so I can get ready to go to the hospital." She shrugged. "I haven't gotten back to Bishop Moore in two weeks. I want to stop by and let him know how Raymond's doing. I said I would, and I'm going to keep my word."

"That's so like you," Cynthia said while she pushed off the bed and walked to her side of the room. "You always do the right thing. I like that about you," she added while she stepped inside a pair of tan loafers. "And," she asked, "How have you been getting to the hospital? You only borrowed my car that one time. I keep telling you to take my ride."

"I told you I take the train to Trenton. Then I catch a bus from the downtown train station to the hospital."

"Child, I must have forgotten."

"You did." Brenda stood. She walked to the compact refrigerator Cynthia and she bought from Target months ago. She pulled out a bottle of grape juice, her favorite flavor. "I've gotten used to the train ride, and I don't want to use your car all the time. You have places to go and on top of that, you work. It's not a hassle. Sometimes I fall asleep on the train so it gives me a chance to get some extra rest."

"Not like you're running up and down the halls at the hospital."

"Girl, stop."

"Tell you what." Cynthia picked her purse up off her dresser. "Let me drive you to church. I'm not due to hook up with my other girls for two hours. Like I told you earlier, I was just going out to grab a bite to eat when you came in. Let me run you by the church. I'll wait for you there. After you finish at church, let's grab a bite. I'll drive you to the hospital before I hook up with my other friends. Just this once, please let me do this. I'll call my girls and let them know to go to the club without me and that I'll meet them there." Before Brenda could object, Cynthia shrugged and said, "I like to drive myself to a club. That way I can leave when I get ready and not when everyone else is ready to leave."

"I feel you on that one," Brenda said. "And I'll take you up on the offer. It'll be cool hanging out."

An hour later they sat outside Salad Express on Broad Street. They sipped lemonade and ate veggie salads. The atmosphere was light, just like the food. It reminded Brenda of how she felt when she was a girl twirling around on her parents' front lawn. Her head would be pushed back like an opened umbrella. Her arms would be spread wide like a soaring eagle's wings. She would be smiling.

"So, what did Bishop Moore say when you told him how your man's doing?"

Brenda stuck her fork into a mound of lettuce mixed with cucumbers, mushrooms and tomatoes. "He was happy. I told him Raymond's getting better like Dr. Kelly says." She shrugged. "I don't see improvement. Raymond still lays in the bed like he's sleeping. It's like his body's a rag." She placed her fork on the table and twisted her mouth. "I hate saying that. That's hard, isn't it?" She looked up at Cynthia.

"I know what you mean. I told you I had a second cousin who was in a coma once. It's the weirdest thing to see. They don't even look like themselves. It's like some part of them isn't there. It's more than their brain not functioning right. It's like some part of them isn't there, but people come out of comas and get on with life." She sipped her lemonade. "My mama said our cousin could hear us when we went to visit. I've heard that before from other people too, so I think it's good that you visit Ray." She paused. "I wonder if they track the progress of coma patients who get regular visitors compared to those who don't. I bet there's a big difference in how the two respond to treatment. What do you think?"

Brenda swallowed a mouthful of salad. "Why do you think I'm at the hospital every weekday night and all day and night on weekends? Like I told you, Dr. Kelly thinks my being there is speeding up Raymond's recovery."

"How long do you think you'll be able to keep it up? You have to be straight with yourself, you know?"

"I know, and it's funny. Bishop Moore asked me that very same question when we stopped by the church earlier."

"It's good you have so much love pointed at Ray."

"Yes. The church added him to the Circle of Prayer."

"Good." Cynthia stuck a forkful of food in her mouth. "Did you ever reach Ray's father?"

"Student Affairs got in touch with him."

"Has he come up—"

"He's busy," she lied. No way was she going to tell Cynthia what Dr. Davis relayed to her about his conversation with Malcolm. Even now the words stung in her ears. "I knew something like this was going to happen to my boy," Dr. Davis told her Malcolm had shouted after she pressed him for the truth. "As much as I hate to say it, Ray's getting paid back for walking off and leaving me like he did." Even more, she wasn't going to tell Cynthia that she'd peeked over Dr. Davis' shoulder while he dialed Malcolm's telephone number. As soon as she saw the numbers appear on the telephone's digital screen, she started repeating them in her head. The first thing she did when she got back to her dorm was call Malcolm. It was a disastrous exchange.

Brenda looked across the cafe table and shook her head as if doing so would erase the memory of her brief telephone call to Malcolm. She glanced into her glass of lemonade and said, "Bishop Moore asked me to update him on Raymond's condition once a week." She placed her elbows on the edge of the table and sipped her lemonade. "Coach Carter and he always ask me about Raymond."

A yellow and black butterfly flew between them. They watched the insect in quiet appreciation. Then Cynthia reached out and tried to catch the butterfly by one of its silky wings.

It flew to the other side of the café.

Brenda turned and watched the butterfly go. She felt that the butterfly had, in its brightly colored wings, brought her a gift. She told herself Raymond was going to pull through and wake up this week. There would be no brain damage for him to contend with. He was just going to sit up straight in the hospital bed, look over at her and say, "Let's go."

"B," Cynthia said in effort to regain Brenda's attention.

Brenda placed the glass of lemonade, now almost empty, on the table. "Sorry, Girl. I was checking out that butterfly. Wasn't it something how it flew between us like that?"

"Yea," Cynthia nodded. She looked across the café for the butterfly, but it was gone. When she faced Brenda again she said, "You were talking about Bishop Moore."

"Oh," Brenda waved her hand. "He knows Raymond's coming out of the coma. He wants to celebrate the change with me. That's why he wants me to keep him updated."

"Do the folks from AME visit Ray?"

"Bishop Moore's visited twice. Raymond's only permitted so much stimulation right now, so the hospital's only allowing him to have a few visitors."

"Have you talked to Ray's father lately? I haven't seen him around?" She tore off a piece of sour dough bread. She was mainly playing with the food now, using it as a distraction when the conversation lulled.

Brenda pushed her chair away from the table and folded her arms. "Like I told you, Student Affairs called him." Her voice was flat. "They told him right after I found out." She met Cynthia's glance.

"Yea, but that was weeks ago. I'm asking you if you've talked with Ray's father recently?"

"He was—" She stopped. She'd lied before. The thought to lie again pinched her. After another second, she said, "He's not concerned."

Cynthia leaned against the spine of her chair. "What?"

"Well," Brenda tried. A second later, her shoulders rose and she blurted, "Raymond's father has a drinking problem. According to Raymond, he's been drinking for years. They're not close." She shook her head. "Not at all."

"Girl," Cynthia said, "Your man really loves you." She picked up a cucumber and stuck it in her mouth. "I know I'm bold and sometimes I talk too much, but I'd be too embarrassed to tell someone my parent was an alcoholic."

"Why?"

Cynthia gawked. "Why?" Her thin pencil lined eyebrows went up like two mountain peaks. "Why?" she asked. "Because it's jacked up to be an alcoholic. Alcoholism is all about pain. Alcoholism hurts everybody it touches." She ran her thumb across her recently polished acrylic fingernails. "I know you're one of those super soft hearted people, B, but surely you know that." She lowered her jaw. "Can you imagine being a kid growing up with a father who's a drunk? People would make fun of you. School would be unbearable. Talk about pain."

She rolled her eyes and tsked. "Any parent who'd bring that kinda ache into their child's life can't love their child. It ain't cool for parents to make choices that mess up their kids' lives."

"But I don't know that people set out to do that," Brenda tried.

Cynthia bit into a piece of sour dough bread. "Well," she said in a raised voice. "We studied Quantum Physics in Science." She chewed the bread. "Did you study Quantum Physics?"

"A little. I know what you're talking about. It has to do with intention."

"Exactly," Cynthia shouted. "And if we create our own reality, what you just said doesn't add up."

"No. I mean," Brenda started to eat her salad again. It was as if the renewed energy in their conversation had reignited their appetites. "I know we create our own reality, but we don't always know what it is we're really creating."

"One thing's certain," Cynthia said. "We're responsible for our own happiness."

Brenda shrugged.

"Not sacrifice, B."

"I know."

"Life's about being happy, not about giving up our lives so other people can be happy while we go on sacrificing-sacrificing-sacrificing."

"It's not that simple, Cynthia."

"Yes it is."

"So you say."

"So I know."

"You have your opinion about things and I have mine."

"But the thing is," Cynthia laughed. "I'm right."

Brenda almost spit out her lemonade she laughed so hard. "Now, that there is your problem."

"I'm not a know it all."

"I know you're not. But you're wrong about sacrificing. I admit, I do give of myself a lot, but with Raymond it's different. If you'd stop thinking every guy was out to play you and let yourself join with a cool man in love, you'd know why I do what I do."

"Quantum Physics says somewhere inside me I already know."

"Then," Brenda said with a wagging finger, "You're saying you know everything."

"Deep down I know everything for my life. Not consciously. I know it in my spirit." She pointed at Brenda. "You know the truth for your life too. How do you think you're able to know if something's right for you or not?"

"Girl, you're really getting into this Quantum Physics."

"It's true. Something in us agrees with our greater source and that's when good things happen."

Brenda wagged her finger. "Now you may be onto something."

"Thing is," Cynthia continued. "We're limitless beings just like our creator. Sometimes it takes a lot of digging to know what you really want. Then," She tilted her head, "it sure nuff takes courage to go out and get what you want."

A lopsided grin lighted Brenda's face. "Now I know why we're roommates." She leaned forward. "You know when you first walked into the dorm, I wondered if we'd get along." She revisited that rainy afternoon two years ago. She'd just come out of the shower when the resident director knocked on the door. A towel was wrapped about her head; she'd recently shampooed and conditioned her hair. She wore a pair of baggy sweats.

"You were sharp as a pen, Cynthia. Me. I was in my usual t-shirt and sweats. You stood next to the resident director cheesing like a cat." She looked at Cynthia until they both smiled. "I thought you wouldn't like me. You looked so professional and there I was, my hair wet and wrapped in a towel, looking as casual as ever."

"You're one of my best friends, B, one of my very best friends. I'm glad the school assigned us as roommates."

"Me too. I've learned so much from you."

"And to think I thought you wouldn't like me because I'm an around the way Sister who does yoga, meditates, is a vegetarian and goes on spiritual retreats. I thought you'd think I was a nut."

"Turns out we were on the same spiritual journey."

"Only difference is the tools we use."

"That and your dreams." Brenda laughed. "Seems like every other day you're telling me about some dream you had."

"Nah, B. Don't joke. It's not funny. Dreams speak to us. It's our subconscious or our spirit talking to us when we dream. You ought to write your dreams in a journal. Dreams can let you know how to deal with things in your life—"

"Yea. Yea. Yea."

"For real, B. Don't trip. Dreams let you know what's coming up next in your life. You ought to listen to them." She paused. "I've been interpreting dreams since I was a teenager."

"Thing is, even after you have the dream, can you stop what's about to happen in your life? Huh?"

"All you have to do is change your mental and energetic focus and your dreams will change. You know how we con ourselves and try to believe a lie's the truth?"

"Yea."

"Especially when we really want something." She shook her head. "Desire can be a bitch. You want something so badly you can't see the truth about it."

"Girl, don't get me started."

"Well, dreams show us the truth about what we're experiencing in our lives."

"So why are they so hard to understand?"

"Honestly," Cynthia said, "If we didn't have so much fear attached to things we want, I think we'd understand all of our dreams. Fear that we won't get what we want makes us force dreams in a certain direction, to mean something deep down inside we know isn't true. You know," she added while she looked across the café. "I hadn't thought of this before but I wonder if that's the reason so many of us don't remember our dreams. We don't want to know the truth."

Brenda watched an elderly Italian couple be seated. She looked at the couple and wondered what her life would be like when she was their age. In their faces it showed that they'd managed to retain their zest for life and, more importantly, their love for each other. She looked at the couple with a longing she hadn't allowed herself to feel since Raymond's accident. She watched the woman with her frail thin legs dotted with age marks and the man with his balding head and his gray moustache, until she heard Cynthia holler.

"B."

She blinked and fixed her gaze on Cynthia. "Sorry. I was thinking. Go on about dreams."

"If you can interpret another person's dreams, you can understand your own. However," she said with a raised finger, "If you struggle to understand your dreams then there's something you don't want to see." She leaned into the spine of the chair. "But that doesn't change anything. The same dreams are gonna keep coming up until you accept the change."

Brenda stared across their table at nothing in particular.

In the quiet interlude, a thought surfaced for Cynthia. The thought troubled her. It came like an old memory charged with hard emotions, returning to disturb the afternoon's calm. She glanced over the rim of her drinking glass and peered at Brenda. She drank her lemonade slowly, as if she didn't want to swallow it. "B."

"Yea?"

"I--" she turned and stared at the checkered design on a nearby waitress' apron.

"Cynthia?"

"I don't know how to tell you this," she said after she faced Brenda again. Her mood had changed. She wasn't smiling.

"What?"

"I can't believe I forgot."

"What?"

"This dream I've had for three days." She traced the edge of the tablecloth with her finger. "It's important. Otherwise I wouldn't have had it more than once. I--"

The sun shone brightly. It cast a warm hue over the city. People talked and laughed around them as if everything in the world were, just now, perfect.

"The dream's about Ray." She paused. "And you."

"Why would you dream about us?"

"You said you don't recall your dreams. Dreams don't mean a lot to you. How else could spirit get a message to you?" Cynthia sighed. "Please just listen. If you get mad, you can take it out on me, but remember, I didn't create the dream."

"Yea. Yea."

"If you don't want to hear it, I'll just drop it."

"If you don't tell me, I'll go around wondering what you dreamed about. So tell me. Just tell me."

Cynthia unfolded then refolded her napkin. "I don't know how to begin."

"Tell me."

"It was summer. Ray lived close to a lot of water, an ocean or a river." She glanced at Brenda. "He tried to walk across the water. He couldn't. Something held him back. There was another guy in the dream. He approached Ray as soon as he arrived at this place. He showed Ray around. The houses looked like sticks. There were no telephones, televisions or electricity. It was like going back in time. Ray worked a lot. He seemed so alone. I heard this rushing wind around him."

Brenda didn't say anything for a long time. Finally, she asked, "Where was I?"

Cynthia looked at the older Italian couple.

"Where was I?" Brenda shouted.

Diners turned and looked in her direction.

"Far away."

"Where?"

"I never saw you in the dream."

"So, what's that mean?"

"It means you and Ray had gone separate ways."

"For how long?"

"Ray's hair was gray when I saw him again. He was still alone."

Brenda grabbed her purse. She nearly knocked the pitcher of water off the table she stood so abruptly.

Cynthia laid a twenty dollar bill on the table to pay for their lunch. "Doesn't mean it will happen," she said. "Ray and you could make sure it doesn't happen."

"It's just a stupid dream," Brenda shouted. She was in no mood to continue the conversation. "And it was your dream," she said when she turned and faced Cynthia. She pointed. "It was your dream."

Cynthia grabbed her forearm. "Exactly, B. It was my dream and you can change it."

Brenda rolled her eyes. "Are you jealous of Raymond and my relationship?" she asked as she stood and walked away from the table.

Cynthia stepped back. "What?" She hurried out of the cafe after Brenda. "B," she cried. "I didn't make the dream."

"But you couldn't wait to tell me about it."

"I didn't want to tell you about the dream, and you know it."

"So why did you mention it?"

"Because I want you to do whatever it takes to keep the dream from coming true."

"Here we go," Brenda sighed, "Another lecture."

"No. Just the truth." She paused. "I won't tell you. I'll ask you, so you can hear the truth come out of your own mouth. What do you think you have without love and joy?"

"Everybody knows the answer to that."

Cynthia grabbed her by the forearm. "Answer the question."

"You'd have nothing." She let out a thick breath. "Now are you happy?"

"That's exactly what I was going to ask you."

Brenda's gaze lowered. Knots of dust blew across the sidewalk then over the tops of her feet. For a second, she watched the debris go. Then, and as if she was suddenly prompted, she raised her head, tightened her grip on her purse and ran down the street.

"How do you feel, B?" Cynthia ran behind her asking. "Are you happy?"

Brenda stood outside Cynthia's car jerking on the locked passenger door handle. The question was too pointed. It was razor sharp. It hurt.

Chapter Twenty-Four

The belief that Raymond would awaken diminished with each passing week. Since his arrival at the hospital, daffodils had gone colorless and bent toward the earth to bid the soil to let them inside, beneath the hardening ground. Several weeks later, the Northeastern part of the United States had become barren, frozen. Icicles hung from houses in places where greenery once clung. Only the thickest shrubs, their tops covered with snow, were indifferent to the cold.

Winter bore down on the city for several months. What didn't change was Brenda's appearance at the hospital. It was as if she was born to sit in Mercer Medical Center's Room 348 waiting for the man she loved to come back to her.

Then winter turned to spring. Tree leaves danced like kites across the sky, their buds hard and ready to explode into matchless color. Like soldiers marching home, time went on. Spring became summer. Butterflies, bees and, at night, fireflies, zipped through the air like fairies come to wish the earth well.

It was Thursday, June 19, 1986. Saturday would mark the one year anniversary of Raymond's accident.

Brenda was watching an episode of *Sanford and Son* at the hospital. During the sitcom, Lamont raced down the house steps at night after he heard a cat yelping. Fred lie asleep outside in the truck's bed, refusing to remain indoors while two empty caskets stayed in the house, Lamont hoping to sell them for a nice profit.

One look at Lamont, his jittery steps and his failed attempts to appear brave, as if he was uninfluenced by superstitions Fred had shared with him earlier, and Brenda burst out laughing. The second time she laughed she glanced over her shoulder. And she saw it. Raymond smiled.

When his face widened, the corners of his mouth turning gently up, she leaped from the chair and screamed. Her voice rose above the loud television, rolled under the door and echoed down the hallway. She pressed a button at the side of Raymond's bed and rang the nurse, the nurse who always came when she called, the nurse who had come to seem like a friend, especially during the loneliest hours late at night when she wrestled sleep and won.

Brenda stood between the door and Raymond's bed. She didn't move until the nurse came. She wanted the nurse to be as shocked as she was. She wanted the nurse to be proud of her and Raymond; their long wait was paying off. She wanted the nurse to see. She wanted the nurse's seeing to be proof that Raymond was getting better, that he was waking up.

She shouted, "He smiled. He smiled. He smiled," as soon as the nurse opened the door.

"Calm down, Sweetheart," the nurse told her evenly. More than twenty years Brenda's senior and despite the fact that her eyes were ocean blue and her hair sandy blonde while Brenda's skin was dark brown, to her Brenda felt like a granddaughter. It was a relationship she'd longed for since she married three decades ago. The fact that her husband and she were unable to have children took that chance from her. Yet, she knew the rules. She had to remain distant with each patient. And so beyond her customary kindness and calling Brenda "sweetheart", she treated Brenda like a stranger.

She walked to Raymond's side and looked at him like she was studying a road map. "Most coma patients make facial expressions," she said while she continued to study him. "But that's not a sure sign of progress. In fact," she said, "Many coma patients make noises and even move their limbs but don't come out of the coma. Ever."

Brenda scowled. The nurse's words felt hard, too factual, like numbers on a spreadsheet. Before she knew it, as quickly as she rang for the nurse, she wanted her to leave.

"Thank you for coming," she said. "I wanted you to know he smiled." She bit down on her lip. "You can go now."

The nurse peered over her wire rimmed glasses at Brenda. "Sure." Before she left the room, she wrote, *"June 19, 1986. Visitor noted facial movement from patient – a smile."*

At the door's edge, she turned. "It's gonna be all right, Sweetheart." She gave a nod. "It's gonna be all right."

The door hissed to a close.

Brenda turned on the small radio she brought to the hospital a month after she began her routine. *"Thank you for joining us here at WJJZ, Philly's smooth jazz station. And now one of Philly's own. "* the announcer's silky smooth voice called out.

Grover Washington, Jr.'s *Sassy Stew* played across the airwaves while Brenda walked to the chair at the edge of Raymond's bed and sat.

Her old trusty friend, her imagination, the tool that filled her with incessant hope but that never brought her what she wanted, went into full swing. She imagined what life married to Raymond would be like. She saw herself laughing and playing with their grade-school children, a boy and a girl. Their daughter had long, thick, wavy hair like hers. Their son was tall and creative; he shared Raymond's passion for running.

She played with their children at a park two blocks away from their home. Each room of their house was filled with love. Family portraits, framed in cherry oak wood, adorned the living and dining room walls. Their black and white terrier barked and ran in the park with them. At night they snacked on buttered popcorn while they watched Disney movies.

An unkind word never crossed between Raymond and her. Days they shared stretched out sweet and slow the way thick molasses oozes out of a canning jar.

She smiled while she dreamed. "I can create the life I want," she told herself. She looked to the bed. Another slow smile went across her face. Belief that she could love Raymond forever made her exuberant. She didn't move until an unexpected thing happened. The event sent her mouth swinging open. Raymond's hand reached out to her.

She grabbed Raymond's hand. It didn't cross her mind to call for the nurse. She thought only of Raymond. Her love for him clogged her thoughts and shut out the noise from the radio, the television and the hum of the air conditioner. Inside her mind there was room for him and nothing else.

"Honey," she whispered while she leaned over his bed. Her breath cooled his face like summer breeze. "Can you hear me?"

He sat up slowly, eyes closed, as if he were merely exhausted.

Her mouth formed into a scream, but shock snatched the sound out of her voice.

He opened his eyes then he stared right at her.

"Honey," she stammered. "Ray."

His mouth worked at a smile.

The hunger in his eyes, the searching, the probing, made her feel hot. She squeezed his hand in an attempt to keep her own from trembling. They held onto one another for long seconds. When she stepped back, her face was wet with tears.

"Anthony, Patrick and Doug visit often," she told him. "Coach Carter comes by regularly. Every time I see him, he asks me how you're doing. Bishop Moore or one of the associate ministers has visited once a week over the last few months."

He looked at her in long sweeping motions. Her hair smelled like fresh apples. Her eyes were full, bright. Her face went up into a permanent smile.

Emotion erupted deep within him, causing his jaws to quake. "Where am I?"

Appreciation she felt for his awakening was replaced by sorrow when he looked at her and asked, "Who are you?"

The question jolted her like a punch to the face. "I love you. I've been here—"

"Where am I?"

She patted his hand. "You're in a hospital. You're at the Mercer Medical Center in Trenton, New Jersey." As soon as she spoke the words she wondered if she had told him too much. She didn't want to upset him.

"Are you my mother?"

A lump formed in her throat. "No. I'm your lady." She leaned across his shoulder. "I love you."

"Where did you come from?" He fell back against the bed – hard. The mattress shook beneath his weight. His pillow almost fell to the floor.

She placed her hands against his shoulders and tried to get him to relax. "It'll come to you." She nodded more to reassure herself than anything else. "You'll remember everything in time." "You will," she nodded again. Then she walked across the room and sat in the chair next to him. *"I've suffered enough,"* she told herself.

She'd spent months searching telephone books and Ohio court records in attempts to locate his mother so she could tell her about the accident, but she'd come up empty. It was as if his mother didn't exist.

To her Raymond's parents, especially his mother, were a blur, and yet as soon as he woke from the coma he asked her if she was his mother. The question was sharp like the smooth blade of a polished knife.

She wanted to strike out, protect herself from the hurt. He had asked her if she, the woman who had been by his side every single day for a year, was his mother, the woman who abandoned him when he was two years old.

If he didn't recall her being at his side, if he never recalled a word she spoke while she sat next to him, then each second she spent in the hospital was wasted for she had only come to the hospital so that he would know that she loved him.

Her arms were folded and pressed against her chest. She was frozen. She didn't move until fear that Raymond would slip back into the coma scared her.

She left the chair and walked to the bed's edge.

He rested on his back; his eyes were open, his gaze was fixed on the ceiling.

She stroked his forearm. "Do you remember me?"

A sigh preceded her next questions. "What is your name? Your name? What is your name? Who are you?"

"Am I Ray-mond?" he asked in a slow voice. "Is my name Ray-mond?"

"Your eyes are rolling. Are you tired?"

"Tire?"

"Sweetheart, do you remember anything?"

"Beach," he said. He looked away from the ceiling to the walls to her. "Sand. Car. Who-was-with-me?"

"Anthony, Patrick and Doug were in the car when the accident happened. You were in an accident."

"At-the-beach?"

"On the way back from the beach."

"Driv-ing? I was driv-ing."

"Yes."

"How long have—" He took in a deep breath. "I been—" He took in another deep breath. "In this bed?"

"Weeks. Months. Do you remember how many weeks are in a month, Raymond?"

He smiled weakly. "Four."

"You do remember." She scooted onto the bed's edge and cupped his head in her arms.

"Your voice." He paused. "It's fa-mil-iar."

"We've been together a long time."

"I love you." The gap in his brows allowed enough room for uncertainty.

She chuckled. "Yes."

"Your voice," he said again.

"I've been here everyday, every single day. I'd go to classes then I'd come and sit right here with you. I'd watch TV, listen to the radio, read, do homework and talk with you. I talked about a lot of things. I hope you remember." She sprinkled his forehead with butterfly kisses. "I love you." She fought back tears. "I love you."

"How did I do in Sci-ence?"

She laughed while she stroked his face. "Since most of the year was over when the accident happened, the university decided to grade you based on what you had achieved up to the point of the accident. She smiled. "You earned honors. You did good." She pulled his face close to hers, until their skin touched. She kissed him fully. She savored the scent of his mouth, the tenderness in his lips.

Warm tears went slowly down her face. She'd missed him. She had been desperate for him to wake up. She wanted to celebrate each word he spoke, each shift of his body, the tug of his hand, the pull of his arm as it circled her back.

"Bren-Brend," he stammered. "Are you the woman I used to love? We went pla-ces to-ge-ther. We had fun. I knew you from school?"

"Yes. I love you. I always love you."

"Are you the la-dee from Penn-syl-van-ia?"

"Yes—"

"I met you at school, a big school." He looked across the room at nothing in particular. "A u-ni-ver-si-ty."

"Yes." She smiled and laughed.

All her life she had waited to be loved like this, to have someone remember her, the sound of her voice, the smell of her skin, the way she moved. All her life she had waited for someone to become stronger the more clearly they remembered who she was. Despite her family and friends' pleas for her to stop catching the train to the hospital, for her to forget Raymond and let the chips fall where they may, she came to Room 348.

Then, and as if a strong wind had risen and had blown out a candle's light, the moment was taken from her. It was stolen in the form of a question.

"Do you know my mo-ther?"

She removed her hands from his head and fattened the pillow for distraction.

He spoke slowly, methodically, more like a robot than a human being. But he wanted to know, "Do you know my mo-ther?"

"No." Her smile was gone. In its place was a stare, a look of utter confusion mixed with hurt.

The questions kept coming.

"How long have-you-been-here?"

"I've been here since you've been here?"

"Since I-have been-here." He tried to nod but his head merely rolled on his neck akin to the way a drunken man's head bobs absent balance or aim.

He needed her. She saw that. She let the pillow go and cradled his head again. She held him in her arms and kissed his mouth so slowly when she pulled up his lips clung to hers. The tugging sensation made the hair on her arms erect.

"You haven't been here one night that I was not here with you."

She pulled him closer to her. She kissed his face then she kissed his mouth. Heat from his body pushed inside her pores and made her feel alive.

"Has my fa-ther been here?"

"No. Dr. Davis from school called him, but he hasn't visited. He said he was scared to fly. He said--" She stopped. She couldn't hurt him, not now, not ever. That day a year ago she'd stood behind Dr. Davis' shoulder just so she could read the telephone numbers to Malcolm's house. As soon as she got back to her dorm she dialed the numbers and heard the voice she'd wondered about for more than a year.

"Hello," Malcolm growled when he answered the phone.

"You don't know me," she began. Her voice quavered. "My name is Brenda," she said slowly. "I'm your son's girlfriend." After Malcolm didn't speak, she continued with, "Your son's been in a serious accident. He's in the hospital. He's at the Mercer Medical Center in Trenton, New Jersey. He needs you."

"You're the one," Malcolm accused. "You took my boy from me," he almost wept. "I waited for months for my boy to come home. I looked for him when he first went missing," he continued, his voice taking on edginess.

"No," she said. "No. No. No." She shook her head. "I told Raymond I wanted to meet you—"

"He got up there to that school and I didn't hear from him," Malcolm whined. "He wouldn't even call except for that one time."

Her memory went back to that spring day, the time when she started to keep secrets from Raymond. She punched star sixty-nine on the telephone that day, but she'd hung up as soon as Malcolm picked up the line. She never told Raymond about that telephone call.

"You were with him," Malcolm blamed. "Getting his mind off what he was supposed to be doing when he got hurt. You took my boy from me then you hurt my boy."

"No," she tried.

"Women," Malcolm snarled.

Brenda's spine stiffened. Her mother's familiar ire found its way inside her thoughts. She became determined to defend herself; she didn't care how mean Malcolm got. "I asked Raymond to call you more times than you can know. Like I told you he's at Mercer Medical Center in Trenton, New Jersey. He needs you and if you hear from his mother, please tell her to come because he needs her too—"

Dial tone – it was the next sound she heard, the drone of a telephone connection gone dead. Since that day she'd called Malcolm a dozen times; not once did he pick up.

As she caressed the side of Raymond's face she wondered why he kept asking her about his mother and father, people who had not once come to the hospital, people who did not seem to care about him.

"How long have you-been-here?"

"Every day," she answered with effort. Her mouth was tight. She reminded herself that he was recently come out of a coma. She didn't want to be short with him. Yet, fatigue from the long hospital stays had worn upon her the way road eats up tire tread. She'd answered his questions before and yet here he was asking them again.

"Did we go to school to-ge-ther? Where do I know you from? How long have we known-each-other?"

"We met in school. We attend the University of Pemberton."

"Penn-syl-van-ia?"

"Yes," she nodded. "That's where we go to school. Remember earlier you were asking me about your grades and how you did in Science?"

"I did?"

"Yes. You did. You did good. I knew you would."

"What else do I do?"

She choked back tears.

"What else do-I-do?"

"You ran track."

"I do?"

"Yes."

"Do I like to run?"

"You were so happy when you ran." She waited until he met her glance then she smiled.

He returned her smile. After that he reached up and stroked her face. "I'm start-ing to re-mem-ber you."

"I love you." She rubbed her nose across his. "I love you so much. I love you. I love you. I love you."

"Were-you-at-the-beach with me?"

"No. I stayed on campus that day."

"You were here-the-most, weren't you?"

"Yes."

"I re-mem-ber your voice." He looked across the room at the chair she'd sat in while she waited for him to awaken. "You sat in-that-chair. Over there," he pointed.

She fell across his chest and squeezed his shoulders until his flesh pushed up between her fingers. Low murmurs crept from her lips while she wept softly. "I did."

Images came at him like moving pictures. "You were stand-ing out-side the ho-tel. You did-n't act like you saw me, but I saw you. Did you see me?"

"I didn't see you right away." When his brows rose, she raised the pitch in her voice and said, "I didn't." She chuckled. "I don't care what you think, I didn't see you. I know you think I did. I can tell from the look in your eyes. You've told me about seeing me on those steps so many times. You remember it because it was the first time you saw me, but it was not the first time I saw you."

His shoulders raised, tightened, then loosened and dropped when he laughed. He moved like his bones were made of rubber. She wondered if he could stand. To her his body looked too fluid, disjointed.

"Then when did you first-see-me?"

"I saw you when Anthony bumped into you outside the cafe, you know that small coffee shop at the edge of campus? I was coming out of a record shop."

"I don't re-mem-ber that."

"I can tell. You're stuck on the hotel steps."

"Did I see you then?"

"I don't think so."

"A man named An-tho-ne was in the car with me. At the beach. When we were com-ing back from the beach. I was driv-ing. Some-one else was there too. Some-one named Pa-trick and some-one named Doug."

"You and Patrick used to be dorm mates. Now you and your friends share an apartment in Bensalem."

"I live in Ben-sa-lem?"

"Yes. You work at the Neshaminy Mall."

"A mall."

"Where a lot of stores are."

"Do I still work?"

"The owner of the electronics store said they'd love to have you back." The taste of his mouth beckoned her and so she leaned forward and kissed him.

"Why do you keep kiss-ing me?"

"Because I love you. Because I'm in love with you."

He broke into a long, slow laugh. "Can I see what-I look-like? What do I look-like-to you?"

"You have gorgeous brown skin. You hair feels soft when I run my fingers through it. I like touching you. You have an infectious smile. You like to laugh." She paused and looked toward the door. "You're insightful and spiritual," she continued. "You value your relationship with our creator. You like spending time alone. You have deep, dark brown eyes that I sometimes think see everything. Your eyes are penetrating." She examined his face. "I feel like you really see me when you look at me. You're happy with a touch of melancholy, like a dash of salt sprinkled over a bowl of sugar, and it all shows on your face." She circled the outline of his face with the tips of her fingers. "I think your eyebrows are thick but not too thick. You're a muscular man. You have strong, full, rounded shoulders. But your greatest asset is on the inside." She kissed him again. "You are a beautiful, gorgeous man. You love people and it shows. That's what really makes you gorgeous. And you're forgiving. You just came out of a coma and not once have you asked whose fault it was that you're here. You don't care, because you don't blame. You take life as it comes. You go with the flow."

Larger chunks of his memory returned to him. "I don't re-mem-ber be-ing that way," he told her.

"How so?"

"I don't re-mem-ber lik-ing my father. Did he come see me? Has he-been-here?"

"Remember, Sweetheart. I told you. Your father hasn't been here. He knows you're here and

I'm sure he wants the best for you." As if she had insight into the workings of father-son relationships she added, "All fathers love their sons."

"Do I have chil-dren? Am I some-one's father?"

She laughed. "Not yet."

"Are you my-wife?"

"Not yet."

"I re-mem-ber o-ther voices. Who else came-here?"

"Coach Carter, Bishop Moore and two ministers from church. Your friends, Anthony, Patrick and Doug, were here every single week. Everyone always told me to say hello to you every day and to let you know how much they love you. I always relayed their messages to you. The hospital only allowed so many people to visit at a time." She gazed across the room. "Sitting here taught me how to relax." She looked up at the ceiling. "I'll never forget this experience."

"How long did-I-go-to-church?"

"Several months. You went faithfully." She sighed. "About two weeks before the accident, you stopped going as much as--"

"Why?"

She shrugged. "I think you wanted balance. I think you wanted to have more fun. You know. Enjoy life."

"Did you go to-the-church?"

"Yes. I go there sometimes on Sunday."

"Why did I stop go-ing as much as I-used-to?" His questions came like a boomerang. Regardless of how many times she answered them, he turned right around and asked them again, trying her patience, causing her to wonder if there was a motive behind his questions, something she couldn't see that would later hurt her.

"Like I said," she repeated, "I think you wanted balance in your life. You didn't want to go to church out of obligation or sacrifice, but because you really wanted to go."

The television hummed in the background. A Clorox commercial was on. In the commercial, a woman kneeled over a clothes basket and beamed while she inhaled the fresh lemon scent of her family's newly washed garments.

They lent the television none of their attention.

"Did I gain ba-lance?"

She shrugged.

"Did you go to-church-with me?"

"Yes."

"Always?"

"Not always."

"Why not?"

She moved back on the bed, away from him. The top of his head no longer rested in her lap. It barely scraped her knee now. "I didn't want to go to church as much as you did."

"Why?"

Irritation crept into her voice. "I just didn't."

"So why did-n't you go more?"

"Raymond, I just didn't." Her brows tightened, began to point. "Can we please change the subject?"

He slurred, "I don't know why you would-n't want to-go-to church more." He'd found something from the past to cling to, to clutch like a life preserver.

"Was I driv-ing back to church when I-had-the acci—"

"No. You decided not to go to church that weekend so you could go to the beach."

"Why did you let-me-do-that?"

"Raymond," she ragged, "You're not a little boy and I'm not your mother. We are responsible for ourselves. That was a choice you made all on your own."

"But-you-let-me-go."

She took in an exasperated breath. "I couldn't stop you."

His voice rose. The monitors at the side of his bed began to peak and zig zag. "If I had gone to church that week-end, I would-n't have had the acci-dent." He struggled to push off the bed. His shoulders quaked with the thrust of his effort, but they remained pinned to the bed. Yet, he continued to struggle to sit up. Despite recently awakening, he was alert enough to know that if he couldn't sit up, he had also lost the ability to run, and in that, he had lost his liberation. For years running had been his rescuer, his way to relax, to brush aside the hard things of life, to convince himself that he had a reason to carry on. Sensing it now gone, he sought someone to blame, to attack, and Brenda, her devotion giving her no other choice but to stay at his side, was the only person present. Aware of her love for the Creator, he saw no weapon greater than religion with which to use to attack her. "You did-n't want to go to church that week-end, did you?"

"I didn't go to the beach with you, Raymond."

"An-swer me."

"I did." She stroked his shoulders.

He jerked free of her grasp. "You did-n't want to go. I re-mem-ber you tell-ing me I was go-ing to church too much." Anger fueled him and he began to sit up. "I re-mem-ber you tell-ing me that too much re-li-gion would drive me cra-zy. If it had-n't been for you, I would have gone to church that Sunday. I did-n't want to lose you." His hands went up, covered his face. "I did-n't want to lose you the way I lost my mo-ther. I stopped go-ing to church for-you."

"So, you do know that you're mother didn't come to see you. You do know that I'm not your mother." She couldn't resist; his anger had pushed up fire in her.

"I for-got," he shouted. "Just like I for-got it was you who kept me a-way from church."

"Raymond." His religious fervor frightened her. To her he used religion to prove his worth, to convince himself that he was good. And, she worried, that he thought she'd prevented him from achieving this. Words she saw in his journal came back to her. The words haunted her afresh. She wanted to rescue him from his self-loathing, but when she looked into his dark, angry eyes, she saw that she could not.

"God knew where I-should-have-been. Why do-you think I-had that ac-ci-dent?" Exhaustion started to set in, but he kept shouting. "I had the ac- ci-dent be-cause I was at the wrong place at-the- wrong time." He took in a deep breath then released it. "I should have-been-at church, but I stayed a-way be-cause of you."

The door opened. Dr. Kelly rushed inside. He was accompanied by two nurses, neither whom Brenda knew. No one spoke to her, not even Dr. Kelly. This time she was merely a stranger in the room.

SECTION II (12 years later)

Chapter Twenty-Five

The project chief marched to the center of the limestone quarry. His stomach hung over his belt; it and his broad, blubbery hips swung while he walked. His brow was wet, dripping with perspiration. The heavy smell of stale sweat clung to his skin. A gale of dust was at his back. It pushed funk off his body and sent the pungent odor into the noses of nearby crew members. For miles, over hills and across barren plains, all he and the men could see was dry, brittle grass.

"Good job," the chief boomed. "Let's get out of here." He raised his hands as if he were a king addressing his subjects. As was customary, a grin lighted his face.

The heavy pickax fell out of Mark's hand. It went into the hard ground with a thud. He'd been swinging the ax, deep breaths and loud grunts emitting from his chest each time he pulled the ax forward, for more than six hours. Yet, the large block of granite he tore at with the ax wasn't halfway broken apart. He reached up and swiped his face clean of sweat with the back of his hand. "Ready to go?" he asked Raymond.

His spine aching to the point where he thought it would break, Raymond took his time standing upright. "Let's go."

They walked slowly back to their lockers. They moved in step, their long legs swinging out and striking the earth at the same time.

Upon entering the locker room, Raymond laughed then he tore off his t-shirt. As long as he'd lived on the island, he was yet to grow accustomed to the fierce heat. As soon as he reached his locker he looked up at the thermometer.

Mark followed his gaze. "Doesn't matter," he laughed. "Whatever that instrument tells you, know this. It's hot as a devil's paradise in here." After he tossed his head toward the exit, he added, "Even hotter outside."

With one hand pressed against his locker, Raymond looked at Mark and said, "Yea. And I know I keep checking, but I'm still shocked that we work all day in nothing but heat." He looked up at the thermostat for the fourth time. "Can you believe it's one hundred and fifteen degrees?" His eyes were wide. "And we're inside and it's the end of the day."

"I believe it," Mark laughed. "I've been living on Madagascar all my life." He tapped Raymond's forearm. "You. You're a newcomer."

"Yea."

Mark grabbed a flimsy paper bag; he'd carried it all week. Except for an overly ripe banana, the bag was empty. He already eaten the rice and beans his wife of twenty-four years packed for him early this morning, devouring the food as if he hadn't eaten in days.

"How long you been living here?" Mark asked, already knowing the answer. Hunger pains knifed his stomach and yet he wore a smile. His was an amiable disposition, had been since he was a little boy.

Raymond pulled on a clean t-shirt, one he hadn't sweated hard stains into. Then he turned and faced Mark. "Twelve years."

They hurried outdoors and walked alongside a group of other tired, hungry men. The men's footsteps quickened the closer they got to a small train station. At the station, a long splintered wood roof covered an equally splintered bench; the roof provided scant relief from the scorching sun.

Even so, the men hurried. They longed for the shelter.

"You like it here, don't you." Mark said more than asked.

Silence was Raymond's answer until Mark bumped his shoulder. "Don't you?"

"Yea. It's a good place."

He studied Raymond's face, it betrayed Raymond's words. But Mark kept quiet. He responded the same way each time Raymond told him that he stayed on the island because he liked the place. He was picking his mother up at the airport the day Raymond stepped off a Delta Airlines flight more than a decade ago.

"Wanna catch a card game after we get washed up?" he asked as soon as they boarded the train.

Raymond rested his head against the back of the seat cushion. He almost drifted off to sleep when the train pulled away from the station and started to bob and weave. "Wouldn't be right if we didn't," he said, his voice growing lazy like his eyes.

Twelve unaltered years, routine and habit forcing each new day to turn out like the one before, passed long and slowly for Raymond, like the train moving from station to station down the uneven tracks. Closer to the shore --as they had for more than a hundred years -- cool breezes lapped off the ocean that surrounded Madagascar, a luscious island off Africa's Southeastern coast. Plump, juicy watercress, pineapple and cantaloupe swung from vines. They were a succulent food that Raymond made part of his meals. The fruit reminded him of his first day on the island. He'd stepped inside a restaurant as soon as he left the airport, one lone suitcase in hand and ordered all three. Sweet liquid dripped down the sides of his mouth that day after he bit into the produce. Since then the island came to him like fresh breaths.

"Will you cook that tasty curry of yours, my good friend? It'll go well with the rest of dinner," Mark said as he elbowed Raymond.

"Sure thing," Raymond answered, his head bobbing more than nodding. He circled his mouth with his tongue. "If you'll make that onion gravy I like so much."

Mark laughed. He alternated between glancing out the window and watching trees, small houses, and passing livestock and turning and looking at

Raymond. "My wife makes that gravy." He laughed again. "All this time you thought it was me?"

Raymond's eyes closed. Had he been at home, he'd be snoring right now. "Yea," he said, his eyes slowly opening, "I thought you were the talented chef."

"Well. It's not me," Mark boomed. He rubbed his hands together. "My wife said she's gonna cook up a feast tonight. It's the end of the work week and as you know she always makes a delicious meal on Friday evening. We'll have good fun dining, playing cards and enjoying the cooling air."

Raymond tried to close his eyes, but he soon opened them again. He knew Mark wasn't going to stop cackling. It didn't matter how exhausted he was, Mark was not going to let him drift into sleep, and so he turned and looked out the window.

Land spread for miles. Over the years, Madagascar, with its farms, national parks, nature reserves, exotic animals and traditions, had unlocked a part of Raymond's unconscious. The first month he lived on the island, he walked around wide eyed. He couldn't stop staring at the colors. Even the sky looked bluer here than any place he'd been before.

He didn't think about Malcolm, not now. But he had the last letter Malcolm wrote him. He kept it folded and stuffed inside a compartment of his suitcase. It was dated November 15, 1987. It read:

Dear Raymond,

Things haven't been going so good with me of late. Never thought it would happen, but I guess all good men grow old in time. I've been to the doctor more in the last six months than I'd been in the last ten years. Doctor said I have high blood pressure and some kidney and liver problems. Tried to tell me it's from drinking, but we both know better than that. I've always taken good care of myself. And besides, if I drank too much I wouldn't be able to go to work every day. I haven't missed a day of work in thirty years. I'm just getting older. I passed out at work three weeks ago. Folks at the plant told me that it took me fifteen minutes to come around. They rushed me off to medical. That's how all of this got started.

Don't you go worrying about me though. I know you think I didn't notice, but I know how you can get to worrying sometimes. I know more about you than you think. I raised you. Remember that.

I'm taking vitamins and some strong prescription medicine now, so I'm on the mend. But I'm tired. I feel so tired sometimes, Son. But don't you go worrying about me. You've got that woman in your life now. And I know how that goes. She's probably taking up every free second of your time. I bet you think you love her. I bet you think you can trust her. Be careful, Son. Women have venom a serpent would be jealous to have.

Your old man's gonna go. Getting tired. Gonna lay down on this old sofa and rest.

Your dad,

Malcolm

The train weaved to a stop. Yards away from the station children played rugby. Raymond heard their bouncy voices as soon as Mark and he stepped off the platform. They weren't one hundred yards away from the station when five grinning kids ran up to Mark and circled him with their eager arms.

"Baba," the kids hollered.

"Come," Mark said. "Let's hurry and get home so we can eat and have lots of good fun." Their arms still entwined around each other, father and offspring walked teeter-totter the rest of the way to their house, a small wooden structure that had periwinkle growing sparsely at its front and sides.

Raymond quickened his pace. "You're gonna run an inch off those long legs of yours," he teased

Hasini, Mark's oldest daughter, before he hurried into his own home.

After he opened his front door, he turned and watched Hasini lower her head and blush.

That seemed Raymond's job, making kids in the neighborhood happy, especially the children who lived at the orphanage two miles away. He laughed as hard as the children did when he told them jokes. It reminded him of home and the few times he laughed, really laughed, when he was a little boy. Playing cards with Mark was another thing he did with such regularity it seemed a trade.

"Be back out in an hour," he called over his shoulder to Mark who stood on his own front porch.

"Of course," Mark nodded. The screen door banged closed at his back and he and the children headed straight for the kitchen where Mark's wife, Sharifa, kneaded a mound of seasoned dough.

Next door for Raymond there was bread on the shelf and tomatoes and goat cheese in the refrigerator. He slapped together a sandwich then poured himself a tall glass of pineapple juice. In the living room, the small radio atop the one bookshelf in his house pushed out music played by jazz guitarists.

When Raymond played the radio, noise from the equipment filled each of the house's three rooms, the living room, kitchen and bedroom. The bathroom, in a corner of the bedroom, was too small to count as a room. It was more like a closet.

Time passed lazily.

A little more than an hour after he arrived at home, a knock at the door stirred Raymond away from sleep. He sat up on the sofa and placed the empty saucer his sandwich once topped on the radio. "Who is it?" he asked as he stood up.

"Come on out," Mark's familiar voice beckoned. "I'm getting a card game going. Jafari and Din are here. They're going to play too."

Raymond smiled at the joy in his friend's voice. He was tired and he wanted to sleep, but he was up for a good game of cards. Moments later the saucer was in the kitchen sink and he was sitting on Mark and Sharifa's front porch.

"Ray," Jafari exclaimed with raised hands as soon as Raymond sat down. "So good to see you again."

"Yes," Raymond smiled. "Just as long as we're not at work."

"We worked hard this week," Din said. "It's time to have some fun."

Mark shuffled the cards and the men settled in for a long night of fun. The children busied themselves in the yard hunting sunset moths. Sharifa talked and laughed in the living room with, Malaika and Pamoja, Jafari and Din's wives. The clamor of their own voices, mixed with sound from a popular television show, blended and filled the house with noise.

Back out on the front porch conversation popped like corn while Raymond and his friends went on about the day just passed, how hard they labored at work and how easy the train ride was from the other side of the island to home. While they dealt and played cards, they hooted and drank pineapple juice, a tart liquid Raymond couldn't get enough of.

Din nibbled cassava peanuts. While he talked, his mouth swinging open widely, his company saw the food mesh together between his teeth. He juggled the peanuts in his hand and tossed them high into the air. Catching them again, he plopped them inside his mouth. It was like he was playing another game in addition to the card game. "How much longer do you think it'll be before we finish building the new school?"

Jafari snorted. "We just got started." He laid down a card. "We have a long ways to go. Gonna be weeks, months," he added while he looked up over his horn-rimmed glasses at Din who continued to chew the peanuts like he didn't have a care in the world.

"Where does all this building come from?" Mark asked while he moved cards around in his hand.

"Island's growing, my man," Raymond enthused. He laid a card down and shook his head. "Madagascar has changed so much since I got here."

"You've changed some yourself old pal," Jafari let on.

"Who?" Raymond asked, his head going back, his brows going up.

Jafari burst out laughing. "You," he shouted. He looked right at Raymond. He didn't bat an eyelash. "You," he repeated. "You've changed a bit. Not much," he quickly added. "Just a little."

Mark gave Jafari, Din and Raymond a wary look. As soon as Jafari met his glance, Mark squinted and let Jafari know to cool it.

"How so?" Raymond wanted to know. He glanced around the table at his three friends. Their planted expressions made it clear to him that they all thought he'd changed in the same way. He was the only one who was ignorant as to what they knew about him.

No one spoke.

"How have I changed?" Raymond demanded. Before he knew it, he was pushing the chair he sat in away from the small table they played cards on.

"Well," Jafari shot Mark a quick glance. When Mark's squint let go and opened, taking the crease out of his forehead, Jafari continued. "You're more relaxed." A smile crept across his face. He told himself not to reveal anything he felt certain Raymond didn't want to hear. "You've learned to soak up the island's sweetness." He gave a nod. "Made yourself right at home." He reached across the table and pulled a card off the top of the deck.

"And you taught us how to play cards," Din enthused.

"Yea, Pal," Jafari laughed. "Brought that right from the States with you. And for that," he looked from Din to Mark, "We are all glad."

"It's good to be here," Raymond said. "This place fits me to a "T." The pace of the island matches my mental and emotional clocks." He nodded several times, his head moving in quick motions. "I'm a simple man." He nodded again. "This is just what I need."

While the men talked and played cards, in the distance, sugarcane and cocoa swayed in the rising breezes that passed over the island. Come morning tropical food and other delicious fruits and vegetables would be stacked tall against wood booths at busy markets situated throughout the island, a true cultural mix of African, Indian and Arabian peoples.

The night went on, mixed with fun, happiness. Then hissing cock roaches made their way from the bushes across the way toward the porch. Their appearance worked like a signal. Wasn't long before the men beckoned their wives and headed for their respective homes.

Everyone left except Raymond and Mark. Their friendship had the deepest root, and besides, there was something Mark wanted to tell Raymond, something he didn't want to let linger until morning.

****

Two months after he landed at Madagascar, Raymond got the job at the construction firm. He'd worked there since his arrival twelve years ago. Working with splintered boards and jagged flint rock had caused his hands to grow calluses. Each weekend he put thick salve on the new cuts that formed during the ten to twelve hour days he put in welding steel and inspecting newly bolted doors and floor frames.

As if he'd only awakened from the coma to be dispatched to a new land, four months after he woke, he caught a flight from Philadelphia to Madagascar. Dreams he had convinced him that he belonged on the island. He didn't tell Malcolm that he was leaving the country. He didn't see a reason to.

Twelve years ago, he and his friends were hanging out at a local jazz club when he broke the news to them.

"All the way to Africa," Doug screamed. "Why do you have to go so far?"

"Yea, man," Anthony lamented. "How are we gonna keep in touch?"

Raymond's mouth swung open to reply. "We can—"

"Who do you know in Ma-da-gas-car?" Patrick wanted to know.

Raymond shrugged. Then he tossed his head back and laughed until spit flew out of his mouth, until his friends looked at him with quizzical stares. He laughed until the tension in his shoulders went into his stomach then moved out through his feet.

Doug ran his tongue across his teeth. He leaned back and stuck his thumbs through two belt loops in the jeans he wore. One of his brows was up, way up. "You know you don't have any business in Africa, doesn't matter where you go over there." He eyeballed Raymond. "You don't know anybody over there. You don't even know anyone who's been there before."

Raymond chuckled. "Not as far as I know, I don't."

Doug's hands balled into fists. He banged them against the table top. The glasses and plates shook. "Damn it, Ray," he screamed. "Why do you have to be the different one? Why do you always have to go so far out of the way when you do things?"

"And what's Brenda think about this?" Anthony asked.

Later that night Raymond did tell Brenda about his plans, his unchangeable plans, to move to Madagascar. It was the third time he'd told her. Like the other times, it was as if she went deaf. She asked so many questions that he ended up repeating himself and telling her about his trip again and again and again.

"Why so far, Ray-mond?" she gritted her teeth and asked. The pain of losing him felt sharp, deep enough to take her life. That night, she wanted to run from her dorm room, but she wanted answers too, and so she stayed. She stayed and rocked her foot. She stayed and nibbled her fingernails. She stayed and played with the ends of her hair. She stayed and she prayed. Hard.

"I told you about the dreams," he said.

"You're running away from me." Tears formed in her eyes and stayed there like drops of water stuck at the bottom of a narrow stemmed glass. They quaked each time she jabbed her finger at him. She was so angry even if Cynthia had been in the room, she wouldn't have lowered her voice.

"You're running from our love," she snapped. "You're so scared of love that you're going all the way across the planet to flee it."

"I had six dreams," he tried.

She waved her hand through the air, erasing the words he spoke.

"Dreams where I was on an island spreading the Gospel, helping other people." He looked right at her, hoping she would accept his excuse, knowing how much she loved the Lord.

"There's just one thing I bet you haven't thought of." She paused. "Not once."

He sat back on the chair at the edge of her study desk. "What's that?"

She took in a deep breath. When she released it, she stood from her bed and shouted. "Not once have you asked me to come with you. Not once have you told me how much you wanted me there with you." As she'd done when Cynthia told her about the dreams she had while they dined on salad at the sidewalk café more than a year ago, scenes that revealed Raymond and her apart, Brenda refused to listen. She stormed across the room and jerked the door open. She waited for him to exit.

He stood and walked out of the room.

When he reached the middle of the hall, she followed him. She shouted another question at his back. "How do you know those dreams mean that you should go to Madagascar?"

He turned as slowly as he'd stood from the chair. He walked back down the hall toward her. When he reached her he opened his arms like a cocoon and she hurried inside. They stood in the hallway weeping and holding and rocking each other for a long time.

"I'll change," she cried against his shoulder. "I'll go to more church events, and I'll never try to talk you out of staying home and not going to church again." She sniffled then asked, "What do you want me to be, Raymond?"

He pulled up on her back then he squeezed her warm, soft flesh between his fingers. He pressed the side of his head against hers then he kissed her. "I don't want you to change. You're perfect."

"Then why?" she cried. "I'll adjust to the island. I came here all the way from Tennessee and I did good by myself. I love people. I've studied other cultures. It won't take me hardly any time at all to blend in."

He massaged her back. "Brenda," he tried, his voice coming out low and soft, hushed up, almost in a whisper.

Her tears picked up. The sound of her crying echoed down the hall. "You're leaving me," she wept. You're not going to something. You're leaving me because you know for sure that I love you, and you can't stand it. It scares you too much. Damn," she moaned. "I never saw it." She stepped back, far enough away from him to see his face. "You're terrified of love. You tell yourself that you're flying to Madagascar to spread love, when love is the very thing you're terrified of. Sweetheart," she said. "I'm not going to hurt you. I'm not your father," she said softly. "I'm not your mother."

She worked hard to make him see how much she loved him. She knew deep in her gut that the dreams he had about spreading the gospel of Yahweh's eternal love on the island were fueled by his fear of love. She knew that he had lived with this fear for so long that he was blind to it.

She had often wondered at his need for solitude. It concerned her since before she went to Tennessee and visited with Victoria fourteen years ago. Her sister had tried to tell her that his need for solitude and seriousness was nothing to dismiss, but she didn't listen. On top of that, she'd heard Raymond create reasons for why he couldn't join Anthony, Patrick and Doug at social events. She didn't see it then but she saw it now. Each denial had signaled "stay back – don't get too close to me".

Chapter Twenty-Six

When Raymond first arrived on the island, Brenda wrote him every day, ending each letter with, *"I love you, Raymond. Please come home soon."* In return, he wrote her two to three times a day, but mailed fewer than half of those letters. He thought about her incessantly, but he was embarrassed for her to know. He wanted to appear strong, not vulnerable. He kept the letters bundled together with a rubber band in a box beneath his bed. On days he starved for her affection, her presence, he pulled the letters out and either re-read them or wrote her another one. It worked for awhile; then six months went by and Brenda's letters to him slowed.

The one time he let go of his determination to not appear vulnerable and pressed her about why she stopped writing him every day, she told him, "I'd rather talk on the phone. You feel closer to me that way."

She was the reason he bought a cordless telephone rather than to keep crossing the yard and asking Mark and Shafari if he could use their telephone while he talked with Brenda. They talked for hours the next four months. Then the bills came and their phone calls dwindled to half an hour once a week.

Brenda initiated the majority of their telephone calls. Raymond told himself not to get into the habit of dialing her up. More often than not emotion came over him when their conversations ended and he put his telephone back in its battery charger.

It was then that he wept. He couldn't imagine that she missed him as passionately as he did her. It seemed impossible to him that any other human could love someone as deeply as he loved her. Yet, he was afraid of her and how she made him feel, overcome with love. Leaving her, although emotionally wrenching, created a haven for him, a space where he could feel safe from the possibility that she would, after he had loved her for years, leave him. Although he'd been honest with her about dreaming of the island, he knew, despite the dreams, he could have stayed in the States with her. He prayed that she'd believed his reasons for coming to the island, would somehow learn to let him go, even as he longed for her. He'd seen what his mother leaving his father had done to him. Despite Brenda's loyalties, especially while he had laid in a coma, he had no guarantee, no assurance that she would never tire of him, never encounter another man who she'd rather love instead of him. For Raymond, the risks of staying were too high. And yet, the one person he thought about every day, praying blessings upon her, begging for her forgiveness, was Brenda.

Many nights while he lay on his bed, a small cot pushed against the corner of his plain bedroom, he stared up at the ceiling. Scenes from the night years ago when Brenda and he had wrapped their bodies together like strands of thick, melting chocolate shimmied and danced across the ceiling.

Brenda's last phone call to him came a year into his stay on the island. That day, after he ended his telephone call with her and went outdoors, he spent the next two hours talking with Mark about missionary work.

Much had changed on the island since then. After all, that night was more than a decade old. A dozen new small schools had gone up. There wasn't a single village without a clean water well. In addition, international trade laws eased and Madagascar began to ship more of its products overseas.

Raymond still kept Malcolm's letter folded in a flap in his suitcase and he was still in love with Brenda.

****

The card game over and Din, Jafari and their wives gone home, Mark sat on Raymond's front porch. More dirt than grass filled the yard, much of it blowing its gritty way onto the porch which Raymond rarely swept.

A tall, wiry man whose family root went as deeply into Madagascar as the roots of the bamboo trees that populated the island, Mark listened to Raymond with curiosity. He was twenty years Raymond's senior. His body had held up well over the years. His was a thick, deep laugh that went several yards out from wherever he was when he chortled.

"You know how many times we've played checkers," Mark said. He paused, looked down at the board then he looked up at Raymond again. "I don't have a chess game. If I did, we could play chess." His gaze lowered to the board again. "I think it's more of a thinking game. What do you say?"

"I think I don't want to think for awhile," Raymond answered. He scooted his backside into the small folding chair at the table's far right edge, across from Mark.

"You," Mark shouted. "You're saying that?" His smile was friendly, safe. "You," he teased, "The great thinker?"

Raymond laughed then he picked up a handful of black checkers and juggled them. "Me?"

"Well, it is fitting," Mark said. He no longer wore a smile. In its place was a somber expression. "I noticed it during the card game."

The checkers stilled in Raymond's hand. "Noticed what?"

"You look tired, Friend. And," he added. "Put your checkers on the board so we can get started."

One by one, Raymond placed the checkers across the board. "Who's going first? You or me?"

"Your move," Mark nodded.

"I am a little tired," Raymond disclosed.

Mark sat back in the folding chair wide eyed, stunned.

Raymond penned his attention to the checker board.

"You're admitting that you're not a super hero." Mark released a thunderous laugh. "That's a first for you." He watched Raymond jump one of his red checkers and move it off the board. "Talk with your lady friend lately?" He smiled and gave a quick nod. "That always helps."

Raymond stared at the checker board.

"Don't want to look me in the eye?" Mark chuckled.

After shrugging, Raymond answered, "Concentrating on the game, Man. I ain't hardly going to let you beat me tonight. I can get you in cards, but you've beat me nearly every checkers game we've played since we started playing."

Mark studied the board then he moved a red checker forward. "I thought maybe you didn't want me to know what you were thinking." He laughed. "You know about this uncanny ability I have to pick up what another person's thinking when they look me right in the eyes. And you're easy," he added after Raymond remained silent.

"Yea. I know," Raymond responded dryly. His mouth was twisted, tilted way up on one end, like his teeth had sunk into a sour lemon. "You can read me like an open book." He twisted his mouth even more. "I'm that transparent. You said you've known all about me since the day we met."

"I wouldn't dare say I know all about you. I was born with an uncanny ability to know what people are thinking. We're too layered for me to know all about you or anyone else."

"Remember when we first met? I was getting off the plane at the airport. You were picking your mother up."

"Yep."

Raymond moved a checker forward and jumped two of Mark's checkers. "I knew we were going to be friends right from the start."

"Ray-mond," Mark said. He enunciated Raymond's name with slow precision.

"What?" Raymond was yet to look up from the checker board.

"You don't have to get that wrapped up in the game. We have all night to play this game. Have some fun. There's no hurry," he said right before he added, "Why won't you at least look up?" He studied Raymond's posture, his tight shoulders, his rounded back, a back that had become almost curved at the top because Raymond often walked with his head bowed and his gaze pointed toward the ground – then he laughed. "Your face and your back give you away, Man."

"What?"

Mark waved his hand. "Aw. Never mind." He leaned forward and moved a red checker two spaces forward.

Raymond shrugged. He kept his head down. "I'm studying the game. And I heard you," he laughed, "About not getting so into the game." He laughed again. "I know what you're trying to do. You want to shift my focus so you can start jumping my checkers and do what you always do."

"What's that?" Mark teased.

"Beat me like a rented government mine mule."

They enjoyed a spurt of laughter.

"Ever hear from your lady frie—"

Raymond's hand went up, like a wall, to keep the question from penetrating. "We aren't keeping in touch anymore." He looked up. "She wasn't who I thought she was. She wanted me to be someone who I'm not, someone who I'm not willing to be."

The words worked, for awhile. Raymond had tried them out so many times, he believed them.

"Sure she wasn't trying to surface another part of you?"

"Do you know her?"

Mark smiled. "I haven't been so fortunate."

Raymond rolled his eyes.

"You devote more energy to this woman than to anyone else. It doesn't matter if you're happy when you speak about her the way you did when you first arrived here. It doesn't matter if you're angry when you speak of her. You focus more of your energy on this woman than on anyone else." He tilted his head. "Gotta be a reason for that."

Silence.

Then Raymond released a thick breath. "I was in a bad accident before I came here. She – Brenda – was with me at the hospital." He released another breath. "I appreciate all that she did. We loved each other. I thought we were meant to be together. I thought we would marry, raise a family and enjoy our lives together." He shook his head after he looked up and met his friend's gaze. "I really did."

Mark held his tongue.

A moth landed on Raymond's shoulder. Rather than shoo the insect away, Raymond leaned back in the chair and put distance between himself and the checker board.

"I do appreciate her. I don't know if I would have come out of that coma had she not been there." He shook his head and looked across the yard at nothing in particular. Even as he spoke he could see Brenda's braids taking on a reddish hue as temperatures rose back in the States.

It was summer in America. Daffodils, tulips and lilacs were in full bloom. Tennessee and its rolling hills were alive with wildlife, NHRA races at Bristol Thunder Valley and children playing. He knew Brenda was in those hills. She loved the outdoors.

Even now on the other side of the world, he could see her ascending a narrow trail at the lower elevations of the Smoky Mountains. She might be riding a horse; she might be on foot. The ends of her hair would blow in the wind. Her heart would get lighter the further she went into the heart of nature. And, he knew, as a stab of emotion went against his heart, more than likely while she traveled through the mountains she thought of him. Truthfully and as much as he didn't want to admit it, he hoped she thought of him just now. The same way she had sat at his bedside while he was in the coma, and as little as he expected her to after twelve years apart, he hoped that she continued to hold to him with thoughts of love. He refused to declare it, even to himself, but he longed for her. His soul ached for her, and yet, he would not call, write or visit. In no wise was he willing to admit how connected to her he was.

"She was there everyday," he told Mark flatly. He watched a bird flutter its wings then open its feathers and soar across the night sky. "She was the only person who came to see me everyday. After I woke from the coma the hospital staff told me that she spent each night right by my bedside."

Mark wanted to leap from his chair and shake Raymond. He wanted to demand that he stop this foolishness of running away from the woman he loved, but he remained seated.

"My father didn't visit once."

His voice trailed off; it sounded like it was coming from a man several yards away. He thought about the letter he kept in his suitcase. He wondered at his father's health, but only for a second.

"I didn't expect him to visit." He stared at the checker board then he quickly looked up. "I already told you that my father and I don't have the best relationship. My mother walked out when I was two years old, but you already know that too." He shrugged. "There's not much new to tell."

"Why did you come this far to get away from her? You know you love her."

"Yes," Raymond admitted with a deliberate nod. "I love her. I never said I didn't." He sighed. "But I have to sacrifice my feelings and what I want for God. It's not the easiest—"

"Why?"

Raymond's brows widened.

"Why do you have to sacrifice for God? Why?" Mark paused. "Are you sure you're not sacrificing to earn your biological father's love?" Before Raymond could interject a word to defend his beliefs, Mark added, "You know often the people we spend the rest of our lives striving to please are our parents."

He sighed. "We all make mistakes, Ray, even our parents. If we don't get our parents' love and acceptance right from the start, and every day, we can spend the rest of our days trying to gain their approval through countless relationships. Relationships with colleagues at work. Relationships with lovers. Relationships with our children. Relationships with our neighbors. Our relationship with our Source. The relationship we have with ourselves." He sighed. "When we're children we like to think that our parents are infallible, but they aren't." He chuckled. "Our parents had parents too, people who made mistakes with them. Me, I think the best way to right the equation is to forgive and to love." He shook his head. "I don't think there's any other way. Our resistance to doing those two simple things has created a world of religion. And now we say we have to do everything except forgive and love, but that's what we can do to bridge the gap of error." He smiled. "What do you think, my friend?"

Raymond studied the game board. He jumped two of Mark's red checkers. After twelve years, it was yet to occur to him that Mark cared little over whether he won or lost the game. He still hadn't realized that Mark played the game as a way to spend time with him, as a way to deepen their friendship.

"Ray?"

"What?"

Mark laughed. "Oh. So you did hear me. When's the last time you spoke with your lady friend?" He peered at Raymond. "You say her name's Brenda, eh?"

"You're the clever one," Raymond said with a raised finger that he wagged. "I like your style, Mark. You can be smooth when you want to be."

They met each other's glance and grinned.

"And to answer your question, I already told you. I haven't talked with Brenda in over eleven years."

"It's been that long? You better pick up the phone and call her." He backed away from the game board. "I'll leave now if you want me to so you can call her. We can always catch up with the game some other time. That is," he pried, "Unless you plan on flying back to the States sometime soon."

Raymond's brow tightened. He spoke in a loud voice. "I told you Brenda's not the right woman for me. Yes," he conceded. "She was there for me when I was at the hospital, but I don't know what she wanted. I don't know why she came there every day. I'm not inside her head. We always have a motive when we do things. You know that." He searched Mark's face for agreement; there was none. "You told me that more than once yourself. Plus," he added, tossing his hand up. "She might have moved. I mean, it's been eleven years since we spoke. She could be married now for all I know," he said, the volume in his voice lowering.

"Yes. She might have married," Mark shrugged. "But you don't know that for sure, and," he added, "are you sure you're not being blind, my friend? I think childhood and early adult pains you went through have blinded you to the love your lady friend and you share, to the love perhaps you will only share or experience with her." He examined Raymond curiously. "What if the Creator brought you two together? Come on, Man," he pleaded. "Let the scales fall away from your eyes. You've been hurt, but it's time to let go and move on. The love of your life is right there in front of you. You don't even have to wonder who she is. You know who she is." His shoulders arched. "Do you know how many men are waiting for that, to know who their woman is?" He opened his hands. "It'll hurt like mad if you fly back to the States. Besides my wife, you're my best friend. I don't want to see you go, but more than having you here as my good friend, I want to see you go home to the woman you love."

"You don't get it," Raymond begged. "Brenda is loving. I'm not disputing that. I thanked her I don't know how many times for every second she sat at that hospital with me."

"Who took care of you when you came out of the coma? Who let you stay with them? I'm sure you had to learn to use your limbs again, feed yourself, talk and so on."

An icy glare filled Raymond's eyes. "Brenda."

"Why does it make you so angry that—"

"I'm not angry."

"That she loves you. And I'm not going to let you cut me off and run away with your quick interruptions. No," he said with a jerk of his head. "No more. You know what you're doing is foolish."

"She tried to turn me away from the Lord."

"How so?"

"She wanted to spend more time with me, doing things out in the world."

"That's bad?"

"It's—"

"Excuse me for interrupting, but I gotta ask before I forget. Is Brenda's desire to be with you foreign to you? Kinda like shoes that feel way too big, but only because you have yet to realize how big you really are?"

"Don't get philosophical with me."

Mark laughed. "You. You? You're telling someone not to get philosophical? You're the king of being philosophical. Are you kidding?"

"Okay. You're right. That is one of my MOs. But I don't want to keep revisiting my relationship with Brenda. It hurt me a lot to let her go, but it was something I had to do."

"Why?"

"Why do you insist upon discussing this?"

"Because you're my friend. Because I care about you."

"I guess I should believe you. You never met her, so you wouldn't have any other reason to want to see us together."

"Glad to hear you say that. Maybe you're no longer thinking someone's out to get you."

Raymond tried to smile, but Mark's words struck a sore spot; they created an unease that prevented him from showing gladness. "I'm not that suspicious," he said. "I do a lot of things on the fly. I go with the flow a lot of times."

"We were talking about Brenda."

"Nothing's going to change. She's who she is and I'm who I am."

"That's for sure."

"Okay," Raymond nodded. "Sometimes I miss her. But I don't miss her all of the time," he lied. "She did a lot for me. Don't think for a minute that I don't value her."

He decided to be blunt. He was tired of being labeled 'emotionally distant'. He wasn't. He was giving. As a volunteer, he helped build houses, schools and clean water wells in town. He gave to charity. He prayed for others. He didn't attack folks with gossip or slander. He was thoughtful and proved it each time he spoke.

Sure. He was quiet and he kept to himself. But when he connected with others, he connected through a pipeline of love. Yet, for some reason people didn't see him that way. He heard whispers that he was aloof. He didn't agree with the judgment but he didn't attack. He was a man of peace. Rather than to speak up, he swallowed the painful accusations.

Over the years he had become expert at repressing his emotions. It was easy. He kept to himself so often throughout his childhood that he knew how to masquerade anger, fear and hurt, emotions he labeled bad, emotions he forced behind a gentle smile. It worked like a charm. People might consider him to be aloof, but no one except his father knew his smile was, at times, a blanket that concealed his rage and his desire to flee.

"I sent Brenda I don't know how many thank you cards. I thanked her for coming to the hospital and staying with me each time we talked on the phone. I thanked her every time I wrote her a letter. I thanked her as soon as I woke up from the coma. I thanked her every single day while I was still living in the states. But you see," he went on. "I never told you this before."

He locked gazes with Mark. "She wanted me to stop going to church," he tried, again blaming Brenda for his involvement in the accident. "If I had gone to church the way I used to, I wouldn't have gone to the beach that day."

Mark shook his head. "Stop it with all this religious defensiveness. I've known you for twelve years. Sure. You keep to religious traditions, but not to the point of allowing your religious beliefs to control your life." He scowled and shook his head again. "You're using religion as an excuse. It's your new set of legs now." He blew out a breath of air. "I hope you didn't make Brenda feel that she was the reason you got hurt. I hope you didn't tell her she took you away from the church and that's why you were in an automobile accident." Pursing his lips he added, "I hope not, because you don't believe that," he said. "Religion was just like a straw, right there, ready for you to pick up and try to hurt Brenda with so she'd back away from you." He laughed dryly. "It must have scared you something awful when you woke up from that coma and found out she was still there, loving you. Probably would have been easier for you if she had left."

Raymond leaned forward in the chair, trying to get Mark to see his point of view. "I wouldn't have had the accident if I hadn't listened to her asking me not to go to church like I used to. I wouldn't have gotten hurt. I would never have gone into a coma, and I'm not blaming her," he added. "It's the truth. I'm telling you the truth."

Seconds later, Raymond hated the thought filling his head. He'd yearned to release it into a string of acidic words, not an ounce of regret or gentleness among them, since the week after he awakened from the coma.

He wanted to be heard.

"I know this sounds horrible, but I'm going to say it anyway. I've wanted to scream this at the top of my lungs for the longest time. I am tired of people making me feel like I owe Brenda something. I didn't ask her to come to the hospital. I didn't even know she was there."

Mark fell back in his chair so hard the front legs bounced up off the ground.

"Oh, don't look so shocked," he told Mark with a wave of his hand. "And," he added, his voice calmer, "I'm sure her presence had something to do with my waking when I did." He shrugged. "I guess. I don't know, but the hospital staff told me it helps when a patient has someone who loves them nearby often, and Brenda was that person." He took in a deep breath then he released it. "But she came to the hospital on her own. I didn't tell her to come. I don't owe her anything. It's bad enough," he went on, "To feel like you owe your parent for not walking off and leaving you. I've carried that weight for I don't know how long. I don't want to carry any more weight." He frowned.

"You loved her long before that accident. Sure. You've had a few relationships while you've been here on the island, but none of them satisfied you fully," he said, shaking his head. He didn't mince words. "How many more chances, how much more time, do you think you'll have to love Brenda on this earth?" He leaned across the game board. "That's what I'm trying to get you to see. You said you loved her from the first time you saw her. You told me that you always felt safe with her. She didn't abandon or mistreat you. She didn't put you down. Don't you think loving her was a good thing?"

He didn't wait for Raymond to answer. "She took you down a new path with the way she loved you. She was the person you had courage to love in return. Do you know how freeing love is, Man? Do you know the gift this woman gave you? She opened you up to receive love, the greatest gift. Are you going to sit over there like that doesn't mean squat to you? A woman loved you like no one else had before and you're going to write that off?" He pounded the table. "When are you going to stop trying to live with your head and start living and loving with your heart?" He shook his head. "You're missing the purpose for being here. This is not about sacrifice, Ray. It's about love. Don't let this chance slip by."

Chapter Twenty-Seven

It was October 28, 2000. Raymond had been in the United States for less than two hours, flying into Tennessee from Madagascar, hoping to find Brenda. The only address he had for her took him to Virginia's former home. A neighbor had been trimming the hedges to her front lawn when Raymond pulled in front of the house, the place from which Brenda had defended her love for Raymond to her older sister.

"Who're you looking for?" the woman asked, watching Raymond crane his neck, trying to see through the house's front windows.

"Virginia Wilson," he said, turning and walking down the house's front steps.

The woman lowered the clippers to her side. "She don't live there anymore." She told him, "She moved awhile ago." She gazed across the yard at nothing in particular. "About eleven years ago I'd say." A smile lighted across the woman's face. "She got married to that Scott Lowry. He's doing all right for himself folks say. Yep," she continued, again raising the clippers and commencing to trim her hedges, "She's Mrs. Virginia Lowry now."

"Do you know where they live?"

Sighing the woman said, "That's not my business to tell."

"I'm a good friend of her sister, Brenda's."

The woman gave him a cautious glance.

"We went to school together in Philadelphia, the University of Pemberton."

"Well, the woman said," twisting her mouth. "Everybody knows where Scott Lowry lives anyway. That ain't been no secret for years." Placing the clippers on the ground and moving toward her front steps, she said, "Give me a minute."

When she exited her home and returned to the yard she handed Raymond a sheet of paper. "It's off Alcoa Highway," she told him. "You'll find it. It's not too far from the airport."

"Thank you," Raymond nodded. "Thank you," he repeated, stepping off the lawn and closer to his rental car, a black and silver Toyota Celica.

Less than half an hour later he sat in the Toyota staring up at the expansive, three story house. He drove slowly up the long side driveway, parked and exited the car. As soon as he stepped on the front porch he heard dogs barking inside the house. He stepped back and wondered if guard dogs were also outside the house, if he should have waited in the car and honked the horn.

"May I help you?" a doorman opened the front door and asked.

"Hi," Raymond said, extending his hand. "My name is Raymond Clarke. I was looking to speak with a Mrs. Virginia Lowry."

"Just a moment, please," the doorman said, turning away from Raymond and walking toward the house's winding staircase. "Mrs. Lowry," he called up the stairs.

"Who is it?" Virginia asked, descending the staircase and nearing the door. Before the doorman answered her, she was at the door. "Hello," Virginia said. "May I help you?"

Raymond extended his hand again. "My name is Raymond Clarke. Your sister and I were very close back in college."

"So, we finally meet," Virginia smiled, stepping onto the front porch. "It's nice to meet you," she said, shaking Raymond's hand. "Brenda always had the kindest things to say about you. She thought the world of you."

Raymond smiled nervously, hoping that time had not robbed him of a second chance at love, expecting the worse. "I appreciate you telling me that," he nodded. "The feeling was mutual."

"Are you living in Tennessee now?"

"No," Raymond answered, shaking his head. "But," he added as he turned and glanced over his shoulder, "It sure looks like a beautiful place."

"It is," Virginia assured him. "This is home for us."

His gaze roved, his mind searching for something to say. "So, Brenda's doing good?" he begged more than asked.

"She lives about ten minutes from here."

"Oh," Raymond responded, excitement filling his voice.

Virginia searched his face. She knew he loved her sister in a way perhaps no other man would, but she also knew she couldn't reveal Brenda's whereabouts. She couldn't risk Raymond and Brenda meeting, stirring familiar passions. The timing was all wrong. "I know you're not going to want to hear this," she stepped forward and told Raymond, raising her hands as if preparing to brace his fall." She searched his face again. "Brenda's married. She has a son."

"Oh," Raymond responded, his breath catching in his throat, his mind facing the changes that time had brought. "Well," he tried, eager to distance himself from Brenda's sister. "If you see her, tell her I said—" He shook his head. "No. Don't tell her anything. I-I-I was out of the country," he stammered. "I just ah—I just thought I'd try to stop by and say hello."

"Okay," Virginia nodded, looking out over the road that stretched out in front of Scott and her house, expecting Scott to arrive home soon. "I understand."

"I'm gonna go now," he said, backing off the porch. "It was a pleasure meeting you." Remembering his manners, he approached her and gave her a gentle hug. "Thanks for your time." He hurried toward his car, gulping in air, fighting back tears.

He backed his car down the driveway, waving to Virginia out the window. As soon as he reached the main road, he pressed the accelerator with force, his thoughts racing. He almost cursed Mark for encouraging him to return to the States, for forcing him to relive the stinging pain of loss. By the time he reached Alcoa Highway, tears were streaming down his face and he had started to pound the steering wheel, angry with himself for leaving Brenda twelve years ago, for sending her into the arms of another man.

He wasn't on Alcoa Highway ten minutes when he slowed to a red light, a BMW pulling up to the light, across from him. When the light turned green and the two cars passed one another, Raymond almost turned around, something about the BMW's passenger, her mocha skin and shoulder length curls, beckoning him. The BMW not fifty yards down the highway, Raymond pulled onto the highway's shoulder, turned and looked back. In the distance, he saw a little boy in the BMW's backseat facing the rear window, waving to other drivers and passengers on the highway, an effort at play, something Raymond had done when he was a kid traveling somewhere with Malcolm, trying to pass the time while he waited for them to reach their destination.

Raymond sat on the side of the highway for several minutes, struggling not to turn around and chase after the BMW, trying to convince himself that as it had happened absent forethought or conscious plan, Brenda and his paths had crossed serendipitously again. Finally, he put the car in 'drive' and pulled back onto the highway. He headed North toward Ohio, recalling the words Virginia had spoken, coaching himself to move on.

****

It was mid-evening on Thursday, October 28, 2000, when Raymond reached Dayton, having driven the three hundred plus miles from Tennessee to Ohio non-stop. Soiled pieces of crumpled newspaper, old baseball magazines, dirty socks and empty prescription pill bottles littered the living room floor. Cock roaches scurried across the room, careful to remain mostly beneath the newspaper and magazines. A musty odor hung in the air. It almost turned Raymond's stomach when he entered the room. Although fifteen years had passed since he'd been inside the house at 527 Green Street he knew where everything was. The living room sofa, chairs, television and the kitchen table were exactly where they were the day he walked out of the house fifteen years ago and caught a cab to the downtown Greyhound bus terminal.

Stale lunch meat, empty juice bottles and balled up napkins were spread across the kitchen table. Raymond's gaze swept back and forth across the room. Outside it was raining. From where he stood in the kitchen he could hear raindrops landing against the roof and the sides of the house.

Curious as to his father's whereabouts, he headed toward the stairs. The stairs creaked beneath his weight. When he reached the top, he stopped. The house was so quiet he heard the furnace humming in the basement. When he was a boy he used to be afraid of the big gray furnace pushed into a corner of the basement. It looked and sounded like a monster to him, especially when it clanged and shook. Malcolm sent him to the basement for punishment for the first time when he was three years old. A saucer had cracked when it slid to the floor after Raymond went to his toes and reached way up to the top of the counter.

There were sugar cookies on the saucer and Raymond wanted them. "I'm sorry," three-year-old Raymond pleaded with tears in his eyes. It was no use.

"Go to the basement," Malcolm ordered with a shove to Raymond's back. The shove forced Raymond down the first set of steps leading into the basement. He cried and begged his way down the remaining steps. "Go stand behind the furnace," Malcolm told him. "And don't come out until I come and get you."

Two hours later, Raymond was asleep on the floor clumped in the fetal position when Malcolm clonked his way down the stairs to get him. "Aw, sleep," he growled. Then he turned and walked back up the stairs. He left Raymond asleep on the hard floor for another three hours before he clonked his way back down the stairs, kicked Raymond awake with the tip of his work boots and told him to, "Get up and come eat dinner."

Thunder cracked and Raymond jumped. After he collected himself, he went slowly down the upstairs hallway. The first room he entered was Malcolm's. As usual, the curtains were drawn. They were the same heavy, drab curtains that were hanging at the windows on the day he left home more than a decade ago. Jeans and sweatshirts were tossed across the arm of the one chair in the room. A load of clean week old laundry was spread across the king size bed. The carpet was worn, parts of it so bare the wood subflooring showed through. Thick dust coated the bedroom furniture. The room was so dirty Raymond was scared to run his hand across the top of the dresser.
He looked around the room. It seemed to have everything in it except his father. He started to leave but turned back at the edge of the door. Without thinking about it, he walked to the chair and picked up Malcolm's jeans and sweatshirts. Then he hung the clothes up in the closet. He thought about folding the laundry on the bed, but after he turned, scanned the room again and saw that it was in absolute disarray, he decided to leave the clothes strewn across the bed.
Out in the hallway again he noticed the plants on the long bureau. He took note of the fact that half the plants were so dead they stank. He tossed the dead plants out and watered the plants that had managed to survive. He emptied the bathroom garbage, put a new liner in the basket and carried the full bag down the steps.
Halfway down the stairs he heard a noise. It came from the attic.
The climb to the attic was arduous. The wood steps were fragile; Raymond feared that they would give way. After he reached the top of the attic steps, he opened the overhead door, craned his neck and

looked across the floor. Six raccoons toyed with an empty box in the center of the floor. The animals didn't run or move when they saw him. After he closed the attic door Raymond made a note to call the local Animal Control Office first thing in the morning. "They probably think they're family, as good as cousins," he moaned while he closed the overhead door and climbed back down the attic steps. Back in the hallway, he hurried past the two guest bedrooms. Both rooms were neat. He knew that they hadn't been touched or slept in for years.

After he passed Malcolm's room, he made his way back down the living room stairs. Re-entering the kitchen, he wondered where his father was. The longer he stayed in the house the sharper pangs of fear stabbed at his back. "Malc—" he called out.

He stopped. It had been too long since he had seen his father, so he edited himself and shouted, "Dad?"

He ran inside his old bedroom. His heart pounded in his throat. The room was empty. All of his dresser drawers had been yanked open. His mattress was tossed on its side, exposing the silver box springs.

He hurried back into the living room, snatched the front door open and peered outside. Soon he was standing on the front porch.

Much of the street was unchanged. Ms. Nipson peeked out of her living room drapes at him. He saw Stanley's Pontiac parked in the driveway next door. He almost laughed. "Two of the supposedly coolest and toughest guys in town never, not once, struck out on their own." He mused. "The only time they left home was when they got in trouble and went to prison." It amazed him that he used to be so scared of Stanley and Joey that he did whatever they told him to do without so much as a second thought.

He thought about walking next door and knocking on Stanley's father's door and asking if he'd seen Malcolm, but he decided against it. Instead, he went inside and sat on the sofa. He tried to think of where his father could be. He worried that he might have taken ill and fainted while out grocery shopping. A second later he sprang from the sofa and went back out on the front porch. He was startled to see Malcolm's old trusty Mustang in the side driveway. The next thing he knew he was running up the kitchen stairs again.

In his father's room on the side of the bed closest to the wall he saw what he feared. The thinning body of an aging man was slumped on the floor and buried beneath a mound of blankets.

"Dad," Raymond tried. He shook Malcolm for several long seconds without result. He pulled back the blankets, rolled Malcolm onto his back and gasped.

Chapter Twenty-Eight

Malcolm sat up with effort, as if he was hoisting a three hundred pound man onto his shoulders rather than simply pulling his torso up off the carpet. When his lips parted, the white cottony substance filling his mouth stretched across his teeth. He stared at Raymond for a long time. "So —" he said. His hands went toward his own face then they went out toward Raymond. They landed gently against the sides of Raymond's cheeks. "Son," he cried. "Son."

"I've been waiting for you." His breath was funky, akin to the scent of thick, curdled milk. Crust was caked at the corners of his eyes. The cottony saliva circled his mouth and dribbled down his chin. He hadn't showered or washed in two weeks, but he didn't seem to notice. The one thing that was missing was the familiar scent of alcohol on his breath.

Despite the fact that he didn't want to bring shame to his father, Raymond stepped back. Each time Malcolm opened his mouth, stank whisked, strong and offensive, up Raymond's nose. It took a great amount of effort for Raymond not to cover his face with his hand.

"Where have you been, Son?" Malcolm asked while he struggled to gain his footing. He was on his knees, looking up at Raymond who loomed, like a giant, over him.

Raymond tried to answer, but words failed him. Yesteryear flooded his thoughts. He remembered the afternoon Malcolm ordered him into the basement to stand behind the furnace. He recalled the times Malcolm forced him inside the living room closet then locked the door and kept him there for hours at a time. He remembered the beatings that drew blood. But he couldn't recall a time that he spoke with his father in the middle of the day when liquor wasn't thick on his breath.

"I called that school," Malcolm said. He stretched forth his hand. Raymond grabbed it, and hoisted his father off the floor. "I spoke to Mr. Davis. He said you weren't going to the University of Pemberton anymore." He looked at Raymond. "When did you graduate?"

"It's good to see you, Dad."

Silence filled the room. After a few seconds, it began to feel awkward so Malcolm spoke. "It's good to see you too, Son." He swallowed hard. He spoke carefully, so as not to allow emotion to fill his eyes. "I thought about you every day."

"I got your letter."

"What letter?" Malcolm sat on the edge of his bed. It's the place where he'd originally meant to land two hours ago before he got dizzy, lost his balance and fell to the floor. He'd tried to get up but his chest ached, so he lay still and before he knew it he'd fallen asleep.

Raymond's face drew down, evidence of shame. "Sorry I didn't get in touch sooner."

Malcolm shrugged. "Don't worry about it." He paused. "Are you talking about that letter I wrote you twelve or thirteen years ago?"

"You always did have a good memory," Raymond tried. Here he was with his father, the most important man in his life, and he didn't feel comfortable enough to have a simple conversation with him.

Malcolm patted the empty space on the bed. "Why don't you sit down?"

It took a second but Raymond did oblige. "You said you were having health troubles in your letter."

Malcolm released a thunderous laugh. "Those were the good times," he said. He shook his head. "Those were the good times."

Raymond's eyes swelled. "Things have gotten worse?"

"Let's just say that I'm not the young thoroughbred I used to be."

Raymond didn't say anything.

"Liver, kidneys, my knees, my heart, my back." He shook his head again. "Everything's bothering me." When he coughed Raymond cringed. He'd heard the long cough for years, but this time it was deeper, harder and went on longer than it ever had before. For the first time in his life, he was afraid that Malcolm might not make it.

"I cleaned the place up a little," Raymond said in effort to keep silence at bay. It was hard being alone with his father; it always had been. If he was younger he'd go outside for a run to clear his head. But he was older now and his own knees had started to bother him. "I'll help you clean the place real good later today, after we both get some rest."

Malcolm smiled at the side of his head. "I sure am proud of you, Boy."

Raymond gave him a quick glance. "So, how have you been doing?" He paused and added, "For real."

"I ain't gonna die tomorrow, if that's what you're asking."

After he rolled his eyes Raymond said, "That's not what I'm asking. I'm asking how you're doing. Are you going to the doctor regularly? Are you taking your medicine? I saw a lot of empty prescription pill bottles when I came into the house earlier."

Malcolm's brows rose. "How long have you been here?"

"I got in about half an hour ago." This was the most he could remember talking to Malcolm in his entire life. They didn't even talk this much when they drove to Cincinnati and watched the Reds play baseball, times that were happy for both of them.

When he saw the expression of disbelief on Malcolm's face he added, "I looked for you the first time I came upstairs, but I didn't see you. I walked all the way through the house, then I came up here the second time. That's when I saw the blankets on the floor and realized that it was you who was under them. Did you fall?"

"Yea. I was trying to sit on the bed and I got dizzy."

Raymond studied his face. "Do you get dizzy a lot?"

Malcolm laughed. "Worried about your old man?"

"A little." He nodded reluctantly. "A little."

"Okay," Malcolm smiled. He couldn't remember the last time someone worried about him. "So, did you graduate and where were you all this time?"

"I didn't graduate." He bowed his head then quickly raised it again.

"Awww," Malcolm moaned.

"I'm gonna get my degree," Raymond interjected. "I'm gonna stay here for awhile." He paused. "Until you get on your feet. While I'm here I'm gonna take courses at the University of Dayton and get my bachelor's degree. If I want to go after a Master's degree later, God willing, I'll have time to do that."

"Do what you can when you can," Malcolm said. "Don't wait too late. I learned that the hard way."

Raymond almost laughed. He didn't think his father had dreams. For years, to him Malcolm had been a man who existed just so he could be angry and take his angst out on him. "Like for what?"

"Oh there were times," Malcolm said crossing then uncrossing his legs. "When I thought I wanted to meet another woman." He twisted his mouth.

"Really?" Raymond leaned forward on the bed. "I thought you were finished with relationships years ago."

"I did too," Malcolm laughed. "But I got good and lonely after you ran off to college." A second later he changed his tone. He hadn't known what to do with himself the last fifteen years. He didn't want to say or do anything to push Raymond away again. "I mean, after you went to college."

"It's all right."

"You're here for longer than the weekend?"

"Like I told you, I want to help you get back on your feet. I think I'll stop by UD tomorrow and see what I need to enroll there so I can finish up my bachelor's degree in a year."

"Transfer your credits?" Malcolm said lazily and in effort to keep their conversation rattling along.

"Yes." He leaned to the side and bumped Malcolm's shoulder. "So, have you been seeing your doctor regularly and taking your prescription pills?"

"Let's see," Malcolm said as if he was waiting for the answer to come to him. "Last time I went to the doctor was three months ago."

"That's not bad."

"Yea. For awhile they had me going once a month."

"Are you serious?"

"It's the old man's liver and his kidneys," he said as if he was talking about someone else. "Doctors were worried that my liver and my kidneys were going to go on me. My liver's big, twice as big as it should be. At least that's what the doctors tell me. I guess they know what they're talking about."

"Do you feel any different? You know," Raymond shrugged. "From the way you felt when you were younger."

"You too?" Malcolm laughed.

"What?"

"You think I'm old too?" he laughed again.

"I don't think you're old, but you're not as young as you used to be." He nipped at the chuckle that threatened to slither out of his mouth. "I'm not as young as I used to be either."

"True." Malcolm could feel the old bitterness returning. He pushed it away.

"So how do you feel?"

"Tired a lot."

"As tired as you told me you felt when you wrote me that letter years ago?"

"Not that bad. I wasn't going to the doctor a lot when I wrote you that letter. After that I started keeping my doctor appointments faithfully. I haven't missed one doctor appointment in thirteen years."

"Good," Raymond nodded. He paused. "Have you been hospitalized?"

Malcolm shrugged, as if to do so would diminish the impact of his answer. "A couple of times. I'd passed out while I was at work and I passed out a few times while I was shopping at the grocery store." He shrugged again. "You know how people get excited when a good man goes down," he laughed.

"When's the last time you were hospitalized? And thank God for the people who called the ambulance when you passed out and got you the assistance you needed. Probably helped bring you to your senses."

"Don't forget who's the father here," Malcolm told him. He chuckled to let Raymond know he was joking.

They spent the next half hour talking about Malcolm's health and the possibilities of what Raymond could do if he did stay in Dayton for a year or more. Then Raymond got up, ran the vacuum cleaner, washed the dishes and dusted the furniture. Malcolm tried to help but his body wouldn't let him do much.

Chapter Twenty-Nine

Malcolm woke early like he always did. It didn't matter how exhausted he felt or how little he'd slept the night before, come seven o'clock in the morning he was up. After he showered, he climbed out of the stall and looked at himself in the bathroom mirror. Water sprinkled his hair and clung, like wet beads, to his back. The first thing he saw was his scruffy beard. He'd let it grow over the month that Raymond had been home.

"*I ought to shave,*" he thought to himself. But he just ran his hand across his beard, the sharpest points pricking his fingers, making him feel alive. Then he turned and walked out of the bathroom. The first thing he did when he reached the kitchen was to put the whole chicken he bought from Kroger yesterday in the crock pot. It was a tradition he started years ago when Raymond was a kid. Since then he'd always made sure they ate a big meal on Thanksgiving Day.

He reached beneath the cupboard to the spot where he used to keep bottles of Steel Fervor and Southern Comfort and pulled out the crock pot. After he seasoned the chicken with Lawry's salt and margarine, he placed the meat inside the pot. Then he washed and diced eight sweet potatoes which he sweetened with syrup, margarine and sugar before he placed them in the oven. Then it was off to Joe's Diner.

It took the old Mustang awhile to start. "Come on, baby," he pleaded while he tapped the car's dashboard. Someone who didn't know him would think he was talking to his girlfriend.

Fifteen minutes later, he was five miles down the road and walking through the door of his favorite diner calling out, "How's it going, Joe?"

"Malcolm," Joe tossed his hand up from where he stood behind the grill. When he waved, thick country gravy dripped down the sides of his hand. "How's that son of yours?"

"He's good. In college at UD and all."

"Yea?" Joe said while he wiped his hands on his apron.

"Yea."

"Good for him."

Malcolm sat on a stool in front of the cash register. After he folded his arms and placed his elbows on the counter he asked, "Today's probably a slow day for you, hunh?"

"No," Joe laughed, his back again to Malcolm and his attention on the turkey he was frying on the grill. "Thanksgiving is one of our busiest days of the year. We'll be busy non-stop from noon until we close." He glanced over his shoulder. "As often as you've come in here on T-Day over the last ten or so years, you ought to know that." When he faced the grill again he was chuckling.

"So when're you closing today?"

"At six o'clock." Joe smiled. "With Ray back home and all, something tells me you came in here to get a large serving of mashed potatoes and gravy." He laughed. "I know how much you and Ray like our mashed potatoes and gravy."

They chatted for the next ten minutes, until Joe bagged up six heaping scoops of mashed potatoes and three cups of homemade onion gravy and handed both to Malcolm.

"Have a good one," Joe said when Malcolm reached the door. He was Malcolm's only friend.

They met the day Raymond's mother walked off. Malcolm had come to the diner to grab a bite to eat.

That day, over thirty years ago, after he filled his stomach with a serving of cornbread, black eyed peas and Cornish hen, Malcolm ambled back in his car and drove two miles further into town. He stopped off at Crown's Liquor and bought his first bottle of Steel Fervor. Over the years, despite how much he'd kept to himself, he always stopped by Joe's Diner and chatted, especially on days when he felt his lowest. He and Joe had come to know each other so well over the years, Joe felt like a brother. He even told Joe about his wife leaving him to raise young Raymond alone.

"You too, Joe," Malcolm responded. "Thanks for the grub, and Happy Thanksgiving, Man. Hope you get home to enjoy the holiday with your family."

"I will," Joe assured him. "Say hi to Ray."

Malcolm nodded. "Yea." He pushed the door open and walked outside, his wallet twenty dollars lighter.

Three hours later chicken was browning, the sweet potatoes were done and Raymond was still asleep. The living room sofa was covered with sections of the *Dayton Daily News*. The front door was open, letting in a chill. It was only twenty-nine degrees outside and the threat of an early snowfall hung in the air.

"I know how hard it must have been raising your son on your own," Ms. Nipson told Malcolm. She stood on the front porch holding a lemon cake with icing dripping down its sides. The cake was covered in plastic wrap.

"Thank you, Ms. Nipson," Malcolm said. He stretched forth his hand and took hold of the cake. The thing he wanted most right now was for Ms. Nipson to leave. He knew she was the biggest gossip on the block, maybe in the entire city. He'd never seen a woman peek out of her curtains so much in all his life. If anyone saw her standing on his porch, he knew folks would start to talk, and he didn't want that.

"People in this neighborhood are always talking about how you're over here by yourself." She craned her neck and tried to look inside the house. "But I could have sworn I saw that son of yours home a few times." She craned her neck and tried to look inside the house again.

Malcolm moved to the side and blocked her view. He searched for something to say that would turn her away from the door and send her back across the street.

"It's good if your son is home. We're all getting up in our years," she said. "Those of us who had children took care of them. It's only right that our children take time out of their busy lives and come around and see about us now."

Malcolm nodded. He worked hard at a smile but only a pinched grin came.

"Dad," Raymond called out from the edge of his bedroom. It was eleven o'clock and he had just gotten up. "Where're you at?" He peeked around the corner. He almost laughed when he heard Ms. Nipson's voice at the front door. He knew how much his father disliked her.

"Is that Ray?" Ms. Nipson asked in her high pitched craggy voice.

"Yes," Malcolm told her. He glanced over his shoulder with a look that let Raymond know he didn't want him to come to the door. "He just got up." He smiled a 'thank you' to Raymond when he stayed put at the edge of the hallway. "You know how kids are these days," he continued when he turned around again and met Ms. Nipson's curious glance.

"Well, tell Ray I said 'hi'," Ms. Nipson tried again. "You two stop over sometimes. I'll make you both something delicious to eat."

"Thank you," Malcolm said. "And thank you again for the cake. You shouldn't have gone to the trouble but we appreciate it." He watched her walk back across the street. When she reached her front walk he closed the door.

As soon as Malcolm made it back to the sofa Raymond broke out in a rip roaring laugh. "So you have a girlfriend."

"Don't start," Malcolm said. Before he knew it, he was laughing too.

"She might be nosy," Raymond said. "But I heard she can cook. I bet that cake's delicious."

"Probably is," Malcolm said while he headed for the kitchen.

Raymond followed him. "What's that I smell? Don't tell me you cooked."

"Aw," Malcolm said. "I stopped by Joe's and picked up a few things. I put some meat in the crock pot and I made some sweet potatoes."

"Where are you going?" Malcolm asked when Raymond turned to walk out of the kitchen.

"To get washed up and put on some clothes then I'll come back and help. I can cook the macaroni and cheese and make some string beans."

Forty minutes later he sat at the kitchen table next to his father struggling to think of something to say. Despite his angst, words would not come. He twisted his fingers and stared at a spot of grease that had splattered and remained against the wall over the years.

Since as long as he could remember he'd always wanted to talk with Malcolm more. When he was a boy he told himself that his father and he would become friends after he grew up, became a teenager, a man nearer his father's age. Then he got older and they talked less. It hurt deeply, but Raymond kept that hurt locked in, trying to hold the ocean inside a soda bottle. He didn't tell anyone about how he felt yet the impact of the bottled feelings seeped into all of his relationships. It was the reason he felt ill-at-ease being alone with Malcolm right now.

He stopped twisting his fingers, stood and walked to the stove. He busied himself by scooping food into large bowls. "How did you sleep last night?" he began in choppy speech, like he wasn't certain what he wanted to ask.

Malcolm knew Raymond was fishing for conversation. He could tell by the sound of his voice. He was familiar with this awkward dance. He wished they'd move past it once and for all, but no matter how hard they tried to mature their relationship they kept getting stuck. They never made it all the way to love. "I slept all right." He shrugged and sipped his cup of hot black coffee. "You know me." He shrugged again. "I'm always up bright and early." A long dry cough exploded from his mouth so forcefully his shoulders quaked.

"You're the one who knows how to get a good night's sleep. You always did have a hard time getting out of bed in the morning."

Raymond chuckled. "Nah. I learned how to get my butt out of bed when I started going to college." He shook his head and brought days of rushing off to class to remembrance. "I had some early courses." He sat down at the table next to his father. Before either of them spoke another word he bowed his head. "Dear Lord," he began, "Thank you for the food—" He stopped praying and glanced at Malcolm.

Malcolm quickly closed his eyes and bowed his head.

"Dear Lord," Raymond began again, his head bowed and his eyes closed. "Thank you for this delicious food you have blessed us with. Thank you for allowing me to get back into school to finish my degree. Thank you for Ms. Nipson bringing this delicious cake over for dessert. Thank you for all of our blessings, Dear Lord." Without intent and even as surprise to himself, he reached out and took hold of Malcolm's hand. "And thank you Lord for letting my father and me be together this Thanksgiving." He nodded once. "Thank you."

When he opened his eyes he was surprised to find his father looking at him with arched brows. They stared at each other briefly then they grabbed their forks and knives and dug into the food filling their plates. They didn't talk at all. Their elbows bumped the few times they leaned over their plates and scooped up forkfuls of food which they quickly shoved in their mouths out of hunger and out of a sense that they lacked things to talk about. The one respite for Raymond was his knowledge that Malcolm didn't talk much with anyone.

"That was a nice blessing you prayed over the food," Malcolm finally said.

Raymond met his glance. "Thanks."

Malcolm stuck a mouthful of chicken in his mouth. "Besides going to school, are you going to do anything else while you're home?"

"Want to go to Cincinnati and catch a baseball game?"

Malcolm stared across the room at an old green and brown dinosaur drawing taped to the wall. It was signed and dated "Raymond Clarke, January 15, 1971". Over the years, all but one end of the drawing had fallen away from the wall. The white construction paper the picture was drawn on hung mostly toward the floor now. The writing was curvy, uneven, the mark of a child who was trying too hard to sign his name just right.

"Sure," Malcolm answered. "But, I was thinking more about what you're going to do to have fun while you're here." He washed the chicken down with a swig of coffee. "I know you don't just want to sit around here fixing the place up and looking out for your old man."

"You're not old," Raymond said after he swallowed a bite of macaroni and cheese.

"Well," Malcolm laughed. "I'm sure not twenty-two anymore." He cursed then said, "I'm fifty-two years old."

"That's not old."

"Well, this old body's not holding out so good anymore. But," he quickly added. "I don't want you worrying about me." He didn't give Raymond a chance to speak. "I see you looking at me when you think I don't see you looking at me." He laughed. Then his voice grew suddenly somber. "Don't know how much time I've got here." He smiled weakly when he turned and looked at Raymond. "Glad to see you home. Glad you could come back," he added just before he shoved a forkful of string beans in his mouth. But," he sighed. "I don't want you worrying about me. That's what I did too much of. I worried about everything and before I knew it I was drowning my worries in liquor."

Raymond gawked at his father then quickly adjusted his stare. He leaned back in the chair, circled his mouth with his tongue and looked out the window.

"Night after night I did." He chuckled. "Oh, who am I kidding?" he said. "I did it all the time." He turned and looked out the window too. "When wasn't I drinking?"

Raymond sat silently. He knew his father knew the answers to the questions he asked. What stunned Raymond was the fact that his father ever worried at all. He'd always seen Malcolm as a Superman of sorts, certainly not an ordinary guy trying to find his way in the world. To him, his father had always talked and carried himself like he had all the answers. Scared. Weak. Worried. Those words never crossed his mind when he thought about Malcolm. After hearing his father's confession the words were all he could think about. He wondered why he'd been so afraid of a man who had frailties of his own. He wondered why he'd worked so hard to gain the acceptance of a man who could break as easily as a reed.

"All that drinking's caught up to me now," Malcolm went on. "I'm paying the piper. Backs always hurting. I try to avoid facing it but I know the doctors are right. It's all down hill from here." He swatted at the air. "Oh, they don't come right out and say it that way," he explained. "They're real nice in that doctor kinda way when they break it down to me, but one thing's sure. I'll be in their offices a lot more as the weeks, months and years go by."

"Things might take a turn for the better," Raymond said. "Miracles do happen."

Malcolm eyeballed him. After a lengthy pause, he asked, "You'd want that for me?"

"Absolutely," Raymond said. He leaned over his plate and shoved a forkful of mashed potatoes and gravy in his mouth.

Malcolm went to staring at the side of Raymond's head. When Raymond turned and met his glance, he looked away and sipped his coffee. He didn't eat as much as he used to; he was certain Raymond had noticed. He'd lost fifteen pounds in the last six months alone, and he hadn't wanted to lose the weight. It scared him that his body was doing things, performing in ways he did not recall telling it to. He definitely didn't want to be tired all the time. Sitting at the table next to his son seemed like hard work. Already he was exhausted and he'd barely lifted his hands to his mouth a dozen times.

"I don't want you to be sick," Raymond said after he sipped his grape juice. He shrugged. "Why would I want that?"

Malcolm leaned aimlessly to the side, his fatigued body refusing to sit straight then he pushed his teeth together and sat erect again. "Aw. You know we've got history."

"Yea, Dad. And it's not all bad." He kept talking. "I used to think it was all bad but it's not. I guess it depends on what you want to focus on. There were a lot of good things that happened between us too." He glanced at his father then quickly turned away. "Not as many good things as I wanted or wished there were." He paused. "Not even now, but there were good times. It wasn't all bad," he reiterated.

"You're right. We had fun at those baseball games."

"And driving over to Joe's Diner to pick up food on Thanksgiving was always good. Sure was better than eating chicken from Chick Fix."

"Sorry about that," Malcolm said.

"Yea." Raymond nodded once then repeated, "Yea."

"Think I'm gonna kick the bucket?" The laugh started slowly, quietly then it gained strength and became a full blown uproar.

"We all are one day. I came home to check on you and to see you. If you think that's a crime or that there's something wrong in me for having done that--"

"No. No. No," Malcolm said with a wave of his hand. "I'm glad you're here." He reached out and placed his hand on Raymond's shoulder. His hand felt heavy, the way it always had. "I thought about you a lot while you were gone." An old thought popped into his head. "I was going to ask you this before but we got sidetracked." He took his hand down off Raymond's shoulder. He played with his food for awhile then he ate several forkfuls of string beans. When he stopped chewing he asked, "How's that lady friend of yours?"

A shrug preceded Raymond's answer. "Her sister said she's doing good."

Malcolm gawked. "You haven't seen her?"

"I haven't talked with her in years."

"I thought the two of you went to school together?"

"We did. We both went to the University of Pemberton. That's where we met."

"So?"

"Dad, I was in Africa for the last twelve years."

"What? What are you talking about?"

"I caught a plane to Madagascar twelve years ago." Before his father could ask him a series of questions, he quickly added, "It's an island off the coast of Africa."

Malcolm's mouth hung open.

"It took the help of a good friend," he said, smiling at the memory of Mark, "to realize it, but I was running away from strong feelings."

Malcolm was hushed. He didn't barge in on Raymond while he talked, not this time. His curiosity was peaked to the point where he couldn't find words to express his shock. He felt like he was listening to a stranger.

"It had nothing to do with you." Raymond paused. "At least I don't think it did. I kept the letter you wrote me." He chuckled. "The only letter you ever wrote me. I kept it tucked in a pocket of a suitcase I took to the island."

"I didn't know they had islands in Africa."

"You know, Dad, in a way I guess all land is an island. Every land is surrounded by water."

"Yea. So, why did you go to this island? Finish telling me what you started to say."

A familiar icy chill raced up Raymond's spine. He was angry, outraged at his father for even slightly attempting to tell him what to do. It was for this reason that he left his father hanging in limbo for several seconds. He wanted to make him wait before he answered his question. That way he wouldn't feel as if he was doing his father's bidding, a thing he vowed never to do again the day he packed his sports bag, left home and caught the Greyhound bus for the University of Pemberton.

"I had dreams about the island," Raymond finally responded. Years ago he would have feared his father's certain ridicule but not now. He still expected Malcolm to laugh and he knew the laughter would hurt, but it didn't wield enough power to keep him from saying what he wanted to say. He realized that he had grown up and for that he was glad.

"While I was recuperating from an accident I was in, my doctor suggested that I write down my dreams in a journal. I'd been keeping a journal for awhile, but I'd never written my dreams down before." He sighed. "Anyhow, the first time I had the dream I didn't pay it much attention. Then about two days later I had the very same dream again. I was standing on a piece of land. The land was surrounded by clear blue water. This guy walked towards me and extended his hand." He smiled. "To this day I know that guy was my good friend Mark. I met Mark as soon as I stepped off the plane. He was at the airport picking up his mother."

"So you left your lady friend to be with this guy?"

"No," he shouted. "I didn't even know the dude. For all I knew at the time it was just a dream. He just happened to become a good friend of mine. He's married and has kids."

"Oh."

Raymond scowled. "You always did think I wasn't hard enough."

"No. I thought you didn't have enough friends."

"You? The guy who never had anyone call for him except a bill collector." He laughed, his mind going back to those uneven days. "A few maddening phone calls from the hounds and you never fell behind again."

"Surprised you remember that summer. You couldn't have been a day older than six years old when I went into debt buying that Corvette so we'd have a second car. Sold that car a year later."

"I remember. I also remember that you didn't have friends. As far as I know you still don't." He grinned. "But it was good to see Ms. Nipson stop by earlier and drop off that cake."

"She's just a nosy neighbor and you know that." Raymond shrugged. "Things change."

"Nothing's changed. At least not in regards to Ms. Nipson or any of the other neighbors around here."

"Speaking of neighbors, how are Stanley and Joey? I haven't seen them around."

Malcolm let go a rip roaring laugh. "They're in the big house. Even without being here for awhile I thought you'd know that." He paused. "Where else would those two be?" He laughed. "They sure didn't go to college."

"I hoped that they would've learned to make different choices."

"It's cool to break the law in places like this." He sipped his coffee until he felt warmer. "You know that."

"Hoorah for ghetto living."

"No, Ray. It's not about that. It's about what a person's used to. And enough of that anyway," he waved. "Why did you leave this woman you loved so much? Sounds like you turned around and did to her what your mother did to me."

The words came like a sack of bricks. One by one they landed hard and bothersome inside Raymond's psyche. In effort to lighten their blow, Raymond stared out the window. He watched a trio of birds flutter their wings and play in a tree in the back yard. "I never thought of it that way," he said. He continued to gaze out the window. "But I guess you could look at it like that." He twisted his mouth. "I never did," he shrugged. "I never did."

"Well, that's what you did." Malcolm's voice took on an edge. "Just sitting here looking at you while you tell me this brings back those old hard feelings." He shook his head. "I tell you that hurt." He banged his fist on the top of the table.

"I didn't mean to hurt Brenda," Raymond tried. "And we didn't have children together. We aren't even married."

"She called here once."

Surprise filled Raymond's face. He turned and met his father's glance. "When? And how did she get the number?"

"I don't know how that woman got my telephone number. I figured you gave it to her."

"I didn't give her your phone number. I don't know how she got it. Unless she went to Student Affairs and got it. You called there enough for--"

"I was only trying to reach you, Ray."

"What did she say when she called? How long ago did she call?"

Shame stretched Malcolm's face, made it long. He nibbled his lip.

"She told me about the accident."

"And?"

"And," he bowed his head. "And," he looked up and repeated. "I should have visited you in the hospital."

"Now that I think about it, when I woke from the coma Brenda told me that she called you. She said you told her that your car was too old to make it up there and that you were afraid to fly. I had no idea that you were afraid to fly."

Malcolm peered down at the table then he looked up. "I've always been afraid to fly."

"Why didn't you ever say anything?"

"Because I wanted you to think I was strong."

"You're my father. What kid doesn't think their father is strong?"

"Yea. But I had problems."

"We would have done a lot better if we had talked after I was old enough to understand what was going on. You certainly didn't go out of your way to hide your troubles from me."

"I drank a lot in front of you—"

"I was thinking more about the abuse, the physical and verbal abuse."

"Let's enjoy Thanksgiving dinner."

"You asked me why I went all the way to Madagascar. I was running from someone who loved me, and I'm starting to see why. I wasn't trying to repeat what Mom did when she walked off and left. I'd never want to repeat that. Brenda doesn't deserve that. No one deserves that." He glanced at his father. "You didn't deserve that."

"I never thought you'd see it my way."

"It's not about seeing it your way." He looked hard at his father. He shrugged. "I don't know where she is." He sighed. "I don't know anything about her, my mother, but I love her. That's what Bishop Moore and everybody tells me. We've got to love."

"Who's Bishop Moore?"

"A pastor at a church I used to attend back in Philadelphia." He shook his head. "I haven't seen or talked to him in years either."

"Damn, I missed out on a lot of your life," Malcolm said, looking down at the table. When he raised his head, he asked, "Ever try to find her? Your mother," he mumbled.

"Nah," Raymond answered. He shook his head and gazed across the kitchen. "I didn't." Maybe I just love an ideal of what I think she'd be like if she had stayed."

"Ah," you didn't need to go hunting for her," Malcolm said, swatting a gnat. "You had me," he grinned.

"I don't know the reason she left beyond what you told me. It was a pathetic thing for a mother to do. Truth told, Dad," he twisted his mouth and said, "I don't hardly think about her. She used to pop into my mind sometimes when I'd see a mother with her kids on campus. But as I've gotten older, she's faded, further and further out of my memory.

But," he sighed, "it was horrible of her to just leave like that."

"Not to mention how hard it was on her husband."

"Dad, I'm sorry you thought I was a burden to raise." He paused. The next words accused; they were meant to. "Maybe I felt like such a burden for you to raise because maybe you didn't love me either."

"Still think that way?"

Raymond's eyebrows rose. "I'm saying it now."

"You're attacking me."

"No I'm not. And maybe that's part of what's been troubling you all these years. Maybe you think everyone is out to get you. I'm not out to get you, Dad. I did want to get even with you for years. I wanted you to feel all the hurt that I felt when you shouted at me and when you locked me in the closet and when you told me to go into the basement and stand behind the furnace for hours when you knew how scared I was of being in the basement alone while you stayed upstairs watching television or drinking."

"Son." He waited for Raymond to meet his glance. "I apologize for all the pain I caused you. I really do. All this time by myself I saw a lot of things."

"Yea," Raymond nodded. He didn't know what else to say. This was all new to him. He'd spent his life bickering with his father, silently hating him. Before he knew it he was shoving mashed potatoes and gravy and macaroni and cheese in his mouth with a speed that concerned him. Yet, he continued to eat as if he was famished. He didn't want to face his father. He could not blame Malcolm's meanness on alcohol. After all, liquor not once lifted itself off the table and poured its way down Malcolm's throat. Malcolm had chosen to drink, day after day, he had.

"*No*," Raymond told himself. Malcolm was accountable for the harm he'd caused him. It was Malcolm's hands who had punched, slapped and pushed him. It was Malcolm's voice that had cursed, shouted at and accused him of being less than human, of being an animal, a beast. It was Malcolm who told him that he was never tough enough, that he was weak. It was Malcolm who not once, even now, told him that he loved him.

Despite this knowledge, Raymond told himself to appreciate this huge step forward his father was taking by apologizing for the hurt he'd caused him throughout his life. He *tried* to appreciate, but he was seething. The more Malcolm apologized the more he wanted to haul off and knock him on his ass. Not even his religious training could bolt down the rage he felt boiling beneath his skin.

"Ray," Malcolm placed his hand against his son's forearm. "Did you hear what I said?"

"Yea," Raymond grunted. "You apologized." He nodded. "Thanks. I appreciate that."

"I regret how I treated you."

"Why don't we just eat and enjoy the first Thanksgiving dinner we've had together in God only knows how long." He rocked his legs back and forth beneath the table. "I certainly don't remember having many peaceful times with you. Usually I'd be getting the crap beat out of me."

"Ray—"

His hand shot up. "No." He continued to rock his legs beneath the table. "Let's just take it slow for now. There's so much water under the bridge, we can't deal with it over one meal." He gritted his teeth. "That won't work. Tomorrow I'll help get the house fixed up. It's already dirty again and the pipes are leaking." He tightened his brow. "I don't want to live in a broken house."

"Sure," Malcolm nodded. "Sure." He toyed with his food then he said, "It's okay with me if you use the telephone to call your lady friend while you're here."

Raymond looked at his father with a softened gaze. "She's married, Dad. She and her husband have a son. I stopped by her sister's on my way here." He turned away from his father, blinking away tears. "It's over." He tossed his hands up. "I made the wrong choices, made a mess of things."

Chapter Thirty

Raymond and Malcolm spent the rest of the week washing and painting the walls, vacuuming and shampooing the rugs and dusting and rearranging the furniture. Raymond did most of the work because Malcolm's health kept him confined to the sofa for long stretches. When they finished, the house looked so good Raymond felt ready to invite company over.

It was another several weeks before Raymond re-established the few friendships he'd had from high school. Over the next months, and though still easily fatigued, on Mondays, Wednesdays and Fridays, Malcolm started his mornings with a slow walk around the block. He was proud of his effort. His doctors told him that the walks would pay off in huge dividends over time. Malcolm believed them. Raymond believed Malcolm when he told him that his doctors said his health was fast improving.

Less than fourteen months after Malcolm began his morning walks, on Sunday, July 22, 2002, Raymond graduated from the University of Dayton with a bachelor's degree in engineering. The ceremony was held at the Dayton Convention Center. Malcolm was there, having driven Raymond to the convention center. He stood, cheered and clapped wildly as the Dean of Engineering called out Raymond's name and handed him the degree. After the ceremony, Raymond and Malcolm dined at Joe's Diner, enjoying loud laughter and joke telling with their longtime family friend.

Raymond also landed a full-time job at Guardian Industrials as an electrical engineer, and entered into a string of monogamous relationships with women, each woman as hungry for love as he was, howbeit none of the relationships developing into rewarding romances that extended beyond a year.

****

That was five years ago, before the United States invaded Iraq . . . before the housing industry came crashing down and subprime mortgages saw global economies panic and wobble beneath one of the hardest recessions to hit developed nations.

For Raymond and Malcolm, it took many long nights of discussion, many of those conversations ending in tears and loud arguments, but father and son found neutral ground. It was upon this ground that they lived out their remaining days together. For both of them it was rewarding. It wasn't what they wanted, but it was enough. They certainly weren't Cliff and Theo from *The Cosby Show*, but they didn't hate each other anymore, either.

They were Christmas shopping at the Dayton Mall when Malcolm told Raymond that he felt out of sorts. "I just don't feel good," he kept shaking his head and saying. "I want to go home."

Raymond quickly obliged. He'd learned not to play with his father's health. He'd called the ambulance enough times over the last two years to know that his father really wasn't doing well physically despite how positive his mood was at times.

"Why don't we sit down," Raymond offered. He moved their shopping bags into one of his hands and guided Malcolm to a mall bench. After he got Malcolm seated he asked, "Want me to get you some ice?"

"No." A long dry cough shook its way out of his mouth. With it came a lot of spit and film. "I want to go home. I want to go back to my own house."

"Do you feel well enough to sit here while I pull the car up so you don't have to walk far to reach the car?"

"I can make it."

The pasty look on Malcolm's face and his dry, chapped lips didn't sit well with Raymond. He was scared. If he could carry his father to the car he would, but the mall was packed and they'd parked at the back of the lot.

As soon as he exited the mall, Raymond took off running. He ran past cars and holiday shoppers until he reached his car, a used Honda Accord. Then he jumped inside and hurried back to the front of the mall. After he got Malcolm inside the car, he laid the passenger seat back, took off his coat and draped it over Malcolm's chest and shoulders. "I'm gonna stop by the hospital—"

"Take me home," Malcolm insisted. His breath came out in thin breaths. His lungs hurt when he inhaled and his lower back ached due to his failing kidneys.

"Dad, I really think we should stop by the hosp—"

"If it makes you feel better," Malcolm said in a thick raspy breath, "Call 911 as soon as you get me home if I'm not doing better, but," he added, "I think the car ride'll settle me down. I just needed to get out of that mall," he said as he ran his finger around his shirt collar.

Raymond was silent, dread cramming his thoughts.

"Ray," Malcolm said several seconds later.

"Okay, Dad," Raymond nodded. "I'll take you home. Although," he added as he listened to his father struggle to breathe, "I think I should take you to the hospital."

Malcolm shook his head. "I ain't going in if you do, and I'm in my right mind, so by law, you can't force me to go."

"So, calling 911 was just a ploy?" Raymond gritted his teeth and asked.

"Just take me home," Malcolm demanded. "Back to everything I'm familiar with." He coughed a long, dry cough. "It's my home," he leaned forward and shouted.

"You were born at Miami Valley Hospital," Malcolm said, edge going out of his voice. A slow smile went across his face.

"Dad," Raymond frowned. He turned on the radio but it didn't take his mind off his father's struggles to breathe.

"You were."

"No need to get nostalgic."

"I was born there too." His entire body ached when he laughed. It had been that way for the last week. He just didn't say anything to Raymond. "Who's from Dayton who wasn't born at Miami Valley Hospital?"

Raymond sped down I-75 North until he reached downtown Dayton then he turned off the interstate and hurried down side streets until he pulled in front of 527 Green Street. It took him five minutes to get Malcolm from the car to the house. "Dad, lay on the sofa," he said as soon as he got Malcolm in the living room. "I'm going to call 911, have someone come to the house to at least look at you."

The next sound he heard was a loud bang, the thud of a heavy weight that had fallen without intent, like a rock, to the ground. When he turned away from the telephone, he was shocked to find his father sprawled out on the floor, inches away from the sofa. "Dad," he shouted over his father. When Malcolm didn't revive, Raymond reached down and with a single grunt, he lifted his father onto his shoulder then he placed him across the sofa. Then he dialed 911. Afterwards, he ran inside his bedroom, yanked the blanket off his bed and covered his father with the blanket to keep him warm.

While he waited he berated himself for not driving Malcolm straight to the hospital. Then Malcolm started to revive.

"Ray," he said struggling to sit up on the sofa.

"No, Dad," Raymond told him. He placed his hand gently across his father's chest and lowered him to the sofa again. "Rest. You need to rest. The ambulance is coming."

"There's something I gotta tell you," Malcolm said. His voice continued to come raspy, with a great deal of struggle. "I shouldn't have treated you so badly all those years."

"Dad."

"No," Malcolm tried to shout, but his voice merely came out in a whisper. "I was wrong. I was mean. I drank too much. I cursed too much. I should have never, not once, hit you. I took all of my hurt and all of my fears out on you and you were always a good son. Ray, look at me."

Raymond turned and met his glance. "Yes?"

"You are a very good son. You are a very good man. I wish I was more like you. You taught me the things I should have taught you. All my meanness was because of me. It had absolutely nothing to do with you. I love you, Son." He reached up to grab Raymond's neck, but he ended up falling back on the sofa. "I love you, Son," he whispered. "You're the best friend I ever had." Then he closed his eyes and went into the sleep men don't wake up from.

Chapter Thirty-One

It took Raymond two months to sell the house on Green Street. A week afterwards, he boxed up the last of his father's belongings he hadn't sold at yard sales. Items in tow, he bought a one-way USAirways ticket to Philadelphia. Besides Dayton and Madagascar, it was the only other home he'd known.

He moved into a three-room flat off Broad Street in Center City. The only semblance he kept of Brenda was the picture he framed of her in gold. It hung above the top corner of his bedroom dresser. In the living room, a faded black and white framed portrait of Malcolm and Raymond, their arms draping each other's shoulders, was placed in the center of the coffee table. Joey had taken the picture at Malcolm's request after Raymond and Malcolm returned from a Cincinnati Reds baseball game, the Reds having recently beaten the Pittsburgh Pirates. Raymond was six years old. He and Malcolm wore red and white baseball caps tilted on the sides of their heads, both of them grinning.

In between working full-time as an electrical engineer at TriMon Incorporated, a construction company, and dates with women he didn't feel much interest for but who kept him from feeling lonely, Raymond flew to Detroit and caught a Lions game from the sky box with Patrick and Doug.

Anthony no longer pounded his way through beefy defenders for a first down. His uniform was retired five years after he hung up his cleats. He was a Hall of Famer who continued to receive accolades and cheers when he ventured out in public, which for him, a fun loving extrovert, was often.

After the games and on two to three weekends throughout the summer, Raymond hung out with his trio of friends. They told jokes, laughed like a bill collector had not once knocked on their front door, barbecued steak and hot dogs and listened to good jazz. They visited hot spots in Detroit until it felt like they were teenagers again learning their way around UPemb's campus.

It went this way for forty more years, until Raymond and his friends' hair turned gray and their backs began to ache, not to mention the stiffness that had moved into their knees. Arthritis hit Raymond the hardest. It got to the point where on most days he was unable to walk down his outside apartment steps. He was in pain all the time. If not for the weekly telephone calls to and from his good friends Anthony, Patrick and Doug, all who were happily married and had been for more than thirty years, Patrick to Sandra, Doug to Linda and Anthony to a woman he met after college named Larissa, Raymond would think his life was full of only pain. He was tired of hurting.

SECTION III

Chapter Thirty-Two

"Hurry up," a teenage mother, her naturally blond hair recently braided and fashioned with colored beads, demanded of her three year old daughter.

Several feet ahead of the mother and daughter, a man wearing jeans and a heavy wool coat told his five-year-old son, "Hold my hand and keep up."

Everyone was in a hurry.

Raymond walked around the people. He leaned most of his weight on his cane while he shuffled through the Philadelphia International Airport.

"There's Gerald," he heard a trio of college co-eds shout. He followed their pointing fingers to a tall, stocky guy who reminded him of Doug.

Here and there he noticed overweight men pushing controls that lined the sides of their mobile chairs. Their fat fingers darting up and down, they zipped around young couples who moved toward airline boarding sections.

Grandmothers pulled their handbags against their hips then they took off in a gentle trot. Their worn knees sent their thighs crashing against one another, making it hard for them to run. The farther they hurried through the airport, the wider their smiles became. They were so eager to meet their grandchildren who were visiting with them over the winter holidays that they almost sprinted through the terminal.

Alongside the grandmothers, military personnel moved like sentries through the airport. Their uniforms were starched and neatly pressed. Their faces were set; they knew where they were going as they clutched new orders.

Radio station WDAS played local phenomenon, Patti Labelle, singing *Joy To The World* over the loud speaker. Her rich, strong voice went across the airwaves with as much force as the large 747s flew across the clear skies outside.

Large green wreaths decorated with red and white silk ribbons hung from the terminal ceiling. A vibrant energy infused the airport. Lovers, children and the hopeful were coming home. It was a time of rejoicing.

Outside the airport more than a foot of snow blanketed the ground. Icicles hung from the roofs of the huge airline hangars. Maintenance crews sped across the ground outside on mobile carts. Further away from where the crews worked, jets inched down runways.

Despite freezing temperatures – newscasters reported that the warmest Philadelphia would get for the day would be twelve degrees – thousands of people hurried through the airport. Shuttle buses escorted travelers from the terminals to the large outdoor parking lot which was almost filled to capacity. Interspersed with the shuttle buses were lanes of cars. Horns honked. Passengers jumped out of parked cars, grabbed their luggage and ran inside the airport. Baggage attendants worked hard for good tips.

Amid the hustle, amid the crowds, the music and the chatter, Raymond hurried toward Southwest Airlines domestic baggage claim area. Even if he went to his toes, he wouldn't be able to spot Brenda. They were older now, their backs curved, their joints achy and slow to move. Sixty years had passed since they last saw one another. They were in their eighties with sharp minds and fragile bodies.

While each of them made their way through the terminal, they told themselves to run, to move faster, to hurry and spot one another, to be together -- now. Howbeit their limbs would not cooperate. They weren't the young couple they were when they saw each other outside the University of Pemberton's campus hotel more than sixty years ago.

Raymond shuffled toward Southwest Flight 671. He smiled at everyone he passed. He waved at children and nodded at men and women. He had always wanted to love Brenda. It took him decades to realize this truth, and now that it was upon him, age could not hold him back. Nothing would prevent him from savoring Brenda's love. Nothing would stop him from loving her now. Nothing.

The cherry wood cane Mark made for him five years ago proved valuable. He pressed down on the flat handle; it fit his palm sweetly, and moved his arthritic limbs closer to Brenda. He felt no pain; he didn't notice the constant limp in his forward movement. Rather than to focus on the hard years, the mental and emotional inflexibility that had found its way into his legs, Raymond listened to his heart. Brenda taught him, especially over the last six months, that he could trust his heart. His heart thumped like a drum meant not to cause alarm but instead to keep his life moving forward at a pace he could maintain.

Their second chance at a life full of love's rewards came six months ago, on what began for Raymond as a common Tuesday, a predictable day replete with repetition.

Sun rays poured into his three-room flat through the naked window. Two minutes passed before he sat up, the mattress center sunken and soft, on his twin size bed. On a bad arthritis day, it took him ten to fifteen minutes to sit up.

After he pushed his feet inside the house shoes he kept beneath his bed, he scooted into the bathroom. It was just around the corner from his bedroom. He could find his way in his sleep; he'd made the trek so many mornings before over the last twenty years.

He brushed his teeth with his favorite cinnamon flavored Crest toothpaste. Then he washed his face with the one white wash cloth he kept folded over the towel rack.

The battery operated clock on the wall ticked off five more minutes before he returned to his bedroom. On this day, he dressed in his favorite tan khaki pants and blue and white striped cotton shirt.

He was always presentable. He always found something to care about in his day. After he dressed, he made his way into the kitchen where he poured himself a tall cup of dark cherry coffee.

Birds chirped outside the kitchen window. They made so much noise he turned and looked at them. Four Robin huddled and flapped their wings on the lower limbs of an oak tree that stood like a faithful friend at a corner of the apartment.

While the quartet of birds sang one chorus after another, Raymond sat in the kitchen enjoying the coffee. He took his time drinking it. The last drops were cold by the time he drank them. He had no place to go. The day before he pulled his metal carrier, the one with the wheels, out of his bedroom closet and went to the ShopRite three blocks into town. He stocked up on toilet tissue, bread, spaghetti, rice, fresh broccoli and spinach, bananas, and thinly sliced roasted turkey breast.

That day at his apartment in West Philadelphia while birds chirped outside his kitchen window, he heard the telephone ring. He thought it was Doug. Since he had returned to Philadelphia from Ohio, Doug and he played cards and checkers together several times a week. Weekends they went fishing.

It was Doug who kept him apprised of how Anthony and Patrick were. Because Raymond didn't travel long distances anymore, it was Doug and his wife Linda who flew out of town to visit with their friends once a year. Doug always brought word back to Raymond on how their friends were faring. Major holidays, the quartet caught up on old times while they laughed, sipped caffeine free coffee or tea and chatted over the telephone. They were the sweetest times, gone like fresh rain down into each man's soul.

Anthony lived drama free in Michigan, a welcomed respite for the former athletic all star who once couldn't get enough of the limelight. Forty years ago his name was freed of speculation around the 1984 shooting after witnesses stepped forward and implicated Walter and Michael as the club shooters during a separate drug related murder trial that got Walter and Michael each a thirty year prison sentence.

Over the years, Anthony's wife, Larissa, had been his balancer. Anthony and Aretha broke up one year after Anthony got drafted into the NFL. Aretha's jealousies, her need to hold onto Anthony at all cost, became too burdensome. After Aretha stormed inside Anthony's hotel room before a playoff game, threw a lamp across the wall, accusing Anthony of cheating on her with a team cheerleader, and cursed Anthony out in front of his teammate, Anthony called their relationship off. Aretha spent the next two months calling and paging him in effort to win him back, but Anthony never returned her calls or her messages. They hadn't seen or spoken to each since the hotel room incident.

Unlike Aretha, Larissa was a woman who felt comfortable in her own skin. She didn't cling to Anthony, nor did she allow him to disrespect her or make a lie of their union by living a bachelor's life while she lived the life of a doting wife back home.

Anthony and Larissa blended well together; they were a good team. A gentle yet resilient soul, Larissa knew when Anthony was trying to manipulate her into going along with a plan, a new get rich business scheme or a marketing stunt that would put them on the front cover of *Ebony*, *Today's Black Women*, *Essence* or *Black Enterprise* magazines. She knew when to put her foot down; she also knew when Anthony was putting up a tough front but hurting or feeling small on the inside. It was for this reason that she was always loving and gentle yet decisive. She knew the nature of the man she had promised to love.

Patrick and Sandra made their home in Prairie City, Oregon. After more than fifty years of marriage, the expansive open land and wildlife still called to them. As far as Raymond could tell, the couple that seemed created to love each other would be buried in the Beaver State. Their three children, two sons and a daughter, left Oregon after they graduated from high school. They came back to visit Patrick and Sandra throughout the year, but their lifestyles led them to big cities like New York, Philadelphia and Atlanta.

****

Certain it was Doug calling to update him on their friends Raymond took his time getting to the telephone. A duo of squirrels had joined the birds at the foot of the oak tree. Across the hall in his bedroom, Raymond lifted the receiver out of its cradle that day six months ago. "Doug," he said as soon as he put the receiver to his mouth.

The line went silent.

"Hello?" Raymond tried again.

"Oh," a woman said softly on the other line. She sounded faint, like surprise had suddenly crammed its way inside her voice.

Raymond waited. He didn't want hope to betray him, so he told his mind to hush. He couldn't believe he had heard a familiar tone in the woman's voice, a sound that had for so long seemed too far away, gone – forever.

He toyed with the top button on his shirt. "May I ask who this is?"

After several seconds of awkward silence, ire began to arrest his battered sense of hope. His voice took on edge. "Who is this?"

"Ray," the woman tried. "Do you remember me?"

Raymond took in a deep breath. He placed his free hand along the top edge of his bed's headboard to brace himself against rising emotions.

"Ray. Raymond," the woman's voice said. "It's me. Brenda."

His mouth went "Oh," as he sank onto the edge of his bed. It was all he could do not to weep. As it was, his legs and hands were trembling, making it hard for him to be steady.

He didn't want her to think that he'd gotten soft over the years. He didn't want her to think he wasn't strong, so he bit in his tears and started with, "It's so good to hear your voice. Are you still home in Tennessee? "

They talked on the telephone for more than three hours that day, he in his apartment in Philadelphia and her, in her home in Tennessee. After that first telephone call, they talked two to three times a day, every week.

Raymond was always at home when Brenda called. If she didn't call him by ten o'clock in the morning, he picked up the telephone and called her, and he always called her at night before they both retired to bed. He refused to squander a second chance. He grasped it, appreciated it. This chance at agape romantic love had always been his. The difference was that this time he knew it.

Since that day six months ago, Brenda revealed to Raymond that her husband had transitioned four years earlier. "The first years without him were hard," she told Raymond, "really hard. My husband was a good man," she continued. "Ours wasn't a passionate marriage, but it was good, and we raised a wonderful son." Raymond could hear the smile in her voice. "Our son owns a string of soul food restaurants in Tennessee and Georgia. He's doing very well. He's married now," she'd continued, her voice beginning to sound distant. "And you, Raymond," she said, her voice lowering to a near whisper, "have always been in my thoughts. I couldn't wash you out of my heart if I tried, and I did try." Her voice broke. "I was a faithful wife. I was a good wife, but you," she said, her voice breaking up again, "I never could forget you."

"After awhile I started making telephone calls. Through Internet searches I located Anthony who gave me your telephone number." She paused, "I'm so glad we found each other again." She took in a deep breath. "You do something good to my heart."

****

A myriad of voices surrounded Raymond at the airport. Some of the voices were dry and gruff; just by their sound Raymond knew that they belonged to men who were as aged as he was. Some of the voices were light and bouncy, like they belonged to a child. Some of the voices were high pitched and squeaky. All of the voices were filled with excitement and energy. Raymond felt as if he was amid a symphony of human sound. Just for a second, he closed his eyes and focused upon the person he had seen the last time he was in love.

He neared baggage claim. Brenda had given him her flight number, but she had not remembered to tell him where they would meet once she arrived at the airport. His head told him that she'd remain at the gate and wait for him to pick her up there, but his spirit told him to head in another direction. Rather than waste time and effort trying to force the universe to submit to logic, a futile task that had always found him frustrated and angry, he listened to spirit. He let joy and peace guide him. The emotions took him closer to the baggage claim area.

The clocks on the walls moved as quickly and as slowly as they always had. Nothing about the clocks had changed, and yet to him the time it took to reach the baggage claim area was only seconds, despite the fact that he had been inside the airport for more than twenty minutes.

Brenda leaned over the baggage claim turnstile and grabbed her brown leather shoulder bag. It was crammed with clothes and two pairs of walking shoes. She'd send for the rest of her belongings in the coming days. Right now she just wanted to see Raymond. She wanted to touch him. She wanted his breath to warm her skin. She wanted to hold him and be held by him. She wanted him.

When she turned from her place at the crowded baggage claim area, her once dark brown hair now entirely grey, she heard a familiar voice call out, "Brenda. Sweetheart."

She ran toward that voice. Just past the baggage claim area, her eyes met Raymond's. His frame was smaller to her, his back curved, his legs somehow shorter. Noticing Raymond's cane and limp, she hoped the years had been kind to him, not causing him pain. His skin was as wrinkled as hers, pinching the corners of his eyes and mouth as he smiled at her.

She pulled at her blouse collar. When she did, Raymond noticed the brown age spots spread across her hands. He almost looked down at his own hands, glad that they'd taken on similar signs of agedness.

Brenda continued to hurry toward Raymond. As she did, her bag slid down off her shoulder and her pocket book landed on the floor.

She watched tears stream down his face. He wept unashamedly, as if they were alone in the airport. His tears spoke to her; they told her that he had always loved her.

Brenda shook and wept. Nothing else mattered anymore. Her entire earth experience she had wanted Raymond more than she had wanted anyone else.

She started to run again. Her legs were still nimble. Gentle country living had kept years off her face and frame. She felt equally fit.

"Darling," Raymond cried out. He bit down on the ache arthritis jolted his limbs with and trotted toward her, his weight shifting from side to side, so that he appeared to be wobbling, not running.

"Darl-ing," he called out, emotion catching in his throat. "Oh, Brenda," he said as their eyes locked. He looked at her longingly.

They hurried into each other's arms. They held onto one another tightly while they rocked from side to side.

Around them travelers moved away from the baggage claim area; their newly acquired suitcases hung over the arch of their shoulders. Several of them turned and stared at Brenda and Raymond, curiously admiring an older couple's open display of love and affection.

"I love you, Raymond. I love you. I love you. I love you," Brenda wept, kissing the sides of his face. She raised her hands and offered herself to him.

He basked in her love, returning her kisses. Then he took her hands inside his and looked at her longingly. A slow smile went across his face. He realized he'd gifted her with the very thing Yhwh had always given him – love.

She pulled him closer to her, until the heat from his body went inside her skin. She held him until her body felt hot, until she felt like she stood next to dancing flames. As Raymond's and Brenda's bodies merged, their love went out like a prayer. It rose above the ceiling. It rose above doubt. It rose above fear. It soared.

Read More Books by Denise Turney

Love Pour Over Me

Portia (Denise's 1st book)

Long Walk Up

Pathways To Tremendous Success

Rosetta The Talent Show Queen

Rosetta's Great Adventure

Design A Marvelous, Blessed Life

Spiral

Love Has Many Faces

Your Amazing Life

Awaken Blessings of Inner Love

Book Marketing That Drives Up Book Sales

Love As A Way Of Life

It Starts with Love

Love The Journey

Gada's Glory

Escaping Toward Freedom (new book)

Visit Denise Turney online –
www.chistell.com

Made in United States
Orlando, FL
05 June 2025